Gypsy Magic

Karli,
Best wishes!
Tonya Royston

Tonya Royston

GENRE: PARANORMAL THRILLER/YA/PARANORMAL ROMANCE

This is a work of fiction. Names, places, characters and incidents are either the product of the author's imagination or are used fictitiously, and any resemblance to any actual persons, living or dead, businesses, organizations, events or locales is entirely coincidental.

GYPSY MAGIC ~ Book One of The Gypsy Magic Trilogy

Cover Design by Jennifer Gibson

ISBN: 1530218721
Print ISBN: 9781530218721

First Publication: MARCH 2016

Lost and alone in the woods, I never expected him to find me...

When a twig snapped behind me, I turned but saw nothing. A gust of wind whipped my curls across my face. As I reached up to push them aside, hushed voices whispered in the breeze and I looked up to see hundreds of black birds circling overhead. They cried out, some of them flying into each other.

Panic ripped through me as another stick broke. I scanned the surrounding woods, but all I could see was white. The birds' squawking grew louder, sounding like they were closing in on me. When I shifted my gaze up to them, they scattered as if threatened.

Quiet followed, but only for a moment before the sound of galloping hooves erupted in the distance. The thundering intensified as the land trembled beneath my feet, and I couldn't tell if it was one horse or several. All I knew was that it or they were coming closer, roaring behind me like a freight train about to hit.

Then the pounding stopped. Silence surrounded me, and I swallowed nervously, not trusting it. Holding my breath, I spun around to come face to face with the muzzle of a black horse less than an inch away. Nostrils flaring, its breath blew against my cheek.

I stood still, paralyzed as my fear of horses returned with a vengeance. I had nowhere to go. I was at the mercy of this beast. Closing my eyes, I did the only thing I could think of. I prayed.

GYPSY MAGIC ~ Book 1 of The Gypsy Magic Trilogy

Gracyn Picrcc is starting over. She has a new home, a new boyfriend, and a new horse. Everything is perfect, or so it seems. Because Gracyn left a secret behind. In her quest to erase the memory of that stormy night, she forces herself to study hard, her sights set on an Ivy League college.

But her attempts to stay focused are derailed when the neighbor suspected of murdering his sister returns to town. As if that isn't enough, her senses begin to change in ways that aren't physically possible. As hard as she tries to find an explanation, there isn't one.

Gracyn soon learns that things are not what they appear to be. Even her sister who took her in is hiding something. Will Gracyn continue pursuing her goal of getting accepted to a top-notch university, or will the secrets of the past and present ruin her future?

Also by Tonya Royston

The Sunset Trilogy

Book 1 – Shadows at Sunset

Book 2 – Silence at Midnight

Book 3 – Surrender at Sunrise

1

I didn't know I had a sister until I was fifteen years old. The day my mother sat me down and told me about Becca changed my life.

I had always wanted a sister, something my mother knew. When I asked why she had kept my sister a secret for so many years, she explained that she'd become pregnant with Becca while in college, something she wasn't proud of. Young and confused, she had given the baby up for adoption. Ten years later, after finishing graduate school and accepting a job with the State Department, she got married and had me. But I never met my father. All I knew was that he had died in a car accident before I was born, forcing her to raise me on her own.

Everything had worked out fine, at least until recently when my mother turned down a promotion. The position was in Moscow, and she refused to move me overseas for my senior year of high school. When I found out about her sacrifice, I was determined to make it work. It was perfect timing, too, with the promotion announced just days after a horrible incident I wanted to forget.

I pitched ideas to my mother to keep me in the states while she took the job, including alternatives such as boarding schools or staying with a friend. She turned down every single one. Then, to my surprise, Becca invited me to live with her and her husband. It was her idea, too. I hadn't wanted to ask her since we had only visited each other a couple of times. I didn't feel like I knew her well enough, but she seemed to have no reservations.

So here I was, driving along a back country road in Sedgewick, Massachusetts, hundreds of miles from Bethesda, Maryland, the only home I had ever known. I slowed when I read Becca's street number on a mailbox, careful not to turn too quickly and send the boxes piled up in the seat next to me crashing into the door.

The scenery here was picture perfect with clouds dotting the blue sky and green everywhere from the lawns to the leaves. Colonial houses sat back from the road, surrounded by maple trees and towering oaks. This was where my sister lived, and it would be my home for the next year.

I turned off the music and rolled down my window, taking in the crisp air. It smelled fresh, so different from the stagnant humidity and oppressive heat that sucked the life out of me in Maryland at this time of the year.

The car crept along the gravel, the tires crunching over the stones. I smiled as I spotted white flowers between the driveway and the post and rail fence. Birds chirped and a woodpecker drilled into a nearby tree. What a tranquil setting. I felt like I'd driven through the gates of heaven.

Becca and Gabriel's log home was nothing like the white colonials I had passed on their road. A wicker bench sat on the front porch and log beams angled up from the sides, meeting at the top. Large windows reflected the sky and treetops. The property was private and secluded, hidden from the road and neighboring homes.

I pulled up to the house, ignoring the weathered barn in the rearview mirror. It reminded me of the horses Becca and her husband owned, tarnishing the peace I sensed from my new home. I had an unshakable fear of horses ever since I'd fallen from one on a trail ride. After that, I had sworn never to get near them again, and yet I was now moving to a horse farm.

Pushing my worries aside, I focused on the house looming before me, not the large animals far behind the pasture fence. Hopefully, they'd never know I was here. I shifted into park and turned off the engine. With a sigh, I removed my sunglasses and tucked a stray curl behind my ear. After a long day of driving hundreds of miles, I had finally arrived.

As I stepped out of the car, the front door to the house slammed shut. Footsteps thudded on the wooden porch, and I turned to see Becca rushing over to greet me. A huge smile beamed on her face, her silky blonde hair hiding the straps of the purple tank top she wore with jeans. Her figure was slim, one of the many things we had in common.

Two shepherd-like mutts, one black and the other one white, followed her. I remembered them from my visit last summer. The black dog was Scout, the white one Snow.

Becca bounded down the steps and ran toward me. "You made it! Come here, sis!" Before I knew what was happening, she threw her arms around me.

"Hi, Becca," I said as I gave her a quick hug, my voice sounding weak from the long drive. I couldn't match her energy, at least not after ten hours in the car. "It's good to finally get here."

Becca pulled away from me, a genuine sparkle in her blue eyes, another trait we shared. Except hers weren't hampered with bad eyesight like mine. Without my contact lenses, I needed to wear glasses if I wanted to see farther than two feet in front of me.

"How was your trip? Are you tired? Hungry?" she asked.

"Fine, yes, and yes," I answered with a smile. I stepped away from her and shut the car door, each movement feeling so good after sitting all day. "It's just great to be done with that drive. Although I still can't believe I'm doing this."

"What do you mean?"

"Moving here. I never thought Mom would allow it."

Becca shrugged. "You're eighteen, and she obviously trusts you. You're old enough to be on your own even though you're still in high school."

I thought about what she said, realizing I had told myself the exact same thing every time I doubted moving to Sedgewick. "I suppose you're right. But listen, about this whole thing, I can't thank you enough. You and Gabriel."

"Nonsense. You don't have to thank us. We're family, and we want to help you. Besides, it's going to be fun." Becca draped her arm around my shoulders, leading me to the house as the dogs sniffed at my heels. "I'm really looking forward to this. I always wanted a sister. We can have girl nights where we stay up 'til midnight talking about boys and eating ice cream. I'll get to relive high school, without the homework."

"Lucky you," I groaned as we climbed the porch steps. "What does Gabriel think about this?" I'd only met her husband once last summer when I had visited. He seemed nice enough, but I didn't want to cause any problems between him and Becca.

"He's fine with it. He stays in Boston several days every week since his shifts at the hospital are really long, so he's glad I'll have some company. He also hinted that maybe once you get used to the routine around here with the dogs and horses, we can take a few vacations. It's been hard for us to find someone to take care of the animals so we can get away."

I stopped, glancing across the driveway at the horses grazing in the distance. One of them snorted as a gentle breeze whispered through the leaves. "I don't think that's a good idea. Dogs, I can handle. But horses make me nervous."

Becca chuckled. "Then I'll have to help you get comfortable around them. Our gang will love you. But don't worry about that tonight. There will be plenty of time for you to meet them later."

"Much later," I couldn't help adding.

Grinning, Becca changed the subject. "I suppose you'd like to see your room."

"Sure. But won't I be taking the same room I stayed in when I was here last year?"

"Yes, but you won't recognize it. I redecorated it for you."

"Really? You shouldn't have. It was fine the way it was." I couldn't imagine why she felt she had to make any changes. The room had everything I needed a bed and some furniture for my clothes.

"I wanted to. Besides, it was missing a desk which I'm sure you'll need. And that old quilt was nasty. I had a lot of fun shopping which, by the way, is something we need to do lots of." She gestured for me to follow her. "Come on. I can't wait to show it to you."

The house was cozy and rustic as I imagined any horse farm would be. In the living room, a dark green couch and matching chairs faced a two-story stone fireplace. Centered under the coffee table was a tan rug covering the hardwood floor. Two log posts marked the beginning of the kitchen. Pendant lights hung above the island, their reflections shining on the black granite. Oak cabinets the same color of the walls lined the back between stainless steel appliances. A table was tucked into an alcove surrounded by floor to ceiling windows, a wrought iron chandelier above its center. Not a single curtain blocked the view of the yard and woods.

Becca led me across the living room and up the hardwood stairs. At the top, we continued down the hallway along a railing that overlooked the kitchen. She stopped at the only door at the end and turned to me. "Ready?"

"Of course. I'm sure it's gorgeous."

Becca pushed the door open and gestured for me to walk in first. As I stepped into the room, my jaw dropped. Gone was the old furniture and ugly orange quilt I remembered from last year. A queen-sized bed with a burgundy comforter and matching pillows piled up against an oak headboard took center stage. Two nightstands with lamps sat on both sides of the bed. A dresser and mirror had been placed along the inside wall across from the window. The sheer white curtain rippled in the wind, brushing against the desk in front of it. Between the walk-in closet and private bathroom stood a tall chest.

The only thing I wasn't sure I liked was the picture hanging above the bed. The three black horses galloping across a snowy field was another reminder of the horses who lived here and my fear of them. I contemplated asking Becca if I could remove it, but then decided not to. I didn't want to hurt her feelings after all the trouble she'd gone to for me. It was beautiful, not to mention fitting for a farm. Perhaps I could live with it. If I ever decided I couldn't, I'd paint something else to hang in its place.

Ever since I could remember, I loved to draw and paint. At a young age, I used up a box of crayons nearly every week. These days, I preferred watercolors, painting everything from cathedrals in the city to park landscapes. I wasn't very good at people or animals, though. I never seemed to get facial expressions right. Inanimate subjects were easier to replicate.

I walked across the room, leaned over the desk, and swept the curtain aside. All I could see was blue sky and green treetops, quite the difference from my room in Bethesda overlooking the rooftops of neighboring houses. "Wow! Becca, this is amazing. You shouldn't have done all this," I said as I turned around. "I'm only going to be here for a year."

A warm smile spread across her face. "How can you be sure? You never know. You might want to hang around a little longer."

"Or by next spring, you and Gabriel could be counting the days until my graduation."

"I doubt that."

It was my turn to smile. "Okay, hopefully not. But seriously, this is too much. I don't know what to say."

"You don't have to say anything. It was my pleasure. I waited a long time to have a sister. And I don't have anyone else to spoil."

"You mean for now. You could have a daughter someday."

A dark shadow raced across her blue eyes, then vanished as quickly as it appeared. "If that ever happens, it'll be pretty far in the future." Becca clasped her hands together. "Okay. Do you want to start unpacking? I can help you carry your things up here."

I shook my head with a tired sigh. "No. It's getting a little late, and it was a long day. I think I'll just get what I need to take a shower and change. The rest can wait until tomorrow. But thanks for the offer."

"Of course. What are sisters for? If I can't help you with your bags, how about I order us a pizza?"

"You read my mind," I said with a grin. "You really are going to spoil me."

"You got that right. What do you like on your pizza?"

"Anything but anchovies," I replied.

"Me, too. I'll go call it in. Then I'm going to run out to the barn and finish up the evening chores while you get settled. I should be back in twenty minutes or so."

"Okay." I watched her start to leave before calling out her name. "Becca?"

She stopped, spinning around in the doorway. "Yes?"

"Thank you. You have no idea what all of this means to me."

A soft smile formed on her lips, and her eyes filled with happiness. "I think I do. And you need to stop thanking me. You'd do the same thing if you were in my shoes. I'll see you downstairs in a bit." With that, she turned and disappeared around the corner.

Her footsteps faded in the distance until silence took over. I scanned the room, amazed at the beautiful furnishings. But it wasn't the ornate bed or new dresser that choked me up. It was the fact that Becca, the sister I barely knew, had put so much effort into my homecoming. She made me feel more welcome than I ever could have expected.

A heartfelt smile settling on my lips, I left the room to return to my car and get what I needed for the night.

After lugging my suitcase and overnight bag up to my room, I went straight to the bathroom and unpacked my hairbrush, toothbrush, shampoo, and other personal items. Not wanting to clutter the counter, I opened a side drawer. Expecting it to be empty, I gasped at the contents–toothpaste, deodorant, hand soap, tampons, and...a box of condoms. A handwritten note on top of the toiletries read, "Help yourself to anything you need." A little smiley face had been drawn at the end. I shook my head with a chuckle, leaving the items where they were before piling my things into the drawer below it. I couldn't help wondering what my mother would think.

The muffled ringing of my phone broke through the silence as I placed my last toiletry in the drawer. Forgetting the surprises Becca had planted in the bathroom, I rushed back to the bed and dug into my purse. I found my phone just in time to answer it before the call would have dumped into voicemail. My mother was trying to reach me for the tenth time that day. Or was it the eleventh? I had lost count, but I knew if I didn't answer it, she might not get on the plane the next day.

"Hi, Mom," I said, sitting on the comforter.

"Gracyn, honey, are you there yet?"

"Yes. I pulled in about twenty minutes ago. I was going to call you. I just wanted to unpack a few things first."

"Well, I wanted to make sure you made it safely. I was worried about you being on the road by yourself all day. I'm glad you're there."

"Mom, are you sure you can handle being across the ocean from me?"

"No, I'm not. But I'm working on it. So, how's it going so far?"

I glanced across the room at the bathroom, thinking about the box of condoms as heat raced into my cheeks. "It's...interesting."

"What?" my mother gasped on the other end. "Honey, if you're having second thoughts, we don't have to do this. I haven't left yet. There's still time to change your mind."

I let out a reassuring sigh, smiling even though she couldn't see me. "No, Mom. Everything is fine. Really. You don't have to worry about a thing. I'm going to be happy here, and Becca has already been wonderful. You should see how she decorated my room. It's gorgeous."

"Take a picture and text it to me. I'll feel better if I can see where you are."

"I will."

"So you're really okay?"

"Yes. Stop worrying. This is good for me. I mean, I'll be going to college a year from now. This will help me get ready for that."

"You have a good point." She paused, then continued in her typical business-like tone. "My flight leaves first thing in the morning, as you know. I emailed you my pay schedule today so you'll know when your deposits will hit." She had insisted on covering my food, gas, and anything else I needed in spite of Becca's offer to pay for those things. Both of them refused to let me chip in with what I had saved from my summer job as a lifeguard, leaving those funds for clothes, books, and of course, painting supplies.

"Mom, you already told me you'd email the schedule to me. I'll check it as soon as I can."

She ignored my calm tone, continuing with things she didn't need to tell me. "I'll be online as soon as I get over there. If there's anything you need, anything at all, don't hesitate to email me. I don't care if I have a hundred messages in my inbox when I get there. Just don't forget the time difference. I may not be able to respond right away."

"I'm not going to send you a hundred emails. Please, stop all this fussing. I'm going to be fine." *Except maybe for the horses,* a voice slipped into my thoughts. Where had that come from? I shook my head, annoyed at my inner self. Now was not the time to worry about that.

"You're sure?"

"Yes, Mom. I can take care of myself. And if there's anything I need, I'm sure Becca will help," I stated, hoping to put her worries to rest.

"You're right. I'm sorry. I should trust the two of you more. It's just going to take some getting used to. You're my baby girl." Her voice faded at the end of her sentence as if she was fighting back tears.

Her sentiment caught me by surprise, causing a lump to form in my throat. Until recently, she was the only family I had. As much as I was ready to move on, I would miss her. Swallowing hard, I resolved to stay strong for both of us. "Mom, you're doing the right thing. I know how excited you are about this assignment. I want you to go over there knowing I'm proud of you."

"You are?" she asked quietly.

"Yes." I suddenly felt more like the mother in this conversation. "Now I need to go. Becca ordered a pizza, and I want to hop in the shower before it gets here."

"All right," she said, her voice strong and confident once again. "Have fun and tell Becca again how much I appreciate everything."

"I will. Have a good flight tomorrow."

By the time I hung up, I was wondering if I'd ever get her off the phone. I stared at the blank screen for a moment before dropping it onto the bed. Then, trying not to give my mother another thought, I returned to the bathroom.

Fifteen minutes later, my damp curls plastered against my gray sweatshirt, I left the room to join Becca in the kitchen. As I reached the bottom of the stairs, Becca was shutting the front door behind the pizza delivery boy, a flat white box in her hands. The house smelled like greasy garlic, making my stomach rumble.

"Perfect timing," I said with a smile as I approached the island.

Becca placed the pizza on the counter before taking plates, glasses, and napkins out of the cabinets. "What would you like to drink?" she asked.

"Whatever you're having."

As she turned to the refrigerator, I carried the plates and napkins to the table. She wasn't far behind me with glasses and a two-liter bottle of Sprite. After setting them on the table, she retrieved the box from the island and placed it in the center of the table.

"Mm," I murmured. "That smells good."

"Help yourself," Becca offered as she sat down across from me.

Lifting the lid over the pizza loaded with cheese, onions, and peppers, I said, "I talked to my mom before getting in the shower."

"Yeah? How did that go?"

I cringed as I pulled a piece of pizza onto my plate. "Weird," I answered, looking up at Becca. "Just like it is when I call her *my* mom. Technically, she's your mom, too."

As Becca reached for a slice of pizza, she caught my eye and shook her head. "Maybe biologically, but I never knew her. So she is *your* mom, not *our* mom."

"Do you resent her for giving you up?" I asked, curious.

Becca's soft smile didn't waver from my question. "Not at all. I had a wonderful family. I think she was very brave and selfless to give me up for adoption. But let's not talk about the past. Why was your call weird?" she asked before taking a bite.

"I think she's still a little nervous about everything."

"You don't mean letting you live with us for the year, do you?"

"Well, yes, that's part of it. But not because she doesn't trust you or me. I think it's just because of the distance. It's the first time we'll be living away from each other since I was born. It's going to take some getting used to, for both of us."

"Of course. That's to be expected. At least you can keep in touch easily with email and texts."

"True. And like I told her, this year will be good for me. It'll give me a chance to be on my own before college."

Becca raised her eyebrows. "You're not entirely on your own. You have me and Gabe."

"I know. But I don't want to be a burden. I want to take care of myself."

"You are *not* going be a burden. But speaking of taking care of yourself, you're on your own tomorrow. I have to work. Unfortunately, it's a Monday, and that's a busy day at the bank."

"No problem. I'll probably just unpack all day."

"Well, one day this week, you should stop by the high school. You'll want to know your way around. And maybe you could stop in the office and meet the staff."

"Good idea. I might head over there on Tuesday. It's going to be strange not knowing anyone this year."

"If I can get a day off this week, maybe we can go shopping. I can't make any promises, though."

"That's fine." I took another bite of my pizza before continuing. "So what is there to do around here? Anything fun?"

"That depends on your idea of fun. It's a small town. Gabe and I enjoy walking the dogs and taking the horses out for trail rides."

"Sounds exciting," I teased, my tone more sarcastic than I intended, although Becca didn't seem offended.

She laughed softly. "Now you're just making me feel old. But I guess that's what being married has done to me. I'm sure once you meet some of your classmates, you'll have tons of things to do. That reminds me, this might be a good time to go over the house rules."

I sucked in a deep breath, surprised and confused. "Rules?"

"Yes," Becca said. "Don't worry. There are only two. Rule number one, don't drink and drive. If you're at a party and there's any drinking, whatever you do, don't drive and don't let anyone else drive you. Call us and we'll come get you. No questions asked. Other than that, you're free to come and go as you please. If you stay out overnight, just let us know."

"Wow. I wasn't expecting that. Too bad your rule will be wasted on me. I don't drink, and I really don't party, so you don't have to worry about any of that."

Becca chuckled. "And here I was trying to be the cool big sister. Good for you."

"What's rule number two?"

Her eyes sobered as she swallowed another bite of pizza. "Don't ever go into the woods alone."

2

"*Don't ever go into the woods alone.*" Becca's warning echoed in my thoughts for the rest of the night. When I asked why, her answer that bears lived around here did little to comfort me. From what I knew about bears, the kind that lived in the east did their best to avoid people and rarely attacked. I couldn't shake the feeling that she wasn't telling me something. It wasn't what she said, but how she said it. Her grave voice and solemn expression chilled me to the core. As she went on to mention a few teachers she knew, she acted as though her warning had never been spoken. It was as if it had been as casual as asking how my day was, forgotten a moment later.

I forced myself to brush it off. I didn't want Becca to think I had an overactive imagination which I certainly did not. We stayed up late, talking until eleven o'clock when we both yawned and said goodnight.

By the time I woke up the next morning, I suspected Becca had already left for work. Still sleepy, I sighed and squinted at the nightstand clock. Ten-thirty. Sunlight filtered in through the sheer curtain flapping in the breeze. The chill in the air reminded me that I wasn't in hot, muggy Maryland anymore. The only time I felt cool in August back home was when I cranked up the air conditioning. But this chill came with a silence void of the hum of air conditioners. It came from the cool temperatures outside, and it felt refreshing.

I lingered under the heavy comforter for a few minutes, knowing I had a long day of unpacking ahead of me. I was in no hurry to get started.

As I closed my eyes, hoping for a little more rest, the silent morning came to a screeching halt when the dogs started barking. Even from behind my closed door, I heard them clamoring about downstairs. My heart racing, I shot up, now wide awake. After Becca's warning about the woods, an unsettled feeling washed over me.

I grabbed my black-framed glasses from the nightstand before jumping up. The wooden floor was cold under my bare feet, but it was the last thing on my mind as I hurried out of the room and down the hall in my oversized black T-shirt and gray pajama pants. I flew down the stairs and rushed to the front door where the dogs paced. Their tails swished behind them, and they seemed more excited than upset.

Curious, I sidestepped to the nearest window and peered outside. At first, I didn't see anything but my car in the driveway and the horses grazing beyond the wooden post and rail fence. But when I swept my gaze toward the barn, I noticed a red pick-up in front of it. A figure approached the truck, tossed a bulky sack on his shoulders and disappeared into the barn.

After retrieving my tennis shoes from the coat closet, I slipped them on and escaped outside onto the porch. The dogs bounded ahead of me in a blur of black and white. Goose bumps prickled my arms and I rubbed them, realizing my jackets were still packed up somewhere in the trunk of my car. Music thumped through the air, drowning out the chirping birds in the distance.

I jogged down the steps and across the gravel to the barn. The truck had been backed up to the entrance, its bed loaded with stuffed burlap bags. The dogs scampered around the pick-up, sniffing the tires. Scout promptly lifted his leg over one of them. Ignoring the dogs, I stopped and scanned the open barn for a sign of life, but no movement caught my eye. All was still within the shadows.

I frowned, wondering where the guy had gone when he walked out of the barn. He hesitated for a moment, then continued toward me. His dark hair had been pulled into a ponytail, and a few stray strands fell beside his face. A single hoop earring gleamed in the sunlight and his tanned forehead glistened with sweat. His army green cargo shorts were ripped at the knees, his hiking boots scuffed. The sleeves to his untucked, half-buttoned beige shirt were rolled up to his elbows, and a silver feather pendant dangled from a black rope around his neck.

"Hi," he said as he stopped in front of me, his warm brown eyes meeting mine.

I threaded my fingers through my crazy red curls, wishing I'd brushed my teeth and put my contact lenses in before rushing outside. I could only imagine how awful my freckles looked without any make-up covering them. If I had known the delivery guy looked like he belonged on a Rolling Stone magazine cover, I would have cleaned up. But it was too late now. My first impression had already been made.

When he spoke again, he seemed a bit flustered. "Sorry. I didn't realize anyone was home. Was the music bothering you? I can turn it down." He shifted his weight as if he was about to head for the truck.

"No," I said, finally finding my voice. "I just wasn't expecting company, that's all."

He chuckled softly, flashing his white teeth. "Me, neither. Becca's never home when I make this delivery and sometimes Gabriel is here, but I never expected...well, you."

I wasn't sure what that was supposed to mean. If he was trying to confuse me, it was working. Especially since I had woken up only a few minutes ago. "And I didn't expect the dogs to interrupt the first morning I had to sleep in all summer."

"Again, sorry. I'm making my rounds like I do every Monday." He paused, studying me as he scrunched his eyebrows. "Becca didn't tell you to expect visitors?"

Becca hadn't told me a lot of things, including the real reason I shouldn't go into the woods. I wasn't too surprised at an unexpected visitor. "No, but I just got in last night and we had a lot to catch up on."

"How long are you staying?" he asked.

I felt a small smile flutter across my face. "For the year, actually. I'm moving here."

"Really? That's cool. Where from? And do you have a name?"

My smile widened as I relaxed. "I'm from Maryland just outside Washington, DC, and yes, I have a name. It's Gracyn. I'm Becca's sister."

"Oh, then welcome to Sedgewick. I'm Alex. And don't let the delivery job fool you. My real gig is playing guitar in a band. At least for the summer. Once school starts next week, it's back to the books for another year."

"Do you go to Sedgewick High?"

He nodded. "One more year."

"Good. Now I can say I know someone. I'll be a senior there, too."

"Cool. So what brought you all the way up here from DC?"

"Maryland," I corrected.

"Okay, Maryland," he repeated with a soft groan.

"My mom took a job in Russia, so Becca offered to let me live here for the year."

"That was nice of her. What do you think so far?"

Considering Becca's warning to stay out of the woods, truthfully, I was a little spooked. But I kept that to myself. "It's too soon to tell. I haven't even unpacked yet."

"No? I'd offer to help, but I've got a schedule to stick to or the boss will have my hide."

"That's okay. I don't have anything else to do today. Besides, I'm not going to start until I get some coffee and breakfast." I looked down at the gravel, feeling compelled to explain my mousy appearance. "If I look like I just woke up, it's because I did," I said before lifting my gaze to meet his eyes again.

He grinned as he tilted his head to the side. "Hey, I didn't say anything. This might be a little forward, but would you like to come out Thursday night to hear our band? We're playing at The Witches' Brew. I know, don't say it. It's a pretty stupid name for a bar."

I couldn't help laughing. "It is a weird name."

"Well, it's a weird town," he muttered under his breath, dodging my gaze. When he shifted his eyes back to mine, his exuberance returned. "So how 'bout it? If you say no, I'll just have to make sure I leave one of the bags in the truck so I have an excuse to come back and ask you again."

I smiled nervously. I couldn't help wondering if he was asking me out on a date. *Don't be ridiculous,* I scolded myself. *You're a wreck right now. What could he possibly see in you?* Regardless of his intentions, I was tempted to accept. I didn't have any other plans except to work on my painting or search the internet for something new to read. Besides, I knew no one, except Alex now, and maybe I'd meet some of the other kids in my class. "Sure. Why not? It'll be nice to get out."

Beaming, he pulled his phone out of his back pocket. "Awesome. Just let me get your number and I'll text you the address."

"I can probably find it. I mean, how many bars are named The Witches' Brew?"

"Damn. You blew my cover. That was just an excuse to get your number."

"You didn't need an excuse. All you had to do was ask." I tried not to grin as I recited my cell phone number.

As soon as he added it, he slid his phone back into his pocket. "Great. We start playing around nine. But try to get there before eight and I'll introduce you to the band. It gets a little crowded, so you'll want to get there early to get a seat, anyway."

"Okay. I'm already looking forward to it." As soon as I said it, I groaned inwardly. I sounded so lame, like I had nothing else to do. *You've been in town less than twenty-four hours. You really don't have anything else to do,* a voice inside my head reminded me. Even though I meant to comfort myself, I felt like a geek next to this cute guy who was obviously much cooler than I'd ever be.

"Me, too," Alex said before backing away. "I'd better get back to work. Tell Becca she needs to warn you when she knows someone will be stopping by."

"I will."

"And I'll text you about Thursday. Don't change your mind."

"I wouldn't dream of it. I'll put it on my calendar as soon as I get back inside." At least I had something to add to my open schedule for the week.

"Good. I'll see you then. Have a nice day, Gracyn." After one last smile, Alex headed to the truck, hoisted a grain bag over his shoulder and carried it into the barn.

Turning back to the house, I wondered if Sedgewick would prove to be more interesting than I expected.

The rest of the day flew by as I carried box after box from my car up to my new bedroom. I was especially careful with my easel and paints, gently setting them beside the desk by the window. Later, once all of my belongings were put away, I'd set up a work station in the corner.

I had just entered my room with a heavy box of books in my arms when I heard my phone ringing. I dropped the box with a thud, causing the dogs to scramble away from my heels. Ignoring them, I grabbed my phone from the dresser and read the caller ID. Samantha. My best friend in the whole world. The one person I would miss the most over the next year, aside from my mother. She and I had practically been joined at the hip since kindergarten. In addition to being in the same class, we had worked as lifeguards at the same pool for the last few summers. We both had our sights set on Ivy League colleges, MIT for me and Harvard for her. Although my money was on Sam. She breezed through school with straight A's while I struggled to earn mostly A's.

We had been nearly inseparable for years, at least until a few weeks ago when something terrible involving her stepfather had happened. She had no idea what that was, and I had no intention of telling her. Ever. Unfortunately, it made me very uncomfortable around her. The move to Massachusetts couldn't have come at a better time.

In spite of it all, I still loved her like a sister. And her phone call gave me an excuse to take a break. "Hi, Sam," I said as I sat down on the bed next to my open suitcase.

"So you're gone one day and you've already forgotten me?" she teased on the other end. I pictured a smile on her sunburnt face, her brown eyes mocking me.

"I could never forget you. You know that."

"Then why didn't you call? I want to hear how it's going. I'm so jealous that you get to live on your own this year."

"I'm not on my own. I'm with Becca."

"You know what I mean. She's your sister, not your mom."

I smiled, remembering the box of condoms in the bathroom drawer and Becca's offer to drive me home from any drinking parties. Not that I'd need either one. "Yeah," I said. "It's definitely a change of pace."

"So, tell me about it. Are you and Becca getting along? Is she cool?"

"Slow down, Sam. Yes, of course we're getting along. I feel more like a roommate to her than anything. But I guess that's the way it would feel. She's not my guardian." I paused, then changed the subject. "How's it going at the pool? Did you work today?"

"Of course. It was hot as hell, as usual. Is it hot up there?"

"No. Actually, it was pretty cold this morning."

"That might be nice now, but just wait until winter. You'll be buried in snow freezing your butt off before you know it," she teased.

"Thanks for the reminder," I said with a groan. "But I'm sure you didn't call to talk about the weather. How's your dad?" He wasn't her real father, but he had married her mother fourteen years ago and she called him dad. Her biological father had been killed in Iraq when she was a baby. That was another thing we had in common, never knowing our real fathers.

"The same. Still no change," she replied, her voice flat.

I sighed, trying not to think about him even though I had asked. A few weeks ago, after my incident with him, he had become very sick. His symptoms of pain and exhaustion quickly took a turn for the worse. He had been admitted to the hospital and, within days, his heart weakened. All I knew was what Sam had shared with me. That he'd slipped into an unexplained coma and was on life support.

I could tell she didn't want anyone to see how worried she was, but I knew she was devastated. She couldn't bear to watch what it was doing to her mother and her twelve-year-old brother. Her mother had fallen into a depression, barely getting through work each day before returning to the hospital. Sam and her little brother were spending a lot of time alone, and I knew it was killing her. She tried not to show it by carrying on with life like everything was fine, but I knew better. "They haven't figured out what's making him sick?"

"No. They don't have a clue. One day he was fine, and the next, he's in a coma. Well, I don't need to tell you that. You already know since you saw him the night before it happened."

I cringed at the one memory of home I was trying my best to forget. "Yes, I do. I'm so sorry, Sam." I didn't know what else to say even though I apologized every time we talked about him. The crazy thing was, I really was sorry.

"You don't have to keep saying that. Now can we talk about something else? Please? Tell me something about Becca or Sedgewick. Anything except the weather since we already covered that."

"There isn't much to tell, yet. But I already met a guy who will be in my class."

"Okay. That's a start. What's he like? Is he cute? And how did you meet him? You've only been there a day. Actually, less than a day."

"He was delivering feed for the horses this morning."

"Ooh, a delivery boy. I like him already," Sam quipped. "Tell me more."

"He was really nice. His name's Alex, and he's in a band. He invited me to hear them play at a bar in town Thursday night."

"You are going, right?"

"Sure. Why not?" I replied flippantly, not wanting to admit it was a big deal. Not only was he the first person I had met, but he was also kind of cute.

"I get it. You like him, so you're taking that 'I don't care' attitude."

I nearly choked with laughter. Sam would say anything to get me to ante up the details. "I hardly know him. We only talked for two minutes."

"I can understand that. So you don't know much about him, yet. But you know what he looks like. He must be cute if you're acting like you don't care."

"He is. But you wouldn't be interested if you were here. He has a ponytail and an earring." Sam liked the preppy boys with clean-cut looks. Short hair, no jewelry, and polo shirts with khakis. "But he had a nice smile. He made me feel welcome which is why I'm going to hear his band on Thursday."

"Wow. It sounds like things are really going well up there. Maybe Becca will let me move in."

My smile faded as I remembered Becca's warning not to go into the woods alone and how Alex had called the town weird. Both statements made me suspect there was more to Sedgewick than peaceful horse farms. "I'm just telling you the good stuff."

"Then tell me the bad stuff, too."

I frowned, realizing I couldn't tell her what Becca and Alex had said. She'd just counter it by telling me I was worrying about nothing. Or she would be worried, and that was the last thing she needed right now. She had her own problems to deal with. "I have a feeling it might be a little boring compared to living near the nation's capital my whole life. It's a really small town."

"What about going to Boston every now and then?"

"I think Boston is about two hours away."

"Then I guess you'll have more time to enjoy nature and paint. Not to mention work on your college applications."

"Yay," I groaned. As Sam rambled on about college and how if I got into MIT and she got into Harvard, we'd be living closer again, my mind wandered. Talking to her reminded me of everything I had left behind. My old life. Friends, or at least one who knew me better than anyone. Familiar places like the Starbucks I could walk to from my house and familiar sounds like the ongoing hum of cars on the beltway. I had stepped outside my comfort zone, although I hadn't been very comfortable back home since Sam's stepfather had gotten sick. I had to admit, pushing all I'd miss aside, I was grateful to escape the constant reminders of that horrible night.

After twenty minutes of listening to Sam and answering her random questions, I said goodbye. We would talk again soon since she made me promise to tell her about the band after Thursday night. Putting the phone down as silence surrounded me again, I resumed my unpacking.

3

Hours later, I had everything where I wanted it. My pants, blouses, and coats hung in the closet, and my shoes were lined up next to the wall on the floor. Sweaters, shirts, pajamas, underwear, and socks were tucked away in drawers. My collection of art books and novels stood between brass bookends on top of the chest. I had placed my easel next to the desk where I could scoot the chair over to it. It was angled just enough so I could catch glimpses of the sky out the window between brush strokes.

Framed photographs were clustered on the corner of the dresser. There was one of me and Sam on the steps of the Jefferson Memorial, her straight dark hair the complete opposite of my strawberry blonde curls. Another captured my mom and me at the beach, sunglasses shielding our eyes as our hair blew in the breeze. The rest were of me, Sam and some other friends from school. Some of those friends I would miss, others not so much.

Pleased with my hard work, I sat down on the bed to admire the room. In time, I'd add my paintings to the walls once I finished some of the countryside around here.

I only had a moment to rest before the dogs scrambled to their feet and charged out of the room. Then I heard the front door open and close. Becca must have returned home from work.

I lagged behind the dogs, my bare feet padding softly on the wooden stairs as Becca's heels tapped the floor below. When I reached the bottom, she looked up from where she stood at the kitchen table, her white blouse and black skirt very professional. She held the mail, but seemed to forget about it as she smiled.

"Hi. I didn't want to wake you up this morning before I left for work. But then I felt a little guilty for not saying goodbye. I would have called to check in, but we were really busy. Mondays can be pretty crazy," Becca explained.

"That's okay. I woke up to an empty house all summer. Mom used to leave for work by six," I said as I walked across the room to the table.

"How was your day? Are you all unpacked?"

"Yes. My car is completely empty which is a good thing because I'll probably drive over to school tomorrow."

"Wow. You're fast. I hope you're feeling settled in now."

"I am."

When Becca dropped her attention to the mail, my curiosity about her warning reared up in my mind again. "Becca, I need to ask you something."

"What's that?" she asked, her voice distracted as she opened an envelope.

"It's about what you told me last night. You know, not to go into the woods."

"Alone. I told you not to go alone," she clarified.

"Yeah, that's what I mean. I don't understand the bear thing. Is there really a bear problem around here? It's not every day you hear about bears attacking people."

Becca sighed and shifted her eyes, stalling. A few moments later, she glanced back at me. "I'm sorry about that. Yes, there is something you should know." She stopped, her expression hesitant.

"What?" I asked, wishing she would spit it out.

"It's a long story, but I need to do the barn work and put the horses in for the night. Let me change and we'll go out there together. I'll explain everything while I'm finishing up."

"Becca—" I started to protest, but my voice fell away when she turned and disappeared into the back hall leading to her bedroom. In an instant, I was left alone with the dogs. "Great," I muttered. The last place I wanted to go was out to the barn. Horses made me nervous, and I seemed to do the same to them. Perhaps once Becca saw that horses and I didn't mix, she'd realize I should stay far away from the barn.

Within minutes, she returned, her arms raised as she pulled her long hair into a ponytail. Her skirt and blouse had been exchanged for jeans and a black T-shirt. "Come on," she said, breezing past me on her way to the front door.

Eager to hear the truth, I followed her in spite of my apprehension. We stopped at the front closet to get our shoes—a pair of paddock boots for her and tennis shoes for me. After putting them on, we headed outside as the dogs bolted across the driveway.

The early evening air held a slight chill. I couldn't believe I was wearing jeans and a shirt with sleeves to my elbows, and yet I was comfortable. In Maryland at this time of the year, one step outside in these clothes and I would have been soaked from sweating in the humidity. But here, a breeze blew, pushing a stray curl against my cheek. I drew in a deep breath, admiring the clear sky and lush grass that were so different from the stagnant haze and burnt lawns of August back home.

As Becca walked across the driveway to the barn, I stopped on the last porch step. The barn loomed too close, sending a wave of anxiety through me. Three horses, each a different color, lingered near a gate at the far end of the barn. The dark brown one with a black mane and tail was the tallest. Beside it stood a solid white horse, its coat as pure as freshly fallen snow. But the third one captured my attention. Its reddish-brown coat was sprinkled with white as if it stood in the mist. I'd never seen a horse of that color. It was strangely appealing, reminding me of autumn leaves hiding behind a cloud of fog.

Becca's voice broke me out of my thoughts when she stopped halfway across the driveway and turned. "Gracyn, are you coming?"

"I...I'm not sure," I answered, hesitation in my voice.

She backtracked until she reached me. "Gracyn? What's going on?"

My heart pounded in my chest. From where I stood, I could see that the horses stood taller than the fence. And the top board had to be almost five feet high. My fear was returning in full force. "It's the horses. I'm a little scared of them," I admitted.

"You're kidding, right?" Becca sounded like she didn't believe me. "There's nothing to be afraid of, I promise. Besides, they're out in the field. If they make you nervous, you don't have to stay when I bring them in."

I took a deep breath. Perhaps she was right. As long as they stayed out there, I'd probably be fine. "Okay," I agreed, my voice hesitant.

"Why are you so worried about the horses?" Becca asked as we walked toward the barn. She squinted in the setting sun, her eyes appearing almost translucent.

"I had a bad experience," I replied.

She raised her eyebrows. "You must have met the wrong horse. They're kind of like guys. When you meet the right one, it can be magical."

I chuckled. "You're kidding, right?" When the conviction in her eyes didn't waver, I changed the subject, not sure what to make of her comparison of horses to men. "Okay. Enough about the horses. You promised to tell me about the woods."

A worried frown raced across her face. "You're right, I did." She paused, focusing on the barn ahead before continuing. "A girl was murdered two years ago. Her body was found in the woods."

I drew in a sharp breath. That was the last thing I expected. I couldn't imagine something that horrible happening here. Sedgewick seemed so peaceful and safe. Back in Maryland and Washington, crime was pretty common. But it didn't fit into the picture of a small town tucked away in the rural New England landscape. "Did they catch the person who did it?" I asked.

Becca shook her head. "No. There was a suspect, but they weren't able to prove he did it."

We reached the barn, and I stopped outside the entrance as Becca disappeared into the shadows. After she flipped on the lights, she returned to the doorway.

I stood where I was, lost in my thoughts of the heinous crime. In spite of my better judgement, I asked the question on the tip of my tongue. "How did it happen?"

"She was stabbed in the heart."

I cringed at the image, sickened by the thought of such a gruesome attack. "That's awful. How old was she?"

"Twelve. Her name was Cassandra Dumante, and her family took it really hard."

"I'm sure they did. Especially if they never caught whoever did it. Who was the suspect?"

"Her brother. He was always kind of strange and a bit reclusive."

An uneasy feeling settled in the pit of my stomach. Not only would I have to contend with horses, but now there was a murder suspect in the picture. I'd been here twenty-four hours, and things weren't looking good. "Does he still live here?"

"Not really. He's been gone since it happened. Only the father is here from time to time. But he travels for business a lot, and the mother, well, she pretty much disappeared after the murder."

"Lovely," I said with a sarcastic smile. "I think I liked the bear story better. Does this mean there are no bears?"

Pink tinted Becca's cheeks as she avoided my eyes. "No. No bears. You were right. If one ever wandered into these woods, it probably wouldn't hurt anyone."

I pursed my lips as the knowledge that Becca had lied nagged me. "Why didn't you tell me the truth last night?"

"I'm sorry. Really, I am. I probably should have told you before you decided to move here. But it didn't seem important then. And I wanted to tell you last night, but I didn't want to scare you on your first night here."

"So you lied instead." I couldn't keep the sarcasm from rising up in my voice.

"Yes," Becca said with a straight face. "You'll have to forgive me. I'm a little nervous about this. I wanted your move to be perfect, and I was only trying to spare you the grisly details."

"Then why tell me now?"

"This is one of those times when you sleep on something and wake up knowing you did the wrong thing. I knew this morning I would have to tell you the truth because you're bound to hear about it once you start school."

I softened my expression, finding it hard to stay mad at her when she put it that way. As confident as she seemed, her insecurity about our relationship had just peeked out. And I couldn't fault her for caring too much.

"You're not freaked out, are you?" she asked.

"A little," I admitted. "It kind of tarnishes the image I had of Sedgewick."

"What was that?"

"Peaceful. Unspoiled. Completely unlike Washington, DC."

"It still is. We may never know who killed Cassie, but as each day goes by, it gets a little further behind us. It's already been two years. Even though it's a cold case, nothing has happened since she was found. No murders, kidnappings, or even burglaries. This town is as safe as they come."

I nodded, still unsettled by the notion of a violent crime committed so close to my new home. "As much as I'd prefer not to know at all, thank you for telling me the truth. Is there anything else I should know?"

A warm smile broke out on Becca's lips. "No. That's the only dirty little secret in this town. And if we're good now, I need to get started on the stalls because they aren't going to clean themselves."

When I nodded, she broke her gaze away from mine and disappeared into the barn. Putting my silly fear aside, I followed her. After all, the horses were still outside and I was pretty sure the hay wouldn't jump out and grab me.

Dust swirled around my feet as I walked down the dirt aisle. To my left was a row of four stalls, the doors made of solid wood panels reaching about four feet high. To my right was everything else—a tack room, a feed room, a pile of sweet-smelling hay stacked to the ceiling, and a cement-floored wash stall with a hose curled over a wall mount. Several sets of black nylon straps hung from the walls, and halters with ropes attached to them dangled from hooks outside each stall.

Becca slipped out the far end of the barn and returned pushing a wheelbarrow with a pitchfork sticking out of it. She guided it into the first stall and disappeared behind the door.

I could have headed back to the house, but I decided to stick around. After being alone all day, it was nice to have someone to talk to, although it would be better if the conversation shifted to something a little less depressing. I moved into the stall doorway and leaned against the dusty wall, my hands shoved into the front pockets of my jeans.

"I met Alex today," I announced as Becca scooped up piles left behind by the horses with the pitchfork.

Heaving a mixture of manure and soiled shavings into the wheelbarrow, she barely glanced at me. "Oh, yeah?"

"Yes. I wish you told me you were expecting a delivery."

She stopped, shooting a mischievous smile my way. "Why?"

"You're not seriously asking me that, are you? All you had to do was mention that a cute guy from school would be coming by in the morning to deliver grain. I looked hideous because I'd just rolled out of bed."

"Sorry. I honestly didn't even think about it," Becca said as she scooped up another pile and tossed it into the wheelbarrow. "So, do you like him?"

"Well, yeah, he seemed nice. But I only talked to him for a few minutes. All I'm saying is I wish I'd been prepared so I could have made a good impression since he's the first person I've met from my class."

"I'm sure you did just fine."

"Maybe. He invited me out this week to hear his band play Thursday night."

"Really?" Becca stopped for a moment, holding the pitchfork upright with the tines buried in the shavings. "Are you going?"

"Yes, I'd like to. Is it okay with you?"

Becca shot me a teasing grin. "You're asking me?"

"Yes, I guess so."

"First of all, of course it's okay. But secondly, you don't have to ask. You're an adult in this house, and I trust you. As long as you follow the rules we went over last night, that's all I care about."

I nodded as a smile crept upon my face. This freedom was going to take some getting used to. Even though my mom was nowhere near being a helicopter parent, she had never given me a free rein like this. "Okay. I'll try to remember that in the future."

"Good," Becca said with satisfaction before she resumed cleaning the stall.

Well, that was easy, I thought. *No wonder she needed to warn me about the woods. She won't be checking up on everything I do.* I wasn't sure how I felt about that. With a sigh, I changed the subject. "When will Gabriel be home?"

"Tomorrow, late. I talked to him today and told him you were getting settled in. He said to tell you he's glad you made it here safely and he's looking forward to seeing you."

"That's nice." I suddenly felt a little awkward as I realized how little I knew about him.

"You don't sound very sure of that," Becca commented, practically reading my mind.

I shrugged. "I just don't want to intrude. I hope he knows how much I appreciate this, that's all."

"He does, trust me. And stop obsessing about it. Gabe loves everyone. He wouldn't turn away a stray dog."

"So I'm a stray dog to him?"

"That's not what I meant and you know it," Becca said, a motherly tone slipping into her voice. "Look, he won't be around much because of his job. And once you get busy with school and a social life, you probably won't be home when he is around. But, when you are both home, you're going to learn really fast how easy he is to get along with."

Becca shoveled the last scoop of dirty shavings into the wheelbarrow before tossing the pitchfork on top of the load and walking around to lift the handles.

As she moved into the next stall, she asked, "Would you mind grabbing the hose and filling the water buckets?"

"Not at all," I replied before crossing the aisle to the wash stall. "I can help with anything that doesn't involve getting close to the horses," I added as I uncurled the hose.

We worked in silence for the next ten minutes. Becca finished cleaning the stalls while I dragged the hose from stall to stall, filling the water buckets in each one. When she pushed the wheelbarrow out of the barn, I kinked the hose and carried it back to the wash stall. Then I turned off the water and coiled up the hose.

As I hung it on the wall mount, Becca returned. "Thanks for the help."

Finished, I turned to face her. "No problem. What's next?"

"I just need to measure the grain and then bring the horses in."

My nerves fluttered the moment Becca mentioned the horses. "Then this is when I say I'll see you inside." I brushed past her and hurried toward the doorway, my sights set on the safety of the house when she ran in front of me. She stopped, planting her feet on the ground and blocking me. I skidded to a halt, suddenly worried she'd force me to help with the horses.

"Hey, not so fast," she said.

"You promised I wouldn't have to get near them."

"And I intend to keep that promise. All I ask is that you wait outside the barn until I put them in their stalls. Then you can come back in and meet them, at a safe distance of course."

I shook my head. "I don't think so. I can't. Not yet."

Panic took hold of me as I remembered the trail ride on my eighth birthday that had gone awry. I had been so excited, too. But the moment I'd shown up, the horses began acting strange. They fidgeted and pawed the ground from where they'd been tied to the fence. When the guide helped me up onto a chestnut mare, she tossed her head, the whites of her eyes showing. At first, I almost changed my mind about the ride. But I didn't want to seem ungrateful, so I held on as best as I could while the mare pranced behind the horse in front of her. Halfway through the hour, she spooked and reared up, catching me off-guard. I fell backward, slamming onto the hard ground before she took off without me. The guide rushed to my side, asking if I was okay. I told her I was fine, although my body and my spirit had been bruised. She allowed me to ride with her for the rest of the trail, but I'd been too shaken up to enjoy it. After that, I had never felt comfortable around horses.

"Gracyn, if I'm going to help you get over your fear, maybe you should tell me why you're afraid," Becca prodded gently, breaking me out of my thoughts.

I sucked in a deep breath, meeting her curious stare. "I'd rather not go into it."

"Please. It's nothing to be embarrassed about if that's why you don't want to talk about it. But I'm your sister. It would mean a lot to me if I can share this part of my life with you."

I sighed, not sure what to say. "Will you promise not to force me to get up close to them?"

Becca hesitated for a moment before answering. "Only if you trust me enough to meet them once. After that, I promise."

I wanted to agree to her terms, but fear paralyzed me. On the other hand, if things didn't go well, surely she'd never ask me to get near them again. "Fine. But I have to warn you, this isn't going to be pleasant." I proceeded to tell her what had happened on my eighth birthday, although I left out how skittish the horses had seemed around me. I couldn't be sure I had been what scared them that day, and if I made it sound like that, Becca would probably think I was being ridiculous. I paused at the end, taking a deep breath.

"Do you know what spooked the horse?" Becca asked.

"Well, I didn't see anything. But the guide said it could have been a snake since she'd seen a lot of snakes on that section of the trail."

Becca's expression remained calm and stoic. In fact, she didn't bat an eye. "Then there you go. I think you're letting one bad experience ruin something you could really enjoy."

I averted my eyes away from her, glancing at the fading sunlight beyond the dusty aisle. "I don't know. Horses just aren't my thing. I'm a city girl, remember?" I felt a small smile peek out on my face.

"But you don't know what you're missing. Would you at least try it, for me? You trust me, right?" she asked.

When I returned my gaze to her, confidence radiated in her eyes, daring me to be brave no matter how scared I was. "Yes, I trust you." I heard the words, my voice speaking them as if they'd been pulled out of me by an invisible force.

Becca smiled with satisfaction. "Good. You won't be sorry. Wait outside. As soon as I bring the horses in, I'll come get you. I'm so excited for you to meet them." Without giving me a chance to change my mind, she left me alone as she headed for the pasture.

Against my better judgment, I walked out to the gravel and waited for what would surely be an introduction I wouldn't forget for a long time.

4

In spite of Becca's confidence that everything would be fine, my fear returned when I heard the horses' hooves plodding along the dirt aisle. I fought the urge to flee to the house and never look back. Images from my horrible experience with horses came flooding back to me. I'd been so excited, too. I had begged my mother to go horseback riding for years. Nothing had ever disappointed me as much as that fateful day when I'd fallen. Although the memory of hitting the ground faded over time, I never found the courage to try horseback riding again. I wasn't even comfortable being near horses, but I didn't seem to have a choice now.

A part of me chided myself for my silly fear. How could so many people enjoy horses if they were that dangerous? I needed to get over what happened ten years ago and move on. I needed to trust Becca.

I heard buckets bumping against the stalls and metal latches snapping into place. Then Becca appeared in the doorway, a hopeful look on her face. "Ready?" was all she asked.

"I guess," I answered, still unsure.

"Stop being a nervous ninny." She reached for my hand, clasping her fingers over mine. "Let's do this." A smile flashed across her face before she led me toward the barn.

My feet were heavy, my legs wanting to resist every step bringing me closer to the horses. As nerves raced through my veins, a glimmer of hope took up residence in my heart.

Are you sure about this? I asked myself. *These horses look even bigger than the trail horses from ten years ago.* Then a confident voice rose above my fears. *Stop worrying so much. Becca is here, and everything will be fine. You really need to get over this fear. It's childish and silly, and it's time you grew up.* As the war between hope and doom waged on in my mind, we reached the barn door.

When we stepped into the aisle, the horse with the misty red coat lifted its head and stretched its neck over the stall door. It nickered softly, its big brown eyes studying me.

I stopped, watching in bewilderment as the horse seemed to beckon me to come closer. My pulse slowing, I met the horse's gaze. Its mane was dark red, its forelock long and parted, exposing soft dark eyes. Up close, the coat of mixed red and white was even more striking.

Becca dropped my hand and approached the horse. When she stopped, she stroked it from between the eyes to just above the nostrils. "Gracyn, I'd like you to meet Gypsy." Becca shot the mare a knowing look, and I could have sworn the mare gave a subtle nod of her head.

Gypsy remained calm, watching me as if she knew me which was completely crazy. "She's beautiful," I said from where I stood in the barn entrance. "I've never seen a horse of that color."

Becca smiled. "She's a strawberry roan which is pretty rare. You can come closer. She won't hurt you."

With a deep sigh, I walked toward them. I wasn't sure what I was expecting, but nothing happened. "She's so calm," I murmured in disbelief.

"What did I tell you?" Becca asked with a grin. "Besides, this girl is a present for you. She's yours."

"Wha...what?"

"Yes. Oh, did I forget to mention that when you got here yesterday?"

I did a double take, shaking my head and wondering if I heard her correctly. "Yeah. I think you missed that little detail. But why? I mean, I don't understand."

"Well, it's pretty easy to explain. Gabe and I have three horses, but there's only two of us. Gypsy always gets left behind when we head out for a ride. This one here—" She turned and pointed to the white horse in the middle stall. "Is Cadence. She's mine. And that's Prince." She gestured toward the third stall. All I could see was the back of the dark brown horse sticking up over the wall. "Prince is Gabriel's."

As I listened, my mouth fell open. This was unbelievable. Until twenty seconds ago, I was afraid of horses, and now one would be mine? "Becca, I can see you have an extra horse between the two of you, but I can't accept this. It's just, it's too—"

"Too much?" she asked, finishing my thought. "Then consider it a loan. Or a trade-off. It would be really nice if you could groom and exercise her for the next year. It would be a huge help."

"But, I don't even know how to ride," I said, feeling overwhelmed. "The only time I went riding, I fell, so I'm not sure about this."

"That was an unfortunate accident you need to put behind you. You can learn to ride. Gypsy will take care of you. She'll be a good teacher." Becca chuckled. "You should see your face right now. You look like you just saw a ghost."

I broke my stare away from Gypsy to look at Becca. "I feel like I did."

"Well, don't just stand there. Come closer."

I snapped out of my trance and stepped up to them. The mare backed up and returned her muzzle to the corner of her stall. When I stopped in front of the door, she lifted her head again, chewing on hay that poked out from between her lips.

As she munched, she reached out to me, nudging my arm. Her muzzle felt soft, but the hay tickled a little. I glanced at Becca in disbelief before raising my hand to stroke Gypsy's neck. For the first time since I had entered the barn, I relaxed. I finally believed I could get over my silly fear.

"See," Becca said with a grin. "You guys are going to be great friends. And I'll teach you everything you need to know about grooming, tacking up, and riding."

"Good. Because I know nothing when it comes to horses." *Paint and watercolors maybe,* I thought. *But definitely not horses.*

"You'll learn fast. You'll see," she stated. "Well, I'll give you two some time to get acquainted. I'm going to head in and start dinner. Is spaghetti and salad okay with you?"

"Yeah, that sounds great," I murmured, not taking my eyes off Gypsy as I continued petting her.

"Good. Just come on back to the house when you're ready." Becca gently squeezed my shoulder before walking past me, the sound of her footsteps fading as she left the barn.

For several minutes, I remained beside the stall, stroking Gypsy each time she lifted her head with another mouthful of hay. She was so calm, the complete opposite of the trail horses I had met ten years ago. When the fleeting memory of falling off that day shot through my mind, Gypsy nudged me as if trying to reassure me.

A smile broke out across my face, and a tear of happiness brimmed in the corner of my eye. "Thank you," I whispered, touching her muzzle again.

Something about my horrible experience with horses had always bothered me. Ever since, I'd believed horses were nervous around me, and it made me feel as though I'd done something wrong. Now, I finally felt at peace with myself. It must not have been me. Something else must have frightened them that day.

After petting Gypsy one last time, I pried my attention away from her and headed back to the house, a smile lingering on my face.

The next few days flew by. I couldn't believe how quickly the sun seemed to set each night, even though it stayed light longer than in Maryland. I had more to keep me busy than I had expected. Drive around town, find the high school and the grocery store. Help take care of the dogs, although that really meant let them out a few times each day and make sure they didn't wander off. I barely found time to get started on my next masterpiece, a painting of the farm. I had high hopes of surprising Becca with it, so I dragged my easel outside after she left for work and lugged it back up to my room before she returned home each day.

The horses also took up my time. After ten years of being afraid of them and thinking I'd never get near one again, I found myself drawn to them. I helped Becca feed them in the mornings and evenings. She showed me how to put a halter on Gypsy and lead her to and from the pasture. The horses were calm and patient with me and, before long, I forgot my fear. I couldn't believe it. Not only was I no longer afraid, but they treated me with kindness and an unspoken understanding, as different from my first horse experience as the light of day was from the dead of night.

My mother emailed me as soon as she arrived in Moscow as she promised. She wanted to know how I was doing, if I liked living with Becca so far and if I'd met anyone from my class yet. I couldn't help smiling when I read her emails—all ten of them in two days. I tried to answer all of them, but it was hard to keep up. Finally, in my last email, I warned her that I couldn't respond to multiple emails every day.

The evenings were spent with Becca. We were still getting to know each other, and I grew to love her company. Her easy-going nature and appreciation of the simple things in life was admirable. I hoped that someday I'd end up as happy as she was.

Gabriel returned home Wednesday just in time for Becca's homemade chicken pot pie. He breezed in through the front door, a suitcase hanging from one arm, as I was setting the table. I stopped for a moment, looking up when the dogs scrambled across the room to greet him. Their tails wagged and they whined as he spoke softly, petting both of them between their ears. Once the dogs settled down, Gabriel shifted his attention to the kitchen.

He was just as handsome as I remembered from my last visit. Tall with clean-cut golden hair, blue eyes, and fair skin, he reminded me of an angel. When he smiled across the room at me, I froze, not sure what to say.

"Gracyn," he said, leaving his suitcase behind the couch before walking over to the table. "Welcome. How have your first few days been?"

"Very nice, thank you," I replied as Becca hurried around the island and into his arms.

"Gabe!" she gushed, her face brimming with pure affection. "You're early!"

As she kissed him, I looked down and continued placing the silverware next to each of the white dinner plates. After finishing, I walked back to the cabinets to get glasses.

Gabriel chuckled as Becca peeled herself off of him. "I missed you, too," he said fondly. With a subtle twitch of his nose, he darted his gaze to the kitchen. "Please tell me I smell your pot pie."

Becca returned to the counter where a half-sliced tomato and a knife waited on a cutting board. "Of course. I wanted to make it for Gracyn. I was going to leave a plate for you since I didn't expect you to get home in time for dinner."

Gabriel glanced at me. "You're in for a real treat. Becca's a great cook. I sure miss these meals when I'm in Boston. And it's not just her cooking, it's the fresh vegetables we get from our garden." He loosened the gray tie around his neck and approached the cabinet where he pulled out a long-stemmed glass. Then he reached for a bottle on the counter, popped the cork out of the top and poured red wine into the glass.

"I can't wait to try it. It's been in the oven for an hour and smells amazing," I said, returning to the table with the glasses.

Gabriel leaned against the counter, sipping his wine. "I trust you've been to the other side of the property where the garden is."

"No, actually, I haven't." I shot a curious look at Becca, wondering why she hadn't mentioned it. But I'd only been here a few days and there had been a lot to do between exploring the town and getting comfortable with the horses. Besides, Becca had been at work most of the time. "But it sounds interesting. It must be great to grow your own food."

"It is, although it can be a lot of work," Becca said. "We may need your help next month with the Harvest Festival."

"Harvest Festival?" I asked.

"Yes. Every year, the town holds a huge fall event. They have all kinds of street vendors and entertainment. We take our fruits and vegetables to sell. Some of the other locals also sell produce, meat, and cheese. We always stock up for the winter."

"Isn't that what grocery stores are for?"

Gabriel tossed a knowing smile at Becca before looking at me. "If you want produce covered in pesticides and meat full of antibiotics and hormones. Trust us on this one. Everything we get here is fresh. You won't want anything else once you try it."

I wasn't sure what to think about that, but I let it go. "So where's your garden? I didn't realize there was more to the property than the pasture for the horses and the surrounding woods."

"There's a path behind the barn," Gabriel explained. "If you follow it for about fifty yards, there's a clearing off to the side. We have apple trees, corn, tomatoes, broccoli, lettuce, and a bunch of other vegetables."

"Wow. That sounds pretty cool. I can't wait to check it out." I wasn't sure if I really meant that, but I didn't know what else to say. I mean, it was a garden. Maybe for a married couple, the accomplishment of growing their own food was exciting. But I was perfectly happy going to the grocery store. I had too many other things to do like get good grades and submit my college applications on time than worry about growing vegetables I could just as easily buy from a store.

Gabriel finished his wine and set his empty glass on the counter. "Well ladies, I'm going to unpack and change if it's all right with you."

Becca flashed him a smile. "Of course."

"Great. I'll be back in a few minutes." He headed across the room to grab his suitcase before disappearing down the back hallway.

I approached the island and took a seat on one of the stools across from Becca. She had just finished cutting the last tomato and tossed the slices on top of the lettuce filling a wooden salad bowl.

"So, is the garden a secret?" I asked, half joking.

Becca's eyes shot up from the salad, alarm in them. But it faded almost immediately. She recovered with a faint smile. "No secret," she answered with a nonchalant shrug of her shoulders. "I didn't see any reason to bring it up. Fortunately, the garden is a lot less work than the horses."

"I'm sure it is. I didn't know anyone at home who kept a garden. No one had enough land. It just reminds me that I'm a world away from Maryland."

"I hope that's okay."

"It is," I assured her. "I like it here. I can get back to nature. Or get to know nature for the first time since I lived in the city my whole life until now."

Thoughts of what I'd left behind in Maryland wormed their way back into my mind. Mom getting ready to move to Russia. Sam at her lifeguard post at the local pool. And Sam's stepfather sick in the hospital with a mystery illness the best doctors in Washington couldn't identify. Without any warning, my heart sank. *No! I won't let him ruin my night, or the rest of my life for that matter. I didn't want to hurt him. And I never would have if...*

"Everything okay?" Becca asked, breaking me away from my thoughts.

I mustered a smile. "Yes. I was just thinking about some stuff from back home. But I am hungry. When will the pot pie be ready?" I prayed Becca wouldn't ask any more questions. The last thing I wanted was to dump the one problem I'd left behind in Maryland on her.

"Two more minutes," she answered as she carried the salad bowl over to the table.

"Good. Because I'm ready to eat."

As Becca promised, we dug into the steaming pot pie still hot from the oven a few minutes later. Gabriel emerged from the back hallway wearing jeans and a sweatshirt, joining us for dinner. Then, for the rest of the night, he told me more than I ever cared to know about organic farming.

5

The Witches' Brew was like any bar one might expect to find in a rural New England town. The entrance was buried between two quaint gift shops on Main Street in the heart of town. Neon orange flames flickered under a black pot after the word Brew in the sign above the door. Inside, the lighting was dim and soft music floated over the hum of voices. The bartender hustled to serve the crowd, her long dark hair flopping over her white blouse as she reached for bottle after bottle from the rack behind her. Beer plaques and pictures of the town, some black and white with horses and buggies lined up on Main Street, adorned the walls.

I walked in alone, not quite sure what to expect. The only person I knew was Alex and, since he was in the band, he probably wouldn't be able to keep me company while I waited for them to start. Feeling several sets of eyes on me, I wandered through the bar and took a seat at a tall empty table several rows back from the stage. Placing my purse on the stool next to me, I turned my attention to the guys in black T-shirts and jeans, some with ponytails and tattoos, setting up the microphones and instruments.

As I watched, I wondered for a quick moment where Alex was. But I didn't have to wait long for an answer. He appeared from a backstage doorway, his jeans ripped at the knees and his black T-shirt matching the rest of the band. His hair had been pulled back into a neat ponytail, not a strand out of place. He strolled to the front of the stage, an acoustic guitar in his hands. When he reached a microphone stand, his gaze swept across the crowd until it landed on me. For a moment, he scrunched his eyebrows as if deep in thought. Then he smiled and set his guitar down before hopping off the stage and winding around the tables until he reached me.

"Gracyn!" he said, beaming when he stopped. "I almost didn't recognize you without your glasses. You look nice."

"Thanks." I couldn't help smiling. As opposed to our first meeting outside the barn a few days ago, my glasses were gone and my curls had been smoothed into waves by the hair dryer. Instead of a T-shirt and pajama pants, I wore a black sweater, jeans, and tall black boots.

"I'm glad you came. You didn't have any trouble finding the place, did you?"

"No," I said with a chuckle. "This town isn't that big. I think I've found everything there is around here."

"I bet it seems tiny compared to DC."

I nodded. "But it's nice. It's peaceful and quiet. I like it, at least so far."

It was his turn to laugh. "Just wait until you've been here for a month or so. Once the novelty wears off, you'll be bored out of your mind."

I shrugged. "I don't know. It'll give me more time to focus on my homework and college applications."

"Are you always like this?" he asked.

"Like what?"

"You know, a glass half-full kind of person."

I paused in thought for a moment, my gaze meeting his kind brown eyes. "I guess. I never really thought about it. But when you grow up with a single mom and you hear other kids talking about things they do with their dads, you learn to appreciate what you have. It's no fun going through life wanting something you can never have." When I stopped talking, I noticed a grin on his face as if he expected me to continue.

I was about to say something else when the blond guy who had been setting up the drums approached Alex. "Yo, dude," he said. "Need you back up on stage to finish getting ready."

Alex turned toward him. "In a minute, Derek. I don't want to be rude. This is Gracyn. She just moved up from DC. She's staying at the Morgans' place."

Derek glanced around Alex at me. His dark blue eyes roamed over me for a minute before approval raced through them. "Nice to meet you, Gracyn. No offense, but why in the world would you move to this town from Washington?"

"It's a long story," was all I said. I didn't want to go into the details about what had brought me here, especially since Derek and Alex were needed back up on stage.

"Well then, maybe some other time," he replied with a smile, his eyes twinkling.

I felt a blush race across my cheeks as I sensed a suggestive tone in his voice. I wasn't quite sure what to say and, fortunately, I didn't have to say anything. Alex jabbed his elbow into his friend's side. "Hey man, no flirting with the girl I brought here."

"There's nothing wrong with a little competition."

"Yeah, yeah," Alex groaned with a grin. "Come on, let's get back to work. Gracyn, I'll catch up with you after our set."

"Okay. Sounds good."

As Alex started to walk away, his friend hung back for a minute. "And when you get bored with this geek, you can look me up." His comment earned him a slap on the shoulder from Alex before they both headed back to the stage.

I couldn't help wondering where all that had come from. If Alex's friend had seen me a few days ago in my glasses and pajamas, surely he wouldn't have been interested at all. I wasn't used to attention from guys like this. Perhaps I was more appealing as a big city girl in a small town. Because if they knew the real me, the girl who hid behind glasses, worked hard to get good grades, and painted in her spare time, they would realize that big city girls weren't any more interesting than those from small towns.

As Alex and Derek returned to the stage and continued setting up, the feeling that I was being watched came over me. The hair on the back of my neck stood on edge as chills raced up my spine. I turned around, craning my neck to scan the dimly lit room. Within seconds, my eyes locked on a guy sitting at the bar. He had light brown hair, a scruffy beard, and intense brown eyes. He stared at me, a shot glass filled with amber liquid in his hand. When my gaze met his, he cocked a half-smile and lifted his drink as if in a toast before downing it.

I whipped around in a knee-jerk reaction, feeling like I'd been caught staring. Even though I was as much to blame, that guy gave me the creeps. He appeared to be in his forties, way too old for me. I had no idea what he wanted, unless he liked high school girls. The thought of it sent a wave of nausea over me, reminding me of the way Sam's stepfather had looked at me that night.

When are you going to give that a rest? an annoyed voice trilled in my head. *You are hundreds of miles away from him. The incident happened, and now it's over. The guy is in the hospital with a mystery illness for crying out loud. He's paying for his actions, and it's time you put it behind you. Move on and loosen up. Alex is the coolest guy to ever pay attention to you. Don't ruin this chance to make some new friends. It may be your last.*

As I resolved to heed the warning coming from the wise voice in my head, a waitress stepped up to my table. "What can I get you, hon?" she asked.

I glanced at her, thankful to have a diversion from the guy at the bar. She chomped on a piece of gum hidden by her bright red lips, her brown curls partially concealing gold hoop earrings. A tight black shirt accentuated her full bosom, making me feel a little self-conscious about the tiny curves under my sweater that I owed to the extra padding in my bra.

"Ginger ale, please."

"Sure thing. Anything else? We've got a full menu. Would you like to see it?"

"No, thank you. I just came to hear the band."

The waitress rolled her eyes. "You and everyone else," she muttered before walking away. As soon as she was gone, I sucked in a deep breath and dared myself to look at the man again. But when I turned, his stool was empty.

Good, I thought with relief. *Hopefully that's the last of him.* I spun around, expecting to see the band on the stage. Instead, the guy from the bar stood on the other side of my table, his eyes focused on me. I gasped, clutching my hands to my chest, my heart pounding furiously. My gaze whipped up to his, the image of a young girl who had been viciously stabbed to death flashing through my mind. Becca had said they never caught the killer. It could be anyone, and it would be my luck to catch his attention so soon after moving to Sedgewick.

"Hello," the man said with a warm smile.

I nearly did a double-take. He actually seemed nice. I forced my guard back up, reminding myself that just because he sounded harmless didn't mean he was. I tossed a glance over my shoulder before lifting my eyebrows. "Are you talking to me?"

"Yes. And I'm sorry, I didn't mean to scare you. I haven't seen you around here before."

Think fast, Gracyn. You need to send him on his way. Don't give him any mixed signals. You are not interested. "That's probably because I just moved here a few days ago and this is the first time I've set foot in this bar," I answered coolly, hoping he'd take the hint and move on to someone about twenty years older.

Instead, his expression softened. "I know what you're thinking. Why is an old guy like me hanging around a nice young girl like you?"

At least he knew he was making me uncomfortable.

"I teach History at the high school, so I know just about all of the kids around here. I'm Mr. Wainwright. And you are?"

I frowned, realizing if I didn't introduce myself, he'd find out who I was sooner or later. I might as well get it over with. "Gracyn Pierce."

"Nice to meet you, Gracyn," he said as recognition spread across his face. "So you're Gracyn. You're in my class. Your name was on my roster. Did your family move here over the summer?"

In spite of the hair standing on the back of my neck, I was starting to feel a little more comfortable. If he was a high school teacher, I could at least hope he was harmless. "No. I moved in with my sister, Becca Morgan."

He sucked in a deep breath, his jaw dropping for a split second before he composed himself. "Becca? Is that right? I thought you looked a little familiar. You have her eyes. I'm a...or was, at least, a good friend of Becca's. Mind if I have a seat?"

"I guess not," I responded, still wary of him. For an older guy, he was handsome in a rugged sort of way, but something in his eyes unnerved me.

He slid onto the stool across the table from me. "You're probably wondering why a strange man is sitting at your table."

"Good guess."

"Well, Becca and I go way back. We were pretty close at one point."

"Really? She never mentioned you." Becca was probably ten, if not fifteen years younger than him. When exactly had they been close? It couldn't have been too long ago, but she'd been with Gabriel for years.

He smiled knowingly. "I'm sure she didn't. She goes out of her way to avoid me now."

"Why? What happened?"

Before he could answer, the waitress returned with my soda. I thanked her, expecting her to leave. Instead, she tossed a brilliant smile at my visitor. "Aidan, honey, can I get you another drink?"

"That would be great, Ellie. Bourbon and Coke."

"No problem, hon." After flashing him another flirty smile, she disappeared on her way to the bar.

"Maybe now she won't be so grumpy to waste a table on me with my soda," I commented.

He just smiled, studying me, his eyes intense. The feeling I'd gotten when I first saw him staring at me from the bar returned in full force. My nerves rattled, I shifted my gaze away from him.

An awkward silence came between us while voices hummed in the background and instruments rang out as the band prepared for their set. Finally, I looked back at him, my eyebrows raised. I had no interest in being stared at all night. I didn't care if he was a high school teacher or Becca's best friend in the entire world. "Can I give Becca a message for you?"

A dark shadow raced across his face as he looked down. "No. I have nothing to say to her. She's where she wants to be, and I'm sure she doesn't want our history dredged up again."

"Then why did you bring it up?" I asked.

"Just trying to make conversation, that's all. I'll see you in class, Ms. Pierce," he muttered before hopping off the bar stool and heading back to the bar.

I twisted in my seat to watch him, perplexed by his odd behavior. Trying to put the encounter behind me, I turned around to face forward, my mind churning with questions. What had happened between him and Becca? It was probably none of my business, but I was curious. And if he didn't want to talk to her or see her again, then why had he mentioned her? The whole thing seemed very weird.

With a sigh, I sipped my soda and waited for the band to start. When the lights dimmed a few moments later, the guys on stage took their places behind the microphones and drums. Alex and another guy picked up their guitars when the lead singer turned to them. As soon as he cued them with a nod, they launched into a song that reminded me of a mixture of country and rock.

The band played for two hours. People continued to straggle into the bar until it was standing room only. The waitress refilled my soda three times before I paid the tab and squeezed through the crowd to find the ladies room. By the time I emerged from the bathroom, soft music came from the overhead speakers. The stage was dark and empty, except for one of the band members who was unplugging a guitar.

I scanned the bar, looking for Alex and hoping not to see the History teacher, or as I thought of him, the creepy bar guy. But I didn't see either of them among the crowd of people, talking and drinking, oblivious to my presence.

Giving up, I headed toward the front door. Alex was probably busy loading equipment into a truck or taking a break. He didn't need the extra pressure of being the new girl's escort for the night. I'd see him at school next week, anyway.

As I scooted between bodies, someone behind me tapped my shoulder. I whirled around to see Alex dabbing the sweat on his forehead with a white towel. Wisps of hair hung loose around his face, and he tucked a few behind his ear as he smiled. "You're not leaving, are you?"

"Yeah, I was. It's getting late, and I really don't know anyone."

"You know me," he quipped with a dashing smile. "But I know I was busy for a while. I hope you enjoyed the music."

"I did. You guys are good."

"Thanks. I'm glad you liked it. I know it didn't exactly give us any time to get to know each other. But we're heading out to the lake for a party. Want to come?"

My first thought was that I would have to ask... Who? I had no one to ask. Becca had made it quite clear that she didn't want me asking Mother May I for everything I wanted to do. I was an adult at eighteen, and she respected that.

But I still hesitated. *Seriously?* I chided myself. *A cute guy is asking you to go to a party. What are you waiting for? Say yes before he asks someone else!* By the adoring looks I'd seen other girls throwing his way all night, I was sure he had plenty of choices. Why me? I wondered what he saw in me, but maybe it was time to stop over-analyzing things and go with it. What did I have to lose?

"Sure, why not?" I answered. I didn't need to get up early the next morning. I could stay out as late as I wanted and sleep in.

He grinned, a sparkle lighting up his dark eyes. "Great. Do you want to ride over there with us?"

"It would probably be better if I drive myself so no one has to bring me back here."

"Okay. Well, we're ready to go. Come on. I'll walk you to your car." Alex gestured for me to lead the way to the door. A smiled formed on my face as I squeezed through the crowd, sensing him close behind me. In just a few days, Sedgewick had proven to be anything but boring. I couldn't wait to see what happened next.

6

Derek led the way to the party in the black van the band used to haul their instruments around town. Alex rode with me to make sure I wouldn't get lost if Derek got too far ahead. We reached the edge of town in a few minutes, then left the lights of civilization far behind as we drove several miles through the woods. When we arrived at the party, dozens of cars and trucks were already parked along the side of the road. I pulled in behind Derek's van and shut off the engine. Then the headlights went dark, and pitch black surrounded us.

I stepped out of the car and hugged my arms around my chest in the cool night air, once again realizing I was no longer in Maryland. A jacket would have been nice, but I had figured a crowded bar would be hot. And I never anticipated going to a party out in the woods.

Alex walked around the front of the car to join me as I heard the van doors slam shut. Derek and the rest of the band members darted through the trees, heading straight for the bonfire flickering in the distance. Muffled voices rang out from the party, even as cheers erupted from the crowd greeting the band.

"This seems like quite the party spot," I commented.

"It is, when it doesn't get busted."

"Busted?" I frowned, wondering what I was getting myself into. This seemed like the kind of party I had worked hard to stay away from back home. One with drinking and who knew what else. Even though Becca seemed pretty cool, she probably wouldn't appreciate having to bail me out of trouble my first week in town should the cops show up tonight.

Alex must have sensed my apprehension because he touched my arm. "Don't worry. This is kind of small tonight. The cops usually leave us alone in the summer. They crack down after school starts. Next weekend, there will be almost a hundred kids out here. This crowd is nothing."

"Okay. Good to know."

"And I wouldn't bring you here if I thought you'd get in trouble. That isn't my idea of making a good first impression."

"Thanks." I tried to sound nonchalant, but parties, especially those with drinking, had never been my thing. "So are you going to introduce me around?" I asked as we made our way through the woods, our feet crunching on leaves and snapping twigs. The voices in the distance grew louder as we got closer to the party.

He turned his head slightly, tossing a smile at me, his white teeth flashing in the moonlight. "Sure. I can do that. But I was really hoping we could get away from the crowd. I don't know anything about you, and I'm not going to if you're too busy meeting everyone to hang out with me."

"There's enough time for both. I don't have anywhere to be in the morning. How about you?"

"I have to start my deliveries at eight. But you'd be surprised at how little sleep I need to function," he said as he ducked under a low-lying branch. "Careful." He turned back, holding it up until I passed under it.

"Thanks," I said with a shy smile. Something about him relaxed me, made me comfortable. His eyes met mine for a moment before he continued leading me in between the trees to the party.

When we emerged into the lakeside clearing, the bonfire blazed, sending a column of gray smoke up to the sky. Groups of teenagers lingered around the fire, most of them holding red cups or beer bottles. Beyond the party, the lake rolled out in the distance, exposing the midnight sky. Orange flames reflected on the water while stars twinkled like diamonds overhead.

"Can I get you something to drink?" Alex asked.

"Um, a Coke, if there is one," I answered.

"Should be. I'll be right back." He rushed off, leaving me to wait among strangers.

I was only alone for a second. Derek noticed me and excused himself from a group of girls before coming to my side. The girls watched him walk away, their eyes narrowing at me when he stopped. "Hey. Alex left you alone? Big mistake," he said with a chuckle. He lifted a beer bottle to his mouth, his eyes never leaving me as he took a swig.

"He's just getting me a drink," I explained.

"His kind gesture is my advantage," he said coyly.

I raised my eyebrows, not sure what to think. "Why's that?" I asked, staring across the clearing at the fire. All I wanted was for Alex to return with my Coke.

"Because it gives me a chance to ask if you have a boyfriend. Do you?" He took another swallow of his beer, as if needing a little extra courage after blurting out his question.

"Oh, that's all you wanted? No, I don't. I left Maryland a free agent. No strings attached."

"Excellent. But I'm sure you left some broken hearts behind."

Smooth, really smooth, I thought, lifting my eyebrows again. *Too bad the only broken heart I left behind belongs to a fifty-year-old guy hanging on for his life in the hospital.* I shrugged, brushing off the voice in my head. "I doubt it."

"Oh, come on. You don't expect me to believe that. You're quite a catch. I bet there's at least one guy back in DC kicking himself for not asking you out when he had the chance."

Not sure how to respond, I opened my mouth, but no words came out. Just as the silence hit an awkward moment, Alex returned with a beer bottle in one hand and a red plastic cup in the other. He handed me the cup. "I hope I'm not interrupting anything here," he said, seeming annoyed as he glanced at Derek before an apologetic look crossed over his expression when his eyes met mine.

"Nope. I was just keeping Gracyn company since you left her alone."

"Thanks, man," Alex gritted out sarcastically.

Derek seemed to get the hint. "Well, Gracyn, perhaps we can continue this another time. I'll leave you two alone." Derek winked at me before wandering around the bonfire to a group of girls giggling and throwing rocks into the water.

"Thank you," I said with a little too much emphasis as soon as Derek was out of earshot. Trying not to think of him again, I sipped my Coke.

"No problem. Derek can be a little forward sometimes, but he's a good guy. You'll see. He'll back off."

"Soon, I hope."

Alex grinned. "Soon enough, I promise. He knows I saw you first."

"I'm beginning to feel like a puppy in the store window being fought over by two little boys."

"Sorry. It's not often a pretty new girl moves to town." He paused thoughtfully, then continued. "Come to think of it, you're the first new girl in school I can remember."

"So I'm going to stick out like a sore thumb? I can't wait," I muttered.

"Don't worry. Everyone's going to love you. But I like being the first to get to know you." Alex pointed toward the lake. "There's a picnic table over there closer to the water. Want to sit down?"

"Sure." As I followed him past the crowd around the fire, a few girls glanced at him. He seemed oblivious to the attention. But when some of those same eyes glared at me, I realized that heading off to a private spot with one of the guys in the band might not be the best way to make new friends. Good thing I was kind of a loner, anyway.

When we reached the table, we sat side by side, our backs leaning against the tabletop. We watched the water lapping the shoreline, barely audible over the voices around the fire.

"Did you have a nice time at the bar tonight?" Alex asked. "I hope you at least liked the music."

"Oh, I did. It was great. Except for—" My voice trailed off when Mr. Wainwright crept into my thoughts.

"Except for what?" Alex nudged me, a faint smile tugging at his lips. "Come on. You can tell me. What's bothering you?"

I sighed, staring out at the inky black water. "There was a guy who was kind of weird."

Alex chuckled. "I know Derek can be annoying, but he's harmless. I promise."

I shook my head, turning to look at Alex. "No. I don't mean Derek."

"Then who was it?"

"The History teacher. Mr. Wainwright."

Recognition immediately registered on his face. "Mr. Wainwright's got you this unsettled?" he asked in disbelief.

"Yes. He was staring at me when I first got to the bar. Then he showed up at my table from out of nowhere. What's his story?"

"He's the town drunk. He spends his evenings and weekends drowning his sorrows in a bottle. But in spite of that, he's a great teacher. Everyone I know who's taken his class has said so. If you're lucky, you'll have him for History."

"He said my name was on his roster, so it looks like I do. But why does he drink? What's his problem?"

"I don't know all of the details, but apparently some woman really messed him up years ago and he's never gotten over her."

"Becca," I stated before realizing I said her name out loud.

"Becca?"

"Maybe Becca," I corrected quickly. "It's just a guess. He told me they were close once."

"Hmm." Alex furrowed his eyebrows in thought as he stared out at the lake. "She's what, twenty-five years old?"

"Twenty-eight. Ten years older than me."

"So, he's probably about forty-five. And he's been drinking for over ten years. But even ten years ago, she would have been eighteen. And he would have been about thirty-five," Alex mused. "That can't be right. Or maybe it is. You never can tell about people."

"I have no idea since this is the first I knew anything about him. But you're right, the age difference doesn't add up. I'll have to ask Becca about him when I get a chance."

"Won't that be a little awkward?"

"Maybe. But she is my sister. I'll only worry if I don't know what happened. Especially if he's going to be my teacher for the year."

"Yeah. If Becca's the one who broke his heart, it would be better to find out now."

Curious, I glanced at him. "You don't think he'd hold it against me, do you? I mean, the last thing I need is one of my teachers knocking my grades down because of something I had nothing to do with."

"I would hope not. But he's been pretty miserable for a long time. I remember watching him stagger down Main Street on a Saturday night once when I was a kid."

"Wow. That sounds really sad. I hope it's not because of Becca."

"Who knows? Maybe she isn't the love of his life. And yes, it is sad." As Alex agreed with me, a sparkle lit up his eyes and a small smile hitched across his lips. "Kind of like this conversation. I was hoping to get to know a little more about you, not spend time trying to understand the notorious town drunk."

My hopes fell at the thought of letting Alex get to know me. If I didn't keep the conversation focused on something else like Mr. Wainwright, Alex was bound to ask questions about my life back home. I wasn't ready to tell this cool guy who had half the girls at the party drooling over him that he was sitting next to a bona fide nerd. "Well, I'm sure we won't figure him out tonight."

"I hope not. Because the last thing I want to do is spend the whole night speculating about Wainwright's love life."

"Then tell me, what else should I know about Sedgewick? Give me the good gossip, too. I want to be informed when school starts next week."

"I was hoping to learn more about you," Alex said. "But, I guess that can wait. You know the saying, be careful what you wish for?"

"Yes."

"Then consider yourself warned. There are some real characters, starting with Celeste Hamilton who's had a crush on Derek since the third grade. Derek really isn't into her, at least not yet. Personally, I think they'll end up married one day. But after high school. You know, like one of those opposites attract kind of relationships. And then there's Lacey, Derek's on and off girlfriend. Don't let me forget Zoe, head of the drill team and my cousin. Derek's been in love with her for years, but I won't let him get his hands on her. Or should I say, I wouldn't if he ever got the chance. I'm not crazy about some of the guys she dates, but let's just say her taste has improved a bit over the last two years."

"Why's that?"

Alex frowned, his expression darkening. He shifted his eyes from me to the water. "It's kind of not cool to date a murderer." He paused and, just as I was about to ask what that meant, he spoke again. "But thank God, he's been gone for years."

"Are you talking about the brother of the girl who was killed two years ago?"

He nodded. "Yeah. I guess you heard about that."

"Becca told me. Well, first she told me not to go into the woods alone and then she made up some stupid bear story about it."

Turning to me, Alex laughed. "Bears? Well, I gotta hand it to her, she's at least creative if nothing else." Then his smile faded and sadness crept back onto his face. "As for Cassie, it was a pretty dark time when she was found. I hope you're not going to let that ruin your image of Sedgewick, though. It's actually a peaceful town."

"I can see that. And no, it was years ago. I'm glad I know about it, but I think there's a lot to like about Sedgewick." My hand slid a few inches to the side, brushing against his. The gesture was meant to comfort him and let him know I was having a good time. It seemed to work.

"Hmm," Alex mused, his smile returning. "I'm glad we're making a good impression on you." He took another swallow from his beer bottle as I moved my hand back to my side.

"So tell me more. Are there any girls in this school who don't have a crush on Derek? Or any he's not in love with? And who has a crush on you?"

"You don't waste words, do you?"

"Nope. I just want to know the scoop before the first day. This is very important information." I could barely keep a straight face. The high school dating scene was none of my business and it was completely out of character for me to care. Or was that my old character? Maybe it was time to start over. And maybe it wasn't that I cared so much about these other kids and who they liked, but that Alex interested me and I wanted to know who my competition was.

Alex launched into more gossip, pointing out some of the kids around the fire. I was sure I wouldn't remember any of their names after the party, but I enjoyed hearing the stories. I felt like I'd be a little less of a stranger on the first day of school if I knew something about them. Fortunately, this kept Alex from asking me questions about myself. He'd learn I was a geek soon enough.

All in all, the night was a success except for one small detail. Aidan Wainwright. The memory of him lingering at my table nagged me all night. I promised myself to ask Becca about him before school started on Monday and I had to deal with him in class.

I returned home shortly after midnight. After taking out my contact lenses and changing into pajamas, I climbed into bed. Then I closed my eyes and fell asleep hoping to dream about Alex and what it would be like to be his girlfriend. Because once he discovered the real me, I was sure the only chance I'd have with him would be in my dreams.

Rain pummeled the windshield, the wiper blades pulsing up and down. The storm had come from out of nowhere. Thunder shook the ground and lightning streaked through the black sky above the rooftops. Sam's stepfather slowed the car and turned the wipers up to their fastest speed.

But even that wasn't enough. The deluge of water rushing down the windshield made visibility impossible.

"Sorry about this, Gracyn," he said, pulling into an alley I could only see when lightning flashed. "We're going to have to wait it out."

I glanced at him, noting his wire-rimmed glasses and dark thinning hair sprinkled with silver. His tie was loose around his neck, his button-down shirt wrinkled from a long day. Sam had planned to give me a ride, but when the storm warnings were issued, her stepfather insisted on driving me home.

"Okay," I murmured, not sure if he heard me over the pounding rain. My attention shifted to the river gushing down the windshield as my muscles tightened. I hated being stuck in a car with him for the five-minute ride home, and the fact that the storm was prolonging my misery didn't help.

"We can listen to the radio," he suggested as he turned a knob on the dashboard. Music lofted out of the speakers, but it couldn't compete with the monsoon crashing down on the car roof. All that could be heard was the occasional drum beat.

I offered him a forgiving smile, regretting it at once. "That's all right."

He seemed to interpret my smile as an invitation. His lips curled up as his dark eyes bore into me. I tried to look away, but fear took over when he moved his hand across the console and touched my jean-clad thigh. "You know, Gracyn, you're a very beautiful young woman."

My breath caught in my throat, and I fought back a nauseated gag. I looked down at his hand as he curled his fingers around the inside of my thigh and began moving up my leg. Without a moment of hesitation, I grabbed his hand, stopping him in place before he went too far. I narrowed my eyes, glaring at him. "Beautiful? That's the best you can come up with? If you're going to molest me or seduce me or whatever the hell you're trying to do here, you could at least be a little more creative." Malice seethed from my voice, defiance and self-preservation rising up inside me.

I started squeezing his hand, harder and tighter as my anger channeled into my strength. Something crunched, like brittle bones being broken. But that couldn't be it. I wasn't strong enough, or was I?

Thunder boomed directly overhead, nearly shaking the car. Lightning lit up the darkness in a flash of white. At that moment, his eyes, wide and full of sheer panic, met mine.

I jolted up in bed, my heart racing and my breathing labored. The sheets stuck to my sweaty arms as I leaned back and tried to calm down. *It was just a dream,* I told myself before a snarky voice entered my thoughts. *No, it was a nightmare. A nightmare from the past, and obviously one that won't go away. I told you weeks ago you should have reported him to the cops.*

Closing my eyes, I took a deep breath. *What difference does it make? He's a vegetable in the hospital right now. And he has a broken hand. He got what he had coming.*

My eyes opened as I resolved to put the memory of him behind me. He was hundreds of miles away now. And if he ever woke up and returned to a normal life, he'd stay far away from me if he knew what was good for him.

Trying to forget my nightmare, I noticed the early light of dawn sneaking around the window curtain. Then a sound from the kitchen below broke through the silence. Becca was probably getting ready for work.

I slipped out of bed and grabbed the gray pajama pants draped over the back of the desk chair. Still wearing the oversized black shirt I'd slept in, I pulled on my pants and grabbed my glasses. Wide awake, I headed downstairs.

Dressed in a navy skirt and a white blouse not much lighter than her hair, Becca scurried about the kitchen when I approached the island. I plunked down on a stool and rested my forearms on the granite.

"You're up early," she commented, pouring a cup of coffee. "Want some?"

"No, thanks," I replied, my thoughts on the teacher from the bar. Unfortunately, he wasn't much better than the man haunting me in my nightmares. "I met Mr. Wainwright last night. Apparently, I'm in his class. He said he knew you."

Becca nearly choked. Her hand trembling, she set the mug down before any coffee spilled on her clothes. With a deep breath, she composed herself, then took another sip. "Really? And how was the band?" she asked casually.

"Good. I liked their music. But back to Mr. Wainwright. How do you know him? If you don't tell me what I'm in for, I may have to ask the school to change my schedule. He said you two were close. If there are some unresolved feelings there, I don't want to end up in the middle of it."

A troubled look crossed over her expression, and her smile disappeared. Her shoulders tensing, she looked down at her coffee. "Well, this is certainly unexpected for a Friday morning." She lifted her steady gaze to me, the emotion from a second ago now gone. "I don't know what he told you, but all you need to know is that he's a thing of the past. I moved on, but he seems unable to. I'm sorry he dragged you into this. That wasn't right."

"So you're the one who broke his heart?" I asked, remembering what Alex had told me.

Becca whipped her eyes to the side, scanning the hallway that led to her bedroom. Then she moved closer to the island and leaned across the counter. "I can't talk about this now," she whispered. "Gabe could walk in here at any minute."

"It's true then?"

She didn't need to answer me. The moisture in her eyes gave her away. "Please, I'm begging you to let this go. It's complicated."

"Did he hurt you?" I asked. "Because he was kind of creepy if you ask me."

"No," she said. "It was nothing like that."

I wrinkled my eyebrows, wishing she'd tell me more. But my time ran out. The dogs trotted into the kitchen, their nails clicking against the wood floor. Gabriel followed them, his hair messy in a sexy, just-woke-up sort of way. The white T-shirt he wore outlined his lean muscles, the tails falling over plaid pajama pants. He looked more like a graduate student after a late night of studying than a successful doctor.

"Good morning, ladies. I thought I heard you two." He made a beeline for the coffee as Becca returned her attention to me.

"So, do you have any plans for today?" she asked in a bright tone as if our conversation about Mr. Wainwright had never happened.

Confused, I hesitated with a disappointed sigh. My questions would have to wait for another time. "I'm not sure yet."

"Well, I bet Gypsy would love a good grooming. And if you have a chance to clean out the stalls, I'm sure Gabe would appreciate that," Becca rambled on as Gabriel walked across the family room to the front door.

After letting the dogs out, he returned to the kitchen. "Becca, shouldn't you be going? It's almost seven-thirty."

"Yes, you're right." She took one last swig of coffee before grabbing her purse off the table and stopping beside him for a quick peck on the lips. "I've got to run. You two have a great day. I'll see you later."

Before I could say another word, she hurried out the front door, leaving me alone with Gabriel.

7

Silence filled the room as I sat still, wondering what to do now. First, it was Sam's stepfather, then Mr. Wainwright who I still thought of as the creepy bar guy, and now Becca's husband. I hadn't spent much time with Gabriel, but it looked like that was about to change. I wanted to believe he was a stand-up guy. He was married to Becca after all, and I hoped he wasn't a low-life like another married man I knew.

Gabriel leaned against the back counter, a coffee mug in his hand. "So, what's on your agenda for today?"

I shrugged. "I haven't really thought about it. I might go back to bed for a few hours."

"Late night?"

More like an early morning, I thought. But I wasn't about to spill my guts over my nightmare. I was trying to bury the past, not keep it alive. "You could say that."

I suddenly changed my mind about the coffee. Pushing my chair back, I stood and wandered around to the cabinets. After helping myself to a mug, I filled it with steaming black coffee. It felt good to finally know where everything was in the kitchen. After four days on my own, I no longer needed to guess where the coffee mugs were. I added a dash of the creamer sitting on the counter before lifting it to my lips. "Mm. That's better."

"How about some breakfast? I can whip up some scrambled eggs," Gabriel offered.

I glanced at him, thinking sarcastically to myself, *No, this isn't awkward at all. My sister's husband who I barely know offering to make me breakfast.* As harmless and genuine as he seemed, I couldn't allow myself to accept. "That's very thoughtful, but I'm not much of a breakfast eater. I'm just going to take my coffee upstairs and give my mom a call. I think it's afternoon in Russia right now and I want to catch her soon in case she has any plans for tonight."

"Okay, but you're missing out," he said with a grin.

"Maybe this weekend, then."

"I have to head back to Boston in the morning," he explained.

"Oh, well, then maybe next week," was all I said before scurrying out of the kitchen, careful not to spill the coffee in my hands.

I headed up to my room, my soft footsteps not making a sound on the hardwood floor. Once inside, I shut the door, relieved when I heard the latch click into place, not because I was afraid of Gabriel or nervous to be alone with him, but because I didn't know him very well. I hoped in time, I'd get to know him better and situations like this morning wouldn't bother me so much. Especially if I could put Sam's stepfather out of my mind. Until then, unfamiliar men rattled my nerves.

Shaking thoughts of all men out of my head, I sat down at my desk and grabbed my cell phone. No new calls. I'd received and sent several texts and emails to my mother since she left for Russia, but I wanted to hear her voice. So I found her number and pressed the call button.

I gazed out the window at the clear sky and lush tree branches as the phone on the other end rang. After three rings, my mother answered. "Gracyn! Honey, I'm so glad you called. I was just thinking about trying you, but I wasn't sure if you'd be up yet."

"Hi, Mom. It's good to hear your voice. Texts and emails are nice, but they can never take the place of a phone call. How's Moscow?" *Keep the subject on Mom,* I told myself. *The last thing you want to do is worry her about an unsolved murder and a creepy History teacher who apparently has an unresolved past with Becca.*

"It's okay," she answered hesitantly. "It's very different. I'm starting to settle in and figure out where things are like the grocery store. And I've learned enough of the language to order a coffee."

"Wow. I never thought about the little things like that. It makes moving here to Sedgewick look like a breeze. But I'm sure it's worth it for your new job. I'm so proud of you, Mom. Really, I am."

"Uh-oh. What's wrong?" my mother asked abruptly. How did she do that? It was like she could read my mind. Even now, with several thousand miles separating us, nothing had changed. I still didn't know how I'd kept the situation with Sam's stepfather from her, but I wasn't about to share that nightmare. Some things were better left unsaid.

"Nothing, really," I replied slowly. "Just like you, I'm getting settled in. It's quite a change of pace compared to home."

"Are you sure that's all?"

"Yes. In fact, I already met someone from my class. I think I mentioned in an email that I was going out to hear his band play last night."

"You're right. You did. And that sounds wonderful, honey. I'm glad you're making friends already. So things are going okay? What do you think of Gabriel?"

"He's great. But I haven't spent much time with him. He only came home from Boston two days ago and he has to leave again tomorrow. But he's been very welcoming."

"Good. Are you ready for school?"

"Ready as I'll ever be. I'm registered to start Monday, and I know where it is. There isn't much more to do at this point."

"That's my baby. Always so organized and prepared." Chatter rang out on the other end, and it sounded like my mother held her hand over the phone while she whispered to someone in the background.

"Mom? Are you still there?"

"Yes. Sorry, that was a coworker. I'm still at the office."

"Oh, I guess you would be. I'm sorry."

"Gracyn, honey, never be sorry for calling. But I really should go because I need to wrap up a few things before leaving tonight. Was there anything else you wanted to talk about that can't wait until the weekend?"

"No," I said, a little disappointed she had to go.

"Then I'll call you tomorrow or Sunday. I love you."

"Love you too, Mom." With a sigh, I hung up the call. It felt good to hear a familiar voice, and I had to admit, I missed her. My mother and I were very close since we were the only family we had, at least until I'd learned I had a sister. But even then, we had stayed close.

Tapping my fingers against the desk, I stared out the window as if in a trance. I sipped my coffee, taking in the silence. Quiet like this where one could hear a pin drop didn't exist in Maryland. Even in the dead of the night, sirens often blared and the roar of the beltway was a constant hum in the background. I was slowly getting used to the silence. But it still seemed strange, like the calm before the storm. At least once school started in a few days, I wouldn't have time to watch the minutes tick by.

My thoughts were broken when my phone buzzed from a new text. I picked it up and swiped the screen, smiling when I saw Alex's name. *R u up?* was all he had written.

I typed a message back to him. *Yes. U?* As I hit send, I smacked my hand against my forehead. That was dumb! Of course he was up.

U r funny, he texted back.

As I chuckled at his message, my phone rang. Alex. I answered it on the first ring. "Good morning," I said, my phone clinking against my glasses frame.

"Good morning to you. I trust you made it home okay."

"Yes. I'm learning my way around. How much longer did you stay out last night?"

"I was able to bribe Derek to leave right after you. There will always be those who turn the night into a marathon, but I'm not one of them, at least not when I have to get up for work the next day."

"I thought you said you didn't need much sleep to function," I teased.

"I did, didn't I? I was just trying to impress you. Did it work?"

I laughed. "Only if I need you to stay up all night with me for something. But anyway, getting up for work must have sucked after a long night. Where are you now?"

"I'm used to it. And right now, I'm halfway between the Hamiltons' farm and the Dumante estate." His voice fell on the second name, his tone somber and disapproving.

"Dumante? You mean—"

"That's right. As much as I hate going there, they have animals to feed, too." He paused, then continued in a happier tone. "I'll be there in a few minutes, so I can't talk long. Want to get together tomorrow night? Maybe this time I can learn something about you instead of getting roped into giving you the scoop on everyone else."

A grin crept onto my face even as I dreaded the moment he realized the exotic city girl he had met was really a dud. *Stop being such a martyr. He's going to have to know the real you sooner or later. If you like him, you need to ante up. And if he is genuinely interested, he won't care if you were the biggest nerd or the head cheerleader back home.* "Okay. I'm in."

"Awesome. I'll pick you up at six, okay?"

"Sounds good."

"Great. Well, I have to go. I see the gates of hell waiting for me."

I rolled my eyes at his drama. "Oh, no. Don't let it gobble you up. We have a date tomorrow night and if you're gone, whatever will I do?" I teased.

"Shut up," he said, a twinge of laughter in his voice. "You're not going to let me have any fun, are you?"

"Nope."

"I'm so glad we got that out of the way. Well, I'm pulling in. See you tomorrow."

"Bye." I hung up the phone, my giddy smile fading as I backed up to his reference to the gates of hell. That seemed odd. This Dumante family didn't seem to be well liked. As if I didn't have enough to worry about between Mr. Wainwright and my nightmares, a two-year-old cold murder case was now added to the list. At least I had met Alex. Perhaps he was just what I needed to distract me from all that seemed wrong in the world.

By the time I trudged downstairs the next morning, Becca sat at the table, the newspaper sprawled out in front of her, a corner of it curled up against a ceramic mug. The dogs were sprawled out on the floor by her feet, and the coffee pot gurgled from the counter.

"Good morning," she said as I passed her on my way to the coffee.

"Hi," I mumbled, tired from staying up late reading a new novel I had downloaded. After pouring my coffee and adding a dash of creamer, I joined her at the table. Unlike Becca who'd dressed for the day in jeans and a black shirt, I still wore pajamas. My glasses shielded my eyes, the frames locking some of my curls behind my ears. "Did Gabriel leave already?"

Becca nodded, lifting her eyes from the newspaper. "Yes. A few hours ago. His shift starts at nine. So it's just the two of us for the weekend. And I have a plan." She grinned, her eyes twinkling.

"Dare I ask what it is?" I asked before taking another sip of coffee.

"It's not so terrible. Now that you've gotten comfortable around the horses, I think it's time you learn to ride."

I frowned, thinking over her proposition. I wasn't nearly as scared and opposed to learning to ride as I'd been a week ago. But after ten years of being afraid, it was hard to let go of the fear altogether. "I'm not sure I'm ready for that," I told her.

"Why not? You and Gypsy are getting along great. I don't see any reason to put it off any longer. She needs the exercise and if you're going to learn, you should do it before the weather gets cold."

I stared straight ahead, my eyes drawn to the rustic barn in the distance outside the window. With a heavy sigh, I set my mug down, unable to think of a good reason to refuse her offer. "Okay. I'll give it a shot. But one fall and I'm done. Deal?" I raised my eyebrows at Becca who smiled with satisfaction.

"Deal. You won't be sorry, I promise. Besides, you should trust me more now. I was right about the horses, remember? They love you."

"I know. It's the only reason I'm agreeing to this."

"Well, get some breakfast and meet me in the barn as soon as you're ready." She stood, then carried her dishes to the sink. "I'm going to head out there now and start sorting through the tack." After loading her bowl and mug in the dishwasher, she headed for the door, whistling to the dogs. They scrambled up and followed her outside.

Twenty minutes later, I walked out the front door. After eating, I had changed into jeans and a white T-shirt. My curls fell from a ponytail and contact lenses replaced my glasses. The only thing I wasn't sure of was my shoes. My options were tennis shoes or hiking boots and, after a long debate with myself, I chose the hiking boots.

Outside, the air held a chill, but I could feel the sun gearing up to warm the day. As I walked across the driveway, doubts crept into my mind. *Relax,* I told myself. *How could anything go wrong on a day like this?* Then another voice jumped in. *The very same way something could go wrong in this town. Like a twelve-year-old girl being murdered. See? Things can and do go very wrong anywhere.*

Why couldn't I stop thinking about that? Perhaps because anyone could be guilty, including Mr. Wainwright. I still didn't have Becca's explanation about her involvement with him. Maybe I could get it out of her today. She had said something about not wanting to talk about him in front of Gabriel, but Gabriel was back in Boston. This time she wouldn't be able to dodge me like she had when she ran out the door to work yesterday morning.

The barn smelled like sweet hay and old leather when I passed through the doorway. The horses' hoof beats on the dirt floor and their snorting had become familiar sounds to me over the last few days. Rather than terrifying me, they comforted me now.

Becca emerged from Gypsy's stall, leading the frosty red mare into the aisle before securing the crossties to her halter. As Becca hung the lead rope on a hook, I folded my arms across my chest.

"You never told me about Mr. Wainwright," I said.

Becca froze for a moment, tensing as she turned to me. "What do you want to know?"

"Just what happened between the two of you," I explained as I approached Gypsy and stroked her soft muzzle. My gaze shifted to Becca before I continued. "I don't mean to pry, but he made me nervous. And after what you told me about that girl getting killed, I think I just need some reassurance that he couldn't be the one who did it."

Relief washed over her face. "Is that what's bothering you about him?"

"Yes. I mean, I don't go to a lot of bars. Actually, I never go to bars, and I certainly don't have guys in their forties I don't know approaching me. He was a little creepy."

A huge grin broke out on Becca's lips as a wistful expression crossed over her eyes. "Well, I can assure you that Aidan isn't a murderer and he doesn't go around hitting on high school girls."

"So he's nothing to worry about?"

"I don't know if I'd say that. He's still going to be your teacher, so you will have to worry about your homework."

"I understand." I paused, realizing I was still petting Gypsy's nose. Dropping my hand, I kept my attention on Becca. "Why did he ask me about you?" I probed gently.

She averted her eyes away from me. "I'm not sure. It was a long time ago, and it's not something I want to dredge up right now," she whispered. She looked sad, like she was about to cry, unlike the Becca who loved everything about her life I'd gotten to know this week.

"He didn't hurt you, did he?" I blurted out.

She shook her head. "No. It was nothing like that."

"Okay. Good. Because you just promised me he's harmless."

"I did. And I meant it." As quickly as the pain had spread across her face, it disappeared. "I think we need to get moving with your lesson because I need to get some gardening done." Before I could protest, she spun around and headed for the tack room.

Gaping at Becca's retreating figure, I frowned with disappointment. I'd hoped to learn more about what had happened between her and my future History teacher, but clearly, she'd told me all she was willing to share. At least I found comfort in knowing she was convinced he hadn't killed the girl who'd been murdered years ago.

Shaking those thoughts out of my head, I grabbed a brush from the shelf and began grooming Gypsy. Her coat glistened from every stroke. As I ran the brush over her hindquarters, Becca emerged from the tack room carrying an English saddle, the girth buckles clanking with every step she took.

"Did you get her hooves?" she asked, positioning a square quilted pad on Gypsy's back.

"Not yet. But I will." I tossed the brush on the shelf and reached for a hoof pick. Approaching Gypsy's shoulder, I told Becca, "I have a date tonight." Without waiting for Becca's reaction, I nudged the mare just enough to get her to pick up her leg.

"Really? Let me guess. Alex," Becca said as she hoisted the saddle onto the mare's back.

"Yes. I guess that was pretty obvious." I finished scraping the dirt and manure out of Gypsy's hoof before gently setting it down. Standing up, I noticed a teasing grin on Becca's face.

"It was also pretty fast," she said as she buckled the girth. "You haven't even been here a week."

"I know." I smiled, remembering Alex's nice brown eyes and the way he'd shown an interest in me, something few boys had ever done. Then I shrugged with a frown at that thought. "He's probably only interested because I'm the new girl in town from the big city."

Becca snapped her attention toward me as she secured the girth and let the saddle flap fall over it. "Why would you say that?"

"Because he's a cool guy who's in a band and goes to parties." I almost said drinking parties, but caught myself. Even though Becca seemed okay with that, I didn't need to advertise it and risk getting a lecture. "I'm a geek who gets straight A's and likes to paint. We have nothing in common."

"How well do you know him?"

I narrowed my eyes as a faint smile crossed over my mouth. "I guess I really don't," I answered slowly, realizing he had revealed no more about himself last night than I'd shared about myself.

"Then give him a chance. You never know what could happen." She gave me a sly wink. "Okay, enough boy talk. I'm going to grab the bridle and you need to clean out her back hooves."

Without another word, Becca disappeared into the tack room. I ran my hand along Gypsy's hindquarters to her tail, my thoughts focused on my date with Alex as I forgot I was about to get on a horse for the second time in my life, something I thought I'd never do again.

8

It was no surprise that Becca was right. Gypsy followed my commands like the perfect horse. As soon as Becca helped me climb into the saddle from the mounting block, I took the reins and tried to balance. The mare's movements were soft and fluid, and she responded to my cues as if she knew what I was going to ask of her before I gave each signal.

At first, I felt awkward and clumsy. But Becca's instructions were easy to understand. We only walked, using the pasture while the other two horses remained in their stalls. I learned how to stop by pulling gently on the reins, go forward with a nudge from my calves, and turn in each direction with a leading rein.

After a half hour in the saddle, I felt like I knew what I was doing. I was surprised by how confident I felt in one session. I thanked Becca profusely until she laughed, insisting I was a natural. By the time I led Gypsy back to the barn to untack her, I forgot about my first horseback riding experience that had ended in disaster. Instead, I chided myself for letting one bad experience scare me. Now, looking back, I realized it was an isolated incident, one that must have had nothing to do with me.

Becca quickly showed me how to untack and where to put everything. After turning Prince and Cadence out to pasture, she left me alone, explaining that she needed to head out to the garden. I offered to help, but she refused. "It's very kind of you to offer, but I can't accept. This is your last weekend before school starts. You should enjoy it. Besides, you have a date tonight. You don't want to get dirt under your fingernails today," she insisted. Then she hurried out the barn door with the dogs in tow, not giving me a second to object.

I sighed, turning back to Gypsy. If I didn't know any better, I would have thought Becca wanted to be alone. *That's it,* I thought. *She's probably still upset because you asked her about Mr. Wainwright and she doesn't want you to pursue the subject.* As curious as I was, I had to let it go. It obviously upset her and, regardless of being assigned to his History class, it wasn't any of my business.

Trying to push the thought of Mr. Wainwright out of my mind, I finished untacking Gypsy and led her out to the pasture. As soon as I released her, she trotted over to the other horses. Then I secured the gate and headed back to the house, eager to paint the day away until my date with Alex.

Becca was chopping lettuce, a glass of red wine next to the cutting board, when I marched downstairs to wait for Alex that evening. As I set my purse on the island, she whistled at me.

"What?" I asked with a coy smile.

"You look gorgeous. He doesn't stand a chance."

"Hmm," I mused, sliding onto a stool. "I think you're exaggerating." Secretly, I hoped she was right. I had chosen my favorite jeans for the night. My hair fell in waves over my white ruffled shirt, and I'd added a touch of make-up to my eyes, grateful for my contact lenses.

Becca lifted the cutting board and used the knife to scrape the chopped lettuce into a wooden bowl. "No, I mean it. Is this is a big night or just casual? Because I'm reading hot date off your look."

"I haven't decided yet," I told her with a smile.

Raising her eyebrows, she lifted her wine glass. "So you're a tease?"

"Maybe."

"At least you aren't denying it. What are you and Alex doing tonight? Dinner and a movie? Or something more romantic?"

I felt heat racing across my cheeks. "Alex texted me about an hour ago. We're going to grab some pizza and then maybe head over to his cousin's house for a party."

"That sounds nice. I'm glad you're already making friends. I'm sure it was tough to leave all your friends behind for your senior year."

"Not as tough as you'd think," I muttered, looking down at the shiny granite countertop as Sam's stepfather flashed through my mind.

Before she could ask what I meant, the dogs scrambled to their feet from where they'd been lying next to the kitchen table. They charged across the room to the door just as the bell rang.

"That's Alex." I grabbed my purse and hopped off the stool. "I don't think I'll be out too late, but I'll text you if I'm not going to be home by midnight. Bye."

Wanting to avoid an awkward departure, I rushed outside. "Hi," I said to Alex as I shut the door behind me.

"Hey. What's the hurry?" he asked, standing a few feet away and not making any move to follow me.

I stopped and smiled at him, once again marveling at how comfortable his warm brown eyes and easy going demeanor made me feel. I was even getting used to his ponytail. Tonight, he wore a gray T-shirt that strained against his broad shoulders and hung untucked over his jeans. The silver feather pendant he seemed fond of hung from a black rope around his neck.

"I'm hungry, that's all," I explained. "Wait until I tell you what I did today."

He closed the distance between us, his eyes meeting mine. "I'm all ears."

I nodded toward the driveway where his black Jeep Wrangler waited. "Then let's go. I'll tell you all about it in the car."

"Call me old fashioned, but shouldn't we say goodbye to Becca and Gabriel?" he asked, hesitating.

"It's only Becca because Gabriel's working this weekend. And no, that's not necessary." I lowered my voice and glanced at him from under my eyelashes. "Okay. If you want the truth, she'll probably just say something to embarrass me. So please help me make a getaway."

Alex glanced at the front door as a twinkle lit up his eyes. He grinned, but humored me. "Okay. If it makes you happy."

We hurried down the porch steps and around to the passenger door of his Jeep. I was about to open it when Alex reached for the handle from behind me.

"Here, let me," he said.

I backed up as he moved to the side and opened the door. "Thanks," I murmured shyly, glancing at him out of the corner of my eye.

"No problem." He took my hand as I climbed up into the seat. When he let go, I tossed him a faint smile of appreciation. Instead of shutting the door, he lingered beside it, his eyes focused on me. "You look nice tonight."

"Thank you. So do you."

A wide grin formed on his mouth. As if happy with the way the evening was shaping up, he shut the door and walked around the front before jumping in beside me. When he turned on the engine, I snapped my seat belt into place. Then he backed up and guided the Jeep down the gravel driveway.

Alex turned onto the road, and shadows from the fading sunlight danced across the windshield. "Everything okay?" he asked, breaking the silence between us.

"Yes," I said with a little too much emphasis. When he raised his eyebrows, I continued. "Actually, I'm better than okay. I rode a horse today."

"Hmm," he let out with a deep breath. "And how old are you?"

"Hey! You don't understand. I went on a trail ride when I was eight and got thrown off. It was pretty traumatic, and I've been terrified ever since." I deliberately spared him most of the details. He didn't need to know that the horses had acted skittish around me. Besides, I was trying to forget the entire experience, especially now that I had Gypsy.

"Oh. Then, this sounds like a big accomplishment. I'm happy for you."

"Thanks." I felt flushed and hoped my cheeks weren't bright red. "I also talked to Becca about Mr. Wainwright."

"Now we're getting somewhere. Tell me the scoop. Is she his long lost love? The one who broke his heart?"

I frowned, afraid my answer would disappoint him. "She wouldn't tell me much. She clammed up the instant I mentioned him. Both times."

"That's not good. And you tried twice?"

"Yes. But she told me I was crazy when I asked if he could have killed that girl two years ago."

"Why would you even think that?"

I sighed, realizing that beneath my suspicions hid a terrible secret I never wanted to reveal. "I don't know. Could be the way he was staring at me from the bar or how he showed up at my table out of the blue."

"You really don't like him, do you? Sorry to disappoint you, but school starts in two days. And you're going to have to deal with him since you're in his class."

"I know."

"Well, he's no killer. I could have told you that."

"Okay. Now I feel even better. If both you and Becca are convinced he didn't do it, then he must be innocent."

"Everyone knows who did it."

"The brother, I know," I said with a sigh, wanting to ask why he wasn't behind bars if he'd done it. Instead, I studied the woods passing by. The setting sun sent streaks of dark purple racing across the twilight sky. "Mind if we change the subject?"

"Mind? I'll change it for us." He smiled before launching his next question. "So, Gracyn Pierce, I hardly know anything about you. Let's start with college since that's got to be on your mind right about now. Have you sent any applications out yet?"

"No. But thanks for the reminder. I need to get started on those soon."

"You and me both. But seriously, do it."

His emphasis on the last two words nearly made me laugh. "What? Why do you care?"

"I'm just saying that you don't want to fall behind on them. The last thing you're going to want is to be stuck in Sedgewick any longer than you have to be here."

"Oh, come on. It's not that bad."

"You've been here a week. Just wait until you've been here a month or so. There isn't a whole lot to do."

"I'll keep that in mind. Have you started working on yours?"

"Absolutely. I want them all sent out by the end of September. The earlier, the better."

"Where are you applying?" He didn't strike me as the intellectual type. So far, all I really knew about him was that he delivered farm supplies and played the guitar.

"Everywhere," he responded vaguely. When I gave him an exasperated look, he continued. "As long as it's far from this crazy town, I'm interested. But seriously, I'm applying to a bunch of schools throughout New England. I wouldn't mind moving to Boston. How about you? Do you know where you want to go?"

"Um, not really," I said quietly, not wanting to tell him my sights were set on MIT. It would only expose me as the geek I really was, and I was enjoying the attention I was getting as the cool new girl. "Everything happened really fast with my move, and I haven't had a lot of time to think about college for the last few weeks. But you're right. I need to get started on my applications soon."

"Then you'd better pick some schools," he said.

I nodded, suddenly eager to get away from the subject of college. The more we talked about it, the more likely he'd realize he was sitting next to a first-class brainiac. "So how much longer until we get to the pizza place?" I asked with a broad smile.

"Are you changing the subject on me?"

"Yes. I'm hungry. And pizza is one of my favorites."

"Good. So you like pizza. I'm beginning to learn a little about you."

I couldn't help laughing softly. "Of course. I mean, who doesn't like pizza?"

"Well, you are from the south."

"Oh please. People from Maryland like pizza."

"Really?" he asked with mock surprise. "I thought you Southerners liked collards and grits and stuff like that."

"I think you have to go a lot farther south for those. Maryland isn't in the deep south."

"It is compared to here. Trust me, when the temperatures are in the single digits and the wind chills are below zero, you're going to be dreaming of the South."

I shrugged. "That's hard to imagine right now, although my friend, Sam, loves to remind me about that."

"Who's Sam?" Alex asked, his eyebrows arched.

"Actually, it's Samantha. She's my best friend. Always has been. Always–" I wanted to say "Always will be", but I got stuck because I couldn't be sure of that. If she ever found out why her stepfather was in the hospital, there was no telling how she'd react.

Quiet settled over us as we reached the edge of town. The trees thinned out, giving way to Victorian homes tucked behind white picket fences.

"It must not be easy to have to start over for your last year of school," Alex said.

I took a deep breath, watching the quaint neighborhoods pass by. But images of Sam's worried brown eyes and her frightened expression clouded my thoughts. I vividly remembered the last day we'd spent together, about two weeks after her stepfather had slipped into a coma. She had tried to stay strong for me the night before I drove up to Massachusetts, but I could still see the concern in her eyes. She might have been able to hide it from some people, but I always knew when something was bothering her. And nothing had ever worried her as much as her stepfather's sudden unexplained illness. "It's not," I answered, my voice quiet and wistful.

"I'm sorry. I didn't mean to upset you," Alex said.

"It's okay. It's only natural that you'd ask me about my friends back home. You don't have to be sorry," I said, staring out the window. Only when I finished talking did I look back at him.

"But you turned as white as a ghost when I asked if you missed her."

We finally reached the business section of town. Alex turned down a side street and then into a parking lot. As soon as he stopped behind a brick building, he shut off the engine and turned to me. "I wanted to have a good time tonight and get to know you. But I suddenly feel like I've dredged up something that bothers you."

I looked down at my purse in my lap, playing aimlessly with the strap. All I could think about was Sam's stepfather. I hated it when I was reminded about him. I had never wanted something so horrible to happen, but I was convinced I had unknowingly cursed him. I mean, if I'd had the strength to break his hand, anything was possible. Even though I knew I couldn't be blamed, that he had done a bad thing and was paying the price, I still felt guilty. It was my fault Sam's family was crumbling at her feet. That her mother was slipping into a depression and her brother was drifting away. Her life would never be the same, and it weighed on me every time I thought about it. "It's...it's just—" I stuttered, fighting the urge to open up and confess my part in this.

Don't do it! a voice in my head ordered. *Leave that mess behind. There's nothing you can do. No one can prove you did anything. So let it go and move on!*

"What?" Alex asked, gently touching my shoulder.

I glanced at him, took a deep breath and mustered a faint smile. "Now I'm the one who should be sorry. Can we start over?"

"Sure. But before we do, I just want to let you know that if you ever need someone to talk to, I'm a good listener." He smiled warmly, his eyes meeting mine.

"Thanks." For a moment, I felt a light tingle race through me. Maybe there was a spark between us. But it disappeared quickly, leaving me to remember the ugly past I'd left behind.

Swallowing nervously, I looked out the windshield at the brick wall. I blinked hard, as if closing my eyes could shut out the horrible memory of that night. Then, with a bright smile, I turned back to Alex. "How good is this pizza place? I'm starving."

9

Dinner at the pizza restaurant was exactly what I needed. The cheerful dining room bustled with energy from the crowd. Alex and I ate at a corner booth and several times, I noticed other girls glancing at us. Ignoring them, I gave Alex my undivided attention as we bantered back and forth in what could only be described as a speed dating game of twenty questions. I worked hard to answer everything he asked, but not give away my guarded secret. That I was a dedicated student who had a three-year record of almost straight A's. And until my junior year, it had been straight A's. But last year, I couldn't seem to do anything right for my Literature teacher. The B-minus she had given me pulled my average down, but even an A-minus overall average was a little too nerdy to reveal to Alex.

I tried to squeeze in questions about him. He told me he had lived in Sedgewick his entire life, his father was a doctor in town and his cousin, Zoe, was more like a sister to him because he didn't have any siblings. But getting more information about him than that was like pulling teeth. And I couldn't let it frustrate me since I wasn't telling him everything about myself, either.

After we polished off a veggie pizza, we headed across town to Zoe's party. The stately brick manor with gabled windows on the third floor was lit up like a beacon in the night. Cars and trucks lined the long driveway. Alex drove past them until he reached the loop circling a water fountain with a Greek statue rising out of the middle.

He pulled up behind a silver BMW and turned to me with a grin. "Since I'm family, I always get the good parking spot here."

"Nice," I commented, unfastening my seat belt. I hopped out of the Jeep, approached the back, and waited for Alex. Kids streamed in and out of the front double doors ordained with stained glass. The guys carried bottles while girls teetered on high heels whether they wore jeans or skirts ending half-way up their thighs. I felt a bit understated in my jeans and boots, but dolling it up like some of them had wasn't my style.

When Alex reached my side, he took my hand. "Ready?"

"Sure. This is some place."

"Yeah. It's not too shabby. My uncle is the DA. And my aunt is the only accountant in town."

"Must be lucrative."

Alex looked away, a scowl crossing over his face. "It is when your number one client is the wealthiest businessman in the county."

"Who's that?" I asked, not sure if I'd know who he meant.

"Everett Dumante. Your neighbor and the father of a deceased young girl."

"Oh." I was almost sorry I brought it up and quickly changed the subject. "Where are your aunt and uncle tonight? Dare I even ask if they're home?"

"You may ask. But no, they're not. They spend most of their summer weekends at the Cape. Zoe came home early to hold her annual 'Let's Get Wasted Before School Starts' party."

"So this is a tradition?"

Alex led me up the stairs when he found a break in the trickle of kids going up and down. "Yes, it is. And since she'll be a senior, it's the last one. It'll be the talk of the school on Monday. It will be good for your reputation to be here tonight."

My jaw nearly dropped. I'd never had a reputation before because I had never hung out with the cool kids, let alone gone to parties like this.

Before I could respond, we entered the house and Derek ambushed us in the two-story foyer. "You made it," he said. "And you're not alone, you sly devil." Derek slapped Alex on the shoulder, a sparkle in his blue eyes. "Hi, Gracyn. I hope this one's treating you well."

"Hi, Derek. It's nice to see you again," I replied, ignoring his comment.

Derek's gaze skimmed over us, briefly pausing when he noticed our hands locked together.

Alex paid little attention to his friend. He scanned the party crowd, honing in on a group of girls clustered in an open doorway off to the side. "Isn't that Zoe over there? Don't you think you should talk to her?"

Derek shifted his stare away from me to look across the foyer. I followed his gaze and guessed that Zoe was the tall one with long black hair. She was the center of attention in skinny washed-out jeans, black boots, and a matching V-neck shirt that showed off her tan, not to mention cleavage I would have died for. She held a beer bottle in her hand, her blue eyes anxious as she watched the foyer.

Derek whipped his gaze away from the girls. "Yeah. She's back from the Cape. So what, man?"

"Go talk to her. You're not going to get anywhere with her if you're hanging over here with us," Alex insisted.

"Wait a minute," Derek said, shaking his head. "Why are you suddenly routing for me to hook up with your cousin? You always said you'd never let that happen."

"I'm just saying you should go talk to her. You know, so you'll leave us alone."

Derek grinned like a Chesire cat. "Now the truth comes out. You're so busted, Carver."

"Whatever it takes. Besides, sometimes I need to remember that Zoe can handle herself."

"She sure can. And it's a good thing, too." Derek's expression turned dark. "Because guess who's back."

I pulled my gaze away from the girls, returning my attention to Alex and Derek.

"You're kidding?" Alex asked with a frustrated sigh.

"Nope. Rumor has it he'll be in our class this year."

"What? He hasn't graduated yet?"

"I guess not. He took two years off to travel the world because, you know, that's what one does after one kills their little sister."

I sucked in a sharp breath as I looked at Alex, my eyebrows scrunched with curiosity.

He met my stare before answering my silent question. "Lucian Dumante. He and Zoe were an item up until his sister's body was found. After the funeral, he took off. I kind of figured he'd be back at some point."

"I think you forgot to mention that to me," Derek complained. "I would have appreciated a warning. I was hoping he was gone for good. With him back in the picture, no one stands a chance with Zoe."

"Zoe would be a fool to take him back," Alex gritted out as his gaze swept back across the foyer and landed on Zoe. She instantly locked her eyes with his, her expression cold, warning him to butt out as though she'd heard him.

"Excuse me," Alex said, not backing down from her stare. "I'll be right back." He dropped my hand, crossed the room, and grabbed Zoe's wrist as her friends scattered. Without another look back at me, he pulled her through the doorway and they disappeared around the corner.

"Well," I said, looking at Derek. "There goes my night."

He tried to cheer me up with a smile. "This won't take long. Zoe won't let him monopolize her at her own party. But he has a point. I mean, the guy's a criminal. I know Zoe will probably never choose me, but she can at least do better than Lucian."

"And Alex can talk her out of going back to him?"

"Not a chance. He's wasting his time, but I think it makes him feel kind of macho and all, taking on the role of her big brother."

I raised my eyebrows and glanced at the empty doorway, hoping Alex would return soon. The front door kept opening and shutting as kids came in and out. Cool drafts breezed over me while I waited, wondering if I'd end up standing in the foyer all night. As if reading my mind, Alex appeared a moment later and returned to my side.

He forced out a smile, even as dark shadows lingered in his eyes. "Sorry about that."

"It's okay. She's your family and you have to look out for her."

Alex's expression softened as he took my hand again, threading his fingers through mine. "That's what I like about you. You are so cool." Alex looked up at Derek. "Isn't she great? Man, did I get lucky." He beamed like a little boy who'd gotten his most wanted item on his Christmas list.

"Rub it in, why don't you?" Derek grumbled.

"Hey, cheer up. You've got plenty of girls to choose from," Alex said. "This place is swarming with them." He paused, a teasing sparkle forming in his eyes. "Unless you're holding out for Celeste. Sorry to break it to you, but I doubt she'll be here."

Derek rolled his eyes. "Gee, thanks for reminding me that I'll have to deal with her in two days."

"Come on. She's cute even with her goth style and all."

"She's weird," was all Derek said as his eyes wandered about the party, as if looking for someone new to set his sights on. When he focused on a group of girls beyond the kitchen doorway, a sly smile lit up his face. "I think I see Lacey. Later you two." Without another word, he rushed across the entry hall and disappeared around the corner.

"Well, he sure forgot about your cousin fast," I said.

"Lacey is his friend...with benefits," Alex explained with a grin.

I immediately got the drift. "Oh," I said, my eyebrows raised. "And Celeste? Doesn't she come to any parties?" I asked.

"No, never. She's a loner. She spends all of her spare time riding. She's very talented, from what I hear."

"At horseback riding?"

"Yes. And I'm not talking about just riding the trails. She spends her summers at a bunch of jumping competitions."

"Wow." I couldn't imagine riding a horse over jumps. I had been excited enough to live through my first lesson when all Gypsy had done was walk. "How do you know so much about her?"

"It's a small town and an even smaller school."

"That reminds me. Aren't you going to introduce me around tonight?"

Alex stepped closer to me, a smile on his face. He leaned toward me, brushing my hair away from my ear, the touch of his fingers on my cheek sending a shiver through me.

"I'd rather keep you all to myself." His breath swept along my neck, causing my pulse to quicken and heat to fill my veins. No boy had ever made me feel like this. It was exciting and completely unexpected.

As anticipation raced through me, a voice of caution sounded in my head. *Careful. Don't get your hopes up. He might be interested tonight, but come Monday when he sees you in school, he's going to be as interested in you as Derek is in Celeste.*

Oh shut up! I scolded myself. I was determined to enjoy tonight and not worry about tomorrow.

As Alex lifted his lips away from my ear, I gazed up at him, the noisy kids barging in the front door a blur in the background. "On second thought, I have all year to get to know everyone else."

He grinned, squeezing my hand again. "Come with me. There's a pond out back. And there used to be some swans, but I'm not sure if they're still there."

"Where would they have gone?" I asked as Alex pulled me behind him through the house.

"They usually don't last long. Between the bobcats and coyotes around here, nothing is safe."

We wound our way around the kids clustered in the kitchen and family room until we reached a back door. As Alex opened it, I looked out into the night. "Poor swans. That's horrible."

"It's just nature, Gracyn," Alex said with a chuckle as we stepped outside onto the deck. A strand of white Christmas lights had been twisted around the railing, sparkling in the dark. When the door fell shut behind us, the voices from inside were muted instantly. Alex dropped my hand and wrapped his arm around my shoulder, his body leaning against mine. "Don't worry. I'll keep you safe. Come on."

As we walked down the stairs leading into the darkness, anticipation wormed its way through me. If there had ever been a time to put the rest of the world aside, it was tonight.

10

Stars glittered in the black sky, and water trickled from a fountain in the middle of the pond. I searched for the swans, but if they were out there, the cloak of night hid them. Whispers came from the woods surrounding the pond, occasionally breaking out into a hushed laugh.

I bit my lip, trying to keep a straight face. Apparently, Alex wasn't the only one to bring a date out back for the privacy. Forcing myself to enjoy his company and not worry about anyone else, I allowed him to lead me around the pond until we reached a bench. We sat beside each other, and I leaned against him, enjoying the warmth of his arm over my shoulders.

Alex was the first to break the silence between us. "Why do I still feel like I don't really know you? Your answers to my questions at dinner were pretty vague."

I took a deep breath, not sure what to say. "You figured that out, huh?"

"So you admit it?"

"Maybe, although there isn't much to tell. Besides, I wanted to learn more about Sedgewick and everyone here. You know, since I'm the new girl. And now I feel a lot better about starting school Monday."

"That worried you?"

"A little. I spent my whole life in the same school system, at least until this year. I went to kindergarten with most of the kids in my class. So yeah, I guess I'm a little nervous. Or was."

I twisted around to face him, searching his expression for understanding. In spite of the chill in the air and my flimsy shirt, I was warm from being so close to him. Alex dropped his arm to circle my waist and pulled me closer, causing a tingle to rush through me. He didn't say a word, just studied me with his dark eyes. My heart racing with anticipation, I wondered if he was about to kiss me.

But he didn't move. After a few moments of silence, I smiled shyly. I felt a blush heat up my cheeks, but hoped he wouldn't notice it in the dark. "What?" I asked, breaking the silence.

"I still can't believe you didn't leave a boyfriend behind."

"Believe it," I said a little too quickly. He would understand once he saw me in the advanced classes at school next week. Girls like me spent their fall weekends studying with no time for dates or parties.

Alex continued looking at me, like he could see through me. "But I don't get it. You're beautiful and smart. What are you not telling me?" He asked his last question slowly, drawing out every word.

"Nothing," I insisted, biting back a smile as my heart glowed from the flattery. In spite of it, all I wanted to do was change the subject. "What about you? I see the way girls look at you. How come you don't have a girlfriend?"

Alex grinned as he shrugged. "I went to kindergarten with all of them. And I've dated a few of them, but nothing worked out. I was planning to stay a free agent this year, at least until you showed up."

His words caught me off-guard, my breath hitching as I met his gaze. His focus on me sent my heart into a flutter. I wanted to know why me, but the intense moment pitched my senses into a whirlwind. Before I knew what was happening, he leaned toward me.

His lips touched mine, and I closed my eyes, feeling like I was lost in a dream. His kiss was light and soft, as if he was testing the waters, waiting to gauge my reaction. When I reached my arm up around his shoulders, he deepened the kiss. His lips moved against mine, his free hand trailing up my spine to the base of my neck. I trembled, my head swarming with emotions and excitement. Never had I imagined tonight was going to turn into the best date I'd ever had. Not that I'd had many dates to compare it to.

The moment ended abruptly when two partygoers shuffled through the woods behind us. Footsteps in the leaves grew louder as they came closer. Whoever it was, I hoped they were passing through so Alex and I could get our privacy back.

"Zoe!" a deep, disgruntled voice called.

At the sound of his cousin's name, Alex pulled away from me and my eyes flew open in surprise. Pressing a finger to his lips, he whispered a quick "Shh" as we turned to look behind the bench. All I saw were the trees until a movement caught my eye from the side.

"Zoe! Stop!" A tall guy ran up behind Zoe, catching her around the waist and twirling her around to face him. The two were mere shadows in the woods, their faces barely visible.

I was mesmerized by the male voice holding a hint of an English accent. Tingles crept up my spine when he spoke, like I recognized him. But that was impossible. Frozen, I watched the two of them, unable to tear my eyes away.

"Lucian! I told you, not tonight," Zoe protested, pushing against his shoulders.

I looked at Alex, alarm pulsing through me as I wondered if he'd intervene. But he shook his head, putting his finger up to his mouth one more time to keep me quiet. I followed his lead and turned my attention back to the couple.

"Oh, come on, love. It's been too long. I missed you. Didn't you miss me?"

"Of course I missed you. But you hurt me, taking off like that without so much as a goodbye. And now you think you can come back and pick up where we left off?"

"I was hoping," he said, his tone calmer and his voice a little softer.

"Well, keep hoping," Zoe told him coldly. "Because you're going to have to earn my trust again. How do I know you're not in town for one night and you won't disappear again tomorrow?"

He loosened his hold on her. "I'm not leaving again. In fact, I'm staying for the year so I can graduate. We're going to be in the same class."

"What? Why should I believe you?"

"It's true. Don't lie and say you haven't heard the rumors. I know they've been spreading around here like wildfire."

"I heard them, but I had no reason to believe them."

"Well, now you're hearing it from me. I'm back to stay."

"Really?" She folded her arms across her chest. "I'll believe it when I see it."

"Oh, Zoe," he said, mock disappointment in his voice. "Why waste valuable time? I missed you too much to wait another day. You know you did, too. Admit it."

"I'll admit to nothing. You can't just waltz back into town and act as though everything is as you left it. It's been two years. I've moved on." She stared at him, anger sparking from her eyes.

"No, you haven't," he retorted smoothly, not missing a beat. "I heard you had a fling with Ethan, but you can't fool me. No one can take my place in your heart."

"You're awfully sure of yourself."

"That's because I know what we had. And I'm not going to give up easily. So why don't you just say yes right now? You know you want to," he said, a sly grin sliding over his lips.

"I'm not going to acknowledge that with an answer. If you want me back, it's going to be on my terms. Dinner. Tomorrow night," she said, her voice commanding.

He groaned, snaking his arm around her waist and slamming her against his chest. "I had something a little more intimate in mind," he muttered.

"That's a bit presumptuous, don't you think?" Zoe asked. "I'll give you a second chance tomorrow. But not tonight. I need some time to get used to you being back."

"Aw. Come on, Zoe. I'll be good, I promise. Let me remind you of what you missed."

"I don't need any reminders, Lucian." She raised her hands to his shoulders and pushed, hard.

He loosened his grip, letting her take a step back. "Please, love. Don't make me beg."

"Maybe you should have thought about me sooner."

"I didn't stop thinking about you the whole time I was gone."

"For two years? Save it, Lucian. I risked everything for you, and you repaid me by disappearing from my life."

My jaw dropping, I raised my eyebrows and glanced at Alex. Before I could whisper to him that I'd heard enough, Lucian spoke again. "You know I didn't kill my sister."

My attention snapped back to him and Zoe. As much as I wanted them to go away, I was too intrigued by the murder case haunting Sedgewick.

"I don't know anything, Lucian. I believed in you and I trusted you up until you disappeared. I don't know what to think anymore."

"I'm going to make it up to you. You should have known I wouldn't stay away forever."

"Really? How's that? You didn't even have the courtesy to call me when you got back to town. I had to hear it through the grapevine. And then you show up here tonight out of the blue and expect me to jump into your arms? Save it." She turned and started to walk away, but he grabbed her by the waist in a movement as fast as lightning.

Pulling her to him, he admitted, "You have every right to be angry with me. But I swear, I thought about you every day I was gone. Let me prove it to you. I promise you won't be sorry." He buried his face in her hair, nuzzling her neck.

Another heat rose up in my cheeks as I wondered how far this would go. I suddenly felt like a peeping tom, but as much as I wanted to turn away, I couldn't break out of my trance. I was mesmerized by the mystery and worried for Zoe's sake. *Don't do it,* I thought, wishing she could hear my pleas. *He can't be worth it.*

Zoe's defiant resolve crumbled as Lucian kissed her neck. Her face softened, showing an inkling of forgiveness. But then her frown returned and she pushed him away again. "Tomorrow. That's my final offer. Take it or leave it."

"Fine," he relented. "Dinner tomorrow night. I'll be counting the minutes until I see you again." He lifted her hand to his lips and placed a kiss behind her knuckles. His demeanor calm, he let go of her.

"Save the charming act for someone it might actually work on," Zoe sneered as she backed away. "Tomorrow night. Don't disappear again." With that, she spun around and hurried toward the house, leaving him alone.

After Zoe disappeared, I watched Lucian as he lingered in the shadows. He wore a dark shirt and something metal halfway down his chest caught the reflection of the house lights in the distance. Perhaps a necklace or buttons on his shirt? His hair appeared lighter than Zoe's, maybe a dark blond or light brown. He was tall and lean, but muscular. Frowning, he remained in the same spot for several seconds, his eyes calculating his next move.

Without moving from between the trees, he swept his gaze around him, stopping when he looked in our direction. His eyes seemed to drill a hole through me. I couldn't help feeling like he'd caught us spying on him. His stone cold expression sent a ripple of fear through me, and I wondered what was next. Would he approach us, confront us for eavesdropping?

I swallowed nervously, afraid to breathe. When I dared to look at Alex, he was watching me curiously, almost with a little disappointment. I sighed, offering him a faint smile before glancing back into the woods. But Lucian was gone. There was no sign of him in the shadows where only silence remained.

"Whew!" I said, letting out a deep breath as I turned back to Alex. "Do you think he saw us?"

"Maybe. But it doesn't matter."

"So that was him? The guy everyone thinks killed his sister?" I couldn't resist asking about Lucian. All I could think about was what I had just seen and heard. I had practically forgotten Alex's kiss from a few minutes ago.

Alex nodded with a sigh. "Yes. Lucian Dumante in the flesh," he grumbled. "Talk about killing the mood."

I reached for his hand and squeezed it gently. "I know. The timing sucks. But what did she mean she risked everything for him?"

"Zoe was Lucian's alibi," Alex explained.

"Really?"

"Yes. She claimed they were together when Cassie was killed. It was the only reason they let him go."

"Do you believe her?" I asked, afraid of the answer. An unsettled feeling twisted through me, and I thought about going back to Maryland. But I knew that wasn't an option. Our house was gone, rented for the next two years while my mother fulfilled her assignment. By now, some other teenager had probably taken over my bedroom and decorated it with tacky movie posters.

"Not for a minute," Alex replied coolly. "But it's for Zoe to live with, not me. All I care about is that she doesn't get hurt. And until tonight, she was safe. Now, I'm going to have to keep an eye on her. She's tough, but I don't trust him."

I could see the protectiveness in his eyes and hear it in his voice. "Were there any other suspects?" I asked.

"No. He's the one who found the body and called the cops. She hadn't even been dead longer than an hour. It was awfully suspicious the way he found her so quickly. Which is also weird because he should have known he'd be the likely suspect."

"Hmm." The idea of the young girl's death made me sick to my stomach, and I didn't want to think about it any longer. "Well," I said, slumping back against the bench. "This is not how I expected tonight to end."

"It's not that late. Don't tell me you're ready to call it a night." Alex smiled, but when he caught my worried gaze, his hope faded. "Oh no, you are, aren't you?"

"Sorry," I said with a sigh, feeling drained. Tonight had been a whirlwind from dredging up my buried guilt over Sam's stepfather to a first kiss with Alex to learning that a potential killer who happened to live next door to Becca and Gabriel had returned to town. All in one night. It was just too much to handle.

"I guess we're not going to pick up where we left off when we were so rudely interrupted."

I shook my head slowly. "No. I think the mood's been ruined."

"As long as you haven't changed your mind about me," he said.

"Of course I haven't." I glanced at him as a smile snuck onto my face. "You've been great. If I hadn't met you, I would have spent this entire week alone."

"Good. I'm glad you don't regret meeting me in your pajamas and glasses," he teased.

"You had to remember that, didn't you?" I groaned.

"Yes. In fact, I'll never forget it. You looked so cute, not to mention sexy with that just-woke-up look."

I cringed, averting my eyes to the ground for a moment. "Thanks. You sure know how to make a girl feel special."

"It's a compliment. Every guy wants to know how a girl looks when she wakes up."

When I raised my eyebrows at him, he continued with a smirk. "Just in case. So, are you busy next Friday night? Want to go out again?"

I sucked in a deep breath in disbelief. "What?"

"Friday night? You know, a week from last night? Want to get together or something?" he asked.

"Um, I'm not sure." I had no idea how to tell him I was afraid to accept his invitation. It wasn't that I didn't like him in that way, because after his kiss, I couldn't deny there was a spark. But once he found out what I was hiding, he'd realize he made a mistake asking me out again. I didn't want to get my hopes up, only to be crushed in the end.

"Okay. I get it. You're not sure how to turn me down. No problem. I can take a hint." Alex rose to his feet, turning his attention to the lights sparkling from the deck in the distance. "Come on. I'll take you home."

As I stood up, guilt washed over me. "Alex, it's not what you think. Please don't be upset."

"It's okay. I'm not upset," he said coolly, his back to me.

"Hey." I reached for his hand. As my fingers curled over his, he turned around. "It's not you. I swear. Listen, I'd love to go out with you again–"

"Then let's make it a date for Friday."

"I can't. Not yet. Ask me again on Tuesday."

"Why Tuesday?"

I smiled, dodging his curious gaze as I glanced at the reflection of stars twinkling on the pond surface. "You'll understand soon enough."

A part of me hoped that he'd still be interested in me on Tuesday. But a pesky voice in my head wasn't so optimistic. *You're not seriously expecting him to ask you out on Tuesday? Don't be stupid. As soon as he finds out you're a straight-A student taking all AP classes, he'll be thankful you didn't accept tonight. You're doing the right thing by saving him the agony of having to come up with an excuse to break a date with you. By next weekend, you'll be spending your Friday and Saturday nights reading or painting just like you did back home. It's better this way.* My cruel words snuck up on me, almost pushing me to tears. My inner self could be so mean sometimes.

"I had a great time tonight and on Thursday. You've been really nice and I want you to know I appreciate it," I assured him, trying to sound sincere.

"Why do I feel like you're about to give me that 'I like you, but just as a friend' speech?"

"That's all in your head. Promise me you'll ask me again on Tuesday, if you haven't changed your mind," I said.

"Okay. I promise," he replied, letting out a feeble huff.

"Good. Shall we go now?"

With a deep breath, Alex nodded before leading me back to the party.

11

I couldn't stop thinking about what Alex and I had overheard in the woods at the party. I didn't even know Lucian and Zoe, but knowing Lucian had been the prime suspect in the brutal killing of his sister haunted me. The whole thing kept me up for hours after Alex dropped me off, but I finally dozed off sometime before dawn.

When I woke up the next morning, I gave in to my curiosity. I went straight from my warm bed to the desk, the chair ice cold against my bare legs. But I was too focused on my mission to grab a pair of pants. Instead, I slid my glasses up my nose and turned on my laptop. Outside, sunlight peeked through the branches, promising another gorgeous late summer day. But I didn't give the weather a second thought. All I could think about was learning more about the girl who'd been murdered.

As soon as the computer came to life, I opened up the internet and typed "Sedgewick MA murder" in the search field. Immediately, dozens of articles popped up. They were from The Boston Herald, The Springfield Republican, and numerous other local newspapers. I selected the first article that looked informative, noting its publication date was over two years ago.

With a heavy heart, I began reading. "The people of Sedgewick have always been a bit reclusive. Until now, they've taken great pride in their peaceful town nestled in a valley deep within the heart of the Berkshires. That idyllic reputation was shattered yesterday when the body of twelve-year-old Cassandra Dumante was found in the woods by her brother, Lucian. The cause of death was a stab wound to the heart. The time of death was sometime earlier that day. Lucian Dumante has been named a person of interest, but authorities aren't releasing any information pertaining to his role in this tragic death."

I scanned the rest of the article, disappointed to learn nothing new. Frustrated, I returned to the search engine and scrolled through other links until I found one dated a month later. Clicking on it, I held my breath as I started to read.

"After weeks of gathering evidence and questioning anyone who saw Cassandra Dumante in the hours leading up to her death, authorities have had no choice but to drop all charges against her brother, seventeen-year-old Lucian Dumante. Lucian discovered his sister's body in the woods nearly a month ago after she had been brutally stabbed and killed. The murder weapon was never found after an intensive search of the Dumante property. Police have examined all evidence and concluded it was insufficient to bring a case against Lucian Dumante."

I stopped there, seeing nothing to indicate that an alibi had been the tipping point in dropping the charges against him. Returning to the search page, I scanned the unread options until the cursor hovered on one about the funeral. Swallowing, I pulled up the article.

"All three immediate members of the Dumante family attended the funeral of Cassandra Dumante today. The funeral was closed to the public, but reporters were able to get the following statement out of Everett Dumante, father of Lucian and Cassandra: 'My son did not murder his sister. The truth will be revealed in time, and justice will prevail. Now please, let us grieve in peace.' The millionaire investor promptly retreated into the church, escaping behind closed doors while guards barricaded the entrance. Reporters who got too close to the church or the funeral procession were immediately chased away. Lucian Dumante was granted permission to attend all funeral events, but was taken back into police custody at the end of the day."

I sighed, sickened by the thought of a funeral for such a young girl. I couldn't understand why someone would harm a child. The next paragraph revealed that autopsy test results proved she hadn't been raped. There weren't any bruises, scratches or other signs of a struggle. It seemed as though she'd stood still and allowed her attacker to stab her.

I read more about the family as well, learning that Everett Dumante had made a fortune from investing in start-up ventures around the world. His portfolio included companies in Technology, Automotive, Banking, and Entertainment, to name a few. He had a knack for predicting future trends and had made excellent investment decisions. But his profession came with the price of being away from home for weeks, sometimes months at a time. It was because of his work that he'd been in Paris when Cassandra was killed.

The mother, Genevieve Dumante, had also been out of town when her youngest child had been brutally murdered. Unlike her husband who traveled extensively for business, she preferred Hawaii where she maintained a permanent residence. She rarely returned to Sedgewick, leaving her children with their father who hired a caretaker when he was out of town.

After reading all I could handle, I closed the internet. I removed my glasses and rubbed my eyes. Leaning back, I stared out the window. But the trees and blue sky didn't even register. All I could see was the stony expression on Lucian's face from last night after Zoe ran back to the party. And his eyes, so cold and calculating. The image made my skin crawl, and I couldn't help wondering if he really had killed his own sister.

A thud sounded downstairs, breaking me out of my thoughts. *What am I doing?* I thought. *I'm obsessing over something that happened two years ago! If the authorities didn't have enough evidence to convict Cassandra's brother, then surely he didn't do it. But if he didn't do it, who did?*

"Ugh!" I muttered, shaking my head. *Like you would know. Stop torturing yourself over this! Everyone else around here seems to have let it go, so you need to as well.*

Determined to push the cold murder case out of my mind, I put my glasses back on and shut down my laptop. It was time to stop obsessing about things that didn't concern me and enjoy the one day of freedom I had left before hitting the books for another year.

When Becca suggested I join her for a trail ride that morning, I thought she was crazy. "Becca," I protested, shutting the dishwasher and turning to lean against the counter, a coffee mug in my hands. "I've ridden once. Yesterday. I'm not ready to go out on the trails."

"Really, Gracyn, you worry way too much. Are you saying you still don't trust me? I've been right two out of two times. Come on. The horses need to get out. It'll be fun. I can show you the garden."

"You seem to be forgetting that my fall was out on the trails. I don't think I'm ready for that yet. I'll be happy to ride in the pasture again, with your help of course."

Becca wasn't willing to take no for an answer. "That was over ten years ago. You need to put it behind you once and for all. Gypsy is wonderful. She'll take good care of you, I promise."

I huffed. "That's what the trail guide said years ago." But those horses had also acted skittish around me, fidgeting and pawing the ground, their eyes wide and fearful. Gypsy had never been anything but calm and patient with me. Perhaps Becca was right. Besides, maybe a trail ride would help me forget the murder suspect living next door.

"Please," Becca said. "It's a beautiful day. And I want to hear all about your date with Alex."

A blush raced across my cheeks as I remembered his kiss on the picnic bench before we'd been interrupted. I sighed, smiling at Becca's hopeful expression. "I'm thinking about it. But what if Gypsy spooks at a deer?"

"Deer jump in and out of the pasture every day. The horses don't spook easily, especially at deer. All you have to do is what I taught you yesterday and let Gypsy do the rest. She'll follow Cadence, and we'll just walk, I promise."

"Okay. I suppose I can trust you on this. But just in case, would you mind telling me where the nearest hospital is?"

"Ha, ha," Becca muttered. "Now go get dressed and meet me in the barn in ten minutes."

Without giving me a chance to change my mind, Becca rounded up the dogs and disappeared out the front door. Ten minutes later, jeans and a blue T-shirt replacing my pajamas, contact lenses in my eyes, and my hair pulled up into a ponytail, I entered the barn.

"Just in time," Becca stated as soon as she saw me. "Here." She tossed a nylon halter at me which I barely caught before it almost fell to the ground. "Gypsy is out. You'll need to catch her."

One week ago, I would have said, "No way!" with pure fear. But today, I nodded and walked out to the pasture gate as if I'd led Gypsy in hundreds of times. At least I was relaxing with some things.

After we tacked up the horses meaning Becca saddled them while I watched and took mental notes, Becca led Gypsy out of the barn. Gypsy's red and white coat gleamed in the sunlight, reminding me of a ghost. I still couldn't get over her unusual coloring.

Becca held the reins as I climbed into the saddle and put my feet in the stirrups. As soon as I was seated, she hurried back into the barn to get Cadence. Once mounted, she circled the mare around Gypsy. "You look tense."

"That's because I am," I gritted out. My muscles had locked the moment I climbed into the saddle, and I now realized I was holding my breath. I inhaled, then let the air out slowly.

"That's it. Breathe. It's the key to being relaxed. And horses can sense your tension. Not that it would worry Gypsy, but if your muscles stay bunched up like that for our entire ride, you're going to be awfully sore later on."

I focused on breathing, inhaling and exhaling so deeply that my shoulders rose and fell. "Okay. I'm relaxed, I think."

"Good. Ready?"

"Um, I guess. But shouldn't we be wearing helmets?" I hadn't asked during my lesson yesterday because Becca had been on the ground beside Gypsy the whole time. But I wasn't sure I should ride the trails without one. What if I fell off and hit my head on a rock?

Becca halted Cadence next to Gypsy. "There's no need for that. Gypsy won't let you fall. You're safe. Just give her a loose rein. She knows what to do."

After flashing me a confident smile, Becca nudged Cadence into a walk. She whistled loudly, and the dogs rushed up behind us before bolting ahead of the horses. Neither Cadence nor Gypsy batted an eye at their sudden movement. Gypsy trailed her pasture mate, her pace slow and calm.

Becca led us into the woods on a wide trail. Birds chirped from the branches above, and a light breeze whispered through the leaves. After a few minutes, we stopped. Gypsy halted close enough to nip at Cadence's tail, earning her a warning look from the other mare. Paying the horses little attention, I shifted my gaze to an opening in the trees.

"And I give you our garden," Becca announced with a proud sweep of her hand.

The forest surrounded a field like a protective wall. Corn, tomato vines, lettuce, carrots, broccoli, and other vegetables grew in rows. Trees bearing bright red apples lined one side of the open space, towering over the smaller crops.

"Wow. Becca, this is amazing. Although it looks like a lot of work."

"It is. But it's worth it. You'll see."

I raised my eyebrows, not sure if I believed her. "Back in Maryland, if someone had a ten by ten foot garden plot in their backyard, that was big."

"It's what we do up here. Just like our ancestors did for generations. We'll harvest the crops in another month before it gets too cold. Gabe and I keep what we think we'll need for the winter and the rest goes to the festival where we'll sell some and trade the rest for eggs, cheese and meat."

"I think you mentioned that. So are you going to put me on slave duty to earn my keep now?" I joked with a smile.

"No," Becca said, chuckling. "We just want you to be familiar with the farm and where everything is."

She gave me another minute to study the garden before clucking to Cadence. When the horses resumed walking and I felt myself tense up again, I reminded myself to breathe.

Neither Becca nor I spoke for a while as we enjoyed the scenery. We headed deeper into the woods, up hills, and around bends in the trail. I kept a careful watch on the passing trees, making sure my legs didn't bump against them. As I grew more comfortable with Gypsy, my mind began to wander. To my chagrin, Cassie Dumante returned to my thoughts. "Are you going to show me where the girl was found?" I asked, breaking the silence.

"Is that what you really want to see today?" Becca asked as she twisted in the saddle, her eyebrows raised.

"I guess not," I answered, watching her blonde ponytail sway against her green shirt when she faced forward again. "It's just—"

"Just what?"

I faltered as I debated how much I should tell her about last night. *Tell her everything. What's there to hide? It will be better if you talk about it. She's going to find out sooner or later,* I thought.

"Alex took me to a party last night. Her brother was there. Lucian."

Becca drew in a sharp gasp before composing herself. "I'm not surprised. I heard he returned to town. So you met him, did you?"

"No, I didn't. Wait a minute. You knew he was back and you didn't tell me? Doesn't he live next door?"

Becca turned around again. "He lives at the neighboring estate, but it's not exactly a stone's throw from our house. You have to follow the trails through the woods about a half mile or drive a mile down the road and then up their long driveway. Next door around here isn't the same as it was for you back in Maryland."

"It's still a bit unsettling. I didn't meet him, but I overheard him talking to someone. I'm not sure what to think."

"I know. It was a complicated case. And since he left so soon after they dropped the charges, everyone moved on. His return is going to be tough for some folks around here."

Alex's conviction that Lucian was guilty as sin flashed through my memory, making me quiver in my stirrups. "Do you think he did it?" I asked.

Becca shrugged. "I don't believe my opinion has any bearing on the matter, so I'd rather not speculate on it. All I know is that there wasn't enough evidence to convict him. And one has to believe that if he was guilty, they would have been able to lock him up and throw away the key."

"But–" I was about to ask who else could have done it when she cut me off.

"Gracyn, can we please change the subject? Dredging up the past isn't going to do anything other than ruin this gorgeous day," she said before facing forward again.

I sighed, realizing she was right. She apparently didn't consider our neighbor a threat. Her confidence should have given me comfort, but I still felt uneasy. And talking about the matter would only make it worse. Hadn't I agreed to this ride in part because I thought it would help me take my mind off that horrible tragedy? "So where are we headed now? Do you have any more secret gardens to show me?"

"No. Only the one. This trail will take us to the edge of the Dumante property. From there, it makes a big loop and we'll end up on our farm down by the pasture. It's an easy trail, too. Not a lot of steep hills or rocks."

"Oh, fun. Do we have to ride by the lion's den?"

"Yes, we do. And you're going to have to get over that. This is the best trail for you to learn on," she said. "But enough about our lovely neighbors. How'd it go with Alex last night?"

Great, I thought. We were leaving one dreadful subject for another one. After the way things had ended, I was trying my hardest not to think about Alex. Perhaps that was the driving force behind my curiosity about a two-year-old murder. Because as long as I obsessed over it, Alex was far from my mind.

"Well?" Becca prompted when I didn't answer right away.

"It was fine," I answered half-heartedly.

"It doesn't sound fine. You sound a little disappointed."

After a long pause, I explained the details of the night. I left out a few parts, including my flashbacks of Sam's stepfather, the kiss, and Zoe and Lucian's performance.

At the end of my monologue, Becca turned in the saddle and grinned. "It sounds like you had a great time. And you like him, right?"

"Maybe. But it doesn't matter. Everything will change once school starts."

"What makes you say that?"

"Oh, come on, Becca. You know the real me. I'm a geek to the core, a hopeful for the Ivy League. He's going to be thankful I didn't agree to go out with him next Friday."

Becca shook her head. "You're crazy. That shouldn't matter."

"Well, it does. He's cool, and I'm not. I'm just accepting it now so it doesn't hurt later."

"Maybe you should give Alex a little more credit than that."

"Well, I didn't say no. I just told him to ask me again on Tuesday. So I'll find out soon enough."

"You don't trust easily, do you?" Becca asked.

I shrugged, glancing at the trees. "No, I guess I don't."

"Hmm," was all she said.

I wondered what that meant, but chose not to ask. I had already opened up too much and, like the murder from the past, I wanted to forget the rejection in my future.

From that point, we rode in silence for about ten more minutes. I practiced a few things Becca had shown me yesterday in the pasture. Heels down, thumbs up, shoulders straight and tall. I couldn't believe how easy it was, even though I could feel my leg muscles stretching in a way they never had before. I might be a little sore tomorrow, but it was worth it.

We followed the trail, crossing streams, winding around trees that came way too close to my knees, and going up and down rolling hills. When we reached the top of the tallest hill, Becca stopped without warning, causing Gypsy to bump into Cadence before halting. "What are we doing?" I asked.

Becca nodded her head to the left. "There's the Dumante estate. In case you were wondering."

An opening in the trees on the edge of the trail overlooked a long hill. A pasture surrounded by a wooden post and rail fence rolled out in waves. Three horses grazed in the field, one dark brown in color, one dappled grey, and the third one solid black. A small barn was set off to the side, but it was the huge stone mansion rising up beyond the pasture that made me pause. A column rose up on one end, like that of a castle. Add some fog and it would make the perfect haunted house on Halloween.

"So, this is it?"

"Yes."

"It looks cold. I wouldn't want to live there. I presume you know them?"

"Of course. Everett, the father, is a good man, even though he's gone a lot. And they are the closest neighbors we have."

"That's just...wonderful," I said while thinking to myself, *Lovely. The closest neighbors' daughter was brutally killed somewhere nearby and one of the residents is, or was, a suspected murderer.* Seeing their property made it seem more real. I shuddered, hoping Becca wouldn't linger much longer. I had seen enough.

"Well, we need to keep moving."

I sighed with relief. She must have read my mind. As Becca cued Cadence to walk, Gypsy followed, but I couldn't resist the urge to look back. Twisting in the saddle, I stared at the house again. Before it disappeared behind the trees, someone stepped out onto the deck, his attention focused in our direction. I gasped, my heart accelerating as I whipped around. Closing my eyes for a moment, I inhaled and exhaled just like I had when we first started out on the trail. Questions raced through my mind. Who was that? Lucian? And why did I care so much? We weren't trespassing. Becca knew these trails, and she wouldn't take me anywhere we shouldn't be.

I wanted to tell her someone had been at the house but decided against it. Instead, I tried to focus on the birds and the trees, but even two squirrels chasing each other through the branches couldn't take my mind off what I had seen. And the longer I dwelled on it, the more I was convinced that the person on the deck had been watching us.

12

My first day at school didn't go as smoothly as I'd hoped. First, I slept in and had to rush through my shower. There was no time to blow dry my hair, and it ended up a frizzy mess, leaving my white sweater damp. When I put my contact lenses in, they didn't feel right. A constant irritation poked at my right eye as if an eyelash or a piece of dust had been trapped. As soon as I arrived at school, I raced across the parking lot, paying no attention to the other kids clustered on the lawn. Chatter hummed in the air, but I ignored it as I ran through the front door.

My book bag banging against my thigh, I hurried down the hallway until I found a bathroom and escaped inside. When I leaned over the sink and peered into the mirror, tears brimmed in my eye. I dug my contact lens case out of my bag and removed them, gaining instant relief. Blinking several times, I dabbed at my irritated eye with a paper towel before tossing it in the trash. Then I did what no high school girl ever wanted to do, especially on her first day at a new school. I pulled my dreadful glasses out of my bag and slid them over my nose.

Reluctantly, I stared at my reflection in the mirror. *Wonderful,* I thought. *Now I get to deal with glasses and frizzy hair.* I tried to pat down my curls, but it was no use. My hair had an attitude matching its red color that only a blow-dryer or straightener could tame. I'd just have to live with it today.

As I turned away from the mirror, the bathroom door flew open and a girl rushed in. She stopped as soon as she saw me, studying me with intense dark eyes. A long brown braid fell over one shoulder of her black sweater. Her jeans and boots were also black, making her pale complexion seem even lighter. "Oh my God!" she exclaimed. "You're the new girl. I just heard Derek asking if anyone had seen you." Envy crossed over her face as she frowned.

"Yes, that would be me," I said, wondering how to convince her I had no interest in Derek. "I'm Gracyn. And you are?" I mustered a pleasant smile in spite of the horrible morning that had ruined my mood.

She stepped closer to me, one hand on her book bag shoulder strap and the other one in her front pocket. "Celeste Hamilton."

So this was Celeste. "Hi. It's nice to meet you."

She watched me suspiciously, not responding right away. Finally, her expression softened. "Hi. So you're the girl from the big city. I was wondering what all the fuss was about."

"No fuss," I assured her. "Because, believe me, this crazy hair has seen better days." I pushed a curl behind my ear, tucking it under my glasses to hold it back.

A faint smile peeked out from under her cool exterior. "Maybe. But you're new, and that never happens around here. No one ever moves to Sedgewick. What's your story?"

"It's not that interesting, trust me." I launched into an abbreviated version of how I'd ended up in Sedgewick. Sixty seconds later, I stopped.

"I know the Morgans. Becca is really nice. She's friends with my mom."

"She is? Well, I feel lucky to have her as a sister. But that aside, I want you to know I have no interest in going out with Derek."

Celeste's jaw dropped, her face turning bright red. But she quickly recovered with a bored shrug. "Wise choice. He gets around a bit, if you know what I mean."

"I kind of noticed. Good thing I met Alex first."

"Now this is starting to make sense."

"Why's that?"

"Derek always wants the girl Alex has. Those two have this weird sibling rivalry thing going on, even though they're best friends."

"Well, after today, neither one of them are going to think I'm that cool."

Celeste raised her eyebrows. "You just moved here from DC. Sorry, but I don't think that's possible."

I reached into my book bag and pulled out a wrinkled piece of paper. Opening it, I showed her my schedule. "See. AP classes. That's my secret. I'm just here to get the best grades I can and get into a good college." I almost said Ivy League, but changed my mind at the last minute.

Celeste read it and then lifted her gaze to me. "You really think this will deter Alex Carver?"

"Yes."

She laughed, shaking her head. "You must not know him very well yet. But I see you have Mr. Wainwright for sixth period History. I'm in that class, too."

My memory of Mr. Wainwright, aka creepy bar guy, returned when she mentioned him. *There's one more thing to love about this day,* I thought sarcastically. But I forced myself to smile. "Good. Now I know someone in one of my classes."

At that moment, the bell rang, reminding me that I couldn't stay in the bathroom all day no matter how badly I wanted to hide. "Oh, crap. I'm going to be late to homeroom, and I haven't even found my locker yet," I moaned.

"That's just the one-minute warning bell. Come with me. The senior homerooms and lockers are all in the same hallway."

"Thanks," I said with relief before following her out of the bathroom.

The hallway bustled with activity as students gathered along the lockers. Voices rang out and metal doors slammed. I bumped into several kids as I jogged to keep up with Celeste who hurried through the crowd, weaving around bodies. She turned the corner at the end of the hall, then led me through a doorway and up a stairwell.

"I like your boots, by the way," Celeste said, glancing at me over her shoulder.

"Thanks." This was probably where I should have returned the compliment, but I couldn't tell where her boots ended and her jeans began with all that black.

We reached the top of the stairs, and she led me down the next hallway. At the end, we made a left into another corridor. Only a few students lingered since most had gone to their homerooms.

Locating my room number, I stopped outside the door. "I guess I'll have to find my locker after homeroom."

"Yeah. The late bell's going to ring any second. I'm in a different room, but I'll find you before first period. See you!"

I was one of the last students to trickle into the room. As I slipped down the last aisle to take a seat in the second row back, the other kids watched me. I looked down, trying to appear as though I didn't notice their stares. But I did, and I hoped they would lose interest in me soon.

Homeroom lasted a few minutes, but it felt like an eternity. After the announcements and roll call, another bell rang, letting us out for five minutes before first period. I jumped to my feet and grabbed my book bag, anxious to get out of there. Some of the students stared at me, whispering to each other at the same time. I couldn't help feeling like they were talking about me, and I couldn't get out of the room fast enough. I raced out the door, pushing my way through the crowd. I had memorized my locker number, so I didn't need to find my schedule in my book bag. Not waiting for Celeste, I plowed through the sea of students.

As soon as I found my locker, I unloaded a few notebooks from my bag to make room for the textbooks that would be handed out during the day. Before I finished, Celeste appeared. "Oh good, you found your locker. I was going to see if you needed some help with that. What class do you have first?"

I looked at her, not sure what to think. She had seemed leery of me in the bathroom less than ten minutes ago and now she was acting as though we'd been best friends for days. "Calculus. You?"

"English Lit. Yay," she groaned. "What time do you have lunch?"

I pulled my schedule out of my book bag. "Twelve-thirty."

"Me, too. I'll save you a seat. You know, I thought after I heard Derek talking this morning, I wouldn't like you. But you're not what I expected. I'm so glad I ran into you in the bathroom," she said.

As she rambled on about helping me find my way around, I started to tune her out. I just wanted to organize my stuff and find my first class. As I shut my locker, prepared to make a getaway, I saw Lucian and Zoe marching down the hall.

Zoe's ebony hair hung over her shoulders, her blue eyes cool and confident as she occasionally glanced up at Lucian when he spoke. With an arm draped over her shoulders, he acted like he owned the world. He had short light brown hair, a shadow of stubble across his chin, and haunting green eyes. A silver cross dangled from a chain around his neck, the metal glinting in the light against the black shirt outlining his broad shoulders.

Students moved out of their way as they walked without missing a beat. When they passed me, Lucian shifted his gaze to the side, meeting mine in a moment that knocked the wind out of my lungs. His expression was cold, his eyes narrowed, raising the hair on the back of my neck.

I whipped my attention back to Celeste who was still talking. I hoped she wouldn't realize I'd lost track of what she was saying. She stopped in mid-sentence, glancing at Lucian. "Well, look what the cat dragged in," she muttered sarcastically.

"What?" I asked, noticing out of the corner of my eye that Lucian and Zoe had stopped at a locker.

"Lucian Dumante. He's back." Her voice dripped with disdain.

"So I've heard."

Celeste pried her eyes away from him, shifting her gaze to me. "I can't even look at him. I don't know how anyone could let him come back here. If his father didn't fund half the school year with his property taxes, that bastard never would have been allowed to return."

"I take it you don't like him," I commented. Come to think of it, no one seemed to like him except Zoe who had forgiveness written all over her face today.

"No. And you shouldn't either. Did Becca or anyone else tell you about Cassie?"

I nodded. "Yes," I replied soberly. "It's very sad."

"Sad?" Celeste asked, her voice and expression filled with anger. "It's horrific. Unspeakable. I know they couldn't find enough evidence to prosecute him, but everyone knows he's guilty. And the way he did it was despicable. He doesn't deserve to live, let alone enjoy the life he has."

"Those are some pretty harsh words," I said quietly even though she wasn't the only person who thought Lucian had killed his sister.

"Sorry. I can't help it. I just don't know how anyone could do that to a child. And she was his sister." She paused, guilt creeping into her eyes. "Sorry again. I'll try really hard not to talk about this anymore. That's probably not what you need on your first day at a new school. Besides, I don't want you to think our town is full of murderers. It's actually very peaceful. Before Cassie was killed, I think the cops around here were bored. The only crime we ever had was an occasional spray-painted mailbox and drinking parties down by the lake. Other than that, all they had to worry about was patrolling Main Street and making sure Mr. Wainwright got home after he had too much to drink which was, and still is, just about every night."

"Yeah. I heard about that, too," I said with a deep breath. Interesting how the same stories continued to surface. Not in the mood to talk about the murder or Mr. Wainwright, I suggested, "Maybe we should get to class."

"Yeah. You're right. Do you want me to show you where your room is?"

"No. I think I can manage."

"Okay. If I don't see you between the next few classes, we'll meet up at lunch. We should exchange phone numbers, too. If you want, I mean. It would be nice to have a new friend this year, that's all," she said before waving and disappearing into the crowd.

My Calculus class was half-full when I walked in and took a seat three rows from the front. After hanging my book bag on the back of the chair, I reached for a notebook. As I plopped it on my desk, I heard someone sit down beside me.

"Good morning, Gracyn," said a familiar deep voice.

Alex. What was he doing in this class? AP Calculus was reserved for geeks and nerds like me. I turned my head to the side to face him. "Hi," I said with a faint smile. On his desk was a notebook, a sharpened pencil stuffed into the spiral binding. "You're in this class?" I asked in surprise.

He smiled, lifting his eyebrows, his brown eyes amused. "Don't look so shocked. Cool guys can be smart, too." He still looked like a rock star with his dark ponytail, earring, and tight black T-shirt.

"I guess they can," I said slowly. "Sorry. I just wasn't expecting to see you in here." I reached up, twirling my hair around my finger. I knew I was a wreck between my awful curls and glasses, but it wasn't much different than our first meeting.

"I wasn't expecting to see you in here, either."

"Yeah? Well, this is me. Glasses and AP classes. I didn't want to say anything the other night."

"I guess I can't blame you. I wasn't all that forthcoming myself. I didn't know if you'd be impressed or turned off by the fact that I'm planning to apply to Harvard's pre-med program."

"Really?" To say I was surprised was an understatement. "What about music?"

"It's a fun hobby, but I'm not going to count on that to pay the bills. Besides, my dad's a doctor and his father was a doctor. It runs in the family. Although, I'm not doing this just because my parents want me to. I'm fascinated by medicine." He paused with a grin. "Okay, that's my story. Your turn."

"Um, I just want a good education in a field that has some solid job prospects. I like to paint, but that's not going to pay the bills, either. So I'm planning to apply to MIT for engineering."

"You like to paint? Why didn't you tell me that Saturday night?"

Didn't he hear that I was hoping to get into MIT? I found it strange that he was more interested in my painting. "It didn't seem...well, it just didn't fit into any conversation."

"I asked you tons of questions. You could have brought it up at any time."

Guilty as charged. "Maybe you're right. But I wasn't sure what you'd think."

"I'm a guitar player who delivers grain and hay in the summer and wants to be a doctor. I think a girl who has a hobby she's passionate about and some real career aspirations is pretty cool."

"How was I supposed to know that?"

He flashed a reassuring smile. "How about just trusting me next time, okay?"

A small grin slithered across my lips. "I'll try."

Before he could say anything more, the bell rang. A few students darted into the classroom, taking the only seats left at the front. As a hush settled over the room, the balding teacher wearing a plaid shirt over his round belly stood up behind the front desk. He began the roll call and, while I tried to listen for my name, all I could think about was Alex. It seemed like we had a lot more in common than I ever would have guessed.

After reading the last name, the teacher passed out the class syllabus. As papers shuffled in the front row, Alex reached over and poked me in the side. When I looked at him, my eyebrows raised, I noticed a folded piece of paper in his hand. I snatched it and held it in my lap where the desktop hid it from the teacher's view.

Looking down, I opened the note. "Now will you go out with me Friday night?" Alex had scribbled on the paper followed by, "P.S. You look cute in your glasses."

I whipped my eyes toward him as soon as I finished reading his note. He smiled with a wink and then turned his attention to the front of the class. My heart glowing, I slipped the note into my book bag before reaching for the stack of papers from the girl in front of me. As I took one and passed the rest behind me, I bit back a huge smile. Things were starting to look up.

13

When Celeste and I arrived at our History class that afternoon, Mr. Wainwright looked exactly as I remembered with shaggy light brown hair and a thick five o'clock shadow across his face. He nodded at me as soon as I walked in, but I turned away before dragging Celeste to the back of the classroom. We stayed there until the period ended and the bell rang.

Books slammed shut, voices broke out, and notebooks shuffled as students gathered their things. Glancing at Celeste, I packed up my things and stood, anxious to escape.

"What's your next class?" she asked, hoisting her book bag over her shoulder.

I didn't need to look at my schedule to answer her. I'd been looking forward to my last class all day. "Art. You?"

"Gym," she said with a groan.

"Look at the bright side. If you get all sweaty, at least you can go home right after that. There's nothing worse than having gym first thing in the morning."

"I'd rather not have it at all. I should be able to opt out of it since I have my riding," she grumbled.

"Well, you can doddle to Gym, but I want to get going. Art is the only class I have that should be fun."

"You're weird," Celeste teased as though we'd been friends a lot longer than a day.

"Gee, thanks. Come on, let's go."

We walked up the aisles side by side, reaching the front at the same time. Celeste headed for the door and I started to follow, hoping to escape. But I didn't get so lucky.

"Gracyn. Can I see you for a minute?" Mr. Wainwright asked as I passed his desk.

I stopped dead in my tracks, staring straight ahead at Celeste for a moment. She whirled around to look at me, her eyebrows raised. "I'll wait for you," she mouthed before disappearing out into the hallway.

Turning to face Mr. Wainwright, I noticed out of the corner of my eye that the last student had left the room. An uncomfortable silence even more awkward than our meeting at the bar filled the room. "Yes?" I asked.

"I wanted to see how your first day was going," he said as he walked around his desk and stopped in front of me, blocking my path to the door.

"It's been fine," I answered, wondering if he really wanted to ask me about Becca.

"Good. I just want to make sure you feel welcome. I'm sure moving to a new school for your senior year isn't easy."

I shrugged. "It's no different than going to college, I suppose."

He smiled, the skin crinkling up around the corner of his eyes. "Except that it's not college. You're in a small town high school. I might be a teacher, but I know how cliquey this place is."

"Then I must be doing something right. Everyone's been really nice, at least the kids I've met so far."

"Good. I'm glad to hear that." When he remained standing in my way, I glanced around him, hoping he'd get the hint. Instead of moving, he said, "I didn't realize you wear glasses."

I snapped my gaze back to him, alarm racing through me. Why did he care? "My contacts were bothering me today. I must have gotten a piece of dust in them or something." I paused, searching for the best way to excuse myself without being rude or sounding as frightened of him as I suddenly was. I took a deep breath, noticing Celeste still lingered out in the hallway, waiting for me. "Um, I need to get to my next class."

"Oh, yes," he said, breaking his stare away from me. "I'm sorry." He stepped beside his desk, opening up my path to the door. "Have a good afternoon. I'll see you tomorrow."

"Okay. Thanks," I murmured as I hurried past him and out into the hall. I practically smacked into Celeste in my rush to get away. My heart pounding, I looked at her, shook my head, and then started walking down the crowded hall.

Celeste jogged to catch up as we dodged the other students. "Hey, not so fast! What did he want?"

I glanced at her. "I have no idea," I muttered, rushing through the crowd until I reached my locker. As I opened it, Celeste leaned against the one beside it.

"Well, don't sound so upset. He can ask me to stay after class any day. He's dreamy."

I paused, my History book in mid-air as I forgot that I was about to put it on the shelf. "Dreamy? You sound like you're from the sixties."

"Okay, how about gorgeous or totally hot?"

"That's a little better. But aside from any word you choose, you can have him. He gives me the creeps." I finally slid my History book onto the stack of textbooks on my locker shelf.

"Why?" Celeste asked, sounding shocked.

"It's...a long story." I wanted to tell her about meeting him at the bar last week, but there wasn't enough time. "I'll explain later. Right now I need to get to class and you don't want to be late to Gym."

Celeste rolled her eyes. "Ugh. Thanks for reminding me."

"What are you complaining about? You must be pretty athletic if you ride horses."

"Kicking a soccer ball or hitting a baseball with a bat is a far cry from horseback riding. I'm a complete klutz on my own two feet, and everyone knows it. I'm always the last to get picked for teams."

I shut my locker and adjusted my book bag strap over my shoulder. "Well, at least you only have to suffer through one more year of it, right? Now I have to run if I'm going to make it to Art on time." I backed away from my locker, eager to be on my way. But Celeste didn't move, a frown on her face. "Celeste?"

She huffed, reluctantly stepping away from the lockers. "Yeah, yeah. I'm coming."

We hurried down the hall until we went our separate ways. I couldn't believe I'd lost so much time getting to Art class as it was the only one I looked forward to. I had hoped to get there a little early to meet the teacher, but it looked like I'd be lucky to make it before the bell rang.

With those thoughts, I took off running. By the time I reached the art and photography wing, I was out of breath. I slowed down just enough to slip into the classroom as the late bell rang. The room of misfits and outcasts was deathly quiet when the bell stopped ringing. They stared at me as though they could hear my labored breathing and racing heart. Mortified, I dropped my gaze to the floor and found an empty seat at a table for two out of the corner of my eye.

I lowered into the chair, hoping they would all stop staring. When I dared to look up, no one was paying attention to me any longer. The students sat stone still, as if tormented to be back in school. One girl had pasty white skin, jet black hair, and black fingernails. Another guy had bleached blond hair plastered into spikes and wore a black trench coat. I was probably the only normal one in the class. Even the teacher, a petite woman with frizzy brown hair and black combat boots under her long skirt, seemed eccentric.

After introducing herself, Ms. Friedman proceeded with the roll call in a quiet voice. I barely paid attention since my name was always called close to the end. But then she called a name I recognized. "Lucian Dumante."

Curious, I looked up, surprised.

"Here." The deep voice came from right beside me.

I gasped, daring to glance at the person sharing the desk with me. It was him. He flashed his green eyes at me, studying me like I didn't belong there. I met his gaze and refused to look away, frowning when he took a deep, disapproving breath and shifted his attention to the front of the class.

My heart pounded so hard, I thought it would bust out of my chest. Of all the luck. How had I ended up in the seat next to Lucian? Glancing around, I realized it had been the only one left. And now, it seemed that he was just as displeased to share a table with me as I was to be sitting next to him. But why would he care? He didn't even know me.

It must be that you stand out from everyone else in this classroom. You're the only one not wearing all black, I thought sarcastically. Even Lucian was wearing a black T-shirt. I glanced at him again, noticing how well his broad shoulders filled out the shirt.

I continued to study him out of the corner of my eye, the silver cross hanging from his neck striking me as odd. A religious symbol seemed to be the last thing someone so dark would wear. As curiosity burned through me, I heard my name. "Gracyn Pierce," the teacher called.

"Here," I said, cringing when I felt the other students staring at me. I hated drawing attention to myself. Fortunately, when the teacher moved on to the next name, everyone in the room appeared to forget about me.

Art class seemed to last forever. The teacher passed out a syllabus and rambled on about the different art styles and content we would explore over the year. I tried to concentrate on each word she said, but I was painfully aware of Lucian's presence next to me. Even though I avoided looking at him, I noticed every move he made out of my peripheral vision. When we shuffled papers about, my movement was stiff. I tried to stay as far from him as I could, afraid I'd make one wrong move and accidentally bump him with my elbow.

When the bell finally rang, he jumped up and raced out the door before I gathered up my book bag. My gaze followed his dark figure, my jaw dropped in surprise at his abrupt getaway. *How rude,* I thought. *He didn't say a single word to you. He could have at least said 'hi'.*

Shaking thoughts of Lucian out of my mind, I packed up my things, ready to head home after an exhausting day.

Before I escaped to my car, I made one last visit to my locker. As I stuffed textbooks into my bag, groaning inwardly at the homework I had to complete tonight, Celeste appeared. "Well, that was traumatic, but I survived. How was Art?"

I shrugged, pulling the sides of my bag together and tugging on the zipper. "Fine."

"Oh, no. What happened?"

"Nothing. I said it was fine."

Celeste smiled knowingly. "I don't believe you. I have a sixth sense about these things. I can tell when people are lying most of the time. So fess up. What's bothering you?"

"I just have a lot of homework already."

She raised her eyebrows. "And?"

I sighed with a frown. Scanning the other students in the hallway, I didn't see Lucian anywhere. I couldn't explain why he made me so nervous aside from the notion that he could have killed his sister. Unless it was the way he had watched me and Becca from his deck yesterday, assuming that had been him. But neither compared to the icy stares he'd given me in class. If looks could kill, I'd probably be dead.

"It's really nothing, but Lucian's in my Art class. I was late, and the only seat left when I got there was next to him."

"That explains the weird vibe I'm getting from you. Ew. I'm so sorry you had to sit next to him. Did he say anything?"

"No. Not one word," I said before sliding my book bag strap over my shoulder and shutting my locker.

"That's good. Take it from me, you don't want to get to know him. He's really bad news."

"I'm getting that." I shuddered as his cold stare flashed through my mind. But the silver cross he wore also lingered in my memory, making me wonder if there was more to him than the rumors indicated. "At least it's the only class I have with him."

"I just wish he had never come back," Celeste said as she searched the sea of students in the hall. "The last two years were great. He should have stayed away forever. But I guess he had to come back sometime."

"Why do you say that?"

Celeste tore her eyes away from the crowd and looked back at me. "Because he has a gorgeous estate all to himself and the prettiest girl in school has only been in love with him forever. He knew she'd take him back in a heartbeat, which I noticed already happened."

"Well, as much as I'd love to stand here and talk about the guy, I should probably get going. I have a ton of homework." I patted my book bag, wondering if I'd be able to get Celeste to talk about something else tomorrow. If I couldn't, then I'd be in the market for a new friend. The last thing I wanted was to listen to her go on about Lucian all year. I didn't need any reminders of him, especially after he'd been so cold in class.

Celeste looked down at her watch. "I have to go, too. I have a lesson in an hour, and I can't be late. And I still need to stop by my locker."

"Then I guess I'll see you tomorrow?" Even though I said it like a question, I knew the answer. Celeste had appointed herself as my new best friend, and there wasn't anything I could do to change her mind short of being rude. I sighed, thinking about Sam. I really missed her.

"Yes, of course. Have a great afternoon and don't study too hard. It's only the first day. You don't want to get burned out."

After a quick goodbye, we rushed off in opposite directions. I weaved around the students, then down the stairs and through another hall until I approached the door. As I started to push the lever, a tan arm reached around me, beating me to it.

"You weren't seriously going to leave without saying goodbye, were you?" a familiar voice asked.

A smile broke out across my face and I turned to look at Alex as he opened the door. "Sorry. I guess I wasn't thinking because I already have so much homework," I said with a groan, walking outside into the sunlight.

Students lingered on the lawn and in the parking lot, gathering with friends before leaving. We wandered around them before stopping at the edge of the sidewalk. "Yeah? Me, too," Alex said. "So, am I too nerdy for you now?"

His eyes met mine, warming my heart. I still couldn't believe he was just as much of a brainiac as I was. I never should have judged him by his long hair and earring. "Of course not," I assured him with a soft chuckle.

"Then why are you laughing?"

"Because I was worried I'd be too much of a nerd for you," I admitted.

He smiled. "And I was worried you wouldn't be smart enough. I have a secret. I like smart girls."

I felt a blush creeping across my cheeks. "Really?"

"Yes." He paused, then asked, "This is why you dodged me when I asked you out for Friday night, isn't it?"

I suddenly felt silly for worrying about something that turned out to be nothing. "Maybe," I replied in a guilty voice.

"If I ask you again, will you accept?"

I nodded with a smile. "I'd love to."

"Then it's a date. Come on," he said, extending his hand to me. "I'll walk you to your car."

Hand in hand, we walked between two parked cars. Halfway across the next open lane, I felt the hair on the back of my neck stand up and my happiness faded. I scanned the row of cars ahead, my eyes immediately locking with a pair of icy green ones. Lucian leaned against a black Range Rover as Zoe curled her arm around his neck, whispering into his ear.

But he paid her no attention. Instead, he stared at me like a lion honing in on a gazelle. I swallowed my fear, taking a deep breath to steady my out-of-control heart. What was the meaning of his apparent hatred toward me? He didn't know me, and I promised myself at that moment he never would.

Whipping my gaze away from him, I forced myself to smile at Alex and pretended I had heard every word he said as we squeezed between two trucks, leaving Lucian safely behind.

14

As the week progressed, my teachers piled on the homework. I had Calculus problems to solve, an English essay to write, and History chapters to read. If Becca didn't insist that I helped with the horses in the evening, I would have been at my desk from the time I got home until long after the sun went down.

The afternoon breaks were what I needed. Between the sweet smell of hay and Gypsy's gentle nudges, my time with the horses helped me recharge. Gypsy seemed taken with me, like she knew she belonged to me. Every time I appeared at the pasture gate, she jerked her head up, her ears pointed in my direction. Then she trotted over to greet me, the grass forgotten.

Looking back, I couldn't believe my fear of horses had disappeared in less than two weeks. Comfort and confidence took its place, so much that I looked forward to returning home each day and heading out to the barn to brush Gypsy, fill water buckets, and help with anything else that needed to be done.

My days at school became fairly routine. Celeste grew friendlier, keeping me company between classes and at lunch. She didn't seem to have any other friends and, since I didn't either, we ended up hanging out together. She talked a lot, even more than Sam. But she didn't spend every free minute obsessing over Lucian's return which was a relief. She only brought him up when she saw him, sometimes shuddering with a grimace and other times reminding me that he was a vicious murderer. I just nodded and changed the subject. If that didn't work, I excused myself even though it often meant making something up.

Alex was the bright spot in my days. He always greeted me with a warm smile, a teasing twinkle in his eyes. Once in the hall, he put his arm around my shoulders, but when I tensed up, he dropped it and moved away. I felt badly, but I'd never had a boyfriend and I wasn't sure how to act. Aside from that, I liked him even more knowing he was just as serious about school as I was.

Derek remained friendly all week, but he avoided me when I was with Celeste. If he saw her from a distance, he turned around and took a detour to his next class. It was obvious from the doe-eyed looks she gave him that she had a huge crush on him. But clearly, he wanted nothing to do with her.

Mr. Wainwright left me alone the rest of the week. He occasionally said hello or goodbye with a smile when I passed his desk, but that was all. To my relief, he didn't ask me to stay after class again. By the end of the week, he was just one of my teachers. I even started to forget our awkward meeting at the bar.

The only thing at school that filled me with anxiety was Art class. Actually, it was Lucian Dumante who sent my heart into overdrive and put me on edge for the entire period. He never said a word to me. No friendly "Hi" or "Hello, nice to meet you." He either stared at me, his eyes cold and unwavering, or ignored me as if I didn't exist. To make matters worse, the day the teacher assigned our seats we were sitting at the same bench as on the first day. So I was stuck next to him for the rest of the year. Art was supposed to be my best class of the day, and instead, it was the worst. I could barely concentrate on the teacher, and all I did was watch the clock, counting the minutes until the bell rang.

After returning home Friday afternoon, I carried my book bag up to my room where I dropped it on the bed. I was exhausted and didn't want to crack open a book until Sunday. As I changed into an old pair of jeans and a T-shirt, planning to head out to the barn, my cell phone rang. I pushed my arms through the shirt sleeves before racing over to my dresser where I'd left my phone. Grabbing it, I read Sam's name flashing across the screen. A smile broke out across my face as I answered the call. "Sam, hi!"

"Hi, Gracyn. How was your first week at school?"

I sat down on the edge of my bed, realizing we hadn't talked all week. She had called a few times when I'd been out with the horses, but we hadn't caught up except for a few short texts. "Good, I guess." *Aside from Lucian Dumante,* I added silently as his angry frown flashed through my mind. Then I cursed myself for letting him back into my thoughts. "How about yours?" I asked, trying to sound carefree.

"The usual. All the same kids, just a different year and different teachers. And a few surprising hook-ups from the summer. But I didn't call you to complain about my classes or gossip about anyone. Dad woke up today."

I sucked in a sharp breath, afraid to believe it. As much as I wanted him to pay for what he had tried to do, for Sam's sake, I wanted him to get back to his family. "What?"

"You heard me. He's awake. Mom's at the hospital right now, but it looks like he's going to be okay."

"Really?" My heart filled with relief, but I felt weak, like my blood pressure had just dropped. "Sam, that's wonderful. Have you seen him?"

"No, not yet. It happened this morning. He's been up all day, talking and eating. He lost a lot of weight since it's been almost a month and he still has a cast on his hand, but the doctors think he's going to make a full recovery."

I resisted the urge to ask about his hand. I was still hoping I'd imagined breaking it and that he really had slammed a car door on it which, according to Sam, was what he'd told the doctors. Pushing that thought aside, I forced myself to remain upbeat. "That's the best news

I've heard all week. I'm so happy for you. Your mom and brother must be so relieved."

"They are. They were so different today, like they snapped out of their depressions. I felt like I was the only one holding up these last few weeks and they were leaning on me. It was really starting to take all my energy. I wasn't sure how I was going to survive the year."

"You're strong. You would have managed if you had to. But I'm glad you don't have to get through this year with that on your shoulders." And now, neither did I. Even after moving hundreds of miles away to Massachusetts, guilt had been eating at me from knowing his condition was tearing up her family. No matter how hard I tried not to, I blamed myself.

"Thanks, Gracyn." She paused and silence fell between us before she continued. "God, I miss you. Do you realize this is the first year we'll be in separate schools, not to mention separate states, since Kindergarten?"

"I know," I replied thoughtfully. "But it was going to happen when we went to college. It just happened a year earlier."

"Yeah? Well, it sucks. We won't get to graduate together now. I always pictured us walking across the stage in our caps and gowns together. And of course, getting our pictures taken together." She paused again. "I'm sorry. I don't mean to dump this on you. I know you only did what you had to."

"It's okay. I know it's not easy." An idea formed in my mind. "Maybe you can come up here for a visit in a month or two. Before it gets really cold."

"That would be great! I'll talk to my parents about it as soon as Dad gets home from the hospital and things get back to normal. I'd love to see the farm and meet your new friends."

"Well, don't get too excited. There's just Alex and Celeste." *Don't forget your Art buddy,* a sarcastic voice piped up in my head. Where had that come from? Frustrated, I frowned, thankful that Sam couldn't see my expression. *Why are you bringing him up every chance you get? He obviously doesn't like you. Or is that it? The more he ignores you, the more curious you are? The classic attention getter.*

"Celeste?" Sam asked, breaking through the voices in my head.

"Yes. I texted you about her, remember?"

"Oh, yeah, now that you mention it, I do. But all you said was goth and loner. Sounds like she's going to make a great study partner," Sam said, her voice a bit condescending.

I couldn't blame her. Sam had my best intentions at heart. If I didn't get good grades this semester, my chance to go to MIT could be ruined. "Celeste is no dummy, I can see that. But if I need help in a class, Alex is probably my best bet."

"Seriously?"

"Yes. He's in all AP classes, too."

"Well, that's a surprise. But even if you don't need help, you should ask him for it."

I shook my head, confused. "Why? That's crazy."

"Let's face it, Gracyn, boys have fragile egos. They want to help us. You know, be our heroes and change our tires and stuff. So whatever you do, don't let him think you're smarter than he is even if you are."

I scoffed at her clichéd relationship advice. "Are you kidding me? This is the twenty-first century, not nineteen-forty. You're not really advising me in the dating department, are you?"

"Yes, I am. At least one of us has a cute boy to hang out with and I don't want you to screw it up."

"Thanks for the vote of confidence."

"You know what I mean. I love you like the sister I never had, so I'm always going to tell it like it is."

"Right back at you," I said, realizing Sam was probably more like a sister to me than Becca would ever be. I glanced at my watch, noticing that time was ticking away. If I wanted to groom Gypsy before Alex picked me up, I needed to get off the phone.

I finally told Sam I had a date with Alex to get ready for, but she didn't let me go until I promised to call her in the morning and tell her about it. I laughed, insisting that nothing interesting would happen which she promptly disputed before hanging up.

A smile lingering on my face, I dropped my phone on the bed and hurried out of the room to head to the barn while the sun was still shining.

Alex took me to dinner at a restaurant known for their local cuisine. All of their ingredients came from farms in the area, reminding me of Becca and Gabriel's garden. The salad I ordered was good, but I honestly couldn't tell the difference from salads I'd eaten back home.

When we stepped out onto the sidewalk, streetlamps lit up the row of brick-front shops. A chill had crept into the air, but I was comfortable in jeans, tall boots, and a sweater. I had learned not to trust the daytime warmth. As soon as the sun went down, long sleeves and pants were a must. Even Alex slipped his denim jacket on before taking my hand.

I turned to him, wondering if he had planned anything for the rest of the night. "Thanks for dinner," I said.

"You're welcome. Thank you for agreeing to go out with me again, smart girl," he teased. "Now, I'd rather not take you home so early. Are you up for some dessert?"

"Maybe. What do you have in mind?"

"Smores."

"Smores?" I repeated, not sure I'd heard him correctly.

"That's right. Derek sent me a text. He's at the lake with Lacey. They've got a fire going, and no one else is there because the football team is having a huge party after the game tonight."

"You didn't want to go to the party?"

He shrugged. "I've been to enough of those parties. It's always the same. All anyone does is get drunk and make out."

I laughed. "And that doesn't interest you?"

"Not when I can spend time getting to know you better and remember it in the morning."

"Good answer." I beamed from his words, my heart nearly skipping a beat when he leaned over to kiss me.

"I was hoping you'd say that," he said before leading me across the street to his Jeep.

Ten minutes later, we pulled up behind Derek's van at the lake. I almost didn't recognize the area without the dozens of cars that had lined the road the last time I'd been here. An eerie silence greeted us when we got out of the Jeep. No music or voices rang out in the distance. Instead, the wind rustled through the leaves overhead and an owl hooted in the distance. The flames of a small fire danced from the clearing beyond the trees, a miniature version of the huge bonfire I remembered from last time.

Alex led me through the woods until we reached the shoreline of the lake. Derek sat next to a pretty brunette, a blanket draped over their legs and his arm curled around her shoulders as he whispered into her ear. He jerked his head up when he heard our footsteps in the leaves.

"Hey, man," Derek greeted Alex with a lazy smile. "Glad you guys could make it. Pull up a chair."

Alex grabbed two folding chairs that leaned against a nearby tree and set them up across from Derek and his guest. He gestured for me to sit in one and then took a seat beside me. Scooting his chair close to mine, he slid his arm around my shoulders. I glanced at him with a smile, enjoying the heat of his touch.

"So you guys skipped the party, too, huh?" Alex asked.

"Yeah," Derek muttered. "Everyone is over there. Mark my words, they're going to get busted. I had enough of that last year."

"Really?" Alex asked, his eyebrows raised. Turning to me, he whispered loudly, "He's just avoiding Zoe now that Lucian's back in town."

"Hey!" Derek grumbled. "I heard that. And in case you didn't notice, I have company tonight."

"Of course I noticed." Alex turned his attention to the girl next to Derek. "How's it going Lacey?"

"It's going," she said, sounding bored. "Who's this, Alex?"

"Oh, sorry. This is Gracyn. I guess you guys didn't meet this week."

"No, I don't think so." Lacey eyed me and recognition crossed over her face. "Wait. I think we might have English together. You're the new girl from DC, right?"

"That's me," I answered with a nod, ignoring her reference to DC. Technically, it was Maryland, but it was the DC metro area. And DC sounded a lot cooler than Maryland.

"Why would you want to move to this hellhole when you were living in a big city?" she asked, her brown eyes fixated on me, waiting for an answer.

"I had to. For my mom. She moved to Moscow."

Lacey raised her eyebrows. "I guess I'd pick small town Massachusetts over Russia, too. Even with all the creeps in this town."

Derek shot her a warning look. "Lacey."

"What? She's bound to notice how weird this town is sooner or later." Lacey paused, turning to look directly at me. "And I'm not talking just about the people."

"What are you talking about?" I asked hesitantly.

Derek sighed, shooting her a disappointed look. "You'll have to excuse my date. She isn't as enamored with Sedgewick as some of us."

"Don't be a jerk, Derek," Lacey said, her eyes narrowed at him before she snapped them back to me. "What you may not know, Gracyn, is that Sedgewick is haunted. There, I said it. You two can't hide the truth from her forever."

I huffed nervously. "Is that true?" I asked, looking at Alex.

No one said a word for a moment. An owl hooted, sounding a lot closer than the last one, making me jump.

Finally, Alex took a deep breath, his expression flat. "There are rumors of some eerie happenings around here, but nothing has been proven."

"Like what?" I asked.

"Ghosts," Derek said.

"Goblins," Lacey added.

"And ghouls," Alex piped up, his laughter barely kept in check.

"Yeah. It gets real scary around here on Halloween. Just make sure you lock your doors that night," Derek added before a wide grin broke out on his face.

My racing heart slowed as I realized their game. "Thanks, guys. You had me going there for a minute. Ghosts, goblins and ghouls. Very creative. Maybe you can tell the next new girl that vampires, werewolves, and witches live here, too."

Derek suddenly coughed, nearly choking on a breath of air. He reached for the beer bottle on the ground next to his chair. After chugging it, his hacking subsided. His face had turned red, but he seemed to be breathing comfortably. Standing up, he let the blanket fall onto his seat. "I need another beer. Alex?"

"No, thanks. I'm driving tonight."

"Not me. Lacey promised to drive if I get too hammered. Or we'll just shack up in the van 'til morning." He winked at her before heading over to the cooler on the picnic table.

I focused on Alex, not ready to dismiss their joke yet. "There are no ghosts in this town, right?"

"Of course not," Lacey said, waiting until I glanced at her to continue. "At least none that have been proven. But the rumors around here will make the hair on the back of your neck stand on edge. That's why I'm high-tailing it out of this town the first chance I get after graduation."

"You're high-tailing it out of here after graduation so you don't have to live with your dad's girlfriend anymore," Alex said.

"You got that right," she retorted.

Alex rolled his eyes with a "here we go again" look. Turning in his seat, he looked back at Derek who stood by the picnic table with a beer bottle in his hand. "What happened to the Smores you promised?"

"Everything's over here," Derek told him.

Alex nudged me. "Wait here. I'll be right back." He stood and joined Derek by the picnic table, leaving me with Lacey.

I smiled at her, feeling uneasy because I hardly knew her. Actually, I hardly knew anyone except Celeste since she had watched over me like a mother hen all week, not letting anyone else near.

As silence hovered between us, Lacey reached under the blanket, pulling out a pack of cigarettes and a lighter. "Want one?" she offered as she lit one.

"No, thanks."

"So, you know," she started before taking a drag on her cigarette. After exhaling a long trail of smoke, she continued. "Hanging out with Celeste Hamilton is like social suicide. Why'd you pick her?"

"I didn't. It was more like she picked me."

"You poor thing," she said.

"What's that?" Derek asked as he returned to his seat, the beer in his hand.

"I was just telling Gracyn that she won't have any friends as long as Celeste is hovering over her."

Nodding, Derek sat down and pulled the blanket over his legs. "Yeah. She's kind of strange. She means well, but once she thinks you like her, she won't let go."

"Is that why you won't go anywhere near her?" I asked Derek bluntly.

He stared at me as Alex returned to my side with a box of graham crackers, a few chocolate bars and a bag of marshmallows. "What'd I miss?" he asked, taking his seat.

I turned to him. "I just asked Derek why he avoids Celeste like the plague at school."

Alex sucked in a deep breath and let out a low whistle. "Oh, Gracyn. That was mighty brave of you."

Whipping around to look at Derek and Lacey, I explained, "She's really sweet, even if she is a little overbearing. And Derek, okay, I know you're out tonight with Lacey and I totally get that, but maybe you should sit Celeste down and talk to her. Tell her the truth. Because she seems to keep hoping she has a chance with you. And as long as she believes that, she could be missing out on someone else, not to mention keeping you on your toes. You can't even take a direct route to your classes."

Derek laughed, his gaze shifting between the three of us. "You're funny, Gracyn. Why don't we put that idea on hold for about a month? Then we'll see if you still think it's a good idea. Look, I have nothing against her. She's a nice girl. I just don't want her to get her feelings hurt."

"Aw, honey," Lacey cooed, running her fingers through Derek's hair. "You're so sensitive. I love that about you."

Derek's face turned even redder than it had been earlier from his coughing. "Okay, time to be mean, then. I can't let my sensitive side show. Scratch what I said. The chick's weird. You'll realize that soon enough."

"Yeah," Alex said, nodding. "She is." He turned to me. "Just be on guard with her. She'll mess with your head and that's the last thing you need this year."

"Oh, really? Like telling me that ghosts live in Sedgewick?"

Alex grinned. "Don't be mad about that. We were just playing with you."

"I know," I said, pursing my lips and pretending to be mad. "But you're still going to have to make it up to me."

"How about dessert?" Alex twisted a marshmallow onto the end of a long stick. After handing it to me, he set up another one.

I flashed him a quick smile before holding the marshmallow over the fire. "I guess it will have to do. For now."

The flames engulfing the marshmallow mesmerized me. Derek and Lacey whispered in the background, and Alex put his arm around me as he held his stick over the fire. For the first time that night, I realized I hadn't thought about my Art class neighbor in hours. In that instant, Lucian's stare returned to my thoughts, sending an icy blast through my veins. Too bad my reprieve had to come to an end. I would have preferred the ghosts, goblins, and ghouls to Lucian. They were child's play compared to the demons he seemed to be dealing with.

15

The next morning, it was almost ten o'clock when I woke up. Wearing gray pajama pants and a navy sweatshirt, I grabbed my glasses and headed downstairs. As I made my way closer to the kitchen, I heard Becca's soft laughter. Curious, I quickened my pace, but stopped dead in my tracks at the bottom of the steps when I saw the scene before me.

Becca and Gabriel were caught up in a kiss. Gabriel's hand had slipped under her short white robe, revealing the curve of her butt and her white panties. I gasped, turning away as I felt a hot blush creep across my face. When I dared to glance at them again, hoping they had noticed they were no longer alone, they were still wrapped up in each other, oblivious to my arrival. Gabriel's golden hair was all I could see as he ducked his head, kissing Becca while the dogs snoozed on the rug under the table.

I whipped my eyes away and cleared my throat, not needing to look back at them when I heard their gasps and a coffee mug clanking against the counter.

"Sorry, Gracyn," Becca said. "You can look now. It's safe."

I turned around, the heat from my embarrassment still warming me. Becca stood behind the island as Gabriel poured a cup of coffee, his back to her. "No," I said. "I should be the one who's sorry. I'm cramping your style."

"Don't be silly," Gabriel said, turning to stand beside Becca and draping an arm over her shoulders. "We just have to get used to having someone else around. We've been kind of spoiled for years."

"We weren't sure when you'd be up," Becca said. "We were killing time waiting for you so we could all have breakfast together. You didn't sleep this late last weekend."

"I know. It was just an exhausting week," I explained weakly as I walked over to the island and sat on one of the stools.

Gabriel set about the kitchen, beating eggs in a bowl and starting the stove while Becca leaned her elbows on the island, her attention focused on me.

"I'm sure it was. High school these days can't be fun," Becca said, earning her a confused look from me.

"You're not that old. It wasn't too long ago that you were in high school."

She shook her head with a sly smile. "It might not have been many years ago, but things have changed a lot. We didn't have smart phones and selfies back then."

"Oh, yeah," I groaned. "That's what's taking up all my time. Try three back to back AP classes and then Art class sitting next to a guy who looks like he wants to kill me all the time."

As the spoon fell out of Gabriel's fingers and sank to the bottom of the bowl with a clank, Becca's jaw dropped. "What's that all about?"

I took a deep breath as Gabriel turned. Both of them watched me, waiting for my answer. "Nothing. Sorry, I didn't mean to scare you."

"But you sound scared," Becca said. "Gracyn, if someone is bothering you, we want to know about it."

My pulse taking off, I realized I never should have mentioned it. Now I had to blow it off before they made a big deal out of it. "I have to sit next to Lucian Dumante in Art class. He seems a bit odd."

Gabriel nodded. "Yes, he's one you should stay away from. It's really bad timing that he decided to come back this year."

"Well, he sort of had to," Becca explained. "He wasn't going to wait until he was twenty-five to finish high school."

"Why finish at all?" Gabriel asked. "He doesn't need a degree or even a high school diploma to work for Daddy."

"Gabe!" Becca snapped. "Everett would not be happy if he heard you speak of him so."

Gabriel shrugged. "He's not here. In fact, he's in town less now than he was before Cassie died. I'm slowly losing my respect."

After shooting him a glare, Becca shifted her gaze to me, her expression softening. "Keep me posted on Lucian's behavior. If he starts to bother you, I'll do something about it."

I nearly choked. "What would you do? Look, Becca, thank you for trying to stick up for me and all, but I don't need you to. I'll get through it. For the most part, he ignores me."

"But you said—"

"I know what I said. It only happened one or two times," I said awkwardly. *More like one or two times every day, but who's counting?* I thought. *Just find a way to change the subject. Having your big sister march into school and try to protect you from your imagination will make you look like a child.* "It's no big deal."

Becca didn't look convinced, but she also didn't press the issue. "Okay. As long as you're sure."

"I am," I insisted, thankful when Gabriel turned back to his cooking and fished the spoon out of the eggs.

"So, tell me about last night. How'd it go with Alex? I like him. He's a nice guy," Becca said.

Grateful to have something else to talk about, I smiled, remembering how safe and comfortable I felt with him as opposed to... *There you go again, bringing Lucian back into your head. You have to stop doing this to yourself!* My frown returned as dark thoughts raced through my mind. *You're just replacing Sam's stepfather with the newest problem, that's all. You are seriously disturbed if you always need a problem to dwell on.*

I shook my head and forced myself to think about Alex with his sleek ponytail and teasing smile. There, that was better. "It was fun. We had a nice time. Aside from him and his friends trying to scare me with ghost stories, that is."

Becca laughed, even as a thoughtful look formed in her eyes. "What was that all about?"

"Oh, something about rumors that Sedgewick is haunted. But they finally fessed up and told me it was just a joke."

Gabriel stopped clanking the pots and pans long enough to look at me. "It's no joke, Gracyn."

As Becca shot daggers out of her eyes at him from over her shoulder, I huffed. "What?"

He smiled, winking at Becca. "It's true that there are rumors around here. Must be all the old folks who have nothing better to do with their time than hope some misguided gust of wind is really their dead friend."

"What Gabe is trying to say," Becca started as she turned back to me. "Is that people talk, but none of it's true. The rumors get a little worse around Halloween, but it's all conjecture."

"Well, Lacey didn't seem to like this town at all. She said the people here are strange."

"That could probably be said about every town," Becca said.

Suddenly wanting nothing more than to change the subject, I hopped off the stool. "Is there any coffee left? I sure could use some."

"Help yourself," Becca said, gesturing to the full pot.

I wandered over to the counter, careful not to get in Gabriel's way as he manned the eggs, hash browns, and bacon on the stove. Helping myself to a mug from the overhead cabinet, I heard Becca ask, "Do you have any plans for today?"

"Just homework," I answered as I poured the steaming coffee. After splashing some creamer into it, I turned around. "Unless we could go for a trail ride. I can always save my homework for tomorrow."

"Is that hope I hear? Do you mean to tell me you actually like riding now?" Becca asked.

"I never disliked it. I was just afraid," I clarified. "So yeah, I was hoping we could ride again today." *As long as we don't ride by the Dumante property, or if we do, no one is watching us,* I added to myself, realizing Becca would probably take me on the same trail again, so it was unreasonable to expect we wouldn't ride by their property.

"Great. Let's all go. The horses never get to head out on the trails all together. They'd love that. What do you say, Gabe?"

Gabriel glanced at us with a smile. "Just tell me what time you girls want to saddle up."

Becca looked at me, her eyebrows raised. "After breakfast?"

"Sounds perfect," I answered before sipping my coffee. A morning out on the trails was exactly what I needed to clear my head before committing myself to homework for the rest of the weekend.

The ride didn't go exactly as we hoped. When the three of us headed out on the trail, dark clouds rolled in from the west. We had only been gone for fifteen minutes before the rain began. It started as a light sprinkle, but quickly intensified into a steady downpour. In spite of the branches overhead, we got soaked.

When the rain came down harder, Becca and Gabriel urged the horses into a canter. Knowing Gypsy wouldn't be left behind at a walk, I grabbed a handful of her mane and leaned my chest against her neck. She raced after the others, her hooves splashing mud all over her neck and belly, splattering my legs in the process.

By the time we returned to the barn, the horses were dripping wet. Water rolled down their faces, and droplets pooled at the end of their manes. I hopped off Gypsy, slid the reins over her neck, and led her into the barn. Becca and Gabriel untacked their horses and turned them out before helping me. I was starting to get the hang of it, but I missed undoing a buckle on the bridle. Becca had to show me what I did wrong before I could pull the bridle off and slide the halter on in its place.

After I led Gypsy to the pasture, I retraced my steps through the barn and headed across the driveway to the house. The rain had slowed to a misty drizzle, but I was cold and damp and I couldn't wait to get out of my wet clothes.

The dogs stood in the center of the driveway, their eyes and ears focused on something in the distance. They stood tall and alert, the hair on their backs ruffled up like mohawks. At first, I ignored them. Whatever they sensed couldn't possibly be enough to keep me from a hot shower.

I had almost reached the house when Becca and Gabriel ran down the porch steps. They stopped beside the dogs, staring down the driveway. "Company's coming," Gabriel stated.

"What?" I asked, confused. How could they be sure the dogs hadn't seen an animal somewhere in the distance?

Becca jogged over to me as the dogs sprinted down the driveway, barking and swishing their tails. When she reached me, she put both hands on my upper arms. "I need you to go inside. Now," she commanded, her tone authoritative, yet calm.

As curious as I was, I nodded. "Okay," I whispered before hurrying up the porch steps and through the front door.

Once inside, I ran to the nearest window and peeked around the curtain. A silver Mercedes pulled up next to Becca's SUV, the dogs following closely behind. Gabriel called something out, although I couldn't hear his words through the glass. The dogs instantly stopped their incessant barking and ran to him, halting at his side.

As the two front doors of the car opened, Becca and Gabriel stood like an army on the front line of a battle, their expressions cold and stoic.

A dark-haired man and a blonde woman climbed out of the Mercedes. Tall and slender, the man wore jeans, a white T-shirt, and a black blazer. The woman's long spiral curls were almost white against her black leather jacket. Her skin was pale and smooth like porcelain next to her red lipstick. In spite of the overcast sky and lingering mist, dark sunglasses hid her eyes.

The couple approached Becca and Gabriel, halting before them. Folding her arms across her chest, the woman frowned as the man spoke. I couldn't hear anything through the glass, but one thing seemed clear. This was no social visit.

After a few minutes of watching the scene outside like it was a silent movie, I ran up to my room. My curiosity killing me, I rushed to my desk and opened the window a few inches.

"—understand," Gabriel said, his voice cool and collected. "We weren't happy when we found out about it, either. But what can we do? Everett practically owns this town."

"And yet where is he? He can't allow his son to move back without making sure he won't hurt anyone else," the man said, his voice full of disdain.

So they were talking about Lucian. This I wanted to hear, especially after the cold looks he'd given me all week.

"We can't assume that will happen," Becca explained. "He wasn't convicted. We have to believe he would be in jail right now if he really had killed Cassie."

"You're living in a fantasy world, Becca," the woman's shrill voice rang out before softening. "She was just a baby. And she was special, like Celeste."

"Of course she was," Gabriel said. "Look, we know you're concerned. We're keeping an eye on things. If we see anything you need to be worried about, we'll be knocking on your door. Promise. You're going to have to trust us."

Silence met Gabriel's words, and I was about to shut the window when the man spoke again. "Celeste is our only daughter. If we lose her, our world will cease to exist. And if you lose her, well, you know what that means."

"Yes," Becca agreed, a serious tone in her voice. "We do. We will be vigilant as you should be as well."

"Of course," the woman stated.

"But for now, all we can do is watch and wait," Becca continued. "He has a right to be here, and there is nothing we can do about it."

"I realize that," the man said. "But when Everett returns, you tell him I'd like a word with him. I'm not going to sit back and wait for the next tragedy to happen. I can't, and neither should any of you. If we do, then Cassie's death will be in vain."

"Cassie's death will be avenged in time," Gabriel stated firmly.

"Thank you, Gabriel," the woman said. "We know Becca will do everything she can to protect us. It's just very bad timing. As long as Lucian was gone, we felt safe."

"We are still safe," Becca insisted, although weakly.

"We could be safer," the man implied.

"No," Becca said before he could say anything more. "I know what you're thinking, and I can't. If I need to, I will be ready when the time comes."

At that point, I raised my eyebrows. None of this conversation was making sense. *That's what you get for eavesdropping,* a voice silently scolded. *Now shut the window because all you're doing is sticking your nose in business that doesn't involve you and letting this nasty damp air into the room.*

I finally closed the window, but I was tempted to reopen it. Lucian clearly didn't like me. If they believed he had killed his sister and that he would eventually strike again, perhaps I would be his next victim. In that respect, what they were discussing could concern me.

After a few more minutes of arguing with myself, I decided to turn away and leave the notion of Lucian killing anyone else out in the cold misty drizzle where it belonged. Only one other question perplexed me. How had I been able to hear every word they said from all the way up here?

16

It was a struggle to get through my homework that weekend. I kept picturing Lucian's cold glaring eyes when I thought about the conversation I'd overheard. And each time, I scolded myself for letting problems that didn't concern me get in the way of my work. I needed to stay focused on school and applying to college. Not on worrying if Lucian had killed his sister. That was better left to the police. If only I didn't have to sit next to him every day, the whole thing probably wouldn't bother me so much.

Sam called again on Sunday, this time to drill me with questions about my date with Alex and share the news that her stepfather would be coming home in a few days. I answered her with as little detail as I could get away with and told her how happy I was for her family. Hearing her voice was a welcome distraction, even if it brought up the one thing in my past I was trying to forget.

When the screeching alarm woke me up Monday morning, my eyes fluttered open as I reached over to shut it off. The red neon numbers read five forty-five in the early morning darkness. Still sleepy, I leaned back down. As soon as my head touched the pillow, I shot up again with a gasp. I blinked my eyes, hard. How were the alarm clock numbers so clear? Had I forgotten to take out my contact lenses last night? Wait a minute, I hadn't even put them in yesterday since I'd spent the day in my room doing homework.

Confused, I turned on the bedside lamp and studied my room. Everything was clear from my computer to the gray sweatshirt hanging on the closet door handle. Shutting my eyes, I counted to five. Then I opened them again, expecting the room to be blurry. But every detail was in focus.

For a few minutes, I sat where I was, staring at the room in wonder. It was a miracle. But...how? I searched my mind for an answer, but there was no explanation. People didn't just wake up to find their vision cured, did they? I had worn glasses since I was four years old. Fourteen long years of getting my prescription checked and trying on frames. Could it be possible that I'd never need glasses again? I couldn't allow myself to hope for that.

Whatever it is, this isn't a bad thing, I told myself. *There's enough going on that you don't need to worry about this. Enjoy it! You deserve to be released from those hideous glasses. And contact lenses were never any better.*

In spite of the words racing through my mind, I made a mental note to ask Gabriel how this could be possible. There had to be an explanation and I'd never be able to sleep at night until I understood how this had happened. Unfortunately, he was in Boston again, so I would have to wait a few days for answers, assuming my vision stayed clear that long.

With a smile, I tossed my covers aside and headed for the bathroom. The world was a whole new place that morning. Everything was clear from the steady stream of water in the shower to the fine print on the shampoo bottle. I could even see my ankles when I shaved my legs. My heart glowed with happiness, shutting out my apprehension over seeing Lucian at school that day. All that mattered was my clear vision.

I kept waiting for one blink to make my world blurry again, but it never did. By the time I got to school, I was grinning from ear to ear. My hair had cooperated this morning and fell over my shoulders in smooth waves. A hint of make-up around my eyes made the blue stand out next to the purple shirt I wore with jeans. I'd never felt so confident, even though my glasses were tucked in my book bag just in case.

As I reached for a book on my locker shelf, two hands covered my eyes. My world went dark and I heard a deep voice behind me. "Guess who."

My breath hitched, my smile growing. This day couldn't get any better. "Hi, Alex."

He removed his hands from my eyes and placed them on my shoulders. Then he leaned in, pushing my hair aside before kissing my cheek. "Good morning. How was your weekend?"

I spun around and leaned against my locker, noticing how handsome he looked in a dark green shirt, the sleeves rolled up to his elbows. "I don't know. I honestly can't remember."

A curious frown spread across his face. "Please tell me that doesn't include Friday night, or I'll be crushed. And you don't want to be the cause of my broken heart, do you?" he teased.

"No, I remember Friday night. How could I forget about all the ghosts around here?"

"You're never going to forgive me for that, are you?"

"Maybe not, at least for a week or so."

"Okay, so what happened that you're not telling me?"

I paused, waiting until his dark eyes locked with mine to continue. "Do you notice anything?" I asked, batting my eyelashes. "Look very closely. The only hint I'm going to give you is that it's not very obvious."

"Gracyn," he groaned. "I'm a guy, and you're asking me to notice something about you that's obscure? How many guys have you dated?"

My eyes narrowed, my mood souring for a moment. He knew very well that my dating history before him involved all of three dates and not one relationship. "Very funny. Okay, I'll give you a hint. It's nothing short of a medical miracle."

"A miracle? I don't believe in those. You know me, I only believe in science and fact."

His words could have just as easily come from my mouth, at least on any other day aside from today. "My eyes," I finally said. "Look at them. What do you notice?"

He studied me, a smile curling upon his lips. "They're blue? Oh wait, they're a different color blue. Are you wearing colored contacts?" he asked.

"No!" I said in one long breath, frustrated. "I don't have any contacts in at all. Can't you see that?"

"Oh, wow, you had Lasik surgery this weekend? No wonder I didn't hear from you. That's awesome. You must love it!"

I bit my lip, wondering how to break it to him. "Not quite. That procedure kind of freaks me out."

"Then how–"

Raising my eyebrows, I shrugged. "I don't know how. I woke up this morning and I could see clearly."

Alex's expression turned serious. "That's not possible," he stated.

"Well, it happened. So I guess it is possible."

"It doesn't make any sense. People don't just wake up with twenty-twenty vision when they haven't had it for years."

"But I did," I insisted, even though I almost didn't believe it either.

Alex held a finger up. "Okay, I'm going to figure this out. Hold on one second." He reached into his back jeans pocket and whipped out his phone. Looking down, he started typing on it.

"What are you doing?"

"I'm looking it up to see if anything like this has ever happened before. Did you try that?"

"No, I didn't have time. It happened this morning, and I had to get ready for school." I had also been too excited to think about researching it on the internet.

Alex stared at his phone, scrolling through the search results.

"Anything?" I asked when he didn't say a word.

He glanced up as he shoved the phone back in his pocket. "Nope. Nothing except a bunch of articles on Lasik. I'll try again later when I have more time. There has to be an explanation."

"That's what I thought. But I'm really enjoying this. I don't know if I want to know how it happened. With my luck, it's some kind of weird phenomenon before my vision goes back to the way it was, or gets worse."

"Well, let's hope that doesn't happen," Alex said with a smile. "Except you look cute in glasses. I might be a little disappointed if you don't have to wear them again."

"You're just trying to make me feel better in case this doesn't last."

"Yes, but I'm also being honest."

A weak smile slid across my lips. "Thanks." I paused, taking a deep breath before I changed the subject. "So, how did you do on those Calculus problems? I feel like that's going to be my hardest class this year."

"I got through them. Why?"

"I got stuck on two problems. It drove me nuts that I couldn't figure them out."

"Want some help?"

I noticed a kind sparkle in his eyes and remembered Sam's advice to let him come to my rescue. Perhaps she'd been right. "I'd love some."

"Cool. It's a date."

"No, it's homework."

"Maybe for you," he quipped with a smile.

I playfully touched his shoulder as the warning bell rang. Locker doors were slammed shut as the other kids finished up and started heading to homeroom. "Okay, fine. We'll call it a study date. Now I need to finish up here and get going."

"Me, too. I'll see you in class." After winking at me, Alex turned and disappeared into the crowd, leaving me alone.

Reaching into my locker, my smile returned as I grabbed my books. All I could think about was that for the first time in my life, my vision was clear. I hoped this miracle never ended.

I saw Celeste for the first time that day at lunch. As I approached the table where she sat alone, I noticed the dark shadows under her eyes right away. Against her black clothes, her skin looked paler than ever. Her hair hung down her back in a long braid and wispy strands fell around the sides of her face.

"Hi," I said, placing my tray of salad and lasagna on the table. "I was wondering if you were here today. I haven't seen you. How was your weekend?"

She glanced up at me, a hollow look in her eyes. "Fine."

I had a feeling she was lying. "You look tired. Everything okay?" I asked before sitting down next to her.

"No," she answered flatly, not offering an explanation.

"Want to talk about it?" I asked, opening my milk carton.

"Not really," she murmured, her gaze drifting across the cafeteria as if she was lost in her thoughts.

"Well, I'm here if you change your mind," I told her, hoping she would trust me enough to talk about whatever was bothering her. After overhearing her parents on Saturday, I suspected it had something to do with Lucian.

As I took a bite of my salad, I smiled at her. "Aren't you going to eat?"

The brown bag on the table in front of her hadn't been opened. "Not hungry." Then she sucked in a deep breath. "Damn it, why does he have to be in this lunch period?"

Looking up, I followed her gaze to see Lucian weaving through the tables, a tray balanced on one hand. His movements were fluid, the rhythm of his walk never changing as he turned each corner. He wore a white button down shirt today, something that surprised me. After last week, I'd been sure the only colors in his closet were black, gray, and dark blue.

He walked around the corner of another table and headed straight for us. I watched him, finding it impossible to take my eyes off of him now that I could really see. As he approached, his gaze met mine for a split second. Confusion in his eyes, he tilted his head for a moment. Then, a faint and almost hopeful smidge of a smile formed on his lips.

I tore my gaze away from him, mortified that he'd caught me staring. Not sure if he had even been looking at me, I glanced behind me, certain I'd see Zoe and have an explanation for his smile. But she was nowhere to be found among the sea of faces in the cafeteria. Heat spreading through my cheeks, I focused my attention on my tray for a moment.

When I looked up at Celeste, she looked nauseated. Staring blankly at the table, she rubbed her forehead with one hand.

"Celeste," I said. "Are you okay?"

"No," she muttered. Shifting her gaze to me, she picked up her lunch bag. "I have to go. I can't stay in this cafeteria as long as he's here. I think I'm just going to spend lunch in the library. Sorry, Gracyn."

Before I could stop her, she stood up and marched to the door farthest away, presumably so she wouldn't have to walk near Lucian who now sat alone at a table by the other door. I dared to glance his way, noticing that he seemed perfectly content all by himself, his attention focused on a book.

Forcing myself to look away before he caught me staring at him twice in a matter of minutes, I took a drink. Then I picked up my fork, wishing Alex, Derek, or even Lacey had this lunch hour as it looked like I could be eating alone for the rest of the year.

Lucian continued to ignore me in Art class, but at least he didn't glare at me like he wanted to kill me. Sitting next to him, I stole a few glances at him as I listened to Ms. Friedman ramble on about sketching still life. Not once did he look my way, making me wonder if I had imagined the semblance of a smile he'd given me in the cafeteria.

I sat on the edge of my seat, putting as much distance between us as I could. The last thing I wanted was to accidentally bump him. As it was, he rattled my nerves from where he sat a foot away.

When the bell rang, I jumped up from my seat and ran to my locker. After gathering my things, I left the school with the rest of the students.

Crossing the lawn, I saw Celeste on the sidewalk. "Celeste! Wait up!" I called, jogging toward her.

My book bag bumped against my thigh as I swerved around the other students, my sights set on Celeste who didn't seem to hear me. She continued walking away, not once looking back. "Celeste!" I called again, out of breath. It seemed like the faster I ran, the farther away she got.

She turned into the parking lot and headed straight across the lanes without bothering to look for cars. Tires squealed as a black Mustang skidded to a stop inches away from her. She halted, stumbling to keep her balance. When she started walking again, a boy with floppy brown hair waved at her from the driver's window.

"Good one!" he shouted. "Didn't you learn to look both ways in first grade? Dork!" As soon as he could get around her, he sped away.

"Jerk!" she yelled, raising her hand, her middle finger directed at the car as exhaust fumes spewed out at her. Then she lowered her arm, watching the car disappear around a corner.

The distraction gave me just enough time to catch up to her. "Celeste," I said, stopping behind her.

She turned, acknowledging my presence. "What?" she asked, her eyes tired and her voice withdrawn.

"I just wanted to make sure you were okay. I hardly saw you today except for lunch."

"I'm fine. I haven't been sleeping well, that's all."

"I'm sorry to hear that."

"Well, it's not–" Her voice dropped off as she narrowed her eyes at me. "What happened to your contact lenses?"

I couldn't believe she noticed. "I...um...I woke up this morning and I could see. It was really bizarre."

"Yeah, that is strange," she said thoughtfully before snapping out of her fog. "But now it makes sense. I never understood how you could be Becca's sister."

"What?" I asked, more confused than ever.

She smiled knowingly, the first genuine smile I had seen on her face all day. The worry that seemed to trouble her disappeared, if only for a moment. But in a flash, the haunted glaze returned to her expression. "We'll talk about it later. I have to go now," she said.

I opened my mouth to try to convince her to stay, but I was a second too late. She spun on her heels and rushed across the parking lot before I had time to take a breath. Realizing I'd have to wait until tomorrow to talk to her again, I whipped around, prepared to head to my car, but Lucian stood in my way.

My heart nearly leaped out of my chest when I looked up into the green eyes I hadn't been able to forget since the first day of school. Holding my breath for a moment, I stood still, mesmerized. My nerves on edge, I couldn't help wondering if those were the eyes of a killer.

Lucian was only a few inches away, his frame towering above me. Streaks of dark blond glistened in his hair and light brown stubble sprinkled his chin. The cross I'd noticed several times dangled against the smooth skin below his open collar. His shirt tails hung loose over the waist of his jeans, his sleeves rolled up to his elbows.

Say something! I told myself. *Don't just stand there like a zombie.* But for once, I couldn't think of a single word.

My mind spinning, my eyes still locked with his, he lifted both hands to my shoulders. Without a word, he brushed my hair behind my ears, his fingers grazing my neck and sending a wave of heat through me. I gasped, surprised by his bold touch.

Lucian pulled his hands away as a faint smile broke out on his face. "I think you dropped this," he said, his voice smooth and low. He held out his hand, his palm open.

My gaze dropping, I saw that he held one of my gold hoop earrings. Immediately, I raised my hand to touch my left ear, then my right. Sure enough, my right earring was missing. "Thank you," I said, taking it from him. As my fingers touched his, a shock jolted me. My heart felt like it nearly stopped, and I hoped he wouldn't noticed my surprise. Concentrating to stay composed, I put the earring back on before looking up at him again.

"No problem," was all he said before shifting his eyes away from me. Then he was gone, walking across the parking lot in long strides, heading for a group of girls. I watched them for a minute, recognizing the pretty girl with long black hair who smiled as he approached. Zoe. I couldn't help staring as he made his way toward her. But when her gaze shot past him, landing on me, I felt a fire spread across my face. My pulse quickened, and I finally found the strength to turn around.

"Gracyn!" a familiar voice said, breaking me out of my trance. "You look like you just saw a ghost."

Great. First Zoe, now Alex. You better hope he didn't see you staring at Lucian, a voice in my head sneered. I blinked hard, trying to get the image of Lucian and the memory of his touch out of my mind, fast. "Hi," I said, hoping Alex wouldn't notice how flustered as I was. "Sorry. I tried to catch Celeste before she left, but she blew me off. I just can't figure her out."

Alex draped his arm over my shoulders. "I wouldn't waste your time trying. Nobody can. Want to get a bite to eat before hitting the books?" he asked.

"I don't know. I have a lot of homework. I might have to try to tackle Calculus on my own tonight." The truth was, I wanted to be alone. Between Celeste's strange behavior and my first real encounter with Lucian who'd never said as much as two words to me even though we were stuck sitting together in Art class, I needed to escape. Maybe I would start a new painting tonight before digging into my homework. Or maybe I would take Gypsy out for a ride. As soon as that thought entered my mind, I pushed it aside. Was I crazy? I had all of three rides under my belt. I couldn't go out alone yet.

Alex lifted his arm off my shoulder and backed away. "You sure? Because I meant what I said earlier. I'm happy to help any afternoon."

"Um, maybe tomorrow. Mondays always wear me out."

"Okay. Tomorrow it is. But if you get stuck tonight, don't hesitate to call me."

"Thanks."

"You're welcome," he said, taking my hand. "Come on. I'll walk you to your car."

17

Becca's SUV was parked in the driveway when I returned home that afternoon. Leaving my book bag in the car, I walked across the gravel to the barn. The dogs scurried about, their noses taking them in zigzags through the grass and around trees.

When I stepped into the barn, a cloud of dust rose above the first stall wall. Wandering around the door, I stopped behind the wheelbarrow as Becca shoveled another helping of bedding and manure. "You're home early," I commented.

After dumping the pitchfork load, she looked up. Her hair had been pulled up into a ponytail, and dust smudged her black shirt and jeans. "I had a migraine and the assistant manager agreed to close for me."

"Then why are you out here? I can take care of this for you," I told her. "You should be resting instead of cleaning stalls. And I didn't know you get migraines."

She nodded, her smile faint. "I knew you'd help if I asked, but I need the exercise. I took some migraine medicine, and it makes me pretty tired when I'm at the bank. A little physical work to get my blood pressure up actually helps. As for the headaches, I've been getting them for about two years now. They weren't too bad when they started, but now I have to take the medicine as soon as I feel them coming on or my day is shot. How was school?"

"Fine," I replied before a grin slid over my lips. "Actually, it was better than fine. Hey, when is Gabriel coming home?"

"Not until the end of the week. Why?"

"Because I want to ask him a medical question."

Becca frowned, her eyebrows scrunching up. But she appeared curious rather than worried. "What about? Is everything okay? You don't feel sick, do you?"

"No, I'm great. It's my sight. I woke up this morning, and my vision was perfect. Twenty-twenty. I haven't had my contacts in all day, and I can see everything. And it's not just clear, it's super clear. I can even read small print from a distance."

"Really?" Becca asked.

"Yes, why? Do you know what could have caused this?"

"Must be all the fresh air and healthy vegetables."

I shot her a look of contempt. "I'm not five, Becca. You can't tell me that eating my peas and broccoli fixed my horrible vision. And I know it isn't the air. Something short of a miracle happened, and I want to know how I can see so clearly."

"Well, I'm not sure Gabe will have any answers for you. He's an ER doctor. His specialty is removing bullets and stitching up stab wounds."

Frowning, I tried to wipe the image of bloodied gang victims out of my mind. "Sounds like fun."

"I don't know how he does it, either, but he loves it. Maybe it's because he gets to play hero. Who knows? But talk to him when he gets back. He might know a specialist he can talk to and ask if there have been any other cases like yours."

"Okay. That would be nice to know," I mused.

Becca tilted her head, studying me for a minute. "You must be enjoying it, though."

"Well, at first, it was really weird. But now I love it. I want to know how it happened because I'm hoping it'll be permanent. I don't want to wake up tomorrow and have to go back to glasses and contact lenses. Or worse, what if I wake up blind?"

"Blind?" Becca coughed out in a chuckle. "Gracyn, that's crazy. I don't think you have anything to worry about."

"How do you know? I would just feel a lot better talking to a doctor."

"And you'll get that chance soon. I'm sure Gabe will be fascinated with this."

"Good. But until then, I'll see if I can find something on the internet. Maybe it's some kind of freak occurrence that happens to one out of a million people."

"Maybe." Becca's soft voice told me she was unconvinced.

"But until I know what happened, I'm keeping my glasses with me, just in case. I don't want to blink and have the world go blurry again."

"Good idea. Although I doubt that's going to happen," she said.

"Why?" I asked, curious.

"No specific reason. I think you found some peace here that you weren't getting in the city. And your body is responding by correcting the deficiencies. Maybe the energy is just right for you here."

"I didn't realize you were into that holistic stuff."

"I'm not, but I do believe our state of mind can impact us physically."

"Then do you know what's causing your headaches?"

Her expression immediately caved into fear. She looked away from me, a deep sadness filling her eyes. "Yes, I do. It started with Cassie's murder."

"Then maybe it's time for you to move away from here."

She snapped her attention back to me as if I'd suggested she live out her worst nightmare. "That's not an option. This is my home. If I have to take migraine medication from now on, I will. Besides, I only get a headache about once a month. It's not every day." Pausing, she resumed shoveling the piles in the stall. "Did you happen to see Celeste today?"

Snippets of the discussion I'd overheard Saturday raced into my mind. I wondered if this was the time to ask Becca about that. "Yes. But she looked awful."

Becca's hopes seemed to rise when I answered "Yes", only to fall when I continued. "Awful? What do you mean?"

"She looked haggard and worn out. She said she hasn't been sleeping well." I searched Becca's face for a sign of her reaction, but her interest disappeared as she tossed another pile of manure into the wheelbarrow. "Why do you ask?"

"Her mother stopped by the bank today. She said Celeste has been having a hard time adjusting to Lucian's return. I felt badly for her. Celeste is a sweet girl and, since you mentioned that the two of you were friends, I thought maybe you would know how she's doing."

"Well, we have lunch together, but Lucian's in the same lunch period. She wasn't eating and, when she saw him, she took off for the library."

Becca seemed to forget about the heavy load at the end of her pitchfork because the shavings and manure fell to the ground before she could dump them into the wheelbarrow. "She's not eating?"

"Just lunch. One meal skipped won't kill her."

Becca began raking the scattered droppings into a pile, rambling on to herself. "She should know better. She needs to keep up her strength. She can't afford to let her guard down, and being tired and hungry will only impede her ability to protect herself, should she need to."

"Excuse me?" I asked, not quite sure what to think about Becca's musings.

"Sorry. I was thinking out loud. Thank you for telling me about Celeste. And please keep an eye on her while you're at school."

"Why?" I asked.

"Her mother is a dear friend of mine," Becca explained. "I would hate it if anything happened to her."

"Happen as in she would be killed? Two weeks ago, you were convinced Cassie's murder was a one-time thing. You told me nothing else like that had happened here and that this town was safe." Panic crept into my voice. I felt betrayed, as if she was hiding something from me.

Becca heaved one last pile into the wheelbarrow and tossed the pitchfork on top of the load. Then she looked at me, complete innocence reigning over her expression. "Yes, that's right. There's nothing to be afraid of." She smiled, her face relaxing. "You need to learn to trust me. Don't forget that I was right about the horses."

Her attempt to wipe away my concerns infuriated me. "We're talking about a murder, not a silly childhood fear."

"No, we're talking about Celeste who is letting fear control her. Fear is never our friend. Fear alone can ruin her. But I'm sure she'll snap out of it soon. She has wonderful parents who will support her and get her any help she needs."

I decided to let it go. Without telling Becca I had heard her and Gabriel talking to Celeste's parents the other day, I'd have a hard time pressing her for answers. "I hope she does. She seems like a nice girl." With a faint smile, I backed up into the aisle. "Well, I'm going to head in and get started on my homework."

"You're welcome to stay and groom Gypsy," Becca offered as she grabbed the handlebars of the wheelbarrow and pushed it over to the next stall.

"Maybe tomorrow," I said before turning to leave. But I stopped when I heard Becca's voice behind me.

"Can you spare a half hour later for dinner? I'd love the company since Gabe is gone. I can whip up some mashed potatoes to go with the chicken left over from last night."

I glanced back at her, hesitating. "Sure. Just let me know when it's ready." Then I headed out to my car to get my book bag, hoping my homework would push Celeste and Lucian far from my thoughts.

"Have you gotten to problem ten yet?" Alex asked, turning around in my desk chair the next afternoon.

I looked up from where I sat on the bed, my Calculus book in my lap. Dropping my pencil in between the pages, I scowled. "Ten? I'm still trying to figure out number four."

A teasing smile crossed his face. "Then it's a good thing you met me. I don't think you're going to get through this class without my help. How far have you gotten?"

With a deep sigh, I shifted my gaze to my notebook and stared at the blank space after the number four. "I haven't. I don't know where to begin." Then I sat up and lowered my feet off the edge of the bed, dramatically shutting my notebook. "It's hopeless. What was I thinking? MIT? If I can't get through this, how am I going to get into one of the top engineering programs in the country? Maybe my brain just isn't wired for this."

"How did you do in your math classes back home?"

Shaking my head, I huffed. "Fine. I never had a problem. It's like ever since I started here, my mind is blocked. And I'm doing really well in Lit when that used to be my worst subject."

Alex laughed. "So, Sedgewick has done a number on you, huh?"

I resisted the urge to throw a pillow at him. "Don't say it," I warned.

"What?"

"You're thinking that it's the ghosts, aren't you?"

"Hey, you said it, not me," he said with twisted grin.

Narrowing my eyes, I scanned the area near me for something to toss at him. But I didn't get the chance when my phone rang from where I'd left it on the dresser. Grateful for the diversion, I crossed the room to see who it was. Sam. I picked it up but let it ring again, debating whether or not to answer it.

"You can get that," Alex told me. "This problem can wait another few minutes."

"That's what voicemail is for," I murmured, setting the phone back down. Whatever she wanted would have to wait. I had to focus on Calculus, and I couldn't afford any distractions.

"You sure?"

"Yes. It's just my friend from Maryland. I can call her back." I returned to the bed and grabbed my notebook. Picking up the Calculus textbook, I reread problem four. "Okay. Help me, please."

Alex joined me on the bed, sitting so close his legs touched mine. I tried to pay attention to the problem, but everything in my mind was a jumbled mess.

"Ah, yes. I remember this one. It was a little tricky."

As Alex launched into an explanation of where to begin, I listened carefully. After he pointed out the first step, I let out a long sigh. I couldn't believe I'd missed it. Smiling gratefully, I took over and stated what the next steps should be.

"That's right. See, you get it."

When I finished the problem, I looked up at him, a knowing look in my eyes. "Now I feel stupid."

"Don't say that. You're very smart. You're just..."

"Distracted. I know."

Alex snapped the textbook shut and tossed it behind us. "So my charm is really getting to you, huh? Yes!" he cheered, his fisted hand coming down in a swift movement.

With all the things I had on my mind, I hated to break it to Alex that he wasn't one of them. Instead, I smiled and slid my notebook to the side. "You figured me out," I lied. "Maybe studying together isn't such a great idea, after all."

"But I just showed you the answer."

"I wish all of the answers were that easy," I muttered, thinking of Lucian, Celeste, the miracle cure to my vision, and Sam's stepfather. I wanted nothing more than to be swept away in something other than reality. My world had become very complicated, and it was beginning to scare me.

"They will be. We have sixteen more problems to work on."

"I wasn't talking about Calculus."

Alex finally got my drift. "Oh," he said, his eyebrows raised and a sly smile on his face. "Come here, then." He snaked his arm out around my waist and pulled me against his chest.

My heart sped up as he leaned toward me. Just as his lips touched mine, my phone chimed again, this time from a text.

Alex lifted away from me with a groan. "Someone really wants to get a hold of you," he commented.

"All right. I'll see who it is." Rising to my feet, I pointed at him. "Don't move. You're on to something."

"Yes ma'am," he said with a mock salute.

Grinning as I felt a rush from being so forward, I returned to my dresser. Without picking up my phone, I swiped the screen. It immediately lit up with a text from Sam.

My mood soured when I read it. *Dad came home today. Life is finally back to normal! Let's catch up soon. We need to plan a visit. I miss u!*

I thought I'd be happy from this news, but anger took me by surprise. Sam's stepfather had done a bad thing and now it looked like he would get away with it. My head told me to let it go, even though my heart knew he didn't deserve to have his life back.

Trying to be happy for Sam, I typed a quick message to her. *Can't talk now. Alex is helping me with homework. Catch you later.*

Before I could turn around, a huge smiley face popped up from Sam. There was no doubt in my mind that she would call later to ask about my study date.

As I returned to the bed, Alex watched me. "Everything okay?"

"Yes. That was Sam. I told her I couldn't talk."

"That's right." He patted the bed for me to sit next to him. As I did, he wrapped his arm around my shoulder and pulled me toward him. "Now, where were we?"

But my mood had darkened, and I hesitated, silently searching his eyes for understanding. Shifting back, I broke my gaze away from his. "Maybe we should get back to the assignment. I have sixteen more problems to finish."

"What's wrong?" he asked, letting go of me, his expression worried.

I shook my head, trying to ignore my apprehension. Somehow, I needed to forget about Sam's father. He was hundreds of miles away, but the idea of him free to prey on another girl nagged me. A part of me wanted him to stay in the hospital because as long as he was there, he couldn't go after anyone else. "Just some stuff I left at home."

"Unfinished business?"

"Something like that."

"Want to talk about it?"

"Not really," I answered before reaching behind me for my notebook. As I dropped it into my lap, I shot a hopeful look at Alex. "Ready to get back to the problems?"

With a groan, he smiled. "Okay. I guess we need to. I can't stay late tonight. We're having a practice session at Derek's."

"Really? Do you do that often during the week?"

"Only when we have a gig over the weekend. That reminds me, we're playing in Boston Saturday night. Want to go?"

I sighed, not sure if I'd have the energy to drive all the way to Boston. "That's pretty far."

"Yeah, it is. You're welcome to ride with us, but we're going to crash at a friend's apartment after we play. It might be a little tight. And by that, I mean sleeping bags on the floor. He only has one bedroom."

As much I would have loved to get away, the idea of staying at a stranger's apartment with a bunch of guys was about as far outside my comfort zone as it could get. "Then I think I'm going to pass."

"No problem. Just think, you'll have more time to paint and maybe get started on your college applications."

"Thanks for the reminder," I groaned.

"Well, I'll miss you, but we don't do out-of-town gigs very often. So don't worry, I'll make it up to you."

"Promise?"

He nodded with a smile. "Of course." Then he grabbed the Calculus book and flipped it open to the pages we'd been working on. "Now, where were we?" he asked.

I picked up my pencil, relieved to have my homework to focus on. Anything else lately was just too overwhelming.

18

For the rest of the week, I reached for my glasses each morning, forgetting I no longer needed them. Every day, it seemed more likely that my vision had been restored permanently. I still planned to ask Gabriel how it was possible when he returned home, but until then, I enjoyed the freedom from glasses and contact lenses. Whether I was at school or in the barn with the horses, I felt like I had a new lease on life.

My homework started to pile up that week. I didn't mind the constant diversion from things I couldn't explain. Like why Celeste looked more tired every day, as though she couldn't catch up on her sleep, and why Lucian seemed to be watching me. He smiled on occasion, and I always glanced behind me, convinced he was looking at someone else. But no one ever lurked in the background. I began to wonder why he paid me any attention without bothering to talk to me. The one time I thought he was about to say something, Alex appeared and pulled me into a hug. Instantly, Lucian's smile transformed to a scowl before he veered off into the crowded hallway. I wrapped my arms around Alex, my gaze following Lucian as Zoe caught up to him, her smile oblivious to his moody eyes. From that point, Lucian wouldn't even look at me again. Or if he did, I never noticed.

By Friday morning, I was ready for the weekend. As I trudged into school with the rest of the students, I prayed that the day would fly by. Weaving through the crowd, I headed to my locker. Reaching it, I opened the door and slipped out of my denim jacket. After hanging it on the hook, I bent down to sort through my bag as a figure in black appeared beside me.

Standing up, my gaze fell upon Celeste. The circles under her tired eyes had darkened since yesterday, if that was even possible. Her long hair fell in messy waves over her black coat and a sullen frown flattened her lips.

"Hi," I said. "Still not sleeping?"

She nodded with a sigh, fatigue shadowing her eyes. "Yeah," she said quietly, glancing down the hall in both directions.

I followed her gaze, but saw no sign of Lucian. "I don't see him, but I'll tell you if I do."

"Thanks. My parents said if I don't start sleeping, I may have to switch schools."

"Isn't that a little drastic?"

Celeste huffed. "Anything is better than staying here. They already met with the principal and asked her to expel Lucian."

My jaw dropped in shock. "Really?"

"Uh-huh," she replied. "But she couldn't. Or wouldn't. The Dumante property taxes fund a big chunk of the school expenses, so it's probably not a good move to kick him out. Even if he did kill someone." Her last sentence rolled out sarcastically.

"No one knows that for sure."

"I do," Celeste stated, her flighty eyes dancing back across the crowded hall.

"Well, he's been back what, about two weeks now? And no one has been killed," I pointed out.

"Yet," she added under her breath.

"Okay, I get that this is really upsetting you. But Celeste, the only one you're hurting by being so overcome by fear is yourself."

She looked at me, her eyes wide and afraid. "You haven't been here very long. You'll understand soon enough."

Without another word, she spun around and took off into the crowded hall. Discouraged, I turned back to my locker, but I couldn't focus on my books. Instead, I thought about Celeste. Even though I didn't know her very well, it upset me to see her like this. She seemed like a nice girl who didn't deserve to be tormented, whether or not her fear was warranted.

The warning bell rang, breaking me out of my thoughts. With a heavy sigh, I reached for my Calculus book, hoping my classes would help me forget why Celeste's fear worried me. Because until Cassie's killer was found and punished, I had to accept the possibility that he could be anywhere.

Alex promised the band they would practice Friday night and he invited me to watch, but I declined. Hanging out in a cold garage all night listening to the same songs over and over again didn't appeal to me, especially since Lacey would probably be there, filling up the air with smoke. Instead, I spent a quiet night alone at home after saying goodbye to Becca and Gabriel when they rushed out the door for dinner at a local restaurant as I was walking in. Disappointed that my questions about my vision would have to wait, I retreated up to my room.

I tried to get a little painting done, but my mind was blank. After staring at the canvas for fifteen minutes, hoping the spark of something to draw would hit me, my phone rang. I reached for it on my desk, a smile crawling over my face when I saw Sam's name. We hadn't spoken since she'd texted me the afternoon Alex helped me with Calculus.

"Hi, Sam," I said, picking up the call. Sitting on the edge of my bed, I stared out the window. Streaks of dark purple raced across the sky behind tall branches. A bat darted by, making abrupt turns as it flew by radar. Within moments, it disappeared. "That was wild," I commented more to myself than to Sam.

"What are you talking about?" she asked.

"Just a bat outside my window."

"Ew. I hope it stayed outside."

"Of course it did. It's gone now. So how's life? Are things getting back to normal?"

"For the most part," she answered, her tone hesitant like there was something she wasn't telling me. "Dad's going to reopen his clinic on Monday, although he's not sure how much he can do until he gets the cast off."

I cringed at the reminder of his broken hand. Until now, I hadn't thought of how that would impact his work as a dentist. He would need the use of his right hand. I didn't mind knowing he was still being punished, but his inability to work was hurting his family and they shouldn't have to pay for his crime. "And when is that?"

"A couple more weeks, I think. Want to hear something strange?"

"Always," I answered, hoping to move on to a lighter subject.

"I overheard my mom and dad talking. She asked him how he hurt his hand."

"Really? I thought he slammed the car door on it."

"That's what he told the doctors before he fell into the coma. But the doctors told Mom that the fractures weren't consistent with his story. If he had slammed a door on it, it more than likely would have been broken from front to back. Instead, it was broken from side to side."

My heart nearly dropped into my stomach, and I fell quiet. I had no idea what to say. Until now, I'd hoped I had imagined squeezing his hand until the bones shattered, trying to convince myself that he must have really smashed it with a car door.

"Gracyn, are you there?"

"Y...yes, I'm here," I said, taking a deep breath. "Sorry, I was just wondering about what really happened." *You mean remembering since you were there,* a voice drilled into me, making me feel worse.

"Yeah, pretty weird, huh?"

"What did he say to your mom?"

"Just that all he remembered was the door, but his memory was pretty foggy. He admitted it could have been something else, but he wasn't sure. He blamed it on amnesia."

"And what did your mom say to that?"

"She dropped it. I think she's just concerned because his practice has been closed for almost a month now. Instead of bringing in money, it's costing him every day. So I know she's worried about that."

"Yikes. Well, I hope he heals fast so he can get back to work," I said, hoping I sounded sincere. "How is everything else?"

"Other than that, it's good. My brother couldn't be happier. And it's nice not to have to cook dinner for an unappreciative kid anymore."

"I bet it is."

"Well, tonight I asked if I could come up to see you and visit some colleges near Boston."

"That would be awesome. What did your parents say?"

"The usual answer–maybe. But as soon as I mentioned you, Dad got weird. His face went white the minute I said your name. Like he was upset or something. Gracyn, do you know what that's all about?"

Of course I did, but I couldn't tell her that. "No," I lied, taking short, shallow breaths as I stared out my window. The sky was almost black now, the branches mere shadows swaying in the breeze. "I don't. Maybe you should ask him." That was a great idea. Let the guy explain to his family what he had tried to do to me.

"I thought about it, but I don't think he wants to talk about it. I've never seen him so freaked out."

"As in mad?"

"More like scared."

"Maybe it's a weird side effect from his coma. Did the doctors warn about any changes in personality? I mean, all of this happened after he dropped me off at home that night. Maybe he relates his illness to me because of that." *Or maybe he associates his illness and broken hand with you because you caused them,* I added to myself.

"I don't know. I didn't go to the hospital when he was discharged. Maybe I'll ask Mom if they warned her about any residual effects of his coma."

"No!" I said sharply in a knee-jerk reaction. As soon as I realized how alarmed I must have sounded, I lowered my voice. "I mean if it is some freaky side effect, you don't want to worry her. She's been through a lot and probably doesn't need more problems right now."

"Yeah, maybe you're right," Sam mused.

"Well, give it some time. Maybe he was just confused." I wished I could think of another explanation other than the truth, but my mind drew blank.

"I hope so." Suddenly, her voice perked up. "But enough about this. It's eight o'clock on a Friday night. Why aren't you out with Alex?"

"His band is playing in Boston tomorrow, and they're practicing tonight. It's kind of nice to have the night to myself."

"You get every night to yourself. What were you doing when I called? Painting? I can't wait to hear about your latest masterpiece."

"I don't have one," I grumbled.

"Why not? That's not like you."

"I know. I just don't know what to paint right now. I started working on a landscape of the farm as a gift for Becca and Gabriel, but I haven't had time to finish it since school started. And I can only work on it when they aren't home."

"You'll get there. I know you. You hate to leave anything unfinished."

I smiled, once again reminded of how well Sam knew me. But a frown took over when I thought about her stepfather's reaction to my name. As much as I hated to admit it, I might never see Sam again after what had happened with him.

We talked for another half hour, and thankfully she didn't mention her stepfather again. As much as I loved Sam, I was relieved when we hung up and silence filled the room. Then, giving up any hope I'd get some painting done, I climbed into bed with a book and read until I fell asleep.

I woke up to the familiar ringing of my phone. Groggy, I cracked my eyes open and saw only pitch black in my room. The clock read two thirty-four A.M. Shaking my head, I let my eyes close and waited for the ringing to stop. It had to be a wrong number. Who else would be calling in the middle of the night?

Mom, I thought and shot upright in bed. Something must be terribly wrong if she needed to call me at two in the morning. She had to know what time it was here and, if she was calling me now, it must be important.

Wide awake, I jumped up and raced across the room to my dresser. Grabbing the phone, I caught it on the last ring. Without bothering to read the caller ID, I answered it. "Hello? Mom, is that you?"

But the line was silent, except for breathing. Someone was there, listening to me. I heard every breath they took, inhaling and exhaling, again and again. "Who is this? Mom, is that you? I know someone's there."

As soon as I spoke, a beep indicated that the caller had hung up. The breathing stopped and, as my heart nearly pounded out of my chest, I pulled the phone away from my ear to look at the screen, hoping to find out who had been on the other end. But there were only two words. "Private Caller."

Frowning, I nearly dropped the phone as my hands trembled. Was this a joke? *It's probably just a wrong number. Stop being so paranoid,* I thought. Then I turned the power off and watched the light from the screen disappear. As an afterthought, I opened the top drawer of my dresser and dropped my phone onto a pile of sweaters. Somehow, I felt much better when I shut the drawer before returning to bed.

The next day, the house was empty when I headed downstairs for my morning coffee. Or almost empty. The dogs were still there, but Becca and Gabriel had gone to Vermont and wouldn't be home until late afternoon according to a note I found on the table. I had the place to myself for the day, and I knew exactly what to do.

After a quick breakfast, I carried my easel and a folding chair out onto the lawn. Sunlight broke through the trees overhead, dancing on patches of grass. I set up the canvas and dove into my painting. For several hours, I pored over every intricate detail of the log home, the trees in the background, and the shades of blue in the sky. I hadn't accomplished much since moving here, and it felt good to lose myself in the colors and brush strokes.

I left my phone where I'd put it in the drawer after being rudely awakened at two in the morning. It was nice not to have any distractions from phone calls, text messages or the memory of the heavy breather that I simply wanted to forget.

When I finished touching up the last detail, I carried everything back up to my room. After sliding the painting onto an empty section of my closet shelf, I looked at my hands and forearms. They were smudged with green, brown and blue marks. The sleeves of my white shirt were rolled up to my elbows, dangerously close to the smears, although I had managed to keep them clean.

I started to head for the bathroom, but stopped when something didn't seem right. It was quiet. Too quiet, even for here.

"Damn it!" I swore, realizing I'd left the dogs outside. In fact, I couldn't remember when I had seen them last. They generally stayed close when someone was outside with them, but Becca had warned me that all it took was a deer or squirrel to lead them on a chase to the middle of nowhere.

Forgetting about the paint on my arms, I ran downstairs and out the front door. My heart sank with worry. I couldn't believe I had let them out of my sight.

I hurried across the front porch and raced down the steps two at a time. The yard was empty and silent, except for an occasional snort from one of the horses grazing in the distance. "No!" I muttered. "Scout! Snow! Come here you two!"

Standing in the middle of the driveway, I bit my lip. A gentle breeze blew a stray curl across my face, and I pushed it away as I waited, wondering where those scoundrels could be.

After a few seconds, Scout trotted out of the barn. As he approached me, Snow appeared in the doorway, her white fur standing out against the shadows behind her.

"Whew!" I said with a sigh of relief. "Don't scare me like that. Come on, you two. Let's go in."

Before I could turn, a movement in the woods caught my eye. Scout lifted his head, his ears pointed toward it. I followed his gaze, and my earlier relief vanished at the sight of a deer. Its head was up, its eyes and ears alert as it swished its stubby tail.

"Don't do it," I muttered. "Please don't do it." What was I thinking? Was there anything more tempting for a dog than a deer? Of course not. Scout launched into a run, charging after the animal as it darted into the woods. Snow followed not far behind. Within seconds, I was left alone in their wake.

"You've got to be kidding!" I ranted, taking off after them. Today had been perfect until now. I couldn't believe this was happening. I was dirty and hungry, but a shower and lunch would have to wait.

I ran as fast as I could, thankful I was wearing my sneakers. Entering the woods, I followed the trail I had ridden twice. Shadows flitted across the dirt path and, as my eyes adjusted to the dim light, I saw Snow's white fur flash between the trees up ahead. At least I was on the right track. "Snow! Scout! Come back!"

I followed her up the hill and past the garden, catching a glimpse of Scout who darted around her. Then the dogs veered off the path, leading me into the forest. I kept calling for them, but they never looked back. The deer disappeared from sight, but that didn't stop them. Determined not to turn back without them, I dodged low branches and jumped over logs. One was so big, I had to stop and climb across the top of it.

I wasn't sure how far I'd gone or how long I'd been running, mostly uphill, when the air turned icy. Stopping, I wrapped my arms around my chest and rubbed my forearms. Shivers skated through me as I stared in the direction the dogs had gone. I wanted to turn around, but I couldn't stop now. I had come this far, and I wouldn't give up.

Taking a deep breath, I forced my legs back into motion. My muscles burned from every step, but I pushed forward.

As I headed farther into the woods, the temperature continued to drop. The leaves disappeared, the trees with barren limbs void of any life, making it look as if it were the dead of winter. Thick clouds dropped from the sky that only minutes ago had been bright blue. I trudged on, but with each step I took, the woods grew darker and colder.

Finally, I stopped, not sure if I should continue. I had lost sight of the dogs and just about everything else. Fog fell over the treetops, draping them like heavy cotton. Mist rose from the ground, blurring the logs and underbrush around me. How was this possible? It had been beautiful all day, and now I felt like I'd stepped into a dense cloud. Fear clutching me, I whipped around, not sure which way I was going or which direction I had come from. I was completely disoriented. The dogs were gone, and now I might not make it home. I didn't even have my phone. A lot of good it would do me where I'd left it in my room.

When a twig snapped behind me, I turned but saw nothing. A gust of wind whipped my curls across my face. As I reached up to push them aside, hushed voices whispered in the breeze and I looked up to see hundreds of black birds circling overhead. They cried out, some of them flying into each other.

No! I thought. *This isn't happening. It can't be. Today was sunny and warm. The weather couldn't have changed this fast. It must be a dream.*

But it was real. Panic ripped through me as another stick broke. I scanned the surrounding woods, but all I could see was white. The birds' squawking grew louder, sounding like they were closing in on me. When I shifted my gaze up to them, they scattered as if threatened.

Quiet followed, but only for a moment before the sound of galloping hooves erupted in the distance. The thundering intensified as the land trembled beneath my feet, and I couldn't tell if it was one horse or several. All I knew was that it or they were coming closer, roaring behind me like a freight train about to hit.

Then the pounding stopped. Silence surrounded me, and I swallowed nervously, not trusting it. Holding my breath, I spun around to come face to face with the muzzle of a black horse less than an inch away. Nostrils flaring, its breath blew against my cheek.

I stood still, paralyzed as my fear of horses returned with a vengeance. I had nowhere to go. I was at the mercy of this beast. Closing my eyes, I did the only thing I could think of. I prayed.

19

"You shouldn't be here," a deep voice said.

I looked up past the horse's wild eyes raging from under its long mane. As my pulse quickened, my gaze locked with a pair of blazing green eyes. I gasped, wondering what Lucian was doing out here and how he had found me. Aside from his light brown hair and pale complexion, his shirt and jeans were as black as the horse he sat upon. His silver cross gleamed in the mist, the religious symbol giving me hope that I would be safe. He held the reins loosely, and his horse pranced in place as though ready to spring into a gallop at any moment. It was massive, several inches taller than Gypsy. A stallion, I presumed. His ebony coat glistened with sweat, his veins rippling like cords under his taught skin. He snorted impatiently, tossing his head.

"I...I got lost," I managed to say. My voice barely a whisper, I wasn't sure he heard me over his horse's flaring nostrils.

Lucian stared at me, his eyes and scowl colder than I remembered. "This isn't a place you want to get lost in."

"I kind of figured that out."

He continued glaring at me, his silence unnerving. I backed up a step as a new panic surged through me. What would he do with me now that he'd found me here, lost and alone in the fog? I didn't know which direction was the way home. I could try to run, but where would I go? And I could never outrun his horse.

As I took another step back, Lucian shifted the reins to one hand and tugged them against his horse's neck. The horse immediately stepped to the side. Then he moved up a few feet until Lucian was directly in front of me. Dropping his arm down to me, he held his hand open. "Get on. I'll take you home."

The breath I held escaped from my lungs with relief. When I reached for his arm, Lucian's fingers curled around my wrist in a viselike grip before he lifted me off my feet. The horse was so tall that I struggled to clear his hindquarters. My leg bumped him a few times, but he didn't flinch. He stood perfectly still as I settled onto his back right behind the saddle. The heat rising from his flank penetrated my jeans, warming me up from the chill in the air.

Lucian never let go of my hand. Instead, he pulled it around his chest. I wrapped my other arm around him and locked my hands together.

"Hold on," he said over his shoulder before whipping the horse to the side in a ninety degree turn. Then we shot forward like a rocket.

I squeezed Lucian and pressed my cheek against his back. He barely moved as if he and the horse were one.

Lucian guided the galloping horse through the woods, missing the trees with inches to spare. They were hard to see in the fog, only emerging from the cloudy mist when we were about a foot away. I flinched every time it looked like we would hit one. After the third time, I closed my eyes and concentrated on the horse's stride. I tried to relax, but it was next to impossible riding on the back of a powerful animal, my arms wrapped around a guy I hardly knew. And what I did know about him was unsettling at best.

I felt the horse fly up and down hills, his hooves crashing through the underbrush and snapping twigs. At least once, I felt him leap into the air. Afraid I would fall, I tightened my arms around Lucian's chest with a death grip, my legs swaying against the horse's sides.

After what seemed like forever, the horse slowed and the sound of his hooves crashing through the leaves disappeared. When the air felt warm again, I opened my eyes to see a pasture rolling out to the left. Two horses grazed under the bright sun, not paying any attention to us as we cantered beside the fence.

When we reached the end of the pasture, Lucian slowed his mount to a walk. Relieved, I loosened my hold around his chest and raised my head to see where we were. The Dumante stone mansion rose up on one side, the barn on the other.

We halted in front of the doorway as steam rose from the horse's sides, his flanks heaving in and out with every breath.

"We're here," Lucian said quietly, dropping the reins and putting his hands on mine. His touch flustered me as he moved my arms to his sides.

I took a deep breath and gulped back a nervous shudder, wondering why he'd brought me to his house instead of mine. When he said he was going to take me home, I hadn't realized he meant his home.

After swinging his right leg over the horse's neck, Lucian slid down to the ground, his back to the saddle. As soon as he landed, he turned and reached up to me. "Let me help you."

"Okay." I moved my right leg over the horse's hindquarters and, facing the horse, slowly lowered myself. But the drop off was a lot farther than I was used to with Gypsy. Just when I thought I was about to fall, Lucian caught me by the waist, steadying me while sending my heart into a flutter. A deep breath filled my lungs as my feet touched down on the grass.

"Thank you," I murmured, turning away from the steam rising off the horse's sweaty flank. When I stopped and looked up, Lucian stood inches away, his hands still on my waist. Trapped between him and the horse, I held my breath, waiting for him to let go of me.

He lingered for a moment, his gaze locked with mine. His stoic expression held no hint of softening. "You're welcome," he finally said, dropping his hands from my sides. Without another word, he turned and slid the reins over the horse's head.

I stepped away, noticing the white lather of sweat on the stallion's gleaming black coat. He swung his head back, glancing at me before snorting and rubbing his cheek against Lucian's shoulders. Lucian swatted him away with a low grumble. "Shade, you know better than that."

The horse sighed with defeat as Lucian looked back at me. "Wait here. I'll just be a minute."

I nodded before watching him lead his horse into the barn. A few moments later, Lucian returned alone.

"That was fast," I commented.

"I have help. The caretaker will finish up with Shade for me."

Lucian stopped in front of me, his expression still serious. I wished he would smile, even faintly so I knew he wasn't going to hurt me. Instead, he looked down at my arms, lifting one. As he studied me, his eyebrows raised, I forgot about the sun warming me from high above. All that seemed to exist was the intensity in his green eyes.

"What?" I asked.

"You were painting today," he stated.

I felt a blush rise up through my cheeks and glanced at the smudges on my arms. "Yes. I didn't have time to clean up."

"Why?"

My breath caught, not from the simplicity of his question, but from the sudden softening in his eyes.

Before I could answer him, he spoke again. "You never told me how you got lost out there."

"I didn't have much of a chance."

"Point taken. But now you do."

"The dogs took off after a deer. I was trying to get them to come home."

A rare smile curled on his lips. "You ended up in those woods because of the dogs?" he asked incredulously.

"Well, yes. I never had dogs before. I didn't know what to do. I panicked. I didn't want Becca and Gabriel to come home and find I had lost them."

His smile fading, he raised his eyebrows again. "So you put yourself in danger over a couple of mutts who would have eventually realized they could never catch a deer? They would have come home on their own."

"I didn't think running into the woods was that dangerous."

"You're from the city, right?"

I nodded, starting to feel the defiance rising up inside me. What did he mean by that? And his cold stare was really bothering me. "I don't understand what that has to do with anything. But I have a question. How did you find me?"

He shrugged. "I was out for a ride and saw the dogs. When you ran after them on foot, I followed you. To make sure you didn't get lost. Those woods can be very disorienting to someone who's unfamiliar with them."

My eyes narrowed as I recalled running after Scout and Snow. "I think I would have seen you. I mean, your horse is huge. He's kind of hard to miss."

"We were pretty far behind you. I knew you didn't see us, and I didn't want to scare you."

I took a deep breath, not sure if I wanted to accept his explanation. In fact, all I really wanted was to forget the whole thing. "Look, thank you for finding me and getting me out of there. But I know where I am now since Becca and I rode by here a few weeks ago."

"I remember. I saw you."

So the person I'd seen that day was him. I knew it! But it didn't make me feel any more comfortable around him. "I saw you, too," I said. "Well, again, thank you. But I'm going take off. I can walk home from here." After breaking my gaze away from his, I started walking along the fence.

I had only taken a few steps when he hurried around me and stopped. "Oh, no," he said. "I'm not letting you go out there alone again. I'll drive you home."

"That's okay, really. Don't worry about me. I'll be fine."

"Yes, you will. Because I'm not letting you out of my sight until I personally drop you off on your doorstep."

"I'm not a child–" I started to say.

"No, you're worse. A child wouldn't have been left alone to roam through the woods."

"What is the big deal about the woods? I don't understand what there is to be afraid of," I said. "Except you. Should I be afraid of you?"

A deep pain flashed through his eyes before he blinked it away. "Don't you think if I had any intention of hurting you, I would have done it when I found you?"

"Maybe. I don't know. But I honestly don't want to speculate on that. Now are you going to move out of my way or not?"

He didn't budge. "You know nothing about this place. Do you have any idea of what is in those woods?"

His question sent shivers up my spine, reminding me of the ghost rumors Alex, Lacey, and Derek had mentioned. Sucking in a deep breath, I shook my head. "I don't care what's out there because I'm not going back to where you found me. I already told you I know how to get home from here."

"And I said you'll come with me." His expression was cold, his tone demanding I obey.

I narrowed my eyes and debated what to do next. How dare he order me around like I was an incompetent child?

Before I had a chance to respond, he smiled softly, changing his tune. "I mean, would you care to join me inside for a snack first? Since we're going to be sitting next to one another all year in Art class, I suppose it's time we get to know each other. Besides, I don't want to send you home on an empty stomach."

That was a little better and so unexpected, causing my defiance to crumble at my feet. As much as I wanted to ask why he hadn't said hello to me in class over the last two weeks, I refrained. Perhaps once I got through his icy exterior, I'd feel better knowing who he really was. "Sure. Why not?" I replied.

"Great." He gestured for me to turn and head toward the house. "After you."

We walked in silence until we approached the mahogany double doors on the front of the mansion. Lucian jogged a few steps ahead of me to get to the door first. When he pulled it open, I noticed right away that it hadn't been locked. I glanced at him, my eyebrows raised as I murmured a quick "Thank you."

It didn't take me long to understand why the door hadn't been locked. As I stepped into the two-story foyer, I barely had a moment to admire the iron chandelier and double staircase winding up from both sides of the room. A huge Doberman charged around the corner, its nails scraping the hardwood floor and its sleek black coat reminding me of Lucian's horse. A silver chain hung around its neck, just like the silver cross dangling over Lucian's shirt.

The dog ran past me as I jumped out of its way, my heart skipping a beat from the surprise. I backed up, watching the Doberman rush toward Lucian. "Halt," Lucian ordered. Without a moment to spare, the dog slid to a stop. It tilted its head, its upright ears pointed at Lucian.

Lucian smiled before shutting the door and approaching the dog. As he rubbed its chin, the Doberman leaned into him, seeming to enjoy the attention. "Good boy," Lucian said. After a few seconds, he muttered, "Release." The dog took a deep breath before spinning around and trotting out of the foyer.

"Wow," I said. "He's huge."

"That was Diesel. He won't hurt you. You can relax."

I found it odd that the Doberman hadn't given me, a complete stranger, the time of day. "That's good to know," I said. "But dog or no dog, I'm not sure I'm ready to relax yet."

Not saying a word, Lucian scrunched his eyebrows.

"Well, until today, you've barely spoken to me. And it's not like you haven't had a chance to say hello in Art class." Not to mention he was suspected of murder and just about everyone I'd met so far was convinced he was guilty. I wasn't sure what I believed, but I knew I needed to be on guard. Rumors like that didn't start all on their own. If everyone believed he had killed his sister, there must have been evidence pointing to it, even if it hadn't been enough to convict him.

"I wasn't sure you wanted me to," he said, sounding defeated.

A pang of guilt shot through me. Who was I to judge him when I barely knew him? Maybe I should give him a chance. Or maybe I should run out the door and never look back. I was so confused that I said nothing in response.

As silence hovered between us, Lucian glanced down at my arms. "Where are my manners? Would you like to wash up?"

"Yes. That would be great," I answered, relieved I had something to distract me from the suspicious doubts racing through my mind.

"This way," he said, leading me out of the foyer. We passed a spacious kitchen to the right before stopping at a narrow door. He opened it and moved out of the way. "Here you go. I'll be in the kitchen."

"Thank you," I said before escaping into the powder room.

After washing the stubborn paint off my hands and forearms, I dabbed them with a towel. My skin was red from rubbing it so hard, but at least I was clean.

When I entered the kitchen, Lucian stood behind the island, slicing an apple on a cutting board. Three pendant lights hung from iron rods above the shiny black granite counter. Dark cherry cabinets surrounded the kitchen, their nickel knobs matching the stainless steel appliances.

I sat down on one of the stools across from Lucian. An assortment of cheese, crackers, and fruit had been placed on a ceramic serving tray. "You don't have to do this for me," I told him, reaching for a grape.

"I know. But I've been on my own since I moved back. This house gets pretty lonely on the weekends. Diesel and the horses are only so much company." He finished cutting the apple and slid the pieces onto the tray.

"What about Zoe?"

He frowned as he picked up a cracker. "She's a nice distraction sometimes. But her social life keeps her pretty busy and I'd rather work on my painting than deal with the drama."

"So you like being alone?"

He shrugged, not bothering to answer my question. "What's your story, Gracyn? Why are you here?"

I huffed with a sarcastic smile. "Because you wouldn't let me walk home."

"No, not here in my kitchen. Here in Sedgewick."

"My mom got a promotion, but she had to move to Moscow. And Becca offered to let me stay with her. I figured I'd rather live here than in Russia for the year."

"Becca is your–"

"Sister. Half-sister, actually. My mom gave her up for adoption years before she had me."

"Really?" he asked, his tone suspicious.

"Yes. Why? Is that hard to believe?"

"No. I guess not," he said before popping a grape into his mouth and swallowing it. "But I'd rather you tell me the real reason you're here."

"I don't know what you're getting at, but that is the real reason," I replied slowly.

Our eyes met, almost in a staring contest. A moment later, he smiled as if he hadn't suggested I wasn't telling the truth. "Are you thirsty? Can I get you something to drink?"

I bit into an apple slice, wiping the juice from my chin. "No, thank you. I'm fine," I said after swallowing. Having something to drink would only keep me here longer, and I wanted to leave as soon as I could.

Nodding, Lucian stared at me, his expression cold again. "You want my advice?"

"Not really."

"Too late. You're going to get it anyway. Pack up your things, run as far away from this town as fast as you can, and never look back."

My breath caught in my throat from the deep warning tone in his voice, and an unsettled feeling washed over me. "Then why are you here?" I asked. "If it's so bad, why did you come back?"

"I had to. It's my home. And as hard as it was to come back–" He paused, blinking back the moisture in his eyes. "I couldn't stay away forever. It's in my blood. This place, the town, the horses. But you don't have to stay like me. You have a choice."

"I don't understand."

"You don't need to. But you should leave if you know what's good for you."

I didn't know what to say to that. Dropping my gaze, I reached for a cube of Swiss cheese. "What's good for me is what's good for my family. And by that, I mean my mom. If I don't stay here, she'll either have to move back from Russia or put me in some ridiculously expensive American prep school over there. It's not possible. So unless you have a convincing reason for telling me I should leave other than some vague warning, I'm here to stay for the year."

"My sister died at the hands of a cold-blooded killer two years ago. I believe whoever did it is still right here in Sedgewick. If that's not a good enough reason for you, I don't know what is."

"I know about that. And don't try scaring me with the part about her body being found near Becca and Gabriel's property because I know that, too."

"Doesn't it frighten you?"

"Well, yeah, a little. It would scare anyone. But I'm not going to live my life in fear."

"I can see that. Otherwise, you wouldn't have ended up lost where I found you."

The cold fog buried in the woods flashed through my mind. Was that where his sister had been found? And I couldn't believe he had brought up her murder when he'd been the only suspect. Desperately wanting to end this conversation, I stood up and pushed my stool back. "Thank you for the snack, but would you please take me home now? I stayed as you asked, but I'd like to get back to see if the dogs have returned."

Lucian popped another grape in his mouth, chewing thoughtfully. Then he offered me a faint smile. "Wait here. I'll get my keys." Without another word, he walked out of the kitchen, leaving me alone.

20

Lucian drove me home as he had promised. After leaving his estate, we didn't say a word to each other along the way. Instead, I shifted nervously in the front seat of the Range Rover as questions piled up in my head, mostly about the fog in the woods. What was that? There had to be an explanation for the change in the weather just like there had to be an explanation about my vision.

When we pulled up to the house, the first thing I noticed was Gabriel's BMW parked out front. My hopes fell into my stomach. If the dogs were still gone, I would have to explain that I'd screwed up. Before the Range Rover came to a stop, Scout trotted across the driveway and I sighed with relief. If Scout was here, surely Snow wasn't far. As Lucian turned around in the driveway, Becca raced out of the house and down the steps until she stopped at the bottom.

Lucian shifted into park and flashed a rare smile. "I told you the dogs would come home on their own."

I glanced at him, my eyes meeting his for a brief moment. "Yes, you did."

He nodded in my direction, looking past me out the side window. "I think someone's waiting for you. You'd better get going."

"Okay." I started to open the door, but stopped and looked at him. "Maybe now you can say hi to me in Art class."

"Maybe," was all he said.

I sighed with a subtle shake of my head. What was I thinking? *Forget about him,* a voice in my mind scolded. *You don't need anything from him. He's got problems that you don't want to be involved with. Now let him be and make sure you never go into the woods again, just like Becca warned you when you first moved here.*

As I stepped out of the SUV and shut the door, Becca rushed over to me, the alarm in her expression changing to relief. "Gracyn! Where were you? We were so worried!"

I watched the Range Rover until it disappeared down the driveway before shifting my attention to her. "I'm sorry. I didn't mean to worry you."

"Well, you did. When we got home, the dogs were running around loose and your car was here, but you were gone. What happened? And why did Lucian bring you home?" she asked, her tone clearly conveying she wasn't happy.

I could have made something up, but I figured it was better to tell the truth. So I relayed the events of the afternoon, even the part about the fog. Becca listened with a straight face, her eyes clouding over with concern when I mentioned the woods where Lucian had found me.

After I finished, she shook her head. "I'm sorry you thought you needed to chase after the dogs. Please don't do that again. If they take off, just be patient. They'll come home. They always do."

"That's what Lucian said."

"Gracyn, about Lucian. You should keep your distance from him."

"Why?" I asked.

"He's not to be trusted."

"He just helped me."

"He brought you home, yes."

"No, he didn't just bring me home. He found me when I was lost. I'd probably still be wandering in the woods if he hadn't shown up. It was so disorienting. I didn't know which way to go."

"That's an even better reason not to trust him. I mean, what was he doing out there?"

"He said he was out for a trail ride when he saw me. He followed me because he was worried I'd get lost, which I did."

Becca took a deep breath. "It's awfully coincidental that he showed up when you needed help."

I could tell I wasn't going to convince her that his intentions were innocent. In fact, I wasn't certain of that myself, so I let it go and changed the subject. "Fine. I'll keep my distance from him. But what was up with the fog? Is that why you told me to stay out of the woods?"

Her eyes shifting to the side, Becca nodded. "That's part of it." Then she looked back at me with a soft smile. "I just want you to be careful."

"Or maybe I should pack up and leave like Lucian suggested."

"Really? Well, I don't know what was running through his head. But believe me, if I thought there was any real danger to be worried about around here, I wouldn't have asked you to move in. Promise me you'll stay away from him."

"I already told you I would. And don't worry. I doubt that's going to be an issue." Somehow, I didn't expect things would be any different at school on Monday. Lucian would probably continue to ignore me as he had over the last two weeks.

"Good. Just make sure of it."

"Trust me, it won't be hard to do. He hasn't spoken to me once in class yet. Next week won't be any different, I'm sure." That may have pleased Becca, but for reasons I couldn't explain, it frustrated me a little. "Look, I'm really exhausted. I just want to clean up and try to forget this afternoon."

"Okay. Gabe's gathering some vegetables for dinner tonight. Will you join us?"

I flashed a tired smile. "Of course. I still need to ask him how my vision was corrected overnight. I've only been waiting all week to talk to him. Just let me know if there's anything I can do to help."

Finally, something to focus on other than whether or not a killer had just saved me. With a sigh, I headed up the porch steps, ready to hide in the comfort of my room for the rest of the afternoon.

Dinner that evening was pleasant, but Gabriel didn't have any answers for me about my vision. "There has to be some explanation," I insisted as the three of us sat down at the table with plates of pasta smothered in homemade tomato sauce.

"I'm sorry, Gracyn," Gabriel replied before sipping his red wine. "I talked to my colleagues, one of whom is an ophthalmologist, and there are no documented cases of vision being restored like you experienced."

"Then it can't be possible," I mused, twirling linguini around my fork while my mind churned. All I could think about was my eyesight. I'd been convinced Gabriel would have an explanation. Never had I expected he'd give me no answers.

"Did you search the internet?" Becca asked me between bites.

"Yes. Several times. But I found nothing," I replied.

"Then it must be a medical miracle," Gabriel said with a grin, earning him a cold stare from me.

"You're a doctor. You shouldn't believe in miracles," I told him. "I know I don't."

Becca and Gabriel shot each other a knowing look before shifting their eyes to me. "If it's not a miracle and there's no medical explanation, then what do you call it?" Becca asked.

I was stumped. Huffing, I looked down at my plate. "I don't know. Magic maybe?" I suggested, raising my gaze to them.

"Then there's your answer," Becca said with a sly smile. She took another sip of wine before glancing at Gabriel. "We've got a lot of work to do with the festival coming up in two weeks. I can't believe the summer went by so fast again."

"I know," he replied. "We need to get there early, too, before the Dumantes sell out of their prime rib. I'm definitely stocking up on it again this year."

As they continued talking about the harvest, I ate quietly even though my appetite had disappeared. So it was magic? Or at least that was what Becca seemed to think. I was so confused and disappointed. I needed an explanation. Perhaps I should find another doctor.

No, you're not going to another doctor. Look at what happened to Sam's stepfather. The doctors didn't have an explanation for his illness. Sometimes they don't have all the answers. When are you going to accept it? It's been a week now. This seems to be permanent, and I can think of much worse things to have to deal with. The voice in my head had a few good points, one of them being that I didn't have time between my classes and homework to search for a doctor. And how would I explain that to Gabriel? I supposed I could chalk it up to looking for a second opinion, but I didn't want to offend him.

As Becca and Gabriel continued rambling on about the upcoming festival, I was grateful they didn't mention Lucian or my afternoon in the woods. I wanted to forget about that, but unless I was thinking about my vision, my mind wandered back to Lucian.

Becca and Gabriel were no help tonight. They were completely wrapped up in planning for the Harvest Festival. Personally, I didn't see the big deal. They wouldn't buy or sell anything that couldn't be found in a grocery store. So for most of the dinner, I tried to focus on the meal rather than unpleasant thoughts of Lucian and how my eyesight had been fixed. As soon as I finished eating, I excused myself and, after clearing away my dishes, retreated upstairs to my room.

Hours later as I read a book by the light of the bedside lamp, my phone rang. I reached for it on the nightstand and swiped the screen. It was Alex. I was wondering if he'd call tonight. "Hi," I said, forgetting about the book on my lap. Leaning back against the pillows, I stifled a yawn.

"Remember me?" he asked, his teasing voice rising over the muffled chatter and music in the background.

"Of course. How's Boston?"

"Awesome. We just finished up, and I wanted to call you before it got too late. It's probably a good thing you didn't come with us. The bar was packed tonight."

The idea of losing myself in a crowd appealed to me now more than ever before. What a great way to stop myself from thinking about my vision, Lucian, and even Sam's stepfather. "As much as I'd love to be there, it wasn't the bar that kept me home. It's the sleeping arrangements. I still want to hear you guys play again."

"Oh, but the sleeping arrangements would be a lot more fun if you were here."

"Maybe for you," I retorted.

"Or maybe not. Let's just say if we ever sleep together...um...I mean in the same room, I'd prefer that it wouldn't be with a bunch of other guys."

Even though Alex was miles away on the other end of the phone, I felt my cheeks burning. "Okay," I rolled out slowly. "I'm not sure what to say to that."

"Am I embarrassing you?" he asked.

"A little," I admitted.

"Then we can change the subject. How was your day? Did you do anything interesting?"

I paused before answering, debating whether or not to tell him about the woods and Lucian. But then I remembered the ghost rumors he and his friends had told me. If I described the woods from today, he might think I made it up. So I opted not to say anything about that or Lucian. Alex was one of many who believed Lucian had killed his sister, and I didn't need any reminders of that possibility.

After telling him my day had been anything but interesting, I mentioned that Gabriel had no explanation about my vision. Alex promised to talk to his father and see if he had any theories, but I held little hope he'd figure it out. This was bound to remain an unexplained medical marvel. *No,* I thought sarcastically. *It's magic, like Becca seemed to think*. I silently grumbled to myself, knowing I could never believe that.

After a few more minutes, Alex had to go and said goodnight. I hung up the phone and stared at the blank screen, reflecting on the day and realizing I'd spent the entire evening thinking about someone else. Someone with intense green eyes and a troubled soul. Someone who hadn't given me the time of day until this afternoon.

I hoped Alex would soon return to the forefront of my thoughts. He was the guy I liked, the one I wanted to be with and the one who wanted to be with me. Shaking my head, I placed the phone back on the nightstand. *There's no sense in dwelling on this tonight,* I told myself as I picked up my book, a light-hearted college romance that seemed more realistic than my own life.

I tried to read, but the words swam in front of me as my thoughts drifted back to one person. The same one who had rescued me on his black horse. And until I fell asleep, he was all I could think about.

The house was quiet when I woke up the next morning. Only the dogs were around when I ventured downstairs for a cup of coffee and a bowl of cereal. I enjoyed the solitude and read while I ate, trying to keep my mind off recent events.

After breakfast, I returned to my room to take a shower before dragging my books to the library where it would be easier to concentrate. I needed a neutral place where I could clear my head and focus on homework. My grades were top priority for this year, not trying to figure out why the only friend I had obsessed about Lucian's return or thinking about him living alone in the mansion next door and wondering whether or not he had killed his sister.

After tossing my navy pajamas in the laundry, I walked into the bathroom and turned on the water, waiting a minute for it to heat up. By the time I stepped into the shower, it was steaming hot and seemed to wash my apprehensions away. I lathered up my hair with shampoo, wishing I could stay in here, hidden from the craziness that seemed to lurk around every corner in Sedgewick.

But I had to face the day sooner or later. After washing and rinsing off, I turned the squeaky shower knob until the steady flow of water stopped. The curtain wrinkled up as I pushed it aside before stepping onto the bath rug and reaching for the white towel on the toilet lid. I rubbed my legs, abdomen, and arms until they were dry. Then I dabbed at my hair, soaking up as much water as I could. Once I was convinced the towel wouldn't get my hair any drier, I wrapped it around me and tucked the corner under the top edge.

Silence loomed in my room when I approached the dresser and dug through the drawers for underwear, a bra, jeans, and a sweater. I tossed them onto the bed and, with my back to the door, I shuffled my panties up my legs and under the towel. Then I slipped my arms through the bra straps and fastened it behind me. Once it was secured, I unwrapped the towel around my chest and let it drop to the floor.

As I reached for my jeans, my phone rang. Forgetting about getting dressed, I spun around and picked it up off the dresser. But when I looked at the screen, my heart dropped into my stomach. Private Caller. *Not again,* I thought as it rang two more times before I found the courage to answer it.

"Hello?" My fears were confirmed when no one spoke and heavy breathing sounded on the other end. "Who is this? I can hear you, so I know you're there."

Only silence aside from the steady rhythm of someone inhaling and exhaling met my words. Frustrated, I continued. "Look, you must have the wrong number. Don't call me again." Without wasting another moment, I hung up and tossed the phone onto the bed. My pulse accelerated as I stared at it. I knew it was silly to hate the phone, but right now, I looked at it like it was possessed.

My nerves rattled, I felt like I was being watched. The hair on the back of my neck stood on edge, and I took shallow breaths. I turned around, my eyes narrowing when I noticed the door hanging open a crack. My gaze locking on it for a moment, I felt naked and vulnerable. How had I been so careless to leave the door open? *Because no one ever comes up here,* a voice of reason reminded me. *And who would come up here besides Becca?*

Although my thoughts were logical, I wasn't buying them. It wasn't the people in this house I was worried about with a murder suspect living nearby. I'd have to be more careful to shut and lock the door from now on.

Now you're just being foolish, I chided myself. *Do you honestly think Lucian is going to come over here, waltz in through the front door, and spy on you?*

Maybe, I answered. *He didn't exactly give me a warm and fuzzy feeling when I was with him yesterday. I still know nothing about him other than the fact that he may be a murderer. And that's enough to make me lock the doors. All the doors. Especially now that someone keeps calling my phone.*

The thought of Lucian sent a wave of fear through me. What if he was the Private Caller breathing on the other end of my phone? If so, what was he trying to do? Scare me into leaving Sedgewick as he'd advised me to do?

My eyes still on the door, I stooped down and picked up the towel. Holding it against my chest, I walked to the door with slow, heavy steps. I needed to prove that this was all in my head. I was sure no one lurked on the other side, but I'd feel better once I saw it with my own eyes.

Holding my breath, I approached the door and peeked around the edge. At first, I saw nothing. But then a low whine made me jump. Clicking sounded on the hardwood floor, and I looked down at two brown eyes staring at me.

"Scout!" I exclaimed, a relieved smile escaping onto my face. "You scared me! Don't ever do that again!" I clutched the towel against my chest, feeling my pulse slow to its normal rate. I felt silly, knowing the dog was my boogeyman. "Now if you'll excuse me, I'm going to get dressed." I shut the door, making sure the latch clicked into place.

As I walked back over to my bed and tossed the towel on the chair, I shook my head. "I've been reduced to talking to the dogs like they're human. Great. Can't wait to see what happens next," I muttered, sliding into my jeans.

Ten minutes later, I raced down the stairs, my book bag hanging from my shoulder. My curls were still damp since I didn't want to waste time drying them before heading to the library. I considered not taking my phone to avoid more calls from the Private Caller, but then decided it was better to keep it with me, just in case I needed it. I had learned my lesson about leaving it behind yesterday, so it was now tucked in my bag.

When I reached the bottom, I headed straight for the front door. But I stopped dead in my tracks about halfway across the room when I heard a voice behind me.

"Going somewhere?"

I spun around to see Gabriel emerge from the hallway connected to the kitchen. His hair almost matched the golden log walls behind him. His GQ look in jeans and an untucked white shirt did nothing to calm me after the morning I'd had. Not once, but twice in the last ten minutes, someone had crept up on me. I was beginning to feel like I was being watched even though I knew that wasn't true.

"Yes," I said, backing up a step. "I thought I'd go to the library to study today."

He walked toward me, his curious eyes watching me intensely, as if challenging my motives. "Why? Do you have a research project?"

"No. I just find it easier to concentrate when I'm away from home sometimes. I used to study at the library a lot back in Maryland." That wasn't exactly true, but he would never know it.

Gabriel stopped about ten feet away from me. "Oh. Well then, I hope it helps."

"Thanks." I flashed him a grateful smile, not from his comment but from his acceptance of my explanation. "Will you tell Becca I'll be home around four? Maybe we can ride later today."

"Sure. I'll give her the message. She's out right now, but she should be back soon. I'm sure she'd love to get out on the trails today."

"Good." I started to turn away from him, but stopped. "Have a nice day," I said before spinning around and heading for the door.

It wasn't until I was seated in my car, the doors shut and locked, that I realized I hadn't thought to pack a lunch. I glanced out the windshield at the log home that had seemed so warm and welcoming a few weeks ago. Now, it just reminded me of mystery phone calls and a neighbor suspected of murder. My lunch wasn't worth returning to the house after the morning I'd had. I would just have to survive the day without it.

I sighed as I drove away, watching the house disappear in my rear-view mirror until the trees blocked it. After reaching the end of the driveway, I turned onto the road, grateful for the day of studying I had ahead of me.

There seemed to be only one way to keep my sanity. Study hard. Focus on school, get good grades, and submit my college applications as soon as I could. Alex was right. I would be ready to leave this town the first chance I got.

21

Sunday flew by way too fast and before I realized it, I was parking my car in the school lot Monday morning. I had slept well the night before, possibly due to the fact that I'd turned my phone off to avoid another midnight call from the Private Caller.

Alex met me on the sidewalk as I made my way through the crowd. The other students blurred beyond his charming smile and silver earring that glinted in the morning sunlight.

"Man, you're a sight for sore eyes," he said, stopping in front me. His jeans had a frayed rip in one knee and his black shirt matched his ponytail. With his book bag slung over his shoulder, he slid an arm around my waist and pulled me toward him, a sly grin on his face. "Miss me?"

"More than you'll ever know," I replied.

"Good. I like that answer." Then he dipped his head down and brushed his lips against mine.

As he started to deepen the kiss, I pulled back slightly, embarrassed at his public display of affection. I wasn't used to guys kissing me at all, let alone in front of the whole school.

Alex broke away from me, a hurt look in his eyes. "What's wrong? Is everything okay?"

"Yes," I assured him. "I'm just shy." I shifted my book bag on my shoulder as I felt it start to slide down my arm, pulling my sweater with it.

"You're going to have to get over that."

"I'll work on it, okay? You may keep forgetting this, but back in Maryland, I was kind of a nerd. I didn't have a boyfriend."

Alex swept my smooth waves over my shoulder, pushing them behind my neck. "Then those guys didn't realize what they were missing. You look nice today, by the way. I like this new look of yours. I mean, I liked your curls, but straight hair suits you better. It's softer."

I felt a blush race across my face and dropped my gaze to the pavement for a moment. "Thank you." When I looked back up at him, I grinned. "It must be my eyesight. It's so much easier to get ready in the morning now. I can actually see, and I don't have to waste time putting my contacts in."

"How long has it been?"

"Exactly one week."

"Well, maybe it's going to be permanent."

"I hope so because I'm really getting used to it. It would suck to go back to contact lenses and glasses." Just the thought of that made me grumpy. Even if I couldn't explain how my vision had been corrected other than magic as Becca seemed to believe, I was ready to accept it and enjoy it.

"I'm sure it would. So," Alex said, draping an arm over my shoulders as we started walking toward the school. "How was the rest of your weekend?"

I was about to answer him when Celeste darted past us. Long brown hair blew in the wind across her back as she raced up the steps two at a time. "Fine," I answered, my voice distracted as I watched her pull the front door open and disappear into the school. She hadn't even bothered to stop and say hello. But that was probably for the best. The last thing I wanted was to be reminded of how much Lucian frightened her after I'd spent Saturday afternoon with him.

"Really? You don't sound fine." Alex's comment broke me out of my thoughts.

"Sorry," I said, turning to look up at him as I tried to forget Celeste. "I was just thinking about something. But yesterday was very productive. I went to the library and got all my homework done. I even finished the Calculus assignment, well, all except one problem that I wasn't sure about."

"Only one?" Alex asked, sounding disappointed. "Darn. Then how am I going to get you alone one night this week to help you? We have some catching up to do from the weekend. I missed you."

I sensed the teasing hint in his voice right away and felt heat rush through me. *Good lord, girl,* I told myself. *Get a hold of yourself and get your mind out of the gutter. He's just trying to be helpful.* But I hadn't forgotten his suggestions Saturday night, and I assumed he meant catching up on something other than homework.

He pulled me closer to him, and I leaned against him, pleasantly surprised by the kiss he planted on my cheek. Then his hand found mine and we climbed the steps side by side. Before we reached the school entrance, a tingle crawled up my spine. I stopped abruptly, causing Alex to trip before he stumbled to a halt beside me.

As if in a trance, I glanced behind me to see Lucian walking down the sidewalk. His trench coat swayed around his knees, and sunglasses reflecting the blue sky hid his eyes. It felt like he was staring directly at me, even though I couldn't be sure.

With a deep breath, I pulled my gaze away from him. Frowning, I realized that even after the time we had spent together Saturday, nothing had changed.

"You okay?" Alex asked.

I forced myself to smile. "Yes. Sorry about that."

"No problem. But just in case, I'll walk you to your locker and homeroom."

"You're such a gentleman. What have I done to deserve you?" I asked. Composing myself, I focused ahead and hoped that I wouldn't see Lucian again that day until Art class.

My luck held out and most of the day was fairly uneventful. Not only did Lucian steer clear of me, but Celeste also kept to herself. I knew I would catch up with her soon, but I didn't want to listen to her rant about Lucian. I'm not sure what I would have done without Alex. His charm and attention helped me forget anything troubling me, at least most of the time.

But when History class ended, so did my peace.

"Gracyn. Can you hold up for a minute?" Mr. Wainwright asked when I passed his desk on my way to the door.

I stopped, hesitantly turning to face him as I broke away from the other students herding out the door. A moment later, the room emptied, leaving me alone with him. "Yes?" I asked, leaning against one of the front row desks.

Smiling, he turned away from the chalkboard, placed the eraser on the ledge, and crossed his arms over his gray button-down shirt. "You seemed a little tired today. Everything okay?"

"Yes," I said. "Everything's great." *Except this unwanted questioning,* I thought. I wished I knew why he insisted on singling me out. It made me nervous and suspicious. Could he have been the Private Caller on the other end of the phone this weekend? The mere thought of that sent an anxious wave of nausea over me. Trying to push that notion aside, I inched backward.

"You sure about that?" he asked, raising his eyebrows.

"Yes," I stated, but my voice faltered. I averted my eyes away from his and, before I could stop myself, admitted, "Well, no."

"That's what I figured." He took a deep breath, flashing a sympathetic smile when I looked up. "Want to talk about it?"

"Not particularly," I replied. To myself, I added, *Or rather, not with you. You're my teacher, not my friend. And for all I know, you're the cause of my concerns.* I wanted to kick myself for letting him see that something was bothering me. "I mean, it's just normal stuff. Homework, grades, getting into a good college. It's all to be expected."

"Well, I'm always here if you need anything."

I sucked in a deep breath, cringing inwardly. This conversation had just gone way beyond awkward. I glanced at the students outside the doorway, wishing I could escape into the crowd. "Thank you, but I've got everything under control."

"You sure? Because it's a new school and all–"

"Yes," I stated, cutting him off. "I am. So unless you wanted to see me about something regarding your class, I think you should stop asking me if everything is okay."

His expression fell flat as though I'd just slammed a door in his face. "I see. I'm sorry if I made you uncomfortable. That was never my intention. And no, you seem to be doing fine in class. You may go."

My eyes met his for a split second before I ran out of the room. My heart racing, I hoped that would be the last time he singled me out.

I sprinted down the almost empty hall, flinching when a locker door slammed. Footsteps sounded like the beat of a drum as the few remaining students rushed off to class. Then the bell rang, piercing the silence. With a huff, I sped up, thankful I didn't need to stop at my locker.

By the time I reached the Art wing, I was late. Sure that I was about to be scolded by Ms. Friedman, I took a deep breath before opening the door. All eyes in the classroom shifted to me as I hurried to my seat. I muttered a quick "Sorry", hoping she wouldn't say anything. She raised her eyebrows, her stern expression the only warning she gave me.

The other students seemed to lose interest in me after I took my seat beside Lucian. Everyone except him, that was. He stared at me, his intense eyes flustering me as I settled into the chair and dropped my book bag to the floor. He was just as handsome as I remembered with his wavy light brown hair and green eyes. And as intimidating in his black shirt, even with the silver cross dangling from his neck.

His gaze caught mine, holding me captive until I took a deep breath and raised my eyebrows as if to ask, "What?" Then I shook my head and turned my attention to the front of the room.

After the roll call, Ms. Friedman propped herself up on the front desk, her black skirt reaching her booted ankles. "Happy Monday." Her greeting was met with a chorus of groans. "Cheer up, everyone. I have a project I know you're going to love. And this is Art, not Literature or Biology, so you can all relax. It's supposed to be fun, right?"

I smiled, silently agreeing with her. Although this class would be a lot more fun for me if Lucian's presence didn't send my world spinning out of control with mixed emotions of fear and curiosity.

"Good. You're all with me. So this is a group project." More groans, this time even louder, erupted from the students. "I know, you all are loners and you're probably quivering in your army boots at the thought of working with a classmate. But it will be good for each one of you. I want you to pair up into teams of two and paint anything of your choice. Then you'll exchange paintings with your partner and write a thorough critique of their work. I want you to compare their work to other artists throughout history. The goal is to be critical, but fair. I want to read both positive and negative comments in your reviews. Any questions?"

"So we can't just say it sucks?" a guy in the back of the class asked sarcastically. Soft chuckles broke out across the room in response.

"No, Finn, the intent is not to sum up your opinion in one sentence. I want a thoughtful response. And after I grade them, they'll be shared with the person whose painting you critiqued. So be considerate. Any criticism needs to be constructive. And remember, that person is critiquing you." She paused, scanning the shell-shocked students in the room. A group project in Art class was practically unheard of.

"Okay. If there are no questions, I'm going to give everyone ten minutes to find someone to work with. Your assignment is due one week from today, so you'll have plenty of time." Without another word, she hopped down from the desk and circled around to the chair behind it.

Silence filled the classroom for a moment. The fear and tension in the room was thick, and everyone seemed paralyzed. After a few minutes, hushed whispers started to rise above the panic. I glanced at Lucian and then turned to scan the rest of the room. I was quite possibly the most conformed student in this class. The others intimidated me, their angry expressions conveying how much they hated the world. The only person I knew was Lucian, but I wasn't sure I wanted to work on this project with him in spite of the time we had spent together on Saturday.

I felt a light tap on my shoulder and whipped around to face him.

"What do you say? Want to work together on this?" he asked.

Nodding, I met his steady gaze. "Okay," I replied, realizing I had no other choice.

"Good," he said, seeming relieved. "Because I don't know anyone else in here. They were all two grades behind me when I left town. Besides, we're neighbors. That makes it easy, logistically."

"So when do you want to do this? I guess all we have to do is pick a time to meet and exchange paintings."

"Or," he began, raising his eyebrows. "We could work on our paintings together. Unless you already have something you want to use for this."

"Hmm," I replied, my mind racing with reasons why that was a bad idea. "No, I really don't. But can we figure out a plan later? We have all week."

He shrugged. "If that's what you want. What's wrong? You seem upset."

"I'm not upset," I responded a little too forcefully. "It was a rough weekend. After you dropped me off, that is." *And now Mr. Wainwright is acting weird again, just like the night at the bar,* I thought, but I didn't mention that.

"You didn't get lost in another fog, did you?"

I choked out a laugh. "No," I assured him as Becca's warning to stay away from him surfaced in my thoughts. But I couldn't tell him that, either. Pausing, I studied him, surprised to see him smiling. "You seem to be in a good mood today."

"Really? Uh-oh, I'd better change that," he teased. "I can't let anyone know that." He took a deep breath, put on a mocking frown, and narrowed his eyes. "There. Better?"

"No. I liked you with a smile."

As he flashed a faint grin, Ms. Friedman scooted her chair back, the legs scraping against the floor. She stood and circled the desk. Leaning against it, she folded her arms across her brown sweater. "Okay everyone. That's enough time. You should all have a partner now, so we're going to get back to the rest of today's class."

With a sigh, I tore my eyes away from Lucian and tried to listen. But I barely heard a word. Instead, I watched Lucian out of the corner of my eye, noticing every movement he made and every breath he took. For the rest of the class, I wondered if he wasn't as awful as everyone seemed to think.

When Art class ended, Lucian bid me a quick goodbye before dashing out the door. With a frown, I gathered my things, oblivious to the other kids packing up their belongings. One by one, the students trickled out of the room. I was the last to leave as my thoughts lingered on Lucian. I couldn't decide if I was happy that he'd spoken to me or upset because he'd practically ignored me after the bell rang. Whichever it was, I forced myself to put any feelings about him aside. At least he had warmed up to me a little, and that was progress.

I headed down the corridor and turned into the busy senior hall. I had planned to go directly to my locker, but when I saw Celeste, I stopped. "There you are. Where have you been hiding all day?"

She glanced at me, her expression flat. Dark circles lurked beneath her eyes, and she looked exhausted. "I haven't been hiding. I just wasn't in the mood to talk."

"Well, don't be such a stranger. I missed you at lunch. Will you be there tomorrow?"

"Only if he's not, which isn't likely, so the answer is no."

"Celeste, don't you think you're taking this a little too far? He's been back for a few weeks and no one has died."

Anguish deepened in her eyes. "A few weeks is just a moment in time. It's going to happen again, I know it."

Her warning tone raised the hairs on the back of my neck as I remembered the two suspicious calls I had received. The idea that Lucian was behind them crept into my thoughts. For both my sake and Celeste's sake, I mustered a confident smile, mentally stomping on my doubts.

"Look," I said. "I don't know you that well yet but, from what I can tell, you're really nice and hopefully you think of me as a friend. But don't you think you're taking this a little too far? Maybe Lucian isn't as bad as you think he is. I know I'm new in town, but that allows me to see things without the past blurring the line between what's real and what isn't."

"You have no idea what is real around here," she hissed, her voice sounding angry. "If you even think about trying to convince me Lucian isn't the monster I know he is, then you are not my friend."

"Celeste—"

"No! I can't let my guard down. That's when he'll strike. I knew I shouldn't have started the school year here. I should have asked my parents to let me go to the private school. I don't know how I'm going to make it through tomorrow, let alone this entire year," she muttered before turning away from me. Then she shoved her books in her black bag and slammed the locker door. Without another word, she walked away, leaving me to gape at her back.

My hopes sinking, I realized I might have just lost not only her friendship, but also her trust. As much as I knew she and everyone else around here were convinced Lucian had killed his sister, I didn't want to believe it. If he had, he would have been convicted and locked up. He wouldn't be free to hurt another person. After seeing a sliver of his soft side, I hoped he hadn't done it. I wanted to believe there was more to him than the icy front he hid behind.

With a sigh, I looked away from the crowd swallowing up Celeste. She wasn't coming back, so there was no point in lingering. Instead, I headed for my locker, ready to pack up before going home and throwing myself into my homework or anything else that would keep my thoughts away from both Celeste and Lucian.

22

The week progressed uneventfully after Monday. Celeste avoided me and Lucian ignored me except for an occasional glance my way in class. Alex helped me take my mind off both of them, often flattering me in ways that made me smile and forget anything troubling me at the moment.

Peace returned, at least until Thursday afternoon when I arrived home. Parking in front of the house, I didn't think anything of the empty driveway. Becca wasn't home from work yet as usual, and Gabriel was due back from Boston later that night. *Another quiet afternoon*, I thought, getting out of the car and grabbing my book bag from the back seat. Hanging it on my shoulder, I shut the door and bounded up the porch steps only to skid to a halt when I saw a shoebox-sized package on the doorstep.

Hmm, was all I thought as I knelt down to pick it up. But I froze when I saw my name spelled in letters cut out from magazines. They were all different sizes and fonts, haphazardly pasted together. There was no return address either. Just a postmark from Sedgewick.

I fumbled with my keys until I managed to unlock the front door, fear making my blood run cold. I carried the box into the house, glancing at it several times, not sure if I even wanted to open it. After setting it down on the coffee table, I dropped my book bag on the couch and stood still for a moment, painfully aware of the silence wrapping around me.

"Oh, screw it!" I muttered, running to the kitchen and grabbing a pair of scissors. Holding the blades in my hand, I returned to the couch, sat down, and picked up the box. It was light, but I felt something bulky shifting from side to side as I moved it.

My nerves on edge, I cut the tape around the sides, my heart thumping as I got closer to finding out what was in the box. Cringing, I finally opened it. At first, crumpled newspaper was all I could see.

Holding my breath, I placed the scissors on the table and dug through the paper. Buried under the top layer was a doll with curly red hair. At first, I scrunched my eyebrows, not sure what to think. But when I saw the red stain on her white dress over her heart, I screamed and dropped it as though I had been burned.

My pulse sped up, if that was even possible. I stared straight ahead at the box, wishing it wasn't there, that I was having a bad dream. I closed my eyes and took a deep breath, trying to calm down. *Okay,* I told myself. *Maybe this isn't really happening. Maybe I'll open my eyes and the box and the doll will be gone. It's only my imagination.*

My eyes snapped open and the box was still on the coffee table, the top flaps open. *Imagination, right,* a sarcastic voice trilled in my head. *You're not in first grade anymore. Of course you didn't imagine it. It's real just like your new eyesight. So accept it. Someone is after you. Those phone calls weren't wrong numbers. They were deliberate attempts to scare you.*

That was the last thing I wanted to believe, but I couldn't stop the panic from ripping through me. Trembling, I looked down at the doll on the floor resting on its side next to one of the coffee table legs. All I could see was the back of its curly hair and white dress. From here, it seemed harmless enough.

Biting my lip, I composed myself. I stood up straight and tall, determined not to let this bother me. Whoever sent it wanted to rattle me, and I wouldn't let that happen. With all the courage I could muster, I scooped up the doll and shoved it back under the newspaper in the box. Then I paused, debating whether or not to tell Becca and Gabriel about it.

Undecided, I carried it up to my room and slid it under my bed for now. I wondered what Becca would do if I told her about it. Would she turn it over to the police? Would they be able to get fingerprints off of it and find out who sent it? And then there was the possibility that they'd ask me if anyone had a vendetta against me. How could I tell them the one thing I was trying to forget?

The image of that dark stormy night with Sam's stepfather whipped another dose of fear into me. Thoughts raced through my mind, first of him in the car, then of Mr. Wainwright when he'd approached me at the bar and the two times he'd asked me to stay after class, and lastly of Lucian and his icy glares, hatred spewing from his eyes, at least until he had turned a little nicer. The list of those who made me nervous was too long to even begin guessing who might have sent the doll.

After pushing the box as far under my bed as I could reach, I tried to shake off my fear. *Whoever sent it is trying to upset you. So act like it didn't happen. Like everything is fine,* I told myself. But my words didn't comfort me. Instead, I glanced at the clock. Four-fifteen. Becca wouldn't be home for at least another hour.

Wanting to pass the time quickly, I changed into an old pair of jeans and a brown turtleneck. Then I headed out to the barn with the dogs in tow. I spent the next hour grooming Gypsy and cleaning the stalls, the doll never straying far from my mind. I tried hard to forget about it, but was unsuccessful. Gypsy seemed to sense my anxiety, nudging me while I groomed her, as though asking if I was okay. It was comforting, and yet at the same time, a little odd. How did she seem to know something was bothering me?

After filling the water buckets and putting the horses away, I left the barn. Right away, I saw Becca's SUV parked next to my car. I hadn't heard her pull in, but I was glad she was home.

I jogged across the driveway, feeling a chill in the air. The sun had dropped below the treetops, sending purple streaks across the sky. It looked eerie, quite fitting for the mood I was in tonight. Now I just had to put on a smile and act as though nothing was wrong. I hoped I could pull it off.

When I opened the door, the dogs rushed past me before I entered to find Becca nowhere in sight and the house quiet. "Becca?" I called, shutting the door behind me.

The dogs went to the stairs and looked up before they turned their heads toward the hallway. Becca appeared, her eyes tired as she shifted her hoodie into place. "Hi, Gracyn," she said with a faint smile before stopping beside the island.

"Hi," I said. "I just finished up in the barn. The horses are in, so you don't need to go out there."

"Thanks. I was going to make some dinner while I wait for Gabe to get home. Want to join me?"

"Um, no thanks. I'm not really hungry. But I'll come down if I change my mind."

She shrugged. "Okay. Do you have a lot of homework?"

"Yes," I answered. "And I better get started if I want to finish at a reasonable hour. I just needed a break outside."

"I can understand that. Well, there will be plenty of leftovers for later."

With a smile and a nod, I retreated to the stairs. My feet felt heavy as I climbed up to my room, the anonymous package under my bed filling me with dread. If I stayed downstairs with Becca, I couldn't be sure she wouldn't notice something was bothering me. I felt like I had no choice but to hide. Hoping I'd be able to concentrate on homework in spite of the doll lurking in the shadows, I returned to my room and shut the door.

Two hours later, my stomach grumbling, I gave up on trying to write my English essay. Now wearing flannel pajama pants and a navy hoodie, I dropped my pen and swiveled around in my chair. Standing, I took a deep breath before walking toward the door.

The kitchen was empty when I got there. Even the dogs were absent from their beds. Without giving it any thought, I headed for the refrigerator. But as I opened the stainless steel door, I heard hushed voices.

"Gabe, we have to tell her soon. This isn't going to end well."

Becca's warning struck a chord inside me. I immediately shut the refrigerator and tiptoed over to the hallway leading to the master bedroom. Stopping in the doorway, I continued listening.

"I know," Gabe said.

"I just wish I knew what to do right now," she said. "I never expected this."

"I think the first thing you need to do is sit down and talk to her. There has to be a reason why she hid the doll from you."

I gasped, my jaw dropping open. How did they know about that? As much as I wanted to bust in their room and demand an answer, I stayed where I was, hoping the rest of their conversation would give me some clues.

"She must be scared out of her mind," Becca mused. "I can't imagine what she's going through right now. Everything has been happening so fast. I never thought I'd need to bring her here until at least next year when she started college."

"But she's here now. And someone obviously doesn't like that."

"You don't think—" Becca's voice trailed off.

"Think what?"

"That whoever killed Cassie sent the doll?" Becca asked.

"It's a good guess, although there's no way to be sure," Gabriel replied.

"Well, the fact is, Gracyn's getting stronger. I knew her eyesight would improve over time, I just never expected it would happen overnight like it did."

"Yes. That was a bit of a surprise. She's going to be strong, just like you. So, what do you want to do? Shall we go upstairs and talk to her?" Gabriel asked.

"What, now?"

"Yes. Why wait?"

"I...I don't know. Let me think about it. I don't know what I'm going to say," Becca said hesitantly.

"How about the truth?"

A silent pause followed Gabriel's suggestion. I held my breath, wondering how Becca would answer him as I prepared to jump away from the hallway entrance if I heard their door open.

"That's going to be hard. Of course, I'm going to tell her everything, but imagine her shock. I want to be careful not to freak her out."

Gabriel huffed. "I think that's already been done."

"Yes," Becca agreed with a deep sigh. "You're right. Well, let me think about it. In the meantime, I'm going to see if I can trace the doll's origins. I just have to wait until tomorrow when Gracyn's at school."

"Becca," Gabriel said, his voice full of grave concern. "I don't think I want you doing that. Your headaches are getting worse and more frequent. The more power you use, the worse they get. You need to save it for the garden."

"No, Gabe," Becca retorted. "She's my family, and I'm going to do whatever it takes to protect her. No matter what the cost may be. Someone is after her. That doll was a blatant threat. I'm going to get to the bottom of it."

"And when do you plan to do this? You need to work tomorrow while she's at school."

"I'll figure it out. Don't try to talk me out of it, Gabe. I know you want what's best for me—"

"I want what's best for everyone. I just wish I could do it for you. I hate seeing you in pain. And you know what it means if your headaches get worse."

My heart fell into my stomach. No, I didn't know what that meant, but I didn't like how any of this sounded. If Becca was sick, shouldn't I know about it, too?

"It's inevitable, Gabe. I've lived a long time. The end could be near and I have to accept that."

"Well, I'm not going to. You are too important. I won't lose you."

"I'm sorry, but you know if my time is coming, there is nothing you can do." Becca paused, then spoke again. "But that's not our immediate problem. I will trace the doll this weekend and see if I can find out where it came from."

"I'm not going to change your mind, am I?" Gabriel asked.

"Not a chance," Becca said quietly.

"Fine," he muttered with a sigh. "Then I'll do anything you need me to. I'm here to help."

"Thanks, Gabe. For everything. You know I couldn't get through these times without you. Things used to be so much simpler. I don't know how much longer I can handle this century."

My jaw dropped open, and I raised my eyebrows. *This century? Now I've heard it all. What did that mean?* Unfortunately, I didn't get my answer that night. Her words were the last she spoke before silence met my ears. A few moments later, I tiptoed back upstairs without getting a single bite to eat. After what I'd just heard, food was the furthest thing from my mind.

I attempted to finish my homework, but I couldn't concentrate. My mind kept repeating Becca's words. When the clock struck midnight, I gave up and climbed into bed. In spite of the late hour, I wasn't as tired as I thought. Questions whipped through my head, and it wasn't until I resolved to ask Becca what was going on that I closed my eyes and drifted into a restless sleep.

23

It had to be a dream. I must have imagined the package I received and what Becca and Gabriel said that night. There was no way I could have heard them in their room with the door shut from where I'd been in the kitchen. Or was there?

As exhausted as I was, I woke up several times during the night. Twice, I got up with the intention of drafting an email or text to my mother, but I hesitated, not sure what to say. "Mom, someone might be stalking me." "Mom, I can see perfectly without my glasses or contacts, and Becca is convinced it's because of magic." "Mom, can I come to Russia to live with you?"

Everything I came up with sounded crazy. I couldn't do this to her. She'd be devastated to know what was going on. She would feel guilty and responsible for my problems. And I'd never forgive myself if I interfered with her promotion. Besides, I had no idea what Becca meant by everything she said last night. As for the doll, well, I was freaked out, but I wasn't sure I wanted to run all the way across the ocean to escape. I finally concluded that I needed to talk to Becca about everything as soon as I got the chance.

My eyes flew open at five in the morning, and I was wide awake. The sky outside my window was pitch black, but that didn't stop me from getting up. After a quick shower and dressing in jeans, a black sweater, and boots, I crept downstairs. Fumbling around in the darkness, I grabbed my jacket from the coat closet and slipped out the door.

Once outside, I rushed to my car. Pink rays from the sunrise were inching above the horizon, adding a rosy hue to the sky, and the cold air had left a dew on my car. As soon as I got in and started the engine, I turned the heat up as high as it would go and rubbed my hands together. After flipping on the headlights, I started the windshield wipers to clear away the moisture. Then I backed up and guided the car down the driveway, leaving the doll, Becca, Gabriel, and whatever they were hiding behind me.

The events of the night before haunted me all the way to school. When I pulled into the parking lot, it was empty except for a few cars belonging to the teachers. I found a spot on the far side and left the engine idling as I finished my English essay using the overhead light.

An hour later, after the sun had risen, cars and buses began trickling into the parking lot. After waiting a few minutes for the crowd to disperse, I grabbed my book bag and stepped out of the car. Shutting the door, I fought back a yawn. Exhausted, I had no doubt concentrating today would be a struggle.

At least it's Friday, I thought as I looked both ways before walking across the lane of traffic. Then I frowned. I only had one day of school to distract me before I'd have to confront Becca. As much as I wanted to ask her what was going on, the whole thing made me nervous and jittery. All I knew right now was that I wasn't normal. Between my corrected vision and Sam's stepfather's illness which I had somehow caused, I knew something was different about me. There was no other explanation. Becca was right. I deserved to know what was going on.

You'll get answers soon enough. Don't be too eager, or you'll end up being sorry for what you wished for, I told myself. *Enjoy today and make it last.* Forcing one foot in front of the other, I continued across the parking lot. I reached the sidewalk, thankful the hum of voices from the students hanging out on the lawn drowned out my thoughts. I needed the distraction. The other kids seemed so happy it was Friday, talking to friends about the weekend. I wished I could share their excitement. Their lives were blissfully normal, something I feared I wouldn't have again, at least not for a long time.

As I climbed the walkway stairs, I heard my name being called behind me.

"Gracyn! Wait up!"

Reaching the top, I turned to see Alex skipping up the steps two at a time. He smiled as he stopped in front of me, oblivious to the glare it earned him from a pimply kid in glasses who veered off to the side to avoid him.

"Hi," I said, my eyes meeting his.

"Whoa," he gasped. "What happened to you? You look awful."

"Gee, thanks. Good morning to you, too."

"Sorry," he said. "But you look tired. What's going on?" Genuine concern lurked in his voice.

"I just didn't sleep well last night," I said, not wanting to worry him.

Alex shot me a sympathetic look before grinning. "You should have called me. Maybe I could have told you a bedtime story to help you get to sleep."

I couldn't help smiling in spite of everything weighing on me. "If your idea of a bedtime story is anything like the ghost rumors you told me about a few weeks ago, I'm not sure it would have helped. Besides, I was up long after midnight. I didn't want to bother you."

With a sly smile, he stepped closer to me and wrapped an arm around my shoulders. "You could never bother me. Now come on. Let's get inside. It's chilly this morning."

"That's what jackets are for," I told him as we started heading toward the door. "You should try one sometime," I joked, noting he wore only a black T-shirt with jeans.

"They're overrated. Besides, it's supposed to get warm again later today. The annual Indian summer. Two more weeks of seventy-degree days before we slide into winter. Hope you're ready for it."

I nearly laughed out loud. Between the doll and Becca's secrets, the weather was the last of my concerns. "I say bring it on. You know, we had winter in Maryland."

"Oh yeah, that's the same," he teased.

"No, seriously. We got some pretty big snowstorms. But it usually melted within a few days."

"Well, not here. Once the snow is on the ground, you just end up making bigger piles with every storm."

We walked into the school, and my eyes adjusted to the dim light. The onset of a dull headache from my lack of sleep nagged at me, but I forced myself to ignore it.

As we wound our way through the crowded hall, I let out a soft chuckle. "I can't believe we're talking about the weather. Could I be any more boring?"

"No," Alex stated with a grin.

I shot him a knowing look and rolled my eyes in response.

"Don't worry. I still like you. So what should we talk about?" he asked.

We reached my locker and stopped. I leaned my shoulder against the metal as Alex pulled his arm away from my shoulders and faced me. "Tonight," I answered. "Is there a party at the lake?"

He arched his eyebrows. "Yes. Actually, there is. Do you want to go?" He seemed surprised by my interest.

"Definitely." Anything to get away and not have to think about the doll under my bed. As much as I wanted to know what Becca and Gabriel were hiding from me, it could wait another day. "I suppose you're wondering why I'd like to go."

Alex nodded. "You read my mind. But it's cool. We're not playing tonight, so I'm free."

"Good. When does it start?" I couldn't have been happier if he said the minute the last bell rang this afternoon, but I knew better than to expect that.

"Around eight. They never get going until after dark."

"Hmm. Eight, huh?" I wrinkled my eyebrows, calculating how many hours that would give me at home.

"We could get some pizza in town first," he suggested.

Smiling, I agreed. "That would be perfect."

"I'll pick you up at six."

As I nodded, Lucian walked by, catching my eye. Surprisingly, Zoe wasn't hanging on to him. He headed down the hall, not breaking his stride as the other kids scurried out of his way. He ignored them, focusing straight ahead. Just the sight of his back, his wavy hair brushing the folded collar of his dark green shirt, made me uneasy. I couldn't help wondering if everyone around here was right and he had murdered his sister. In spite of the few times he'd been nice to me, a part of me worried that he had sent the doll.

"Gracyn?" Alex's voice broke through my thoughts.

I tore my gaze away from Lucian as he disappeared into the crowd and looked back at Alex. "Yes?"

"I lost you for a moment."

"Sorry. I thought I saw Celeste," I lied. "I wanted to talk to her this morning."

"Really? Why? She's been acting awfully strange this week. I may not talk to her much, or at all for that matter, but even I can tell she hasn't been herself."

"I know. I've noticed that, too. I haven't known her long, but I feel like I should try to help her out of her funk. From what I can tell, she doesn't have any other friends to turn to."

Alex smiled at me. "Wow. You are so nice. She's lucky to have you looking out for her."

"Well, I'm not sure she's noticed yet."

"Then she's a fool. You really care, which is more than I can say for everyone else around here."

"I would just hate to see something bad happen to her."

Alex raised his hands and placed them on my shoulders. "And that is what I like about you." He leaned in and kissed my lips. When he pulled back, a smile lingered on his face. "Now I'm really looking forward to tonight. You are full of surprises, Gracyn Pierce. I can't wait to see what you have in store for me next."

"Me, too," I muttered, realizing I had no control over that. The next surprise would come from Becca when she told me what she knew about me.

Alex glanced down the hall, his dark eyes locking on someone. "I need to go catch up with Derek. I'll see you later, okay?"

"Make sure you tell him to be at the party tonight. I want to get to know your friends better, too."

Alex grinned. "He'll be there. Don't worry," he said, squeezing my upper arm before taking off into the crowd.

Left alone, I sighed as I sifted through my book bag. I hadn't finished half of my homework, and I could barely keep my eyes open. It was going to be a rough day. The party couldn't start soon enough.

By the time I walked into Art class, I was in a rotten mood. Not only had I felt lost in every class and turned in what I knew was an incomplete History assignment, but I was fighting to stay awake. I slid into my seat at the empty desk with minutes to spare. Lowering my head to lean it on my arm, I closed my eyes to rest for the time remaining before the bell would ring. But only seconds passed before a movement behind me raised the hair on the back of my neck.

Whipping my head up, I took a deep breath as Lucian sat down beside me. He dropped his book bag to the floor and stared at me, his green eyes locking with mine.

"You look tired," he observed, sparing me a meaningless greeting.

"That's because I am," I stated, not offering him any more of an explanation. My gaze didn't waver from his. I desperately wanted to ask him if he had sent the doll to me, but I chickened out.

"Sorry to hear that. But we have to figure out when to get together for our project."

My heart sank at the thought of the assignment. The last thing I wanted right now was to spend time with him, at least not until I found out who was after me. "Oh. I forgot all about that. Great."

"Well, we have to come up with a plan for this weekend. It's due on Monday."

"I know when it's due," I snapped, my short fuse running out. Taking a deep breath, I softened my tone. "Sorry. I've got some stuff going on at home right now, so I'm a little cranky today."

"Anything you'd like to talk about?" he asked softly.

My jaw nearly dropped to the floor, and I forced myself to shut it before he noticed. I couldn't have been more shocked if he'd asked me out on a date. "No, I don't want to bore you with my problems. Let's just decide what we're going to do for the project."

"How about Saturday at noon? My place or yours?"

"Mine," I answered, but then thought twice on it. Becca didn't like him. How would I explain having him over? "Or maybe your place," I heard myself say as fear whipped through me. *He saved your butt last weekend,* I reminded myself. *If he wanted to hurt you, he would have already done it. Just tell Becca where you're going and when you think you'll be home.* My words provided little comfort as the doll resurfaced in my mind and I wondered again if he had sent it. But I didn't change my mind. I would go to his house on a hope and a prayer that he was harmless.

He shrugged. "Sure. No problem. I can pick you up."

I shook my head. "No, thanks. I know where you live and I have my own car. I think I can get there okay."

A subtle smile formed on his face before he caught himself and frowned. "Then I'll be waiting."

When our eyes met again, the bell rang. I shifted my attention to the front of the class as a few students stormed into the room and rushed to their seats. Ms. Friedman cast a disapproving glance their way before launching into the roll call.

I leaned my elbows on the desktop, waiting for my name to be called, but couldn't shake the feeling that Lucian was staring at me. Hoping I was wrong, I glanced at him. He nodded with a brief smile, his intense gaze unsettling me. At that moment, my fatigue vanished. Wide awake, I suspected I was about to spend the next fifty minutes on the edge of my seat, painfully aware of Lucian's towering broad shoulders beside me.

Forcing my eyes and thoughts straight ahead, I sighed restlessly. After what had already been a long day, I was in for an even longer class.

Becca's SUV and Gabriel's BMW were parked in the driveway when I arrived home that afternoon, but neither one of them could be found. The house was quiet when I opened the front door, and I raced up to my room, thankful to be alone.

As much as I wanted to talk to Becca, I wasn't sure what to say aside from, "I heard you talking last night. What am I? How can I hear you from so far away, how did my vision get fixed, and how do you know about the doll?" It was blunt, to say the least. I needed to soften my approach, make my questions less demanding. Otherwise, she would probably become defensive and I didn't want to argue. I just wanted to know the truth. That wasn't asking too much.

Dropping my book bag onto the chair, I pulled off my boots and lay down on my bed. Within minutes, I dozed off, exhausted from my restless night. When I woke up, I barely had time to change my clothes and brush my hair. I replaced my wrinkled sweater with a V-neck burgundy shirt. Still wearing my jeans, I slipped my boots on and ran a brush through my curls. Lastly, I dabbed a little make-up under my eyes to cover up the dark circles.

By the time I ran downstairs, grabbed my jacket from the coat closet, and raced out the front door, Alex was leaning against his Jeep, talking to Becca and Gabriel. The dogs paced along the porch, waiting to go inside.

I walked down the steps, making sure to look only at Alex. I suddenly wanted to get away as fast as possible. Becca and Gabriel made me nervous and, until they told me what they were hiding, it was hard to act like nothing was wrong.

"Hi," I said, smiling at Alex. I stopped several feet away, waiting for his cue to get in the Jeep. "Ready to go?"

"Will you be out late?" Becca asked me.

"Um, I don't know. There's a party, so I guess it just depends on if we're having a good time," I told her, making the mistake of glancing up and catching her gaze.

"Well, if you're not out too late and you're up early tomorrow, Gabe and I are going to take the horses out for a trail ride in the morning. We'd love it if you joined us."

I shifted my gaze to Gabriel who put his arm around Becca. "Gypsy could use a little exercise. So how about it?" he asked.

All eyes watched me, expecting an answer. "I don't know. I have to work on a school project tomorrow with another student," I explained, deliberately not mentioning Lucian by name. But I thought twice about my response, knowing Becca and Gabriel owed me some answers. Perhaps I could ask my questions while we were riding. "Can I let you know tomorrow?"

"Of course," Becca said.

As an awkward moment of silence fell over us, I sidestepped toward the Jeep. "We should probably get going, right Alex?"

He jumped, a little startled as Becca and Gabriel continued to watch me. "Yes. The pizza place fills up fast on Friday night. It was nice to see you again, Becca, Gabriel."

"You too, Alex," Becca said.

"Stop by anytime," Gabriel added.

"Thanks." As Alex slid into the driver's seat, Becca and Gabriel headed toward the porch steps.

I hurried around to the passenger side of the Jeep. Opening the door, I looked up to see Gabriel glance at me over his shoulder, the intense stare in his eyes making me nervous. Breaking my gaze away from him, I hopped into the Jeep and pulled the door shut.

Fastening my seat belt, I looked at Alex. "I don't think I want to come home tonight. I hope this party doesn't stop until the sun comes up."

24

"Well, that was fun," Alex commented as he guided the Jeep down the driveway, leaving the house in the distance behind us.

I relaxed when I glanced in the rearview mirror and saw nothing but trees. Raising my eyebrows, I offered him a faint smile. "What's that supposed to mean?"

"You, Becca, and Gabriel. What was that all about?"

"It's just a little intense right now."

"You can say that again. What's going on with you guys?"

"Nothing," I lied. Well, it was more of a half lie. Becca and Gabriel had no idea that I'd heard them last night, at least as far as I knew. And just the thought of the doll gave me the chills. I felt like someone was watching me, waiting for the right moment to strike.

As Alex turned onto the road, I tried to explain. "I feel like I'm living with strangers sometimes."

"But Becca's your sister."

"I know. But it's not like we grew up together in the same house borrowing each other's clothes and fighting over boys. I didn't even know I had a sister until I was fifteen."

"Really?"

"Yes. I wasn't too happy when I found out, either."

"Why not?"

"I should rephrase that. I was actually ecstatic to find out I had a sister. But I was pretty upset that my mom hid it from me and kept us apart for so long. I grew up as an only child and I'd always wanted a sister."

"Then what's the problem? I thought things were going great with her."

"They were."

"What changed?"

Shrugging, I stared straight ahead at the gray sky above the trees in the distance. "I feel like she's hiding something from me. And I barely know Gabriel."

"You've only been here a few weeks. I'm sure you'll get to know him better over time."

"Maybe," I said with a sigh.

"As for Becca, remember, this is an adjustment for her, too. Maybe she's trying too hard. She's probably worried you won't like living here. And she has a job, so she can't be around all the time. I'm sure it's not easy for her, either."

I wished I could accept his explanation. There was a lot more to Becca than what Alex thought he knew, but I kept that to myself. "You're probably right."

"Of course I'm right," Alex teased, flashing me a soft grin. "Give her some time. It'll work out. You're not feeling guilty for going out tonight, are you? You know, like you should be home spending more time with her?"

"No," I assured him. "I'm right where I want to be. And Becca would never expect me to sacrifice my social life to stay home and play Scrabble with her." *Or tell magic tales,* I thought sarcastically.

That's it! I scolded myself. *You're going to stop this nonsense. This weekend, all you have to do is come clean and ask Becca to talk to you. She needs to explain what she meant last night, and you need to ask her what to do about the doll. Maybe she'll tell you to report it to the police. The point is, you need her help. Avoiding this isn't going to make it go away. But at least for tonight, try to have some fun.*

The voice in my head probably would have continued if Alex hadn't broken my thoughts by placing a hand on my knee. Startled, I turned to look at him.

"You drifted away again. We're going to be in town in a minute. You sure you want to go out tonight?" he asked.

"Yes, I am," I stated with confidence, ready to think about something else. I wanted to have a good time, and that wouldn't happen until I forgot about the doll and whatever Becca was hiding. Changing the subject, I asked, "So who's going to be at the party tonight?"

"Everyone," he answered with a sparkle in his eyes. "I hope you're ready for a wild night."

"You have no idea," I said softly with a deep sigh.

After dinner at the pizza restaurant, Alex and I arrived at the party long after the sun went down. He parked behind the cars already lined up on the shoulder of the road. When he flipped the headlights off, the glare of the taillights in front of us disappeared. Darkness fell over us until I opened the door and the interior light snapped on. I stepped outside onto the dirt, immediately hearing the beat of music and occasional shouting in the distance.

As I shut the door and pulled my jacket around me to ward off the chill in the air, Alex joined me. "You sure this is where you want to be tonight? Because we can always take off. No one needs to know we were even here."

It wasn't the first time he'd suggested doing something else tonight. "Alex, I'm sure. Why do you keep doubting me?"

"It just seems a little out of character for you, that's all."

"We've been here before."

"That was before school started. Those parties were pretty tame."

I frowned, studying his concerned expression in the dim light. His dark hair wasn't even visible, blending into the shadows behind him. "I can handle it." As I spoke, two boys walked by on the other side of the Jeep.

"Hey, Alex!" one of them called, looking our way. "You coming?"

Alex smiled and took my hand. Leading me around the front of the Jeep to the road and his friends, he said, "Of course. Ben, Chris, this is Gracyn."

The boy with thick brown hair extended his arm out to me. "Hi, Gracyn. Nice to meet you. I'm Ben."

I smiled and shook his hand. "Thanks. You, too."

When Ben released his grip, the other boy with sandy blonde hair narrowed his honey-colored eyes at me. "Weren't you hanging out with Celeste Hamilton a few weeks ago?"

I shrugged, not sure how to answer him. Fortunately, I didn't need to say anything.

"What does that have to do with anything, Chris?" Alex asked.

"Just didn't think we'd ever see her here if she's friends with Celeste."

"Well, I'm not sure if I am," I snapped. Then I softened my voice. "At least for now."

Ben watched me curiously. "Sorry about that, I think. Anyway, we're glad you came out tonight. This place is gonna be rocking tonight. Hey Alex, where's the guitar? You guys should play for us out here."

"You know the deal. No stage or electricity, no music. Now are we all going to stand out here in the road or should we get down to the lake?" Alex asked.

"The lake, man. I need a brewski," Chris stated before turning to head through the woods, the rest of us following him.

The music got louder, the bonfire brighter as we approached the party. I barely had a moment to appreciate the stars shining in the sky as my attention was riveted toward the crowd. Kids gathered around the fire, talking, laughing, and occasionally shrieking. Everyone had a drink in their hand whether it was a red cup of beer or a soda. At one moment, the voices quieted and a circle formed around a girl wearing a denim jacket, a black miniskirt, and cowboy boots. Chanting started quietly, then grew louder as she chugged from a cup. When she finished and crumpled the plastic cup in her hand, a satisfied grin on her face, the crowd cheered.

I shook my head, watching her teeter away from the inside of the circle, her strides wobbly and uneven. For a brief moment, I wondered if there was any chance the cops would bust the party. *Don't worry about that,* I scolded myself. *Cops busting this party is at least something that happens to normal kids. You could use a little normal right now.*

I pushed my thoughts aside as we reached a picnic table. Ben and Chris had disappeared into the crowd, leaving me alone with Alex. "Can I get you a soda?" Alex asked.

"No, thanks. I'd rather have a beer." My answer shocked me. I wasn't sure where it had come from, but I wasn't about to change my mind. Maybe it would help me forget about that stupid doll.

Alex's jaw dropped open as he stared at me. "Really?"

I nodded. "Yes. It's a party, right? And I don't have to drive. You're not drinking, are you?"

"No."

"Good. Then I'll have enough for both of us."

Alex raised his eyebrows. "You know, you don't have to drink. No one will think any less of you."

"I know that. I don't want a beer to impress anyone. I just want one because I want one." I couldn't tell him the real reason I wanted a drink.

"Okay. As long as you're sure."

I was starting to get a little irritated by his tone. If he didn't want me to have a good time, then why had he brought me here? *Because you asked him to,* I reminded myself. "I am. If it's too much to ask, I can get it myself."

"Nope. I'm on it."

As he turned and walked away, I felt a little guilty for being so short with him. Maybe he felt like a bad influence on me. Somehow, I'd have to convince him that my decision to have a drink tonight had nothing to do with him, but it would have to wait for later.

Alex returned a few minutes later, a red plastic cup in one hand and a Coke can in the other. "Here you go," he said, handing the cup to me.

"Thank you," I said, meeting his eyes as my fingers wrapped around the cup. Hesitating, I held the drink, suddenly feeling like I'd been pitched into a dream. I'd never had a beer before. I knew what I was about to do was wrong, but it was either loosen up and have a drink or worry about Becca's secrets and the doll all night. The beer seemed like the obvious choice.

My mind made up, I raised the cup to my lips and drank my first swallow. It tasted bland and a little flat, but it went down smoothly, warming me as it settled in the pit of my stomach. Enjoying the relaxing effect it had on my thoughts, I drank several more gulps.

Alex watched me, concern lurking in his dark eyes when I finished the beer. "Hey, slow down. If you've never had a drink before, the last thing you want to do is down the whole thing in thirty seconds."

"Too late. Can I get another one?"

"Gracyn, you need to be careful or you're going to pass out and miss most of the party."

"Oh. Is that all? I can live with that," I said, laughing.

"No, it's not all. If you drink too much, you could end up puking your guts out. Believe me, that's no fun."

"Hmm." I quirked my eyebrows, imagining myself curled up around the toilet. "You're probably right about that."

"Trust me. I've been there. It's one of those moments that'll make you wish you were dead."

Dead. I swallowed nervously as his comment reminded me of a young girl's body found in the woods near Becca and Gabriel's property. And I was supposed to spend tomorrow afternoon with the only suspect, after receiving a blood-stained doll. Realizing I had a long way to go until I forgot all that troubled me, I held my cup out to Alex. "I still think I'd like another one."

"Didn't you hear a word I just said?"

"Yes. I heard you. But it's okay. I know what I'm doing."

Alex huffed. "Fine. One more. But that's all I'm going to get for you. I won't be responsible for corrupting you."

"I'm a big girl, and I will take full responsibility," I assured him in a mocking tone.

"Ha, ha," he mused, snatching the cup from my hand. Shaking his head, he walked back through the crowd toward the keg.

I felt a little unbalanced as I waited. Scanning the crowd, I shifted my weight from one foot to the other, hoping I wouldn't topple over and embarrass myself. But several of the other kids were already stumbling. No one would notice if I was a little tipsy.

Before Alex returned, Derek and Lacey emerged from the crowd clustered around the fire. "Gracie!" Derek boomed, slurring his words a little. "Glad to see you came out tonight."

I cringed at him calling me Gracie, but chose to ignore it. Lacey stood beside him, a cigarette dangling between her fingers, the smoke burning my throat when I caught a whiff of it. "Hi, guys," I said.

"Where's Alex?" Derek asked, looking around.

"Getting me another beer." I hiccupped on the word beer, then bit back a laugh.

Derek looked at me as if noticing me for the first time. "A beer?" he asked in astonishment.

I nodded. "Yes. What are you drinking?"

"Nothing," Lacey said, her expression bored as she took another drag on her cigarette. Then she turned, blowing the smoke away from us. "I'm driving, as usual. I don't drink. That stuff is toxic."

Derek smiled, his eyebrows raised. "That's what I love about you. I always have a designated driver."

"Just don't puke tonight. And if you pass out in the woods again, I'm leaving you there," she warned.

"You passed out in the woods?" I asked him, making a mental note not to do that. I had enough to worry about. I didn't need to risk ending up out there alone again.

"Yeah. A few weeks ago. I drank a little too much of this." Derek pulled a silver flask out of his jacket pocket.

"What's that?"

"Tequila," he answered, his blue eyes sparkling. "Want some? I'll do it if you do it."

"That sounds like a dare."

"Derek," Lacey said. "Leave the poor girl to her beer. She doesn't need any of that poison."

Derek ignored her and pulled two shot glasses out of his other inside pocket. "Don't mind her. She can be a real killjoy," he said, earning him an elbow in the ribs. "Hey, what was that for?"

"Oh, Derek," she said, frowning as she rolled her eyes at him. "Screw you." With a disgruntled huff, she took off, leaving him to gape at her retreating figure.

"Well, she's a lot of fun," I observed sarcastically.

He shrugged, turning his attention back to the bottle and shot glasses. "She has her moments. It must be that time of the month." Seeming to forget about her, he walked around me and put the glasses on the table. As he poured tequila into them, he glanced back at me. "Come on, Gracyn. You're with me in this, right?"

Turning my attention away from the crowd, I stepped over to the picnic table. I had been scouring the party for Alex, but he was nowhere in sight. "Sure. Why not? I'll try anything once," I replied.

"You'd better sit down," Derek told me. "Unless you've done tequila shots before."

"No. Never."

"That's what I figured." When I narrowed my eyes at him, he explained, "Nothing wrong with that. It's good to see you loosening up. I'm just trying to make it as painless as possible."

Laughing, I sat on the bench seat connected to the picnic table. "No pain is good. What else do I need to know?"

"Well, it's best to lick salt first and then chase it with a lime, but I have neither. So we're going to have to suffer through this. Think you can handle it?"

"Why does everyone keep asking me if I can handle it?" I groaned. Without wasting another second, I reached for one of the shot glasses.

"Just watch me." I lifted it to my lips and poured the tequila down my throat before I had a chance to think about what I was doing. I swallowed hard, coughing as it burned my mouth and throat. A few seconds later, a fire erupted in my stomach, spreading its flames through my body. My arms and legs tingled and my vision blurred for a moment, the buzz whipping through me.

"Whoa!" I exclaimed, trying to catch my breath as I slammed the glass down on the wooden table. "That's some serious stuff. Lacey wasn't kidding."

"You were supposed to wait for me," Derek said, sounding hurt. "What was that?"

I smiled, an idea forming in my mind. "Pour me another one. I'll do it with you this time."

"You serious?"

I nodded with a bold grin. "Yes."

Raising his eyebrows, he poured another shot into my glass. "Here you go."

We lifted our glasses and tapped them against each other. Staring each other in the eye, we raised them to our lips and gulped down the tequila at the same time.

The second shot was just as bad as the first one. When it reached my stomach, I felt a wave a nausea wash over me. But it disappeared quickly, and warmth replaced it. The world around me blurred as I gasped, laughing at the grimace on Derek's face.

He shook his head before smiling at me. "How are you? Doin' okay?"

"Sure. But I'm really hot all of a sudden. Where's the fire?" As I pulled my arms out of my jacket, Alex spoke up behind me.

"Over there where it's been all night. What's going on here?" He stood between me and Derek, reaching his arm over us to put a red cup on the table.

I looked up at him after discarding my jacket off to the side. Concern lurked in his eyes, a worried frown forming on his face as he studied the flask and empty shot glasses.

"Derek and I were just having a drink."

"Doing shots is risky business, Gracyn. You've never had a drink in your life and now you're doing shots after a beer?"

Rolling my eyes, I shrugged my shoulders, not caring that I seemed to be in trouble. I glanced at Derek, my eyes begging him to help.

"Geez, Alex," Derek moaned. "We're just having some fun. Lighten up, would you? You're as bad as Lacey tonight."

"That's because we both know we're going to have to take care of the two of you when you get sick all over the place."

"I'm not getting sick. What about you, Gracyn?"

"Nope. I'm good." I smiled at Alex, hoping he'd relax a little.

"Famous last words," Alex grumbled. "Come on, Gracyn. I think you've had enough. I'll take you down by the lake to get some air."

"Maybe I want to stay here."

"Gracyn, be reasonable. You don't need any more tequila. You could get really sick. People can die of alcohol poisoning."

I scoffed as Derek huffed. "I'm not going to die from having a little fun."

"Alex, what's gotten into you, man?" Derek asked. "You used to be the life of the party. You've done your fair share of tequila."

"And I learned my lesson the hard way." Alex looked back at me. "Please, Gracyn."

I shifted my gaze to Derek, shaking my head. "Sorry, Alex. I'm going to have fun whether you like it or not."

"Oh, man, don't do this. Derek, please, back me up here," Alex said.

"No, Alex. You need to be cool," Derek shot back.

Alex stood tall, his expression showing his disappointment. "Fine. Have it your way. But if anything bad happens here, it's on you, Derek." He glanced at me, his eyes still begging me to come with him.

I whipped my gaze away, my mind made up. The tequila felt too good, and I wasn't ready to stop.

As Derek filled the shot glasses, Alex disappeared into the shadows behind us. It was just as well. I didn't need anyone coming between me and my path to oblivion tonight.

25

I wasn't sure how much I had to drink. I lost track of the shots sometime after the third one. Or the fourth one. I couldn't remember exactly when it was. Before long, the voices and faces at the party blurred in the background. I had no idea where Alex had disappeared to and, as hard as I tried not to care, the truth was, I did care. He had been the one steady person in my life since I'd been uprooted from the only home I'd ever known. Deep down, I knew I had disappointed him with my choices tonight. Somehow, I'd have to make it up to him after I sobered up, whenever that might be.

"Gracie!" Derek exclaimed, slapping me on my back after he downed another shot. "I had no idea you could be so much fun. You're a lot cooler than I ever espected." His eyes were bloodshot, his breath reeking of alcohol. But who was I to criticize? Mine were probably just as bad.

I laughed as I leaned against the picnic tabletop for support. Music beat in the distance and the fire blazed, its orange flames dancing under a crescent moon. Suddenly, I felt like I was spinning out of control. Or was the world circling me as if I'd been catapulted into the center of a tornado? My stomach churned, the pizza I'd eaten earlier flip-flopping.

"Whoa," I said, gripping the table, my laughter gone. "I don't feel so good. I need to find Alex."

Derek shrugged, his movement nearly pitching him backward in his drunken stupor. "Nah sure. Go find him. Least he had the sense not to drink this stuff." Derek picked up the flask, but it slipped out of his hands and clanked against the wooden table.

I turned away from Derek and tried to stand up, but my legs wobbled as I put my weight on them. The surrounding woods and kids by the fire whipped past me, and it felt like I was being pulled in several directions at once. The crowd ahead in my sights, I walked slowly, not caring that my path was a crooked zigzag. All I wanted was to stay on my feet. I couldn't fall down. I wouldn't allow myself to admit I was so drunk, I couldn't stand up.

Somehow, I made it to the fire. Voices grew louder, but I didn't recognize any of the kids. Faces flashed in and out of focus in front of me, but I didn't see Alex anywhere. A girl with long brown hair placed her hand on my arm, stopping me. "Hey," she said softly. "Are you okay? You don't look so good."

I swayed like a tall flower blowing in the wind as I looked at her, noticing the concern in her eyes. "I'm fine," I said, pulling my arm out of her reach. Then I turned and walked away from the crowd, muttering to myself. "At least I will be. I'm gonna be okay, I just need—"

At that moment, saliva pooled in my mouth. My stomach started to heave with convulsions, pushing the contents up. Clutching a hand over my mouth, I rushed toward the woods. I wanted to get as far away from the crowd as possible before I threw up. I stumbled a little, dodging the trees I barely saw in the shadows. Branches scraped my forearms, scratching me since I'd rolled up my sleeves when the tequila made me feel warm. I was sure I'd end up with marks, but that was the last thing I cared about right now.

I ran faster, pushing myself deeper into the woods and farther away from the crowd until I could no longer hear any voices. The only sound was that of my footsteps in the underbrush. Finally, I couldn't keep it down any longer. I stopped, dropping to my knees as I retched. The stomach acid burned my throat, even after it was over.

Tears clouded my eyes and rolled down my cheeks as I realized what a mess I was kneeling in the dirt over my own vomit. I took a deep breath and tried to stand up, but my legs were weak and I fell.

The ground was cold and damp, but I didn't care. I leaned on my hands, feeling the dirt creep under my fingernails. All I wanted was for the spinning to stop. My stomach felt a little better, but not much. When my arms buckled under my weight, I lowered my shoulders to the ground. Turning onto my side, I rested my cheek on a bed of leaves. *It won't last forever. I'll feel better tomorrow. Right now, I just need to sleep,* I told myself before passing out.

"Here. Got her?" a familiar male voice asked as I came to.

Strong arms held me, one behind my shoulders and one under my knees. I cracked open my eyelids just enough to see Lucian's face sprinkled with light brown stubble. His green eyes met mine, flashing a split second of sympathy at me from under his cold glare. Then he lifted his hand to wipe a stray curl out of my face.

"Yeah. Thanks for finding her," I heard Alex say. I turned to look up at him, realizing for the first time he was the one holding me.

"No problem. Next time you might consider putting a leash on her."

"No kidding." As I felt Alex walking away, I closed my eyes again, drifting back into my alcohol-induced slumber.

I didn't remember much from that point aside from a few foggy memories of him putting me in the Jeep and buckling my seat belt. As soon as he drove off, the movement lulled me back to sleep.

I was a little more alert when we got home. A little, but not much. Alex helped me out of the car and carried me up to my room. The dogs followed him up the stairs, but Becca and Gabriel were nowhere to be found.

The only light in my room came from the hall as Alex lowered me onto the bed before scurrying about. After opening several drawers to my dresser, he turned around with a pair of gray pajamas in his hands.

Then silently, he helped me undress. I thought nothing of him stripping me down to my bra and underwear. All I wanted was to get out of my dirty clothes that smelled like vomit and damp earth. I could barely hold my eyes open during the process. It seemed like a dream. Even his hands on me, his fingers grazing my skin as he pulled my shirt over my head and replaced it with my pajama top, seemed surreal.

Alex was the perfect gentleman. I tried to unbutton my jeans, but my fingers kept slipping. When he noticed my trouble, he pushed my hands out of the way. "I'll get that," he whispered before easily undoing the button.

As he pulled my zipper down, I gasped. For a split second, I sobered up and stared at him, wondering where this would lead.

Without as much as a glance my way, he tugged the jeans down over my hips. I instinctively grabbed my underwear as it started to slide. But Alex didn't seem to notice. He kept pulling until my jeans reached my ankles and helped me kick them off. Before standing up, he held the pajama pants open and I stepped into them.

By the time the waistband slipped over my hips, I felt nervous and unsettled. Alex's closeness had a sobering effect on me. I'd never let a boy help me get dressed like this. Even in my drunken state, feeling his hands on places of my body that had never been touched before was exciting and intoxicating.

As I sat on the bed, the room started spinning. "I'm sorry," I murmured.

He frowned, stepping back from me. "You're going to be even more sorry tomorrow. We'll talk about it later. You should get in bed." He gestured to the covers behind me.

Nodding, I lifted my knees to my chest and scooted back to the pillows. Alex approached the bed and pulled the comforter over me. "You were right," I whispered, resting my head on the pillow.

"Of course I was," he said with a weak smile. He knelt beside the bed, his face at my level. "I told you I've been down this road before. I tried to warn you."

I watched him through my half-open eyes, studying his dark features and strong jaw. Several strands of hair had escaped his ponytail, falling over his shoulder. "Yeah, you did. I should have listened. I'm sorry."

He shook his head. "You don't have to be sorry to me. You're the one paying the price."

I responded with a soft huff, causing him to flinch backward. "What?" I asked.

"Your breath stinks," he explained.

Shutting my mouth, I placed my hand over it. "Sorry."

"I think you've said sorry about five times in the last two minutes." He stood up and patted my shoulder. "Get some sleep."

As he turned to leave, I shot up a little too quickly. Pain spread through my forehead, but I ignored it. "You're leaving?"

"Yes," he answered, glancing back at me.

"Can we talk tomorrow?"

Alex paused for a moment, his eyes thoughtful as if he was debating his answer. "You may be in pretty rough shape tomorrow."

"You're mad," I observed.

"No. Just disappointed. But we'll talk later. Take it easy tomorrow. Drink lots of water and eat something bland like bread."

I nodded, grateful for his advice. "I will. Thanks."

"Now I'm going to leave before Becca or Gabriel come up here to see what's going on."

Realizing there was nothing more I could say to make up for the night, I nodded before laying back down. After turning on my side, I pulled the covers up to my chin. As my eyelids fell, I heard his footsteps become faint until my door clicked shut. Then I drifted back to sleep, relieved that I no longer felt like I was spinning out of control.

When I woke up the next morning, it felt like a freight train was trampling on my head, back and forth and side to side. My lips were dry, my throat parched, and the taste in my mouth foul. My hair smelled like smoke, dirt, and vomit, and all I could think about was taking a hot shower.

I sat up a little too fast and raised a hand to my forehead. A stabbing pain shot through it as if a hammer was pounding a nail into my skull. Squinting in the sunlight that peeked around the curtain, I realized I wasn't out of the woods yet. I may have made it home, but the misery would linger. *That's what you get for doing shots. One nice long hangover that will probably stick around all day,* I chided myself.

I tried to shake my thoughts out of my mind, but one movement intensified the splitting pain in my head. Rubbing the area above my eyebrows, I took a deep breath. I had to move slowly if I wanted to get through the day.

Relax, I told myself. *It's Saturday. You can rest all day.* As soon as the words registered in my mind, I sucked in a sharp breath. I couldn't be more wrong. Lucian was expecting me at noon to work on our Art project. I didn't even have a painting for him to critique. I could give him the one of the farm I had worked on last weekend, but it wasn't finished and I didn't want to turn it in to the teacher. It was supposed to be a gift for Becca and Gabriel, although I wasn't sure if I'd be in a giving mood until they told me what they were hiding.

But I would have to deal with Becca and Gabriel later. Right now, I had to get moving. I glanced at the bedside clock. Eleven-fifteen. "Crap!" I muttered. I had forty-five minutes to shower, dress, lose the hangover, and get over to Lucian's.

I managed to accomplish three out of four. At exactly five minutes past noon, I stood in front of the mahogany doors of Lucian's massive house. Dark sunglasses shielded my eyes from the blinding sunlight. My mouth tasted minty fresh, and my jeans and black shirt smelled like fabric softener. In spite of my shower-fresh feeling, my stomach lurched with leftover nausea and my head pounded. I had taken some aspirin, but it wasn't working yet.

After ringing the doorbell, I shifted my weight with the folded easel stand in my arms. My other supplies were in the black bag hanging from my shoulder. Within a split second of ringing the doorbell, barking thundered from within the house. I had forgotten about Lucian's Doberman. Backing up a step, I cringed as each bark jolted through my head, causing excruciating pain.

Within a few moments, the barking stopped and I heard shuffling sounds inside the house. Then the door opened.

Lucian stood in front of me, scanning me with his usual cold frown. Diesel hung back behind him, his pointy ears directed at me. "You made it," Lucian commented as if he didn't believe it.

"Of course. We said noon, didn't we?" I made no move to take off my sunglasses as I studied him. He wore jeans and a white T-shirt smudged with black paint. His silver cross hung around his neck, the pendant seeming out of place against his soiled shirt.

"I'm surprised you remembered after last night."

I narrowed my eyes before realizing he couldn't see my expression behind my glasses. "You saw that, did you?"

"Yes," he confirmed coolly. "I was the one who found you in the woods. Seems to be a habit of mine."

I gasped, mortified as I remembered him giving me to Alex. "Oh. Well, thank you. I didn't realize how much I had to drink."

"Obviously." He continued to stare at me as if he wanted to say something more, but he remained quiet.

After an awkward moment, I broke the silence. "We're not going to stand here all day, are we? Shouldn't we get started?"

A faint smile tugged at his lips. "I suppose so." He pulled the door wide open and stepped aside. "Come on in."

I hoisted the easel in my arms as I started to walk in. Before I had taken two steps, Lucian reached for it. "I'll take this for you."

"Thank you," I said with relief.

Lucian backed up, holding the easel as though it was weightless. I shifted my bag strap higher up on my shoulder and walked past him.

Even though I had been in his house a week ago, the two-story foyer and double stairway were still impressive.

Diesel didn't move as he watched me. I tried to ignore him, but it was hard to pretend the huge dog wasn't watching me like I was his dinner. I stopped halfway to the kitchen entrance and turned back to Lucian as he shut the front door.

"Do you want to take your sunglasses off?" he asked.

"No."

He nodded toward the Doberman who stood perfectly still, his eyes on me. "Diesel might feel better if you did."

I glanced at the dog. "Really? Can't you just remind him I've been here before?"

"I can try, but I can't guarantee the results." Lucian's smile faded as he directed his attention at the dog. "Diesel, release."

The Doberman took a deep breath, his body relaxing. Then he turned and trotted away as if he'd lost interest in me. Needless to say, I wasn't disappointed by his departure.

Lucian walked around me and led the way into the kitchen. "Come on in and make yourself at home." He gestured to the table as he walked by it. After leaning my easel in the corner of the room, he wandered over to the stove where a blue flame was heating up a teapot.

As I set my bag down on the floor, Lucian pulled two cups out of the cabinet above the stove. They clanked against the granite, sending a new wave of pain through my head.

"Can you not make such a racket?" I complained, massaging my forehead as I took a seat at the center island. When he darted a surprised look at me, I smiled. "Sorry. My head is killing me. I took a few aspirin, but they're not helping at all."

"Of course not. Everyone knows aspirin doesn't work on a hangover. Especially a tequila hangover."

Embarrassed, I blushed at the memory of last night. "What does work?"

"My tea."

"Yeah, right," I scoffed.

"I'm serious," he said. As if on cue, the teapot started whistling softly, then erupted into a deafening shriek.

"Make it stop. Please make it stop," I begged as another stabbing pain shot through my head.

"Just be patient," he murmured, turning the stove off and moving the teapot to a cool burner. The shrieking sound silenced at once. Then he grabbed a teacup, filled it, and spun around. He approached the island and placed the cup in front of me. "Here. Drink this. You'll feel as good as new in a few minutes."

Hoping he was right even though I doubted it, I reached for the handle. Steam rose from the tea, and I felt heat through the side. "No tea bag?" I asked.

"None needed. I already added the herbs to the water. It's a homemade recipe. You can't buy it in a store."

I lifted it to my face, breathing in the minty aroma. "It smells good. What's in it?"

"It doesn't matter. All you need to know is that this will cure what ails you."

I raised my gaze to look at him, seeing a sparkle in his eyes. Mine still hid behind my sunglasses, otherwise he surely would have noticed that I didn't believe him. "Seriously?"

"The longer you ask questions, the longer you're going to suffer. Just try it. You'll get your answer soon enough."

"Fine." I lifted the cup to my mouth, blowing across the surface for a moment. Then I tilted it against my lips, tasting the herbal tea. It filled my empty stomach with sudden warmth, making me feel alert in an instant.

As I continued sipping it, a miracle happened. My splitting headache and lingering nausea disappeared. Whatever was in the tea, Lucian had been right. It really was a hangover cure.

26

"Wow," was all I said as I sipped the tea. My energy started to return with each swallow. By the time I finished, I felt as good as new. "What's in that?" I asked, amazed as I set the empty cup down.

Lucian grinned, a teasing look in his eyes. "Oh, no. I can't tell you. It's an old family secret."

"Well, whatever it is, it's a lifesaver. You guys should sell it. Seriously. You'd make a fortune."

Laughing softly, Lucian gestured around the kitchen. "I don't think we really need that."

He had a point. "Okay, so don't do it for the money. You could sell it to help your fellow man."

"And contribute to an increased propensity for people to get drunk out of their minds because they know all they have to do is drink some tea in the morning and they'll be as good as new?"

"Well, when you put it that way—"

"Besides, can you imagine the headaches we'd have getting approval from the FDA?"

"I guess I didn't think it through." I paused, then continued when my stomach rumbled. "Hey, do you have some crackers or bread? I didn't get up in time to eat before I came over here."

"Sure," he said, reaching for my cup. "But first, more tea?"

"Yes, please. That would be great."

Feeling better, I removed my sunglasses, folded them, and placed them on the counter. The light didn't bother me at all now that my hangover was gone. I watched Lucian pour another cup of tea and hand it to me.

"That's all I can give you. Any more than two cups and you won't sleep for a week."

"Really?"

Lucian stared thoughtfully at me. "Maybe that's a little exaggerated. But you probably wouldn't sleep tonight."

"Great. That's all I need," I muttered, holding the delicate teacup handle. Flashbacks of Thursday night ran through my mind. I didn't need another sleepless night tossing and turning in bed as I worried about the doll and whatever Becca was hiding. Staring down at the tea, I took another sip.

"Hey," Lucian said quietly, leaning his elbows on the island.

"What?" I asked.

"My tea isn't a reason for you to get wasted again, okay?"

I rolled my eyes with a deep sigh. The thought hadn't even crossed my mind. "Don't worry. I won't be doing that again. Ever." Pausing, I looked back down at the tea. "Even if it did help me forget," I mumbled to myself.

Before I could stop them, the troubles I had escaped last night bombarded my thoughts. My vision, cured by magic. A few heavy breather calls and a suspicious doll from someone who was obviously trying to scare me. Becca's confession that she needed to tell me what I was. Celeste's conviction that Lucian was guilty as sin, and yet, here I sat, alone with him in his kitchen. And no one knew I was here. So much for my plan to tell Becca I would be at Lucian's today. Now I just had to hope he wasn't the murderer Celeste believed him to be and that I was safe, at least for now.

"Forget what?" Lucian asked.

I whipped my gaze back to him, struggling to come up with an explanation. "Just some...stuff."

He smiled knowingly. "You've already been in Sedgewick too long. I can see that. I told you to leave, remember?" He shook his head as he turned toward the stainless steel refrigerator.

When he pulled cheese out of a deli drawer and arranged the slices on a serving tray, my mouth watered. "You should have left while you had the chance," he said.

"It wasn't possible. It's not like I have a choice in this," I replied, choosing my words carefully.

"Sure you do," he stated as he added red grapes and crackers to the tray. Then he placed it on the island before getting two small plates out of a cabinet. "I find it hard to believe a smart girl like you wouldn't be able to do something she put her mind to," he insisted, handing me a plate.

"Is that what you want? For me to leave?" I asked as I took it from him and piled it with cheese and crackers.

"I didn't say that."

"Then why do you keep pushing the issue?"

Lucian took a deep breath from where he stood on the other side of the island, his green eyes concerned. "Because in the last week, you've managed to get lost in the woods and pass out from too much tequila. Somehow, I suspect these things have never happened to you before."

"No, they haven't," I admitted quietly. "Things back home were different. They were normal." At least they had been before Sam's stepfather had gotten sick.

"Are you sure about that?" he asked suspiciously.

"Yes," I shot out.

"Tell me about Maryland and life before you moved here," he said before popping a grape into his mouth.

"There isn't much to tell. My life was actually pretty boring. I lived with my mom. She worked a lot, and I went to school. During the summer, I worked as a lifeguard."

"No wild parties out in the woods?"

I stacked a piece of cheese onto a cracker and held it. "No," I replied with a huff. I was about to take a bite when I hesitated. "Don't you have any food besides cheese, crackers, and fruit?"

"No," he stated. "That's all you get here." Then a sly grin formed on his face. "Of course there's more. But this is fast, easy, and somewhat healthy. An artist's plate."

"I'm sorry. It's nice of you to give me something to eat. I didn't mean to sound unappreciative."

"I know," he said, meeting my eyes again.

His gaze unsettling me, I forced myself to look away. Then I finished the cheese and cracker in my hand and brushed the crumbs off my fingers onto the plate. "Should we get started with our project now?"

"Sure. What are we going to paint today?"

"I have no idea," I admitted. "I was hoping you'd tell me."

He took a deep breath, sorrow washing over his face. "I haven't painted anything I really cared about in two years. At least not since... since Cassie died."

"Oh. I'm sorry."

He shrugged, and I thought I saw tears brimming in his eyes. "Thanks," he said.

"You miss her, don't you?" It was more of a statement, but came out as a question.

He nodded. "Of course. But there's no sense talking about her. She's gone, and nothing anyone can do will bring her back," he said as he started packing up the food. He returned the cheese to the refrigerator, then spun around, the emotion in his expression gone.

"We should get started. What are you in the mood to paint?" he asked.

"I don't know," I answered thoughtfully. "I like landscapes. We could paint your house with the horses in the background. I noticed there's a little fall color in the leaves today. What do you say?"

"Landscapes bore me. I like people. Expressions fascinate me. You can go ahead with the farm, but I'd rather use you as a model."

I chuckled and ran my hands through my crazy curls. "I don't think I'm in any shape to be a model today. I must look like a wreck after last night."

"No," he said quietly. "I happen to think you look perfect."

His words struck a chord in my heart. With a quick breath, I glanced at him, my eyes meeting his for an awkward moment. The silence flustering me, I pulled my gaze away from him. "You are way too kind," I said, feeling flushed.

"Just honest." Lucian paused, only continuing when I looked back at him. "One thing you'll learn about me is that I always tell the truth."

I swallowed nervously, his stare seeming to see straight through me. "Me, too."

"Then tell me what's troubling you so greatly that you chose to drown your sorrows in tequila last night."

"It's a long story," I said.

"I have all day."

"Well, it's complicated."

He cocked a half-smile. "What? Think I'm not sharp enough to follow along?"

"No," I said, shaking my head. "Not at all. I just don't know why you care. It's boring stuff. You know, normal high school girl problems."

"Really?" he asked, his voice skeptical as though he wasn't convinced.

"Yes," I insisted. "We're three weeks into school already, and I haven't even started on my college applications. Not to mention I'm falling behind in my classes. I'm starting to worry that I'm not going to make it this year."

"And none of this has to do with Alex?"

"Alex?" I asked, surprised. "No. He's been great. In fact, I can honestly say that right now, he's the best thing in my life."

"That so? So there's no pressure from him for you to do something you're not ready for?"

If my cheeks weren't already red, they surely just turned a deep shade of crimson. "No," I said. "Why would you ask something like that?"

"Alex has been known to be a ladies man. And you seem, well, please don't be offended by this, but maybe a bit inexperienced."

"Alex has been a perfect gentleman. He's made me feel completely welcome and has been absolutely amazing. If anything, I probably screwed up royally with him last night. But I did not come over here to discuss my dating life with you. I hardly even know you."

"Sorry," Lucian said, ducking his head as he looked down at the floor. "I didn't mean to pry." Glancing back up, he smiled softly. "It's just that I can tell something is bothering you."

"Like I said," I snapped. "I'll feel better once I submit my college applications. I don't like deadlines hanging over my head. Speaking of which, shouldn't we get started? Our reports are due Monday, and we don't even have our paintings ready for each other. Besides, this isn't the only homework I need to do this weekend."

"Sure. We can go now. But don't put too much effort into your homework. It's not like it'll do you any good," he said, walking around the island to the corner where he'd left my easel.

As he picked it up and approached me, my jaw dropped open. "Why do you say that? I'm planning to apply to MIT, and there's no way they'll let me in with anything other than straight A's."

"That's all well and good for now. And I wish you the best with that, I really do. But it's not necessary. Someday you'll realize MIT isn't the answer." My easel in his arms, he headed across the kitchen before stopping in the doorway. "Come on. Let's get outside while the sun's still shining." He nodded his head in the direction of the front door and then disappeared into the entry hall.

My jaw dropped open as I sat paralyzed for a moment. What was that all about? How dare he blow off my career aspirations? I stared at the doorway, lost in my questions and not sure what to say. But apparently, I didn't need to say anything. Lucian seemed to have forgotten our conversation.

I was still trying to shake it off when I heard the front door open. "Gracyn?" Lucian called. "Are you coming? We're wasting daylight."

I jumped off the stool and rushed over to the table to grab my bag of art supplies. "Yes. I'm coming," I muttered.

I attempted to push our conversation aside while we set up our easels outside on the front lawn. Losing myself in my painting always helped me forget whatever was troubling me. After securing a canvas to the easel and getting started with a brush, I focused on the beautiful scene before me. The stone mansion reached up to the blue sky dotted with clouds, the horses grazing in the background.

As I worked the brush strokes, my troubles lingered in the corner of my mind. I could escape for now, but sooner or later, I had to face the truth. The only problem was, I didn't know what the truth was. No one would be straight with me around here. Even Lucian's last comment bugged me. Maybe I could get him to tell me what he meant by that.

When I rinsed my brush in the tiny jar of water, I looked over at him. He sat straight and tall, his eyes focused on his canvas except when he shifted his gaze to me. I cringed at the thought of reviewing a painting of myself, but Lucian had given me no other choice. And the last thing I wanted to do today was argue over what he wanted to paint. I had far bigger problems to deal with.

I couldn't resist stealing glances at him every so often. His silver cross glinted in the sunlight. Diesel stretched out in the grass, his huge black shape a little intimidating even though his eyes were closed as he basked in the warmth.

By the time we finished, the sun was touching the treetops. After bringing our masterpieces in to dry on the kitchen table, we packed up our supplies and carried them back into the house.

I left my easel and bag in the foyer before following Lucian into the kitchen. "That was productive," I commented as I approached the table and stared at our artwork. Lucian's painting was much nicer than I expected. He had captured the image of me from an angle, my red curls hiding most of my serious expression.

"Yes. Very," Lucian agreed.

"I like it," I said, gesturing to his painting. "You can't even tell it's me. It's just a girl focused on her art."

"That was the point."

As I studied the painting, I felt Lucian's stare on me. When I looked up, he smiled. "What?" I asked, feeling self-conscious.

"This was nice. I haven't had a day like this in...well, in a very long time."

"A day like what?"

He quickly looked away from me. "A day of not being judged," he admitted.

I sucked in a deep breath, noticing the sadness in his voice. "I'll take that as a compliment."

"It's been really hard being back here," he blurted out, catching me off-guard. "I see the way people look at me. They stare, like I'm some kind of criminal. And I've heard the rumors. I know they all think I'm a monster."

Not sure what to say, I chastised myself for being afraid to spend the afternoon with him. At this moment, he looked like a vulnerable soul, sad and alone. Instead of saying anything, I just nodded, sympathy crowding my heart.

Lucian shifted his wistful stare to me. "Tell me, Gracyn. Do you think I murdered my sister?"

I gasped, not expecting his blunt question. Pausing, I searched for the best way to answer him. Finally, I said, "I'm pretty sure I wouldn't be here today if I believed that."

"Do you know what happened?"

Memories of what I had learned from the internet about his sister's murder came back to me. "Yes, I know enough."

"Surely, you have an opinion."

I shrugged, desperately wanting to change the subject. "It's really none of my business." *Unless the same person who killed Cassie is after me,* I thought with dread.

"It's everyone's business until we find out who did it and make them pay," he muttered, his voice laced with pure disgust. He took a deep breath, his expression softening. "I'm sorry. I told myself I wouldn't bring this up while you were here, and yet, I don't seem to have the willpower to let it lie."

"That's okay. It sounds like you just want someone to talk to. Like you said last weekend, you're all alone in this big house."

"Yes. It's both a blessing and a curse." He paused, tilting his head as he shot a thoughtful look at me. "Would you like to take a trail ride one of these days before winter gets here? The leaves will be at peak color in a few weeks, and it's really pretty."

"Um, I'm not–" I started to say I wasn't sure when he interrupted me.

"And I mean you on your horse and me on Shade. Not riding double like last time."

I blushed as I remembered holding on to him. He had felt so warm, strong, and balanced. Pushing that memory aside, I shook my head. "I don't know. I haven't ridden out on my own yet. I still can't even tack up by myself."

"That's okay. I can help you with that."

Smiling, I was trying to decide whether or not to accept his invitation when Diesel charged out of the room. His nails scraped against the floor before the front door slammed shut.

Lucian and I turned our heads toward the kitchen doorway at exactly the same moment. Zoe appeared from around the corner, her black hair flowing over her shoulders. She crossed her arms over her red sweater, her icy stare causing my heart to thump nervously. Something told me I had just overstayed my welcome.

27

I backed away from Lucian as I looked at Zoe. I had only seen her from a distance at school and her party, and we'd never met. I had a feeling our imminent introductions would be less than pleasant.

"You have company," Zoe stated coolly, her eyes flashing from me to Lucian. "I hope I'm not interrupting anything." Her voice dripped with sarcasm.

"No, of course not," Lucian responded without missing a beat. "This is Gracyn. She's new this year. She's staying next door with the Morgans."

Zoe glanced my way before redirecting her glare at Lucian. "What's she doing here?"

"There's no reason to be rude, Zoe. Gracyn and I were working on an Art project this afternoon." Their eyes locked, and tension filled the room.

After an awkward silence, I finally spoke. "But we're done now. And I was just leaving." I flashed Zoe a winning smile, hoping to crack her icy exterior, but her frozen expression didn't budge.

Giving up, I walked out of the kitchen, slipping around her. I felt her watching my every move, but I kept my eyes focused on the front door. As I stopped to pick up my easel and bag, Lucian raced up behind me with his painting. "Don't forget this," he said. "And I'll walk you out. Here, take it. I'll carry your easel."

After hoisting my bag over my shoulder, I took the canvas from him. "Thanks."

Lucian walked out with me, shutting the door behind us. Dusk had fallen, turning the sky a hazy shade of gray. Shadows stretched across the yard and driveway, putting a chill in the air and making me wish I had my jacket.

We reached the car and piled everything in the back seat, careful to place the painting on top. I moved to the driver's door, but stopped when Lucian lingered. "Sorry about Zoe. She can be a little standoffish at times."

I shrugged, trying to act like it didn't bother me. But I didn't have many friends and her cold attitude only reminded me of that. "I don't know what the big deals is. We were just working on an assignment."

He smiled. "The big deal is that you're a girl, and Zoe can be very jealous and petty sometimes."

"Then why do you go out with her?"

He looked away, a thoughtful expression crossing over his face. Glancing back at me, he explained, "We have a history. Getting back together seemed like the right thing to do when I got back to town."

I nodded, remembering the night Alex and I witnessed their reunion. I suspected there was more than what Lucian was telling me.

"I'm sorry. I didn't mean to pry. That's your personal business." I shook my head. "I think I'm still a little out of it from last night. Thanks again for the hangover cure."

"You're welcome. But I meant it when I said you can't get wasted again and show up on my doorstep expecting me to help. I might have to let you suffer next time to make sure you learn your lesson."

"Don't worry. There won't be a next time. I suffered enough last night." I smiled, suddenly surprised at how nice today had been. Unlike our previous encounters, today had been almost comfortable. He seemed to have relaxed with me which was a relief. But one thing he mentioned earlier still bothered me. "What did you mean when you said MIT isn't the answer?"

The soft look in his eyes disappeared, his expression turning cold. But he never had a chance to answer me.

"Lucian!" Zoe called from the sidewalk behind us. "Did you forget I'm waiting?"

"I have to go. We'll talk again," was all he said before whipping around and jogging back to the house.

I watched his retreating figure until I noticed Zoe staring at me, her narrowed eyes practically shooting daggers at me. I snapped my gaze away from her before scrambling into the driver's seat. My heart hammering, I pulled the door shut and started the engine. Easing the car down the driveway, I watched the house disappear from sight in the rearview mirror. My frazzled nerves started to calm down until I focused on the road ahead. Then I frowned, realizing I was going back to the very troubles I had run from the night before.

The house was quiet when I returned. After taking my easel, supplies, and Lucian's painting up to my room, I went back downstairs, hoping to find Becca. Both her SUV and Gabriel's BMW were in the driveway, so I knew they had to be here. But only the dogs greeted me when I entered the kitchen.

I stopped at the hallway entrance, debating whether or not to knock on Becca and Gabriel's bedroom door. They could be out at the barn, but the dogs were usually outside with them. It was also getting dark, and they always finished up with the horses by dusk. So I presumed they were here, but the last thing I wanted to do was interrupt them if they wanted their privacy. That could be embarrassing, for all of us.

Disappointed, I opened the refrigerator and reached for a pitcher of juice. As I shut the door with one hand, the pitcher in my other one,

I gasped when I saw Gabriel standing before me. "Gabriel. I didn't hear you." As soon as the surprise wore off, I placed the juice on the counter, forgetting about it. "But I'm glad you're here. I wanted to talk to Becca. Is she around?"

"She's in the bedroom, resting," he explained, his expression showing no emotion.

"Oh," I said with a sigh. "Will she be up later? I assume you two haven't had dinner yet."

"No, we haven't. I was just about to make something, but she won't be joining me. She had another migraine today."

"I'm sorry to hear that. Did she take her medicine?"

"Yes, but it didn't help as much as it usually does. I just gave her a sedative to help her sleep."

There went my plan to talk to her tonight. I had finally mustered the courage to ask her what she was hiding, and now I wouldn't have the chance. The other option was to bring it up with Gabriel, but I wanted an explanation from Becca because she was my sister. "Okay. I guess I'll see her tomorrow."

"Don't plan on that. She just took it and she might be out for most of the day."

"This is starting to sound serious. Shouldn't she see some kind of headache specialist or something? I mean, this can't be good for her."

"There isn't anything they can do other than treat the symptoms. She probably just overdid it out in the garden today. Sometimes the sunlight gets to her," Gabriel explained. He walked around me and snatched a wine glass from the overhead cabinet, then reached for a bottle on the counter and filled the goblet.

When he turned around to face me, he lifted his drink, twirling it in his fingers, his eyes locked on it. Then he looked up with a soft smile. "Would you like a glass?"

"Of wine?" I asked, shocked by his offer.

"Yes."

"But, I'm not—"

"Old enough?" he asked, finishing my thought for me. "One glass of wine never killed anyone. And you're not driving, at least I assume since you were out pretty late last night that you're staying in tonight."

I nodded. "That's a safe assumption." Taking a deep breath, I cringed, the scent reminding me of the tequila from last night. "But no, thank you. I'll pass on the wine."

He shrugged. "Well, it's here if you change your mind. And it might help you sleep."

My eyes flew up to meet his. I tried to find the courage to ask him what Becca knew about me, but I couldn't do it. Right now, I wanted to forget what I had overheard a few nights ago. Maybe I should ask him for one of the sedatives he'd given Becca. A long, deep sleep would be nice.

"I'll keep that in mind," I said slowly. "Well, I'm going back to my room."

"What? No dinner?"

"I'm not as hungry as I thought I was," I replied before turning and escaping up the stairs without another word.

My bedroom provided little comfort. I was exactly where I'd been two days ago with a weird doll under my bed and no answers from Becca. The party last night was already forgotten, but today with Lucian was not. He knew something, too, but I suspected getting it out of him would be harder than pulling teeth. No, I had to wait until I could talk to Becca. I just wish I knew when that would be.

Pacing my room like a caged lion, I had more energy than I expected and it surprised me. *It must be the tea,* I mused, wondering if I'd be up all night as Lucian had warned. *That's okay. I can get my Art review done and maybe some of my other homework. If I can concentrate, that is.*

A frown settling on my face, I stared at the walls, convinced it would be impossible for me to get anything productive done. With a sigh, I sat down at the desk and reached for my phone, needing a distraction. Without another thought, I dialed Alex, disappointed when my call dropped right into his voicemail. "Hi, Alex," I said. "I just wanted to say how sorry I am about last night. I'll be home all night and probably up late. I'm kind of restless, so I don't think I'll be able to sleep. Call me if you can."

I hung up, remembering when he told me I could call him in the middle of the night if I couldn't sleep. I was tempted to take him up on his offer later, but I wasn't sure if he'd answer. I knew how upset he'd been last night, and I didn't blame him. I hoped I could make things right with him, and soon. I needed a friend now more than ever.

As I stared out the dark window, my phone rang from where I still held it in my lap. I jumped with a smile, hoping it was Alex. But when I lifted the phone, my heart dropped at the words displayed across the screen. "Private Caller."

No! I thought. *I can't handle another one of these stupid calls. Just don't answer it.*

The phone chimed four times before it stopped. Dead silence came over the room and I waited to see if my voice mail notification popped up, but it never did. A few seconds later, the phone rang again and "Private Caller" flashed across the screen. Anger mixed with fear taking hold of me, I realized the mystery caller wasn't giving up.

On the fourth ring, I swiped the screen and held it up to my ear. "Whoever this is, for the last time, you have the wrong number. Stop. Calling. Me." Without waiting to hear if they would speak this time, I hung up. Then I tossed my phone onto the bed and closed my eyes, praying whoever it was would leave me alone.

Before I opened my eyes, the phone rang again. With a disgruntled huff, I stood up and pounced on my bed to grab it. I didn't even look at the caller ID this time as I answered it. "I told you to stop calling! This isn't funny anymore!"

"Gracyn?" Sam asked, her voice soft, but worried. "Is everything okay?"

Relief washed over me. I took a deep breath, feeling my body relax with a shudder as I lowered myself onto the bed. "Sam. Sorry, I got a couple weird phone calls tonight, and I didn't even check the caller ID when I answered just now."

"Weird phone calls? What's that all about?"

"I'm sure someone just got my number by accident. Or maybe it's one of those automated systems or something." I doubted it, but I wasn't about to tell her this wasn't the first time I'd gotten the strange phone calls.

"Well, whatever it is, I hope they stop soon. You sounded really upset."

"I was just frustrated. I'm a little on edge tonight."

"Why? And what are you doing even answering my call on a Saturday night? I thought I was going to have to leave you a voice mail. Where's Alex?"

"I'm not sure. We hung out last night, so I'm staying in tonight." I considered telling her about the party last night, then decided against it. The less she knew about what was troubling me, the better. My actions from last night resulted from the crank calls, the creepy doll under my bed, and Becca's secret, all of which I wanted to avoid telling Sam.

"Well, I didn't call you to check up on your dating life, even if it is more interesting than mine. I wanted to see what you're doing next weekend."

"Really? Why?"

"Because if you're not busy, my parents agreed to let me visit."

"Seriously?" Mixed emotions twisted inside me. At first, I was too excited for words. I missed Sam and the normal life I'd left behind. But with all the unexplained things going on, I wasn't sure this was the best time for her to visit. On the other hand, maybe she would put a little normal back into my life.

"Yes. So, should I work on it? Or would another weekend be better for you?"

I paused for a moment before deciding it would be great to have Sam visit for a few days. I needed the distraction, and I could count on her to help me get my priorities back in order. I had no doubt that she'd set me straight on my college applications once she found out I hadn't started working on them yet.

"No, I don't want to wait. Next weekend sounds perfect. You'll have to tell me what time you'll get here."

"I'll let you know as soon as I have an itinerary. Mom was going to make the plane reservations tomorrow as soon as I found out if you were around for the weekend."

"Okay. Is she coming with you?"

"Not sure yet. It will be either her or Dad."

There just had to be a catch to this. I never wanted to see her stepfather again. But how could I tell Sam that I only wanted her mother to come with her without explaining what he'd done to me? "You know, I'm perfectly capable of picking you up at the airport. Maybe neither one of them needs to come with you."

"I tried to tell them that," Sam said with a groan. "But they want to look at some colleges on Sunday before flying home and they're giving me that 'We really want to be a part of your life' guilt-trip. So it doesn't look like I have a choice. It just depends on their work schedules. It might be hard for Mom to get away since September is really busy for her at work."

Great. The one thing that could make me feel better was Sam coming to visit. But if her stepfather came with her, I would just as soon ask her to stay home. *I'm sure he doesn't want to see you any more than you want to see him. He'll probably get a hotel somewhere and let Sam stay here. Just enjoy her company and forget about him. He's not worth all the worrying, especially when you have bigger problems to deal with right now.*

"Okay," I said, trying to sound upbeat.

After talking for another twenty minutes, we said goodbye and hung up. When silence returned to the room, so did my restless state of mind. Leaving my phone on the bed, I stood up and fetched Lucian's painting from the top of my dresser. I sat down with it, studying every line and brushstroke. I had to admit, it was really good. He had a way of putting a lot of emotion into his work. Just looking at the picture brought back the memory of sitting on his lawn under the bright sun a few hours ago.

As if in a trance, I grabbed a pen, opened my notebook, and began to write my review.

Becca remained in bed the next day while Gabriel returned to the garden after asking me not to disturb her. I simply nodded, wondering if I'd ever have a chance to talk to her again. At this point, it seemed like she was either at work or sick. *Just be patient,* I told myself. *It feels like forever, but this, too, shall pass.*

At least I hadn't received any more phone calls from the Private Caller last night. It didn't make me feel much better, but it was a start.

I spent most of the day studying in my room. By early afternoon, I needed a break, so I headed out to the barn. I was grooming Gypsy in the aisle when I heard the hum of a car engine in the driveway. After returning the brush to the shelf where the grooming supplies were kept, I hurried out the door.

The sky was overcast, but the low lying clouds hadn't spilled a single raindrop yet. The air was cool, warranting the long-sleeved green shirt I wore with an old pair of dusty jeans sprinkled with a horse hairs. My wild curls had been pulled up into a ponytail, and I felt them brushing against the back of my neck.

I stopped a few feet outside the barn door and smiled when I saw Alex park his Jeep in front of me. Waving, I tried to rein in the grin I felt spreading across my face. He hadn't called me back last night, making me wonder if he was more upset with me than I suspected. And the longer I waited to hear from him, the more I worried he might not forgive me.

The engine shut off, and Alex hopped out of the driver's seat. After closing the door, he walked over and stopped in front of me. "Hi," he said quietly, shoving his hands into the jeans pockets buried under his navy flannel shirt tails.

"Hi," I replied, hoping to see a sign that I was back in his good graces.

"Sorry I didn't call you back last night. I got your message, but I wanted to see you in person," he said, his eyes shifting from me to the ground several times.

"That's okay," I lied as a lump lodged itself in my throat. Something told me he wasn't here to accept my apology. "So what's up?" I tried to appear upbeat and cheerful, but my tone sounded forced.

"I've been thinking a lot about Friday night, and I think we should take a break for a while."

I took a deep breath, determined to keep my composure. Nodding, I swallowed. "If that's what you want."

"It's not," he insisted, confusing me before he continued. "I liked the old Gracyn. The girl with glasses and the girl who obsessed about her grades. What happened to you?"

"I don't know, Alex. All I can say is I'm sorry. It won't happen again. You were so right about the tequila. That was really stupid."

He nodded, lifting his dark eyes to meet my gaze. "Yes, it was. And I believe you. But I need a little time. I thought we were getting somewhere. If you wanted to have fun on Friday night, there were other ways to do it. Ways that would have involved...well, me."

I gasped, my jaw dropping open. Something Lucian said yesterday came flooding back. This was about sex. It had to be. "Really?" I asked sarcastically. "You're upset because I got drunk instead of making out with you?"

Alex looked down as guilt rose into his eyes. "It's starting to be apparent that I'm a little more into you than you are into me. I'm not used to this."

"I see," I said as my eyes dried and anger replaced my hurt and disappointment. Forcing myself to stay calm, I waited until he looked up to speak again. "Alex, I'm not ready for a physical relationship. I'm not a conquest. I thought I was more to you than that."

"You are," he said sincerely. "That's why I came over here. I'm not the kind of guy who breaks up with someone through a text or email, or even a phone call. I like you, probably too much. And Friday night hurt, more than I expected."

The tables suddenly turned on me as the vulnerability in his voice tore at my soul. Maybe I should give him a little more credit. This was about more than just a physical relationship. "So what does this mean? Are you breaking up with me?"

"I don't know. Let's just give it a week or so. I need a little time."

"Okay," I said, not knowing what else to say at this point. Relationships were new territory to me. As much as I wanted to beg him to give me another chance, I was afraid he'd run away faster if I did that.

"Well, see you," he said before walking back to the Jeep.

No more words were spoken as he hopped into the driver's seat and drove away. I felt a tear roll down my cheek, and I folded my arms across my chest. Watching the Jeep disappear down the driveway, I had never felt so alone in my entire life.

Not sure what to do, I ducked into the barn and approached Gypsy. Then I buried my face against her soft neck and cried.

28

The following week was painful. There was no other way to describe it. Alex avoided me, even in Calculus where he used to sit next to me and offer to help me every day. Celeste was tired and moody. I saw her a few times, but she just said "Hi" before running away. Lucian clammed up again, giving me the cold shoulder as if we hadn't Saturday afternoon together. Every time I saw him in the hall, Zoe clung to his arm and he whipped his eyes away when they met mine.

Becca managed to get to work on Monday, and somehow became unavailable every evening. I had no chance to talk to her, except at dinner and, as luck would have it, Gabriel was home. He had taken the week off to get ready for the weekend festival. So I didn't have a minute alone with her. To make matters even worse, I realized it had been over two weeks since I'd spoken to my mom. We texted and emailed, but I longed to hear her voice. I made a mental note to call her before going to bed one night, just to catch up.

Sam was the only one who lifted my spirits that week. She texted me on Monday with her itinerary for the weekend as she'd promised. She would arrive in Boston early Friday afternoon, putting her in Sedgewick around five o'clock. I couldn't wait to see her. I needed her now more than ever since moving, but she'd never know that. I was determined to be the perfect hostess and show her the good things about living in Sedgewick. If only I knew what those were.

Tuesday evening at dinner, I sat with Becca and Gabriel at the table, twirling spaghetti around my fork even though I wasn't really hungry. I found it hard to focus on food when I had so many unanswered questions. But I didn't want to ask them in front of Gabriel. So I pretended everything was great even though I could tell something was off with Becca. Her eyes, usually so vibrant and alert, were tired and dull.

"I have some news," I said, breaking the silence amidst the forks clanking against the plates. "My friend from Maryland is coming to visit this weekend. Is it okay if she stays with us?"

Becca shifted her gaze to me as soon as I spoke. "Of course. That sounds wonderful. Do you have any plans for the weekend?"

I shrugged. "Not really. She'll only be here Friday night through Sunday morning because she's going to visit some colleges before she flies home."

"Are you going to the colleges with her?" Becca asked.

"No," I said, my thoughts dark as I remembered that Sam's stepfather was bringing her. At least he would just be dropping her off Friday night and picking her up Sunday morning. Hopefully he wouldn't even get out of the car. "I can do that any weekend, and I'm a little behind in my homework. I need to get caught up on Sunday."

"What about Saturday? The Harvest Festival will be going on in town. You girls should plan to come," Gabriel suggested.

"Maybe. What will there be to do?" I asked.

"Oh, there's lots of stuff," Becca said. "During the day, there will be arts and crafts as well as food vendors. That's where we'll be. But as soon as the sun goes down, there's a band and the restaurants set up tables outside where you can eat under the stars while listening to music."

My heart fell as soon as Becca brought up the band. I already knew about the concert in the park. Before my tequila binge, Alex had mentioned they would be playing at the festival. I wasn't sure I wanted to go now, but what else would I do with Sam? Ask her to sit around the house all night and play Scrabble? If I did that on her only weekend here, I'd be the most pathetic friend ever.

"That's a good idea," I said, trying to sound interested rather than depressed. "She'd like that. Will you two be sticking around for the band?"

Becca glanced at Gabriel, concern in her eyes. When she looked back at me, she smiled. "We'd like to, but it'll depend on how the day goes."

I nodded, wondering if she was thinking about her headaches. Before I could say anything more, she and Gabriel launched into a conversation about the festival. My mood suddenly bleak over the thought of watching Alex play on stage Saturday night, I tuned them out and focused on trying to eat in spite of my nonexistent appetite.

Friday afternoon, Lucian was already at our bench when I arrived to Art class. As I sat down and started rummaging through my book bag, I glanced at him. He smiled, catching me by surprise, and I nearly fell off my chair. Instead, the notebook I was pulling out of my bag dropped to the floor, causing everyone including Ms. Friedman to stare at me.

"Sorry," I muttered, reaching for it. I hated drawing attention to myself. Fortunately, everyone seemed to grow bored with me and shifted their focus back to the front of the room.

I sat quietly, drumming my fingers on the table as Ms. Friedman dribbled off names for the roll call. Looking straight ahead, I was painfully aware of Lucian watching me the whole time.

After Ms. Friedman finished, she reached for a stack of papers on her desk. "I finished grading your reviews and will be passing them back. I encourage you all to read my notes and share them with your partner. Overall, I thought they were very well done. I'm impressed."

The students gaped at her, seeming shocked by her comments.

While Ms. Friedman scurried about the room to give each paper back to its owner, whispers rose above the quiet. I looked at Lucian, my eyes instantly locking with his. "What?" I asked, his attention making me nervous.

"How is your day going?"

"Fine," I said, confused by his sudden interest. "Why do you care?"

"I was just making conversation. But we don't have to talk if you'd prefer not to."

"No, I wouldn't prefer that. I'm just surprised, that's all. I don't know why you chose today to be nice. You've ignored me all week," I explained.

Before he could respond, a throat cleared at my side, and I turned to see Ms. Friedman holding my paper out to me. I hoped she hadn't been standing there long. "Here, Gracyn. Nice job. Lucian, I think you'll be pleased to read her review."

I snatched the paper from her outstretched hand. "Thank you," I said, still a little miffed at Lucian.

I was hoping Ms. Friedman would leave, but she remained at our desk. After ruffling through the papers, she found the one she was looking for and extended her arm over me to hand it to Lucian. "Here you go, Lucian. Very interesting. You are years beyond your age. I'm impressed." Without any further explanation, she moved away to deliver the rest of the papers.

I raised my eyebrows, curious. I was about to ask him for his review when Ms. Friedman returned to the front of the room empty-handed. "Okay everyone," she said above the chatter. "Time to get started now." She paused, waiting as the voices simmered down until silence fell over the class. "That's better. I'll finish up a few minutes early today so you all can read what your partner wrote. But for now, let's get to work."

Class that afternoon was the usual. I followed along easily enough, grateful for the break from my academic classes. The time passed quickly, and Ms. Friedman ended early as promised.

I turned to Lucian while the voices in the room started up again. "Here," I said, pushing my review toward him. I was quite proud of what I had written, and I wanted to watch his expression when he read it.

"Thanks," he said hesitantly, seeming a little concerned.

I smiled reassuringly. "Don't worry. It's not bad. I was really impressed with your work. I think you'll be happy with what I said."

His eyes shifting nervously, he took the paper from me. But he neglected to fork over his review of my painting.

"Aren't you forgetting something?" I asked.

"Am I?"

"Yes. Your paper. Ms. Friedman seemed pretty impressed."

"Oh, yeah, that." He finally slid it over to me. But when I tried to take it, he held on to it for a moment. "You know, maybe we should wait. We don't have to do this now, do we?"

My smile fading, my heart nearly fell into my stomach. I had a bad feeling I wasn't going to like what he'd written. "No. Now is a perfect time," I said with sarcastic sweetness. Ripping the paper away from him, I took a deep breath.

I sensed him stiffen as I looked down, first noticing the big capital A circled at the top of the page. But his grade didn't put my worries at ease. If anything, it filled me with dread. Biting my lip, I began to read.

At first, it wasn't too bad. But as I continued, I had to bite back tears. He claimed my brushstrokes were stiff, my lines rigid, and my colors a little off. He went on to state that the piece evoked no emotion, calling it flat and one dimensional. He suggested I find subjects that meant something to me and allowed me to put my heart into my work. In a nutshell, he hated it.

I read the three paragraphs of scathing criticism twice, holding my tears at bay the whole time. I couldn't believe he was so heartless. What had I ever done to make him hate me so much?

As I turned his paper over, never wanting to see it again, Lucian watched me. "Gracyn," he said. "You're mad."

"Nope," I replied, staring straight ahead while I pushed it toward him.

"Yes, you are. Admit it."

I swallowed the lump in my throat and took another deep breath. "No, I'm not mad. Crushed maybe, but not mad."

"I did this to help you."

I whipped my head to the side, tears welling up in my eyes. "Gee, thanks. Everyone needs a little criticism to be helped."

"That's–"

I quickly cut him off. "I said a little criticism. You ripped me to shreds. There isn't one positive thing in there."

"That's not true. You must not have read the very end."

I raised my eyebrows, but didn't take the paper back to find out what he was talking about.

"I said I think you have talent, but that it will only shine through once you lift the darkness from your heart. Find something you love to paint. Give it life. Put your soul into it. That's the mark of a real artist."

"So you're saying I'm not a real artist?"

"That's not what I meant."

"Then what did you mean?"

"Gracyn, you're taking this all wrong."

"Am I?" I reached down for my book bag in anticipation of the bell that would ring any minute. Pulling it into my lap, I glared at him. "This is all I have right now. Painting is the only thing keeping me sane. Thanks for ruining it for me."

Before he had a chance to respond, the bell rang. I jumped up and pushed my way around the other students to get to the hall. Tears clouding my vision, I realized Lucian Dumante was nothing more than an arrogant jerk and I never wanted to lay eyes on him again.

I barely made it to my locker before Lucian caught up to me. As I reached for my jacket, two arms extended on my sides, trapping me. The gray thermal sleeves were the same material as the shirt Lucian was wearing today. Forgetting about my things, I whipped around to meet his familiar green eyes. Leaning against the open locker, I wished I could escape.

But he inched closer to me, his chin spotted with light brown stubble and his expression solemn.

Then I blinked, and everyone in the hallway disappeared. Silence fell over us, the kind of quiet that was so still, I could almost hear my heart beating. I sucked in a sharp breath, not sure what was going on. "What...what are you doing? How'd you do that?"

"Do what?" Lucian asked slyly, ignoring the fact that he had somehow erased everyone around us.

"You know."

"No, I don't. Explain it to me."

"The students in the hall. Where'd they go?"

He smiled with satisfaction. "I dropped a cloak over them so we can get a moment to ourselves. I didn't want to end the week on such a bad note. You ran off before I could make things right."

"What did you expect after you wrote that scathing review?" I shifted my eyes nervously, hoping to catch a glimpse of life around us. But I saw nothing. Not one movement or a single soul.

"That you would take it as I meant it. As a constructive review to help you identify your weaknesses. That's the first step in learning how to overcome them."

"Hmm," I choked out. "You sure thought I had a lot of them."

Lucian shook his head. "If you want to pursue art as something more than a hobby, you're going to need a thicker skin."

"Thanks. Another weakness." I frowned, narrowing my eyes at him. He was simply insufferable.

He paused for a moment, his expression thoughtful. "I think you have a very sensitive soul. But your artwork shows just how tense you are. The fact that your emotions are transparent in your work is a good thing. An emotional artist is a successful artist. You have amazing potential."

"Then why didn't you include that in your paper?"

"Perhaps I overlooked it. The problem is, tension isn't an emotion you want to show in art. You need to loosen up, relax. Show joy, love, sorrow, even fear, but not tension. People cringe at tension, but they're drawn to softer emotions that they want to feel."

He moved a hand away from the wall to touch the side of my face. As he ran his fingers down my hairline to my jaw, a fire erupted under them. My breath catching in my throat, I felt paralyzed, unable to move a muscle. I braced my back against the open locker, thankful my shoulder blades reached each side, preventing me from falling into it.

"You know what one emotion makes for the best art?" he whispered.

I shook my head, my eyes locked with his, my voice lost as I fought to keep my composure. Everything about him captivated me, putting me into a mesmerizing trance.

He leaned toward me, his lips brushing against my ear. "Love," he whispered, his breath warm on my neck.

My heart pounded at a runaway pace while a tingling sensation raced through me, reaching all the way down to my toes. Frozen, I could barely breathe when he moved to face me again, his smoldering eyes studying me as though memorizing every detail.

"I sense you don't have enough of it in your life. Perhaps you haven't found the right person. Or you have, and you're scared to let go," he explained.

I gasped, my mind reeling. "What?" I asked with a deep huff.

He never answered. I blinked again and found myself alone in the crowded hallway. Lucian was gone as if he'd disappeared into thin air. The other students clamored about, talking excitedly and slamming lockers. Two football players wearing letterman jackets barreled through the crowd, laughing as everyone scrambled out of their way.

I looked down the hall in one direction, then the other, searching for Lucian. But he was nowhere to be seen. I shook my head, watching the other students for any sign they knew what had just happened, but they were oblivious. They had no idea that time had stopped for a few minutes, erasing them from the hallway.

But I remembered it vividly. Every word Lucian said was etched into my mind. I wouldn't forget it soon, and possibly not ever. Taking a deep breath, I turned back to my locker, my legs still a little weak. After putting on my jacket, I hoisted my book bag over my shoulder and shut the metal door. Then I turned and began to weave around the students, hoping my weekend with Sam would distract my thoughts away from Lucian's criticism and hallway trick. As if there was a chance.

29

Everything changed the minute Sam showed up. When I heard the car pull into the driveway at five-thirty that evening, I raced outside, careful to keep the dogs in the house. From the porch, I waved as Sam climbed out of the rented sedan and plucked her suitcase from the trunk. I kept my eyes focused on her even though I was painfully aware of her stepfather watching me from the driver's seat. One glance at him brought it all back. His thinning hair, stern expression, and ogling eyes were enough to make me nauseous. But I forced myself to focus on Sam as she carried her suitcase across the gravel.

Brown hair fell to her shoulders, and bangs swept across her forehead. She wore jeans, black boots, and a navy sweater, her jacket folded in the crook of her elbow. With a smile, I headed down the steps to meet her when her stepfather drove away. As soon as the car disappeared, I felt free to enjoy her company.

"Sam! I can't believe you're here!" I said, approaching her.

She stopped and dropped her suitcase to the ground. After pulling me into a quick hug, she stepped back. "It's about time you came down from the porch!" she teased in true Sam fashion, her chocolate-colored eyes sparkling. Then she gestured around her. "This is gorgeous! I can't believe you get to live in such an amazing place. It's like heaven. You never told me how beautiful this is. Do you think your sister and her husband will let me move in?"

I almost felt guilty from her envy. I hadn't enjoyed being here as much as I should have. It was beautiful, but sometimes I didn't see the beauty because I was too busy worrying about our brooding neighbor, fielding crank calls, and wondering what terrible secret Becca was keeping from me. "It may seem nice now, but if you stay long enough, you'll get bored. It's a pretty small town."

"That works for me. Like I do much more than go to school back home anyway. So where's your main squeeze? Am I going to meet him tonight?"

My spirits falling, I reached for her suitcase. "No," I said quietly, not wanting to talk about Alex. "I'll explain later. Let's go inside now. You must be tired from your flight. You can freshen up, and then we'll get something to eat."

I led the way up the porch steps, lugging her suitcase with me. Sam followed me into the house, but stopped once inside as I continued to the stairs. When I realized she was no longer behind me, I turned to see her standing near the door staring in awe at the house.

"Wow!" she gushed, her eyes shining with amazement. "This is something else. It's even nicer on the inside than it looked from outside. I can't believe your sister lives here. It's like she made it over the rainbow. What a life!"

"I know. And she's really happy, too. I keep hoping I'll have half as much when I'm her age." *Aside from the headaches,* I thought.

"Where is she, anyway? I can't wait to meet her. Of course, I'll probably just be jealous and wish I had a cool older sister instead of being stuck with a moody pre-teen little brother."

"He won't be a pre-teen forever," I reminded her.

"No, next he'll be an annoying high schooler."

"Only you won't be there for him to annoy."

She perked up at that thought. "Good point. But where is Becca? I really want to meet her."

"I don't know. If I had to guess, she's probably out at the garden. There's a festival in town tomorrow, so she and Gabriel are packing up their vegetables to sell. I guess it's kind of a hobby of theirs. You'll get to meet her, I promise. Just not now. Come on." I waved toward the stairs. "Let's go on up and put your suitcase away."

Sam crossed the living room and followed me up to my room. Stepping through the doorway, she smiled. "So this is your room. Wow, this is so cool." She walked over to the bathroom and pushed the door open. "You even have your own bathroom. So much privacy. You must love it here."

"It's fine, for this year," I replied. "Feel free to use the bathroom and get settled. I'll wait. Then maybe we can order a pizza."

Sam turned to look at me, disappointment lurking in her eyes. Leaning against the wall, her jacket folded over her arms, she took a deep breath. "Okay, what's going on? First, you mentioned that I won't be meeting Alex tonight, and now we're staying in? What happened to all those parties you've been going to?"

Dodging her gaze, I looked at the floor for a moment. I felt a little guilty for not telling her Alex wanted a break from our relationship, but I only wanted to spare her the awful details of my encounter with tequila and the sickness that followed. "Alex and I are kind of on a break," I finally admitted.

"What?" She gaped at me, her jaw dropping. "Why didn't you tell me? At least then I wouldn't have brought him up. What happened?"

I quickly relayed as little of the story as I thought she would accept. When I finished, I raised my shoulders with a huff. "So that's it. I screwed up, and now he doesn't want to see me anymore. If it makes you feel any better, sometimes when his band has a gig, they practice the night before. So even if Alex and I weren't on a break, you and I would probably be staying in tonight anyway."

"I don't care about that, silly," Sam said as she crossed the room and sat down on the bed next to me. Putting her arm around me, she leaned in close. "I hate to see you upset. Now I don't like him very much."

"But I deserve it."

"No," she objected. "You don't. You made a mistake. Everyone makes mistakes. And it's not like you made out with someone else or that you go out and get drunk every weekend. What a jerk. He could have cut you some slack for the first time."

Taking a deep breath, I turned and scooted back to face her. "You're just trying to make me feel better."

"Of course I am. So what happened this week? Has he talked to you since he told you he wanted a break?"

"No," I said. "Not at all. My week pretty much sucked." I mustered a bright smile. "But it's a lot better now that you're here. And we're not going to sit around all weekend so I can feel sorry for myself. Tomorrow, we're going to the festival. His band is playing and they're really good. You'll like them."

In spite of my cheerful tone, Sam frowned. "Really? Why would you want to take me to hear his band play after what he did to you?"

I shrugged. "Because this weekend isn't about me and my problems. It's about showing you a good time."

"You don't need to entertain me. I'm here because I'm your friend and I want to catch up."

"I know," I said with a smile I didn't need to force. "But I'll be fine tomorrow. And we have plenty of time to talk tonight. So get cleaned up and I'll order the pizza." I jumped up to my feet. "Meet me downstairs in five?"

"Okay," Sam said. "You're really cool, you know that?"

"Must be this northern climate. But I have to order the pizza soon or it won't get here until late. There's only one pizza place in town and they're really busy on Friday night."

Without waiting for her to say another word, I left the room and headed downstairs. After calling in an order for a large cheese pizza and garlic bread sticks, I opened the refrigerator to look for something to drink. As I scanned the shelves, Becca appeared looking freshly showered with wet hair dripping onto her black sweater.

"Hi, Gracyn," she said as I shut the door. "Is your friend here?"

"Yes. She arrived about ten minutes ago. She's upstairs settling in. I just ordered a pizza for us. How was your day?"

Becca slipped around me, poured water from the faucet into a teapot, and placed it on the stove. After she turned on the burner, she smiled. "Good. Better, actually. I feel like I'm finally coming out of a funk. Just in time for the festival, too. I need to be at my best tomorrow if I'm going to get through the day."

"I'm glad to hear it. You look a lot better." And she did. Her eyes were bright and cheerful, her complexion flushed and warm. For once, she didn't look tired and worn out.

"Thanks. Would you like some of this tea? I'm making enough for all of us."

"What kind is it?"

"Cinnamon spice."

I nodded. "Sounds yummy. I bet Sam would like some, too."

"What would I like?" Sam asked from across the room before appearing at the island.

"Some of Becca's tea," I explained. "Sam, this is Becca. Becca, I'd like you to meet my best friend in the world, Samantha."

They exchanged greetings and shook hands. "I've heard a lot about you," Sam told Becca.

"All good, I hope," Becca teased.

"Of course," I assured her.

"Well, why don't you girls have a seat and catch up. I'll bring the tea over when it's ready."

"Thanks, Becca," I said before leading Sam to the couch. As we sat down, Sam turned to me.

"She's great," she whispered. "I love your sister already. You are so lucky."

I raised my eyebrows, not sure what to say. Finally, I answered, "Yes, I suppose so." But doubts crept into my mind as I wondered again what Becca was hiding. She seemed to be in good spirits tonight, but with Sam here, I couldn't ask her the questions that had been on my mind all week.

Sam and I chatted for a few minutes before Becca carried three cups of steaming tea over on a silver platter. She sat down and the three of us talked while enjoying the tea and waiting for the pizza. A few minutes later, Gabriel joined us after he finished putting the horses in for the night.

Sam was enchanted with Becca and Gabriel, asking questions and listening to their stories about the town. I was grateful for their presence tonight. I'd been worried that all Sam would want to talk about was Alex, but Becca and Gabriel provided the perfect distraction.

Later, long after the sun went down and we finished the pizza, Sam and I bid goodnight to Becca and Gabriel and headed up to my room. "Wow," Sam said as she walked over to my bed and sat down on the edge.

"You can stop saying that," I teased, shutting the door. "You've said wow about ten times now."

"I know. I just can't get over your new life. And look at you. There's something different about you, but I haven't been able to figure out what it is all night. So tell me because it's driving me nuts."

I scrunched my eyebrows, confused. "I don't know," I said. "Is it how I look?"

"Yes, and no. I mean, that's part of it. But it's something else."

"My hair?" I guessed.

"Sort of. I love it straight. You rarely wore it straight at home. Do you blow it dry a lot now?"

I suddenly realized what she picked up on. A smile sliding over my lips, I beamed. "Yes, as a matter of fact, I do. And I do a lot of other things differently now that I don't need my stupid glasses or contact lenses."

"What?" she asked, drawing in a sharp breath. "You had Lasik surgery? When did that happen and why didn't you tell me? Seriously, what's with all the secrets?"

"Nothing. And I didn't get Lasik. I don't know what happened. I woke up one morning and I could see. Pretty crazy, isn't it?"

"I'd say." Sam watched me before a grin escaped her lips. Then she turned and scooted back on the bed until she could reach the small square pillow. She grabbed it and threw it at me.

I turned just in time for it to hit my shoulder before falling to the ground. "Hey!" I said, laughing. "What was that for?"

"For everything you haven't told me. So, now that we're alone, tell me what's really on your mind."

My smile fading, I shifted my gaze to the window. Night had fallen, and pitch black rolled out beyond the glass. I was trying so hard to make Sam believe everything was great, and yet she knew something was troubling me. How did she do that? *Probably because she's been your best friend since kindergarten,* I reminded myself. *So come up with something, anything, or you know she's not going to let it go.*

"You're right," I admitted, looking back at her. "I've been so busy getting acclimated to everything around here that I feel like I'm falling behind in my priorities. My grades are not where they should be right now."

"The year just started. You have plenty of time to catch up."

"I haven't started my college applications, either. I bet you've already sent yours out."

"Not yet. But they're on my desk at home and a few are finished. I'm just waiting for Mom to write the checks for the application fees."

"See?" I groaned. Shaking my head, I walked over to the bed and plopped down on my back. I stared up at the ceiling as Sam scooted next to me. "I'm losing it, Sam. One boyfriend has come and gone, and suddenly my life is out of control." That wasn't the exact truth, but it was close enough.

I felt her reach for my hand and squeeze it. "That's what I'm here for. Tomorrow, I'm going to help you get your act together. We'll get you organized during the day so we can enjoy the party. Okay?"

Looking up, I met her warm brown eyes. "Okay. Thank you."

"No problem. That's why I'm here. You need me."

"Yes, I do. You're the best, you know that?"

Sam just smiled before jumping up to change into her pajamas. I lay on the bed for a few more minutes, realizing how glad I was that she was here, even if her stepfather had brought her.

30

The next day, I showed Sam the rest of the property. She helped me with the chores and enjoyed meeting the horses, particularly Gypsy. We took a short stroll through the woods to the garden, although there wasn't much to see now that Becca and Gabriel had cleared out the fruits and vegetables to take them to the festival. I avoided going any farther into the woods. The last thing I wanted was to walk by the trail leading to Lucian's estate. I hadn't mentioned a single word about him to Sam, and I wasn't about to tell her that a two-year-old murder involving the neighbors had yet to be solved.

When we arrived at the festival that afternoon, we wandered through the streets, stopping by some of the vendor tents to look at the merchandise. Booths displaying jewelry, handbags, knitted scarves, and mittens were mixed in with those selling locally grown produce, meat, and cheese. By the time we found Becca and Gabriel, they were sold out and packing up to head home.

"How'd it go?" I asked as Gabriel stacked up the empty crates.

Becca leaned on the table, gesturing to the open space. "Everything is gone. And Gabriel stocked up on some meat for the winter. All in all, it was a good day. It looks like nearly the entire town showed up."

I swept my gaze down the street, watching the people milling about. Even parking had been hard to find this afternoon. "That's great to hear."

"I can't blame anyone for coming out on a day like today," Sam gushed. "Is the weather around here always this perfect?"

I glanced up at the bright blue sky. The air was comfortably warm in the sun, but a bit chilly in the shade. By nightfall, a jacket would be needed.

Becca nodded. "Actually, this festival is known for the weather. Somehow, we always luck out. A lot of people come from Boston and New York for the weekend."

"Becca," Gabriel said, putting the last wooden crate on a utility cart. "I just need to fold up the tables, and we can get going."

"Okay," she said, tossing a smile at him before turning her attention back to us. "You girls look nice. Are you going to stay and listen to the band?"

"Yes," I answered, hoping she wouldn't mention Alex. Although I couldn't help noticing her compliment. I had deliberately chosen my most flattering jeans, a cream-colored sweater, and tall brown boots for tonight. My hair flowed in waves over my shoulders, partially hiding gold hoop earrings. My plan was to show up having the best time possible and let Alex eat his heart out. And maybe I'd find someone to flirt with. A little jealousy might be good for him.

Good luck with that, a sarcastic voice rippled through my thoughts. *Alex was your first real boyfriend. Who are you going to flirt with to make him jealous? Lucian? Yeah, right. He's as shady as they come. And he might not even show up. Besides, if he does, Zoe will probably be hanging on his arm and then he won't give you the time of day.*

Pushing my thoughts aside, I mustered a smile. "Sam's looking forward to hearing the band."

"Not as much as I am to seeing Alex," Sam said, her eyebrows raised at me.

Ignoring her knowing look, I smiled. "What are you doing tonight, Becca? Are you and Gabriel coming back?"

"I don't think so," she said with a sigh. For the first time this afternoon, I noticed how tired she looked, and my heart sank at the thought of her fighting another headache. "We've been out here all day and I'm exhausted. But you two have fun. We won't wait up." There was the carefree big sister I had grown to love over the last few weeks.

"Thanks," I said. "We'll see you either later tonight or in the morning. Come on, Sam. Let's get some dinner before the band starts."

After saying goodbye to Becca, Sam and I headed down the street to The Witches' Brew where tables had been set up along the sidewalk. We found an empty one and took a seat while we waited for menus.

"The Witches' Brew?" Sam asked, glancing at the sign overhead. "Well, that's interesting."

"I know. It's kind of a joke with the locals. Everyone thinks it's a funny name."

"But it's very New England. Reminds me of the witches of Salem. I think it's pretty cool. I know I'm not in DC, that's for sure." Sam's eyes lit up as she talked, her brown curls resting on her shoulders. She looked great tonight in a purple sweater and jeans.

"No, we're definitely not back home."

"But this is your home now," she reminded me.

"Yeah," I mused, nodding. "It is. It's hard for me to think about Maryland these days. I mean, a lot has happened since I moved here. And since I know there's no going back, I think I've accepted that I belong here. At least for now."

"Accepted it? You make it sound like it's punishment."

"I didn't mean it that way. I just don't want to get attached since I'll be moving again after the year is over."

"Good point."

A waitress arrived at our table and handed us a few menus. From that point, we talked less as we studied the entrée selection.

Dinner flew by and, before I knew it, we were wandering through the crowd on our way to the concert. The sun had dropped below the horizon, tinting the sky purple. Streetlamps glowed, lighting up the sidewalk cafes still bustling with patrons. As we approached the park surrounded by a white picket fence, the crowd grew thicker. Kids and adults lingered on the sidewalks and within the fence, many of them holding a drink. The occasional drum beat or guitar chord struck out over the voices as the band set up on the stage.

I led the way, searching for anyone I knew. Weaving around the bodies, I saw Celeste in the far corner. But when I looked again, she was gone. As I scanned the surrounding area to see if I could find her, I bumped into someone. "Oh, sorry," I said, turning to see a pair familiar brown eyes. Mr. Wainwright stood in front of me, his hand wrapped around a bottle hidden in a brown paper bag. "Mr. Wainwright. I didn't expect to see you here."

A lopsided smile crossed his lips. His eyes were bloodshot, his chin and jaw covered in scruff a little longer than usual. "Why wouldn't I be here?" he asked, his words slightly slurred. The whiff of alcohol on his breath didn't surprise me.

"I don't know. I guess you would be," I replied, feeling awkward.

He gestured to Sam who stopped beside me. "Who's this?"

"Um, this is Samantha, a friend of mine from Maryland. She's just visiting this weekend. Sam, this is my History teacher, Mr. Wainwright."

"Hi," she said. "Nice to meet you."

He wobbled a little before another smile formed on his face. "You, too. I hope you're enjoying your visit."

"I am. It's a beautiful town. I told Gracyn she's really lucky. I'd trade places with her any day."

"Well, even small towns have their demons," he said, his smile suddenly gone. Raising his brown paper bag in the air as if in a toast, he nodded. "I hope you ladies enjoy your evening. I'm off to get a refill." Without waiting for a response, he breezed past us and disappeared into the crowd.

"As if you need one," I muttered.

"What was that?" Sam asked.

I explained that Mr. Wainwright was the notorious town drunk, conveniently leaving out the way he singled me out from time to time.

He rubbed me the wrong way, and I couldn't help wondering if he was behind the phone calls and the doll. Shuddering, I realized I was starting to let my fear take over again.

Determined to have a good time, I changed the subject. "But I know you don't want to waste time talking about my teacher. Come on, let's try to get closer to the stage." I spun around and continued leading her through the crowd, the stage ahead in my sights. The instruments and microphones had been set up, but the band members were hanging out below the stage, talking with friends.

I had only taken a few steps when Derek appeared in front of me. He stopped and smiled, his head tilting to one side as he gazed past me. "Gracyn. I'm glad you came out tonight. Who's your friend?"

"Oh, no," I warned. "You're not going after her, too."

"Why not?"

"What happened to Lacey?"

He shrugged. "We're off again. It's no big deal, just the story of our entire relationship. But that means I'm a free agent tonight." His blue eyes hovered on Sam who inched up beside me.

"Hi," she said. "If Gracyn isn't going to introduce me, I will. I'm Samantha, but you can call me Sam. I'm visiting from Maryland."

"It's very nice to meet you, Sam," Derek said, a huge grin spreading across his lips. "Well, if I can't land one big city girl, maybe I can charm the other one."

Rolling my eyes, I searched for the best way to cut off this conversation before it went any further. But I never had the chance. Someone tapped my shoulder from behind and I whirled around to face Alex. At that moment, my courage crumbled at my feet.

He smiled softly, an apologetic look crossing over his face. "Hi."

"Hi." My heart fluttering, I wondered why he was talking to me after giving me the cold shoulder all week. An awkward few seconds passed before I spoke. "What are you doing here? You sure you have the right girl?"

"Yes, I'm sure. If she'll listen to me," he answered, his voice filled with hope.

I folded my arms across my chest and took a deep breath. "Okay. I'm listening."

"I don't have a lot of time, but can I see you tomorrow? I want to talk, just not here. It's too crowded and I only have a minute."

Fighting back a huge smile, I nodded. "Sure." Butterflies rose up inside me. I wanted him back in my life so badly. This past week was the worst one I'd had since moving here, and it was all because I missed him.

"Okay. I'll come out to your place. I'll text you when I know what time I'll be there."

My composure intact, I nodded slightly. "Sam is leaving around ten, so any time after that is fine."

"After ten it is." He offered an apologetic smile, his dark eyes meeting mine. "And I'm sorry."

"We'll talk more tomorrow," was all I said before Sam snuck up beside me. Just like that, the tension in the air dissipated.

"Who's this?" Sam asked.

"Alex. Alex, meet Sam, my friend from Maryland."

As Alex and Sam shook hands and said hello, Derek clamped a hand on Alex's shoulder. "Hey, man. We need to get up on stage. We're opening in a few minutes."

"Got it," Alex said before glancing at me. "See you soon?"

I nodded. I wasn't sure what tomorrow would bring or how I would react to whatever he said, but at least there was hope now.

Alex and Derek walked away from us, their black shirts making it almost impossible to see them in the dark. Then Sam turned to me. "So that's Alex?"

"Yes," I replied.

"He is so not your type," she said. "I'm surprised you two were an item."

I raised my eyebrows at her. "Maybe he is my type and I just didn't know it. But he's really nice, or at least I thought he was."

"And now he wants to talk. He probably wants to get back together with you. What are you going to do?"

"I'm not sure. But I'm not going to think about that tonight because I don't even know what he wants. Maybe he just wants to be friends."

Sam pursed her lips in thought. "Not likely. Guys don't say they're sorry just to have a girl for a friend. My money says he's going to apologize and want to get back together. So you should probably figure out if you want that."

"Since when are you a relationship expert?"

"Hey. I might not have a lot of experience, but I've read more Dear Abby columns than I can count. If that doesn't make me an expert, I don't know what does."

"I'm not even going to acknowledge that with an answer. But whatever happens and whatever I do, you'll be the first to know." I only wished I knew what that was.

Come on, my alter ego began. *You know you're going to get back together with him if that's what he wants. Why would you say no if he apologizes? It's not like you have any other alternatives, or friends for that matter.*

"I'd better be," Sam said with a grin before we turned our attention to the stage.

The band members took their places at the microphones and the music started. The crowd applauded and whistled as the lead singer belted out a fast-paced song. I swayed in time to the music, my spirits suddenly lifted. Sam danced beside me, occasionally looking over at me with a silly grin on her face. I knew exactly what she was thinking–that she hoped Alex and I would work things out. And I hoped so, too.

I started to relax and enjoy myself as we listened to the music. Mr. Wainwright never returned, but a boy approached Sam after a few songs and asked her to dance. Surprised, I watched them. He was in my History class, but his claim to fame at school was as quarterback of the football team. His handsome smile and broad shoulders were enough to sweep any girl off her feet and Sam was no exception. Her face lighting up at the attention, she seemed to forget about me.

I couldn't help smiling. Tonight was shaping up to be better than I expected. But my happiness faded when I felt the hair on the back of my neck stand on edge. A chill ran down my spine, and I turned to see someone across the street from the park. He leaned against the brick wall, his black shape a silhouette in the dark. Swallowing back my fear, I weaved around the people dancing to the music. I didn't know who it was, but it felt like he was staring right at me. Leaving the crowd behind, I walked as if in a trance, pulled by whoever was out there.

When I was about ten feet from the park fence, I stopped, recognizing Lucian in the shadows where he watched the concert from a distance. He had one leg bent, his foot resting against the wall. His clothes were all black, the silver cross hanging against his shirt. A cold expression lingered on his face as our eyes met, rattling my nerves.

Gulping back an unsettled feeling, I turned away, prepared to find Sam. But I couldn't resist sneaking another look at Lucian. When I glanced at the wall again, he was gone. I took a deep breath, trying to relax. Why did I constantly let him get to me? Frustrated, I started to walk back toward the center of the park, but a tall figure blocked my path.

I skidded to a halt and looked up. Sam's stepfather stood in front of me, the steady gaze coming from his narrowed eyes sending panic through me. I fought the nausea in my stomach and took short, shallow breaths. He wore a tan overcoat, his thin silver hair reflecting the dim light. Anyone else might see an older gentleman, but I saw a monster as my memory of the night in his car flashed before me. I could practically feel his hand on my thigh.

I started to run, but he reached out and grabbed my arm, jerking me to a stop and pulling me close to him. A sinister smile slid over his face. In that instant, my vision went blurry. I blinked several times, but all I could see were dark shadows and fuzzy lights in the distance. Tears forming in my eyes, I trembled. What was happening?

"Not so fast," he said. "I've been looking forward to seeing you ever since I woke up in the hospital. You made my life a living hell." He held up his other hand still wrapped in a cast. "You broke my hand, you bitch. I had a real hard time explaining that to the ER."

"What are you doing here?" I hissed, struggling against his grip. But he was too strong, and my attempt to break free only earned me a tighter squeeze.

"You didn't think you'd get away with what you did to me, did you?"

"I didn't do anything to you that you didn't deserve."

"But all I wanted was to have a little fun. Was that too much to ask? I watched you grow up into such a beauty. And red hair is my favorite. Sam couldn't have done a better job picking a best friend."

Sam! Where was she? And how dare he confront me in public like this? "Speaking of Sam, don't you think she's going to wonder what you're doing here and why you have your hands on me?"

He chuckled, a satisfied grin crossing his lips. "I took care of her. That young man was more than happy to take some cash in exchange for keeping her busy the rest of the night. She won't even know you're gone." He started walking across the park to the gate, pulling me beside him.

"I'm not leaving," I said, digging my heels into the ground. But he kept dragging me, causing me to stumble beside him.

"Oh, yes you are. We have some unfinished business to tend to. Come with me and don't make a scene, or I will expose you for what you are," he muttered just loud enough for me to hear. "You don't want to ruin Sam's weekend. I know you'd rather die than let her know you were the one who put me in the hospital."

Adrenaline shot through my blood, but it didn't give me enough strength to break away from him. All I could do was jog to keep up with him as he skirted around the empty perimeter of the park. The rest of the crowd was clustered in the center, and no one seemed to notice I was being taken against my will. Music blasted through the air and darkness draped over us. I could barely see beyond the moisture clouding my eyes, although even without the tears, I wouldn't have been able to see since my clear vision had been snatched away.

"You won't get away with this," I said, wishing I believed it. All I got in response was a sharp squeeze on my arm and an abrupt jerk. Realizing I had no choice, I hurried alongside him, trying not to think about what he was planning to do to me.

31

Sam's stepfather led me down the dark street and then turned into an alley. A few minutes later, we entered a parking lot and squeezed between a few rows of cars until we reached his rented sedan. He shoved me into the passenger seat before slamming the door. My arms and legs trembling, I waited for him to get in the driver's seat.

Thoughts of escaping ran rampant through my mind. I considered jumping out of the car and fleeing across the lot, but where would I go? I could never outrun him, and there wasn't a single soul around to ask for help. Between knowing he would overpower me and not being able to see, I stayed where I was, paralyzed with fear.

After he got in the car, started the engine, and pulled out, I drummed up the courage to speak. "Where are you taking me?"

"Some place quiet. There are plenty of desolate roads around here. I'm sure I can find one where we'll have a little privacy," he sneered as he drove out of town.

I watched the shadows out the window, but everything looked like huge black blurs. I couldn't even see him clearly, my vision was so poor. Shaking, I swallowed as alarm rose up inside me. All I could guess was that he planned to finish what he'd started on that dark, stormy night a few months ago. How had I let this happen? Why had I been strong enough to break his hand then, and tonight, even with my adrenaline running high, was no match against him? His grip on my arm had felt like an iron vice I'd had no hope of breaking. When we got wherever he was taking me, my only chance would be to run.

"Why are you doing this?" I asked, tears rolling down my face. "You're married, for God's sake."

"How observant of you. Well, it's not enough. You're young, so you couldn't possibly understand. But Gracyn, all you had to do was politely tell me no. I would have let you go."

"How can I believe that when you've just taken me against my will?"

"I suppose you can't."

"Then prove you mean it. Let me go now."

He chuckled. "Good try, but no. Not going to happen."

"Why?" I whispered, my voice threatening to break down into sobs.

"Because you broke my hand. And then, I don't know what you did, but you put me in a coma. You need to pay. See what you've done? If you had just told me you weren't into it, I would have found someone who was willing."

Bile burned my throat and I held it back, afraid I would throw up. "What? Have you done that before, cheated on Sam's mom?"

"I had to do something. She works, a lot. She's all business and doesn't understand my needs. Then you came along. You blossomed over the last year, Gracyn. I was watching you for months before I tried to get close to you. And we could have talked first, but no, you had to get all violent on me."

"I was defending myself. And I'll do it again if I have to," I said between clenched teeth.

"I don't think so," he replied smugly. "Whatever possessed you to do what you did then doesn't seem to be in you now. I can tell you're weak tonight. Perhaps my phone calls and gift scared you."

"You made those calls and sent the doll?" I asked.

"Yes."

"But the package was postmarked from Sedgewick," I pointed out. If it really had been from him, I wanted to be sure beyond a doubt. Then again, if he hadn't sent it, he wouldn't know about it.

"I asked a friend to mail it for me from Sedgewick. He was a fraternity brother from college. I told him it was a special surprise for an old friend. That seemed to put his curiosity to rest. I couldn't very well have sent it from Bethesda or any other post office around DC. You would have suspected me right away. And I wanted our reunion to be a surprise. So, Gracyn, are you surprised?"

"Disgusted is more like it," I spat out at him.

He turned the car onto a back road, the headlights shining into the darkness. "My, my, you are feisty. We're going to have some fun tonight. It's a little cool out there, but I'll keep you warm."

"I'll report you this time," I warned. "And I will prosecute you. You'll be punished for this."

He glanced at me out of the corner of his narrowed eyes. "You do that and you won't hurt just me. You'll hurt Sam, her brother, and their mother. Do you want to do that? Be responsible for ruining an entire family? Sam won't be able to go to the college of her choice unless I continue working. And I can't do that from jail."

"You hurt people. I won't allow you to get away with it. How many other girls have there been?"

"Just a few, three to be exact. All over eighteen, I might add. So I've done nothing illegal."

"You raped them."

"On the contrary. They were willing participants. It's amazing what a girl will do for a few hundred bucks."

"Then why me? Why force yourself on me when you can have one of them?"

He slowed the car, pulled it over to the shoulder, and shifted into park. Then he turned off the engine and shut off the lights, sending the world into pitch black. Although I hadn't been able to see much while he'd been driving.

"Because you hurt me. After the stunt you pulled, I need to teach you a lesson."

"You're going to have to catch me first." Before I thought it through, I jumped out of the car and ran into the woods. My arms stretched out in front of me as I used them to feel for branches and trees. I could see dark shapes in the moonlight, but nothing was clear.

I pushed my legs as fast as they could go, tripping and stumbling over tree roots and fallen branches. Breathing heavily, my heart racing, I didn't think about where I was going. I didn't care. As long as I got away from him, I would find my way home somehow.

But I didn't get far. Within seconds, he caught up to me and grabbed my arm. I fell forward from my momentum, but he held me steady. After spinning me around to face him, he laughed. "Thought you could outrun me? Well, I'm back to my normal strength, no thanks to that little trick you played on me. Tell me Gracyn, what exactly did you do to me? Was it a curse? Were you hoping I would die?"

"I...no, I didn't want that. And I don't know what I did," I told him honestly.

"Don't lie to me. Your eyes turned red that night. I saw them. What are you?"

"Just a girl," I said, not sure I believed it myself after overhearing Becca admit to Gabriel that she needed to tell me what I was.

"Yeah, right," he scoffed before forcing me down on the ground and pinning my back against leaves and sticks with his knees beside my hips.

I struggled and squirmed, crying out. "No! Stop! Leave me alone!"

"You're wasting your breath. No one's going to hear you out here in the middle of nowhere."

Without any warning, a dark figure came crashing out of the woods from the side. "You're sadly mistaken," I heard Lucian say before Sam's stepfather was lifted off of me.

As soon as I could move, I sat up and scrambled backward until I hit a tree. I watched in amazement as Lucian threw Sam's stepfather about ten feet in the air. He landed in a heap on the ground, and I blinked furiously, not sure what was going on.

When I heard a low moan from several feet away, my jaw dropped. "How did you do that?" I asked as Lucian knelt in front of me.

He leaned closer, his face coming into focus. His eyes locked with mine, and he reached out to touch my cheek. "Are you okay?"

"Yes, just a little shaken up. But you didn't answer my question. You just threw a full-grown man like he was a football. And how did you know I was here?"

"I saw you leave with him, and I followed. I knew something was up," he said, tilting his head, studying me. "Why are you squinting?" My tears returned, and I shifted my eyes away from him. "I...I can't see. I mean, I can, it's just blurry. I need my glasses, but I don't have them with me. Damn it! I could see perfectly until he found me. Then my vision cut out and I guess it's back to glasses and contacts. Because without them, I'm as blind as a bat."

"That's odd," he whispered thoughtfully.

"What do you mean? Do you know how this happened tonight?"

He never answered my question. Instead, he snapped his attention to the side. "Someone's coming. You're safe now."

As Lucian rose to his feet, I followed him with my eyes. "What about him?" I nodded at Sam's stepfather who was moaning from where he lay in a pile of leaves.

"He will be dealt with. Becca will see to that. I must go now," Lucian said before slipping into the shadows. Hooves pounded against the ground in the distance, growing louder until Gypsy charged out from between two trees. Cadence and Becca followed, looking like a huge white blur to me.

Gypsy cantered toward me and slid to a stop with only inches to spare. She stretched her head down and nudged me with her muzzle. I closed my eyes for a moment, feeling safe. When I opened them, I did a double-take. My vision was clear again. Becca and Cadence no longer looked like a foggy cloud in the moonlit forest. I could see Becca's blue eyes and the folded collar of her white coat as she sat astride Cadence with no saddle or bridle. Everything was sharp and in focus as it had been for weeks.

Becca looked at me, then raised her eyes to look in the direction of the moaning. Her attention on Sam's stepfather, she guided Cadence over to him and stopped the mare before dismounting.

Becca stood straight and confident, her long coat flowing down around her white boots. "Stand," she ordered.

Sam's stepfather groaned in protest. "I...I can't."

Becca took a deep breath, raising her hand. "I'm only going to ask you one more time. Stand up now."

"I—" he began, then screamed out in pain. Clutching his throat, he rose to his feet as if someone held his neck and pulled him up.

Becca lifted her hand while he moved, as though controlling him. "That's better," she said when he stood before her. "Now, what were you doing with Gracyn?"

"I was driving her home," he said quietly before he grabbed his head and cried out. Dropping to his knees, he let out a painful wail.

Lowering her hand, Becca waited for silence before she continued. "I expect the truth."

Sniffling, he looked up at her. "You don't understand. She's possessed. Look at what she did to my hand," he told her, holding up his cast.

"I know all about that. Now rise," she commanded.

Seeming to sense he had no choice but to obey, he stood up immediately. Even though he was taller than Becca, she was clearly in control. "You have sinned, have you not?"

"Yes," he said, his voice sounding like he was in a deep trance.

"You picked the wrong girl to mess with, and now you must answer to me."

"What are you going to do to me?" he asked, his voice fearful.

Becca pulled a silver dagger out of her inside coat pocket. She lifted it to his throat, touching the sharp tip against him. "I'm not sure. You see, I could end your pathetic life right now. Or I could show you mercy. Which would you choose?"

His face turned pale in the moonlight, his eyes wide with fright. "M...mercy."

She smiled knowingly. "I would prefer the alternative, but lucky for you, I do not believe death is the appropriate punishment here. Instead, I shall show you mercy on one condition."

"What's that?" he asked.

"From this moment, you will have nothing to do with Gracyn ever again. You will forget her, and you will return to your family. The only woman you will be with from now on is your wife." When Becca stopped talking, a cloud of fog rose up between them. After it dissipated, she continued. "Now you are free to go. Return to your hotel and pick up Samantha tomorrow morning at ten o'clock as you planned."

He nodded and turned away from her. Without as much as a single glance my way, he walked back to the rental car. The headlights turned on as the engine came to life, and he drove away.

Relieved, I wanted to stand up, but I was overwhelmed. I felt numb, too stunned from everything I'd just witnessed to move.

I was still on the ground when Becca approached and extended an arm down to me. "Come on. Let's go home."

I took her hand and let her pull me to my feet. "What's going on around here? First Lucian, then you. How did you do that?" I asked.

"I'll explain everything when we get home. I don't want to discuss this out here. Get on Gypsy and we'll go."

Scrunching my eyebrows, I looked at Gypsy who stood beside me, her back bare and the bridle missing. I had no idea how Becca expected me to ride without the saddle or reins.

Before I could ask, Gypsy dropped her knees to the ground and lowered her back. I watched Cadence lay down next to Becca, allowing her to hop on behind the withers. As the mare rose to her feet, Becca grabbed a fistful of the mane, never losing her balance.

"Get on," Becca instructed. "What are you waiting for?"

I was dumbfounded. "I can barely ride with a saddle and bridle. You want me to ride bareback with no reins?"

"Yes. You'll be fine. You'll see." When I hesitated, Becca continued. "All the times you were scared and I told you not to be, nothing happened. You know you can trust me. And you can trust Gypsy, too. Let's not stay out here all night. Please. I need to hurry."

Becca's drained voice worried me. I glanced up, recognizing pain and exhaustion in her expression. Without another moment of hesitation, I slid my leg over Gypsy's back. Grabbing a handful of her mane, I held it tightly as she lifted her front end. I felt myself slipping backward for a second before she raised her hindquarters. As soon as her back was level, I straightened my shoulders.

"Ready?" Becca asked.

I nodded, even though I wasn't sure.

Becca nudged Cadence into a slow, collected canter. Gypsy followed, her gait smooth and rhythmical. I hung on, adrenaline still coursing through my veins while the horses traveled through the woods. Riding bareback wasn't as difficult as I expected. Gypsy held her head up, her ears flicking back often as if checking on me. She took the turns and hills slowly, avoiding abrupt changes in her pace or direction.

I soon grew comfortable riding without a saddle and bridle. My ability seemed to have improved greatly since my first few rides. When I stopped worrying about falling off, I reflected on the night's events. I had so many questions, and I suspected I wouldn't have long to wait for answers. Becca had to tell me what was going on now.

32

Gabriel was waiting in the barn doorway when Cadence and Gypsy slid to a stop on the gravel. Stones flew up around their hooves, landing with a pinging sound, and the mares' flanks heaved from their exertion.

Gabriel didn't even look my way as he rushed to Cadence's side. "Becca," he said, his voice worried. She collapsed, falling into his outstretched arms.

I slid off of Gypsy and rushed over to him, but he held his hand out, keeping me at bay. "She's okay. She's just worn out from the power she had to use this week, particularly tonight. Please put the horses away and meet me in the house."

Without a word, I nodded. As he carried Becca across the driveway, I turned to Cadence and Gypsy who stood still, as if knowing to wait for me. I walked between them and stopped when I could see their eyes. "Well, girls, let's go in." Without the aid of the reins, I led the mares into the dimly lit barn.

Prince lifted his head over the door, nickering at Cadence and Gypsy as they wandered into their stalls on their own. His interest in them didn't last long though, and he resumed munching his hay a few seconds later.

I secured the stall latches, then tossed a flake of hay to each of the mares. As soon as I finished, I turned off the light and jogged across the driveway to the house. When I ran inside, shutting the door behind me, the lights were dim and Becca lay on the couch, her eyes closed. I started to rush to her side, but Gabriel intercepted me, a cup of steaming tea in his hands.

"Wait," he instructed. "This will wake her up."

I nodded and stepped back, watching him sit on the coffee table and hold the tea under her nose. She stirred slightly, her eyelids fluttering.

"What's happening?" I asked, alarmed.

"It's just going to take a minute. She'll come to." He placed the tea on the table and gestured to the chair beside the couch. "Have a seat. I think you'll want to be sitting down for this."

Wide-eyed, my heart racing, I started to sit when I suddenly thought of Sam. My butt barely touched the cushion before I jumped up to my feet. "Wait! Sam's still at the concert. I need to go get her." I huffed with frustration when I realized I couldn't. "Crap. My car is still there," I muttered.

"Sam is upstairs, asleep," Gabriel explained calmly. "And don't worry about your car. I'll take you into town to get it tomorrow. You've had a rough night, and I don't want you going out again."

"Why?" I asked.

"Because we need to talk," he said. "Now sit. She's starting to wake up."

Becca's eyes opened slowly and she glanced about, a dazed look on her face. She yawned before sitting up, now a little more alert. "Gabe," she said, her gaze on him. "You're home."

"Of course I am. Here," he said, holding the tea out to her. "Drink this. It will help, at least for a while."

"Thanks," she replied with a faint smile before taking the tea from him. Leaning her elbows on her knees, she sipped it.

Silence hovered for a few minutes before I spoke. "Okay, the suspense is killing me. If you're feeling better, maybe you can explain what's going on. How did you find me in the woods? And how did you do whatever you did to Sam's dad?"

Becca tossed a knowing glance at Gabriel before smiling at me. "I'm not sure where to start, so I'm just going to say it. I'm a witch, Gracyn, and so are you."

My jaw dropped and I swore my heart skipped a beat, her steady expression making the hair on the back of my neck stand up. For a split second, I thought it was a joke. But her eyes said it all. She wasn't making it up. Even as I realized she was telling the cold, hard truth, I didn't want to believe it. "No," I protested, shaking my head. "That's not possible. Witches and magic don't exist. It's crazy. I don't believe it."

"Then how do you explain what you saw?" Becca asked, her voice stoic. "And your eyes. Your vision. I told you that was magic, remember?"

"I thought you were kidding," I muttered, thinking back to that night and realizing she'd been completely serious.

"No. We knew your vision would be restored, we just didn't know when," Gabriel added.

Staring at him, I leaned back against the chair, grateful for its support. "You knew? Why didn't you warn me?"

"Because you had just moved here. You were adjusting to a whole new life," Becca said softly. "We didn't want to scare you."

"Too late. So what does all this mean? And what about Sam's stepfather? If you're a witch, why did you let him go? Why didn't you kill him when you had the chance?"

"That was an empty threat to scare him. We don't kill. It's against our beliefs," Becca explained before a grin formed on her face. "But don't worry. He'll get what's coming to him, trust me."

"Not sure what that means, but okay," I said. "Now back to what you said about me being a witch. Can you please explain how that happened?"

Becca and Gabriel shot each other a look before Becca spoke again. "You are descended from a line of witches dating back to Salem, and even before that. We both are. But our coven here in Sedgewick is a special one. We each have a second half, a soul mate if you will, but not in a romantic sense. It's more like an energy. Each of our lives is connected to one of the most majestic creatures on Earth. The horse."

"Seriously?" I asked.

"Yes. You see, Gypsy is your lifeline. She's your energy, and you are hers. I'm sure you noticed how quickly she took to you and how she seems to know what you are going to ask of her before you ask it. And tonight, you didn't need a saddle or bridle. She carried you home safely because she's bonded to you in a way no other creature can be. She will always protect you. You were born on the same day, and you will die on the same day. What happens to her will happen to you, and vice versa. If she gets sick, you will, too. She also knows when you are in trouble. She knew tonight, and she knew where to find you. All I had to do was let her loose and she led me to you."

I felt as though I'd been thrown into a dream. This wasn't possible, was it? I must have fallen into a deep sleep, and when I woke up, I would return to a world where magic wasn't real, much less a horse whose life was tied to mine through some far-fetched supernatural connection.

"What about the trail horses who seemed scared of me when I was eight? Does that have anything to do with all of this?" I asked.

Becca shook her head. "I'm afraid I don't have an answer. It is possible that they knew you had supernatural powers, thus making them nervous. But nothing like that has happened before. We've always gotten along well with all horses, so it's a bit strange. I trust nothing like that ever happened again."

"No, but only because I never got near another horse after that, at least not until moving here."

"I can understand that. But I'm glad you trusted me with Gypsy."

"Me, too. Gypsy has been wonderful."

"She has," Becca agreed. "She is also the reason your vision improved. Your eyesight became bad years ago because of your distance from her and the fact that you never had the chance to be near her. We knew it would be restored once you moved here, we just didn't know how quickly. Have you noticed anything else?"

I nodded slowly. "My hearing. How can I hear whispers from so far away?"

"It's another power you are getting by drawing energy from Gypsy. You will continue to gain strength and power until you reach the age of about twenty-five. That's when you'll mature."

Staring at the wall on the opposite side of the room, I absorbed all of this. I had more questions than I could count, but I could barely think straight right now. "I was never sick as a child. In fact, I don't even remember many doctor's visits."

"That's because we don't get sick," Gabriel explained. "Our bodies are immune to disease."

My gaze snapped back to him. "What? You're a witch, too?"

"Yes," he answered with a slight nod. "But I'm not as powerful as Becca. She has lived for a very long time. The older a witch is, the more powerful he or she is. That's why Becca came to your rescue tonight and I went into town to get your friend."

"Great. Are there any other witches in this town?"

Becca and Gabriel glanced at each other before Becca answered quietly. "Yes, there are others. We are few in number, but we are strong."

Suspicions raced through my mind, starting with Lucian. I also wondered about Celeste, picturing her tired eyes in my mind for a moment. Could she be a witch, too? But I had so many other questions. Who else was like us could wait. Instead, I asked, "How long were you planning to keep this from me? Don't you think I deserved to know about this years ago?" Sam's stepfather flashed through my mind and, suddenly, it all made sense. This was how I'd had the strength to break his hand. And I must have done something I didn't realize to make him sick.

"We were planning to tell you, but we wanted to wait until you started college. High school is hard enough," Becca said. "We didn't want you to have to move until after you graduated."

"Then lucky for me it happened anyway."

"No," Becca stated. "It didn't just happen. I've been watching over you for a long time. Your powers were growing faster than expected. When you hurt your friend's father, we knew we needed to intervene."

"What?" I gasped. "You knew what happened with him?"

Becca avoided my glare as she nodded. "Yes. I had to keep an eye on things to make sure you stayed safe and that you didn't reveal your power to anyone."

"I guess you blew it," I said. "Because he knows I'm a freak and he's probably going to tell everyone."

"No, he won't. I erased his memory of that night, along with a few other things. As far as he knows, you're just Sam's friend, nothing more."

"How did you do that?"

"It's a simple spell, really. But—" Her voice turned serious. "We do not use our powers to manipulate people. This situation called for it due to extenuating circumstances that required me to protect you. It is forbidden to hurt people or use our magic for personal gain. Remember that."

"Well, considering I don't know how to use it, I don't think you have anything to worry about," I muttered. "How did you know what was going on in my personal life when you were up here and I was hundreds of miles away?"

"Another simple spell. I bonded us when you were young, so that I would know when your powers began to grow. I would get visions, see through your eyes when that started to happen."

"So you knew all about Sam's stepfather when I arrived?"

She nodded again. "Since before you arrived, actually. I was keeping a careful watch over the situation."

"Really? Then why did you let him come here and attack me?"

"I knew he was coming for you, Gracyn. The doll he sent you gave him away. I put a tracing spell on it and found out it was him. But I had to plan things out carefully to protect your friend. I'm sure you would never want her to know what her father tried to do to you."

"No, I would never want Sam to know about that. She'd be devastated. So how did you do it?"

"Last night, the tea you and Sam drank put a spell on both of you. Your tea put a blocking switch on your power that would be triggered the moment you saw Sam's stepfather."

Another mystery had just been solved, I think. "That's why my vision went blurry as soon as I saw him? And I had no strength, either. He pulled me around like a rag doll when I broke his hand with hardly any effort at all last time."

"Exactly. And the spell on Sam made her very sleepy as soon as your spell was activated. That way, she would be safely shielded from the truth about her father."

"Oh." I looked at Gabriel. "Was she okay when you brought her home?"

"Yes," he assured me. "She was fine. When I got to the concert, she was dancing with a young man, but she was getting tired fast. He was more than happy to turn her over to me. She said a quick goodbye and then fell asleep in the car on the way home. When she wakes up in the morning, she'll only remember a fun night. She'll suspect nothing."

"Good," I said, relieved. "But why did you take away my power? Weren't you worried her stepfather would hurt me?"

Becca pursed her lips. "Yes, we knew there was a risk. But I didn't know how else to do it. I had to render you powerless so that you wouldn't unknowingly hurt him again before I had a chance to erase his memory of what you did to him last time. And I trusted Gypsy to take me to you. She came through just as I knew she would."

"Okay, well, perhaps next time you can tell me when you're up to something. Maybe I should know if my safety is at stake."

Becca and Gabriel smiled. "That won't be an issue in the future," Becca said. "You didn't know what you were, but now you do. We won't have to hide these things anymore."

"Will you teach me what I can do? Like spells?" I couldn't believe I was buying into this, but I was curious.

Gabriel took a deep breath. "Gracyn, Becca has only been using these spells to protect you. She already mentioned that using magic for personal gain is forbidden. We use our power for one thing, and one thing only."

"What's that?" I asked.

"The garden," he replied. "Have you ever seen vegetables so healthy using no pesticides or fertilizer? We use magic to grow food, to feed people and allow life to continue. That is our purpose."

"That's it?" I felt like he had just deflated my bubble. "What good is being a witch if we can't use our power to do great things? What about poverty and hunger? Can we use it for a greater good? To help?"

Sadness crossed over both of their faces. "Gracyn," Becca started. "That's extremely noble of you to think of others less fortunate, but there are very few of us. Our power is only strong enough to grow food to feed our families and a few people in town. I wish we could do more, believe me. I've watched the world population grow to a staggering number, and it saddens me to know there is famine in other parts of the world. But none of us have that kind of power."

"Oh." I sighed, picking up on one thing in particular. "What do you mean you've watched the world population grow? How old are you?"

She glanced at Gabriel, as if not sure what to tell me. "Old enough," she said, her eyes still on him.

"Becca, please, enough with the secrets. I think I should know."

She shifted her gaze back to me. "Fine. You're right. I'll tell you the truth. I was born in the year sixteen twenty."

"That would make you—" My voice trailed off as I did the math in my head. Almost four hundred years old? How was that possible? But then again, how was any of this possible? As more questions jumbled around in my head, I finally asked the one thing I hadn't brought up yet. "And our mother? How old is she? And why isn't she here? How does she fit into this? Shouldn't she be the one telling me all of this?"

"That's a lot of questions in one breath," Becca said. "She's not like us, but she knows what we are. I'm going to ask you not to discuss any of this with her. She has enough on her mind with her new job, and she trusted me to tell you the truth."

"Wait a minute. How is she not like us? I mean, if she's your mother, that would make her over four hundred years old. And does that mean Cadence is also several hundred years old?"

At that moment, Becca cringed, bringing a hand up to her forehead. A painful look spread through her eyes as she massaged her temples.

Gabriel noticed her discomfort right away and placed his hands on her legs. "You're starting to overdo it. Drink a little more tea." He helped her lift the cup to her lips, her hands shaking. "That's it."

"I think I need to lie down," she said weakly, her face turning almost as white as her coat. Shifting back, she swung her legs onto the couch and closed her eyes.

Gabriel placed the teacup on the coffee table and turned to me. "I'm sorry, Gracyn, but we're going to have to continue this later. She's exhausted and she needs to sleep now. The effects of the tea are wearing off, and she has a long road to recovery."

"Recover from what?"

He looked at me, his eyes somber. "Becca has lived longer than any witch in our coven. That makes her very powerful. But lately, she's needed to use her power more frequently and it's starting to drain her body. She's trying so hard to hold on and be strong, mostly for you because she knows you'll need her as you learn about what you are and what that means. But eventually, her body will give out."

I felt as though a knife had been driven deep into my heart. Tears formed in the corners of my eyes. "What? You mean she's going to die?"

He nodded, his eyes glistening with moisture. "Yes. But we don't know when. It could be weeks, or it could be years. No one knows. No witch in our history has lived this long. She's very special, but I'm sure you know that by now."

A lump formed in my throat, cracking my voice when I spoke again. "Yes, I do. But I feel like I've only just gotten to know her." Holding my tears at bay, I looked at her. Her light blonde hair framed her peaceful face as she slept, her breaths drawing in and out with a slow rhythm. "What can I do to help?" I asked, my voice barely a whisper, my gaze not leaving her.

"There is nothing you can do," he told me. "Now, I'm going to move her to the bedroom and I suggest you head upstairs. You must be exhausted."

A tear rolled down my cheek as I nodded. "Okay. I'll go. But I don't know if I'll be able to sleep."

Gabriel smiled sincerely. "You still are the girl you've always been. Remember that. Everything is going to be fine, I promise." With that, he stood and scooped Becca up into his arms. Cradling her against his chest, he walked across the room and disappeared down the back hallway.

I stared into space, the silence putting me into a trance. I still couldn't believe everything they told me, but I knew it was true. For the first time in my life, things actually began to make sense. But it frightened me. I had always been a realist, interested in science. Now I would be able to do things that shouldn't be possible. In fact, I had already done things that could only be explained by magic. The comprehension of that was almost too much for me to handle.

I had so many questions. Like how our mother fit into this picture. And how many other witches existed in town as well as around the world.

After several minutes, I stood up and walked across the room. I slowly climbed the stairs, my head reeling from everything I'd just learned. At least one huge weight had been lifted from my shoulders. Sam's stepfather would never come near me again and, for that, I was thankful.

33

The next day, Sam and I had breakfast alone before she packed up her suitcase to leave. We didn't see Becca or Gabriel, but I assumed Becca was still in bed resting. Where Gabriel was, I had no idea. But I didn't particularly care, either. After the previous night, I was happy to spend the morning with Sam who raved about the festival and the concert. She had some amazing memories of the guy she met, the smile plastered on her face all morning evidence of that.

Her stepfather pulled up at exactly ten o'clock. When I heard the car just before the dogs started barking, I glanced at the door, my eyes wide with fear. My heart sped up at the thought of him and memories of last night. But if what Becca had told me was true, he wouldn't remember anything.

Sam led the way across the family room, lugging her suitcase. She wore a black jacket over her beige sweater and jeans, her tennis shoes fitting for a day of walking around college campuses before catching a late afternoon flight home.

I followed her to the door, my heart heavy. *Stop worrying,* I told myself. *Becca promised he won't remember a thing.* Then I realized I wasn't concerned about him. It was that I didn't want to see him, even if he had forgotten and cleaned up his act. Because I still had to live with the memory of his hands on me.

We walked outside onto the porch, and Sam carried her suitcase down the steps as the dogs rushed ahead of her. They circled the sedan while her stepfather stepped out of the car and approached her, reaching for her suitcase with his left hand.

"Good morning, girls," he said with a light-hearted smile. "Did you have a nice time yesterday?"

"Yes," Sam replied. "It was awesome. This was so worth it, even if it was too short."

"I'm glad to hear that," he said before nodding toward the suitcase. "I'll just put this in the trunk while you say goodbye. Gracyn, thank you for letting Sam stay with you. Your sister has a beautiful home. Perhaps I'll meet her next time."

I nearly choked. He had met her, he just didn't remember it. And I doubted Becca would welcome him back here. At least I knew I wouldn't. "Thank you," I told him, forcing myself to smile as my breakfast of eggs and toast almost rose up from my stomach. "I'll tell her." My voice was sickeningly sweet, but he didn't seem to notice.

Fortunately, neither did Sam. As her father walked away, she turned to me. "Okay. You know the drill. Call me as soon as Alex leaves. I want to hear everything."

"But you're going to be busy today. Why don't I call you tomorrow?"

Sam huffed with an eager smile. "No way. This is too important. I want you to be happy, and I know you like him. I'll never forgive you if you make me wait."

"Fine," I agreed with a grin. "I'll call you today."

"Good. Okay, I have to go." She pulled me into a quick hug. When she let go and backed away, she raised her eyebrows. "You know, next year we could be roomies at college. This is just temporary."

The thought of college darkened my spirits. I wasn't sure I would be going after what Becca told me last night. Trying to seem excited, I smiled. "Yes, we could. But if we're not roommates, maybe we'll at least be in the same state. Well, have fun today."

"You do the same," she said with a sly wink before jogging over to the car and slipping into the front passenger seat. Then, just like that, her stepfather drove away. Gone, but definitely not forgotten.

The dogs followed the car until it disappeared from view before they stopped, turned and trotted back to me. They nudged my legs as if they were trying to comfort me.

"Thanks, guys," I murmured, rubbing both of them between the ears. "I know. It's going to be really quiet now." I stood still for a moment, listening to the chirping birds and the occasional snort coming from the horses grazing out in the pasture. It was so peaceful, and I felt like I was seeing the farm for the first time since learning I was a witch. Oddly enough, I didn't feel any different. I still felt like the same girl who knew she had to get back to her homework and strive to earn the best grades she could. The only difference between me now and the girl who had arrived here a few weeks ago was that I could see without my glasses.

You're no longer afraid of horses, a voice in my head rattled off. *And you can hear things from really far away. You're almost a new person. You also have an ex-boyfriend who could be texting you any minute, so get back inside and stay near your phone for the rest of the day.*

My inner self brought a smile to my lips. She was right. Today was going to be great. Alex wanted to talk, and I couldn't wait to hear what he had to say.

With a bounce in my step, I hurried up the porch steps and rushed into the house. The last thing on my mind was the fact that I was a witch. I was determined to push that aside, at least for today.

Alex texted me about an hour later, asking if he could stop by at noon. I quickly responded, telling him that was fine. With an hour to wait, I tried to focus on an English assignment. But after reading ten pages of a Shakespeare play and realizing I hadn't retained a single word, I gave up and got ready for his visit.

I normally didn't primp much in the middle of the day, but I decided to look my best. After changing into my most flattering jeans and a black sweater, I brushed my hair into smooth waves and applied a little make-up. Pausing, I studied my reflection in the mirror. I couldn't help wondering if I looked like a witch. I scrunched my nose and made an angry, wicked face, but all I saw was a teenage girl. Relaxing my expression, I continued to gaze in the mirror, noticing I didn't look any different.

I felt a little different, though. Apart from the whole witch thing, a heavy weight had been lifted from my shoulders, raising my spirits. I no longer had to worry about Sam's stepfather telling her or anyone else that I'd broken his hand and cursed him. She had a good father now, someone who would stay true to her mother, even if it had been forced upon him. All I wanted was for her to be happy, something she deserved.

Stepping away from the mirror, I hurried out of my room. I rushed down the stairs, noticing once again how quiet things were. I still hadn't seen Becca or Gabriel yet today, but that didn't bother me. They had answered a lot of my questions last night, and the rest could wait.

I escaped outside and wandered across the driveway, my boots crunching on the gravel. My sights set on the pasture, I went straight to the fence. Gypsy lifted her head and whinnied when she saw me. Then she trotted over, stretched her neck across the top board, and nudged my arm with her muzzle.

"Hi, girl," I said, stroking her face. "So, there's a lot more to this than you've let on, huh?"

She gazed at me with her soft brown eyes, moving her head in a subtle nod.

"Are you admitting it?" I asked with a chuckle. "I guess we'll be spending a lot of time together. Seems like we're stuck with each other."

My comment earned me another nudge. I rubbed the fur between her eyes, once again amazed that horses no longer scared me. After a few seconds, the purr of an engine rumbled from down the driveway.

As it grew louder, Gypsy whirled around and headed back to Prince and Cadence.

I turned, smiling at the sight of Alex's Jeep. Waving, I jogged over to the driver's side after he parked.

"Hi," he said as he stepped out and shut the door. "Man, am I glad to see you."

"You are?"

He nodded with a grin. "Yes. I should have asked you to stay last night. We finished up around eleven and then went to a party."

I sighed, knowing exactly where he was going with this. "But you were worried I would drink too much again."

"No. Not at all," he said, as though the thought had never crossed his mind. "I just didn't think to ask you to stay. I know you're upset with me, and you have every right to be. Besides, I wouldn't have blamed you for turning me down, especially with your friend visiting. Speaking of her, did she leave?"

"Yes. Her dad picked her up about two hours ago. And she probably would have loved to have gone to the party, but she's touring a few colleges today, so I'm sure it's better that she didn't."

"Well, I noticed you were gone after our set. I hope you at least enjoyed the concert."

"Of course," I said a little too quickly, knowing I had missed most of it. "Listen, I don't know about you, but I don't want to stand here in the driveway. Want to come up on the porch?"

"Sure."

I led him up the steps and we passed the door until we reached the wicker bench at the far end. Sitting down, I looked out across the sunny driveway at the barn. Alex sat next to me, and I could see him studying me out of the corner of my eye.

Biting my lip, I turned to him. "So, you said you wanted to talk. I'm listening."

"Yes." His dark eyes studied me for a minute, his expression serious. "I'm sorry. I acted like a jerk. I shouldn't have brushed you off like that for one lousy night. Everyone is allowed a mistake from time to time. God knows I've made my fair share of them, including having too much to drink, so lucky for you, it's unlikely that you'll ever have to scrape me off the ground."

I chuckled. I couldn't imagine Alex drinking too much. He was so level-headed. He seemed to make good decisions, and yet he was popular with the other kids. "That's okay. If it happens, I'll give you another chance. I owe you that much after my night of tequila."

"No, you don't. I think we're even," he said, a hopeful look in his eyes. "I'm afraid to ask. Am I forgiven?"

I hesitated, not wanting to answer right away. He should be made to sweat, if only for a minute. Shifting my eyes to look out over the railing, I paused.

"Gracyn–" he prompted.

"I'm thinking," I said, my thoughts spinning with everything that had happened in the last twenty-four hours. Being with Alex helped. Somehow, he calmed me down, made me feel normal even though I knew for a fact that I was anything but normal.

"Can you think a little faster? The suspense is just about killing me."

Laughing softly, I turned to face him. "Okay."

"That's it? What does that mean?"

"I forgive you, that's what it means," I said.

Relief spread across his face, followed by happiness. "You really are great. I probably don't deserve you."

"Sure you do. And you know you're going to repay me for making me go through hell last week."

"Anything," he said, a twinkle in his eyes. "But first, there's something I have to do." He put both of his hands under my jaw and lifted my chin.

I scooted closer to him, letting my eyelids fall as his lips touched mine. Wrapping my arms around his shoulders, I lost myself in his kiss. The world seemed to fade away into the background, allowing me to forget everything else. I would have given anything for this moment to have lasted forever.

When Alex broke away from me, I opened my eyes and saw him staring at me, a curious look on his face. "So, you were saying? What will I be doing to repay you?" he asked.

"Let's just say I'm going to enjoy having my own personal Calculus tutor this year."

"What?" he asked, acting surprised. "You already had that. You know I'll help you any time you need it, day or night."

"Not last week."

He looked away for a moment, a frown on his face. "I was a jerk, and I apologized."

"So here's the deal," I said seriously. "Promise me that whatever happens, we'll stay friends."

"If you're breaking up with me now, I'm not making that promise."

Smiling, I shook my head. "No, I'm not. I just don't know what the future holds. And I need you, one way or another. Last week really sucked. I don't want to go through that again."

"Stop worrying. We'll be fine. We have an incredible year ahead." Alex ran his hand down my arm until he reached my hand and threaded his fingers through mine. With a gentle squeeze, he said, "That reminds me. I want to ask you something very important."

"What's that?"

"Will you be my date for the Homecoming dance?"

My heart soared at his invitation. "Yes," I answered immediately. "I would love to."

"Perfect. Boy, I'm glad I didn't screw up so badly that I lost my chance. Thank you."

"For what?" I asked, confused.

"For being awesome."

"You, too. Last week was horrible, but I've put it behind me. I'm just glad you're here now." With a smile on my face, I turned and leaned back against the bench as he shifted to face forward. Sighing, I dropped my head onto his shoulder. Hand in hand, we took in the silence, enjoying the peace. At that moment, I felt good. A lot of things were behind me now and, whatever the future held, I knew I could handle it if I had Alex by my side, as a friend or as more.

After Alex left, Gabriel took me into town to get my car. When we returned, I retreated up to my room and spent the rest of the day on my homework. I even pulled out some college applications to review. Time flew by and, before I realized how late it was, the sun had set and the sky outside my window had faded to dark purple.

When my stomach started growling, I shut my History book. I could come back to it later, but for now, it was time to take a break for dinner. I was about to leave my room when muffled hoof beats pounded in the distance. At first, they were so soft, I barely heard them. But they grew louder, coming closer. Curious, I went to the window and looked outside.

The black shape of a horse and rider appeared in the shadows extending across the trail entrance at the back of the driveway. I immediately recognized Lucian and Shade, the silver cross hanging around Lucian's neck once again noticeable next to his dark shirt. Steadying the huge horse, he watched the house.

I swallowed back the chills sweeping through me, wanting to move away from the window, but powerless to do so. What was he doing here? His presence reminded me that he had come to my rescue not once, but twice. I wasn't scared of him now, only curious.

He looked up at my window, but I didn't move my gaze away from him. Instead, I waved. Without returning the gesture, Lucian spun Shade around and they galloped off into the woods. Within seconds, the thundering hooves could no longer be heard.

Taking a deep breath, I found my composure. At the moment, his reasons for riding over this evening were of little consequence. I had made peace with myself for what I had done to Sam's stepfather and I had reconciled with Alex. My life was good, and no one was going to ruin it tonight.

I was something I had never thought existed. I was a witch. I had a supernatural connection to a horse. I had strength and power beyond human limitations. I had a lot to learn about what I was and what I could do, but I was ready. I would stand tall and face my uncertain future with confidence. Tomorrow would bring a new day and with it, a new beginning.

Don't miss

GYPSY SOULS

Book Two of The Gypsy Magic Trilogy

Now Available

www.tonyaroyston.com/books

Acknowledgments

I want to start this section by thanking anyone who decided to read this story. Whether the synopsis drew you in or the cover captured your interest, thank you for taking the time to be part of this!

To my mom, thank you for your help, your support, and most of all, your interest. It means the world to me that you have become involved in this process. I couldn't have gotten this far without you!

To Jennifer Gibson for the beautiful cover and bookmark designs. Your talent is amazing. Thank you for the images that helped bring this story to life!

To Jaclyn for beta-reading this story and giving me your honest opinion. You helped me make the story stronger and gave me the confidence to publish it!

Lastly, to my family, coworkers, and friends as well as everyone mentioned above. Thank you for listening and supporting me. It's been an incredible journey and it wouldn't be nearly as special if I didn't have all of you to share it with!

About the Author

Tonya lives in Northern Virginia with her husband, son, two dogs and two horses. Although she dreamed of writing novels at a young age, she was diverted away from that path years ago and built a successful career as a Contracts Manager for a defense contractor in the Washington, DC area. She resurrected her dream of writing in 2013 and hasn't stopped since.

When she isn't writing, Tonya spends time with her family. She enjoys skiing, horseback riding, and anything else that involves the outdoors.

More information about Tonya and her writing can be found at www.tonyaroyston.com.

Made in the USA
Middletown, DE
07 March 2019